WHEN HE CAME BACK

a novel

Jessica A. Briones

WHEN HE CAME BACK

Copyright © 2015 by Jessica A. Briones

Cover Design: Indie Solutions by Murphy Rae, www.murphyrea.net

Editing: Holly M. Kothe and Kerry Genova with Indie Solutions, www.murphyrea.net

Formatting: Wendi Temporado with Ready, Set, Edit, https://www.facebook.com/GetReadyGetSetEdit

For my boys.

You guys are my everything!

"I love you without knowing how, or when, or from where,
I love you simply, without problems or pride:
I love you in this way because I don't know any other way of
loving..."

-Pablo Neruda

CHAPTER ONE

Claire

Ever since Claire Monroe had been discovered at an exposition by an influential financier and his wife, her paintings had been sought-after commodities. Some of the most prominent businesses in Toronto wanted her art displayed on their walls. The point of view of a young artist in love with nature and all it had to offer was a refreshing perspective. Every flower, hill, and person had a story, brought to life with every brush stroke and brilliant combination of color.

The execs at the King Edward, one of Toronto's most prestigious hotels, were no different. She watched mindlessly as the hotel manager flipped the pages of her portfolio, which lay open in the middle of the large round table. A few hmm's and ah's were the extent of her vocalization. The big guns wanted locals. If all went her agent Rae's way, Claire would be obligated to honor a contract that would require she submit three paintings by September. She looked at her watch—she had two months to create her heart out.

"Do you have a website?" asked the hotel manager.

"No."

"Facebook, Twitter? Anything?"

"I'm not on social media," Claire responded to a question that had been asked a million times.

A website and any form of social media would mean a type of exposure she couldn't afford.

She'd just moved back home to Springridge, a small town that afforded her the anonymity she relished when she lived in Ottawa. Eight months in and she'd been thrust into notoriety. It made her nervous—she had secrets that any type of publicity could expose—her son Charlie being the biggest secret of all. However, she had to make a living, even though at twenty-one, she had inherited a hefty trust fund. But she wanted to live a simple life. She wanted to raise a humble and kind child. Most of all, she wanted to show her son that hard work paid off, that nothing came easy in life.

"How does that sound to you, Claire?" Rae asked, breaking through her thoughts.

"How does what sound?" she asked the three faces staring back at her.

"September. Does that give you enough time to complete the work?"

"Yes. That's plenty of time. But I have one condition."

The sounds of traffic and people chanting on the streets traveled through the revolving doors into the lobby, distracting them from their meeting.

"Which is?" asked Stephanie, the hotel manager.

2

"It's on my time, my ideas. I don't want any pressure from management. I will keep you posted as to the progress," she demanded, not that she was in a position to make demands. "Give me an idea of what you're looking for, and I will work very hard to give you what you want."

She had her son to think about. Charlie always came first. He was a busy boy who loved sports—baseball in particular. She was determined to be a present and supportive parent, everything her parents weren't. She'd give up anything that jeopardized his happiness—she'd done it once before when he'd been nothing but a tiny dot on a printout from her sonogram. She'd protected him fiercely then, and wouldn't hesitate to do it again.

The sounds outside were getting louder. It didn't escape her attention that the crowd gathering on the sidewalk was mostly women. Girls, actually. They had signs, magazines, cameras, and smartphones at the ready. She wondered who they might be waiting for. She could see the exasperation on Stephanie's face as the woman studied the growing crowd outside.

"As long as the job is completed by the deadline, I have no problem with your suggestions. Do you, Stephanie?" said Alexa.

As the hotel manager opened her mouth to speak, there was a commotion just outside the revolving doors. Girls were screaming something Claire couldn't understand, a jumbled chant that echoed off the century-old marble walls of the hotel lobby and restaurant. The dining area was set in the large, open lobby, sticking to its original character.

"Well then, we're all set," said Rae.

"I hate to cut the meeting short, ladies," said Stephanie. "It seems our high-profile guests have arrived. I'm going to spend the rest of the weekend arranging security and keeping teenage girls from sneaking into the hotel. Miss Monroe, it's been a pleasure. I look forward to seeing what you come up with. Rae, I'll email you the contract and specifications. Alexa, I'm sure I'll see you around."

Alexa, the interior designer in charge of the project (as well as her best friend), had to practically drag her out of Springridge. Claire hated coming into the city, and the drive was as expected, a slow one. Traffic was an endless epidemic infecting most big cities—Toronto wasn't immune. Claire was aware what a huge opportunity this was for her; however, if she could have conducted this meeting from her living room, she would have been a lot happier. Alexa's excitement over this opportunity was infectious, and she already had some idea of what she would paint. But she couldn't wait to get home to her son.

She smiled to herself then, despite her doubts and fears. She loved having her own house and being around her family at last. Growing up, things hadn't always been easy for Claire and her brother. Her parents were absent parents; the allure of Paris and London was more appealing than sticking around to raise Claire and Hunter. After the death of Alexa's mother, Claire's parents had taken in her best friend, and there was a noticeable shift in parental responsibility. With one more mouth to feed and the unimaginable support Alexa would need to cope with her mother's death, the crack in their familial unit was sealed. They finally became the family she and Hunter wanted, and the family Alexa would need. They'd stuck together ever since.

As the screams reached a deafening level, Claire longed for Springridge. The small town had grown in the six years since she'd been gone. Nestled against the picturesque Niagara Escarpment and skirting around horse and produce farms, the modern fit nicely with the old. Although at times, the small town seemed to fight against the monopoly that wanted to turn it into a city. She hoped that the manic race to further populate it would stop. Claire loved the simplicity it offered, the safety one blindly accepted, and the closeness a community had endured for almost two centuries. With that thought in mind, she pushed away from the table, gathered her portfolio, and began digging through her large bag for her car keys.

"Okay, the firm's contract has been faxed to you?" asked Alexa.

"Yes," answered Rae.

"Sign it and get it back to me as soon as possible. I want to seal this deal. I don't want this contract to go to anyone else, Claire."

"Thanks, Alex, for all your help."

"You did this on your own, Claire. You're very talented. I'm just glad you've decided to do something significant with all that talent. This is a long way from your market days."

It had been a warm, sunny Saturday. Claire had just finished setting up at the coveted rented booth in front of Joe's Ice Cream. Financier Michael Jameson and his wife Isabella had given in to the undeniable urge to explore the booths of local farmers, bakers, and artists that shut down Main Street for four hours every Saturday from May to October. That pit stop changed Claire's life forever.

They bought a painting and, unexpectedly, returned the following week. Michael told her he knew someone who'd been inspired by her art and purchased two more. She'd been okay with him buying the paintings and didn't think anything of his purchases. When the man returned several weeks later with check book in hand and bought three more, she got a little curious. He mentioned they were gifts. She sold out, and thanks to him, her art was exposed to the world.

"Those were the days…" she said and stared at her friend.

"Okay. I really have to get going. I have a client meeting for a job I'm going to be doing in Cabo."

"San Lucas?" asked Claire, excited.

"Yeppers!" said Alexa, wiggling her eyebrows.

"Let me know if your client needs any art."

"I will. Okay, I really need to get going. I'll see you Sunday, Claire."

"I'll be there. Charlie lives for those Sunday barbecues."

"It's the first of the season, and I love that he makes you—" the roaring screams from outside cut her off, making the three women look up.

"Jesus. Well, good luck getting through that. I need to head back to the office. We'll be in touch, Claire," said Rae.

"Yes. Take care. We'll talk soon."

Alexa's attention was fixated on the commotion by the doors. Claire shook her head as a very large black man dressed in a fitted black T-shirt yelled orders to an equally large white man. Between them, a body huddled, covering his head, protecting it from the hordes. Two more bodyguards followed them. Claire continued digging for her keys in her oversized purse, eager to get the hell out of there.

"Holy shit!" exclaimed Alexa, reaching to grab Claire's arm.

"I know! I need to get a smaller bag—I can't find anything in here," said Claire, laughing and assuming Alexa's exclamation was about her purse that had once doubled as a diaper bag. It was old, but she loved it for the very reason Alex hated it. It fit everything and anything.

"Claire?" whispered Alexa. The alarm in her voice had her looking up at her friend and then wincing at the strength Alexa used as she locked her hand around Claire's wrist in a painful grip.

"Alexa, what the hell? You're hurting..." she began but stopped at the look on her friend's face.

She followed Alexa's gaze and was met by the icy green stare of Austin McKinley, world-renowned rock star, lead singer of Yellow Scarlet, and father of her only and beloved child. She could feel the color draining from her face. Alexa's grip seemed to be the only thing holding her up.

What the hell were the chances?

"I have to get out here," she said, unsure if she'd actually spoken the words out loud.

The knot in her throat made it hard to swallow, and she reached down for her cold tea to ease her suddenly parched mouth. It'd been six years since she'd last seen him, since she stood in front of him and told the biggest lie of her life.

Telling him she didn't love him anymore had shattered her. All so he could go follow his dream. She hadn't wanted to hold him back. She took a deep, steadying breath and hoped the fear she felt all of a sudden didn't incapacitate her. Her heart was beating frantically, her chest felt heavy as she tried to coax some air into her lungs—the tea hadn't helped.

"Breathe, Claire," whispered Alexa as they both stood watching his stunning six-foot-three frame making its way towards them.

He'd changed. His height wasn't a big shock; he'd always been tall. What shocked her was his build—big and muscular. He'd gotten a tattoo. Four peacock feathers climbed up his arm from his wrist, the tendrils wrapping around his arm leading to a colorful sleeve tattoo. The green and turquoise feathers disappeared up his shirtsleeve, accentuating a defined bicep. She looked up to his face and noticed a smirk playing on his lips. The first thing he'd ever given her was a peacock feather on a trip to the zoo. She'd painted it and given the painting to him. She couldn't help but wonder if the decision for the artwork on his skin was intentional.

Her gaze wandered to the fitted shirt he wore that clung to a sculpted chest, and she knew he was hiding rippling abs. She had bought the magazines, seen the posters—none of which did him justice. Her eyes moved back to his face. Day-old stubble covered the soft skin she remembered. Dark circles shadowed his eyes—he looked exhausted. Despite his smirk, his eyes were devoid of any emotion. His enticing full lips reminded her of how much she'd missed the feel of them against hers. She brought her fingers to her mouth, feeling the ghost of a touch she hadn't felt in years. Memory was a funny thing, she thought as her body reacted to the sight of him. The hair she loved running her fingers through was longer, the ends curling out from beneath a beat-up baseball cap at his nape. She snapped her eyes away from his and looked up at Alexa, who was smiling her brilliant smile as if nothing about this little reunion was unsettling. She would have laughed too if she wasn't so scared of what this encounter meant. The time had come.

"What the hell are you smiling at?" she asked her friend.

"He's hot, Claire, and from the looks of the suitcases being brought in, it doesn't look like he's here for an overnight visit."

"I have to go," Claire repeated.

Alexa kept her from moving, her grip tightening even more on Claire's arm.

"Too late. Relax. You'll be fine. Say hi and then leave. If you run away, he'll question it."

"I can't face hi—"

"Claire?" Her name came out a questioning surprise in his deep, husky voice.

"Hi—" she started, her voice catching on the dryness of her throat. She cleared it and tried again. "Hi, Austin," trying desperately to convey a confidence she didn't feel.

"It's been a while. How are you?" he asked.

"I'm good, you?"

"Hmmm, getting by. You know how it is."

"No I don't, actually. Listen, I'd love to stay and chat, but I have to go. I'm—"

"Hi Alexa, how've you been?" he said, cutting Claire off midsentence and turning to her friend.

"Great," she responded, that bloody smile plastered on her beautiful face.

"I have to go," said Claire once more to no one in particular.

She was going to pass out. The one bite she'd had of her cucumber sandwich was threating to come back up. She pressed her fist over her stomach, trying to control her emotions and bodily fluids.

"Yeah, you were saying. Why are you in such a rush? I have to check in. If you wait, we can grab a drink, catch up."

Claire looked up at him, dumbfounded by the request. "I can't. I have to get back to work."

"Where do you work?"

"I paint," she said to him as his lips turned up into a knowing smile. "I just signed a contract with the hotel," she informed him, waving her hand at the expansive lobby. "I need to get started."

"You always did beautiful work. Do you have a studio?" he asked with genuine interest.

"I have one at home," she said nervously.

"Where's home these days?"

"Springridge. Look, I really need to get going."

"Springridge, really? You did always want to settle there. I have some interviews today, but maybe I'll see you around. I'm going to stay with my parents for the summer."

"Your parents?"

"Yeah, they moved back a week ago—though their stuff's been here for a couple of months. They bought a nice property up in the Escarpment."

"Your parents are living in Springridge?" she asked, flabbergasted by this revelation. The town was small; she could run into them. She didn't want to think what this meant with Austin back in town. Their families knew a lot of the same people, most of which still lived in Springridge. The thought that someone could have said something about Charlie nearly had her running to her parents' house to grab her son and escape…again.

"And you're staying…with them?" she stammered.

"It's what I said. I need to chill. It's been a crazy few years. I'll be there tomorrow," he whispered, leaning into her and winking. "Maybe you and I can meet by the pond. You know, for old time's sake."

She looked up at him, startled by the mischief in his voice. She didn't miss the vindictive gleam in his eyes.

"I'll pass, thanks."

"Are you sure, darling? Others would jump at the chance

11

to frolic under a weeping willow. Is the willow still there?"

She stared at him, offended and unable to come up with a response malicious enough to affect him. She turned away from him.

"I'll call you later, Alex," she said and attempted to walk away.

His grip on her arm was like a shock to her already rattled senses, despite his cunning words. She hated herself for reacting to him.

"Come on, sweetheart, a little touch here and there between old friends won't hurt anyone. Where there are no feelings..." He shrugged. "Well, there are no feelings."

"Who are you?" she asked, unable to mask the hurt from his words.

She might have deserved his anger. Hell, she'd expected it. But she never imagined he would be so cruel. It was obvious his wounds were still raw—her own self-inflicted wounds hadn't completely healed either.

There was a minute or two of uncomfortable silence. Claire looked anywhere but at him—she could feel his gaze on her. He'd always been good at calling her bluff, and she was sure that if he looked into her eyes he would call bullshit. At the sound of his name, the three of them turned. A sharply dressed man was gesturing with his head for Austin to join them.

"You're being summoned," said Alexa.

"Looks that way. I need to check in. Claire, Alexa, it was

nice seeing the two of you," he said.

The brush of his shoulder against hers was a strategic maneuver. One that left his scent lingering in the air around her. But the sting of his touch, no matter the subtlety, was heartbreaking.

She risked a look in his direction. His head was bent, listening to whatever the man who'd called him was saying. As they spoke, he reached out for a paper that the concierge slid over to him. The shorter man kept talking as Austin looked over the piece of paper, signaled for a pen, and scribbled something on it. The girl behind the counter handed him what she assumed was a key card. He looked at her, said something, and the girl blushed and batted her fake lashes. She slipped another piece of paper towards him. Austin took a look at it, smiled at the girl, and slipped the paper into his back pocket.

"Well, there's a rock star move if I've ever seen one. Any money that's her number sh—"

"I don't care!" Claire snapped.

Just as those words slipped past her lips, Austin looked up, holding her gaze. She wondered briefly if he'd heard them. That thought quickly vanished as he turned on his heel and walked away. In those brief few seconds, she saw the resentment and, if she wasn't mistaken, the anger he held towards her. She let out her breath and squeezed her eyes shut in an attempt to keep the tears she hadn't let spill in years from making a rare appearance. It took a second for her to realize that Alexa held her arm once again. Claire swung her arm free from her friend's numbing grip and turned her panic-stricken face toward her.

"What the fuck am I going to do? I have to go. I have to go get Charlie," she rambled.

"Relax, Claire. He's checking into the hotel. He won't be there until tomorrow. Besides, you knew this would happen at some point. You can't keep Charlie from him forever."

"I'm not ready to tell him, Alexa."

"So when then? When will you be ready? Charlie needs his father, Claire. That boy worships a man he's never met. He needs to know his father, and Austin needs to know his son. It was just a matter of time."

"I'm scared..."

"I know you are, sweetie, but these are the consequences of your decisions. Everything will turn out, you'll see."

"And if it doesn't? What if Austin decides to take him from me, then what?"

"Then you could be in for the fight of your life, but I doubt he will do that. Austin is a good man, Claire. I know it's been years, but people don't change too much."

"He hates me. Did you hear how he spoke to me? God, I can't think right now. I have to get to my son."

"Please try to calm down, Claire. I don't want you driving like this."

"I'll be fine. I'll call when I get to Springridge."

"Promise?"

"I promise."

Claire grabbed her things and headed towards the side

door entrance in order to avoid the mayhem of fans in front of the hotel. Her quick steps took her past the bank of elevators. She glanced in one of the cars to see Austin standing in a corner, fiddling with his phone. As if sensing her presence, he looked up at her, a somber look on his face. Her steps faltered, but she couldn't bring herself to look away as the doors slid shut. She watched the numbers light one by one as the elevator climbed, stopping on the number nine. She stared at the number until her vision blurred with tears she was unable to stop from spilling. Years of secrets and lies had caught up to her, and she was helpless to stop the storm that was brewing.

"Claire?" She turned at the sound of her name.

"Jackson? Hi, how are you?" she asked the band's drummer as she wiped at her eyes. "Wow, it's been ages. I can't believe you guys did it...I um..." her voice was shaking with pent-up emotions.

He was Austin's best friend, and hers too, to a certain extent. They'd all hung out together countless times. He'd more than once confided in her, taken her advice on all things teenager. In that moment, there was none of that camaraderie, but an awkwardness that filled her with discomfort.

"Hey, are you okay? Why are you crying?" he asked, concerned.

"I'm fine, just caught off guard, that's all."

"Yeah?"

"Yeah. I'm fine," she said and turned to walk away.

"Claire?" Jackson called. She turned slowly. "I know things didn't end great with the two of you. I don't really know what happened, except that the break-up did a number on him. He doesn't talk about it. He doesn't talk, period. It changed him, Claire," he said, waiting for her reaction. All he got were silent tears and a nod. "He's not the same guy. He doesn't smile, doesn't enjoy life anymore. I think he does this for us; his heart isn't in it anymore. Anyway, for what it's worth, he never forgot you. In fact, I don't think he ever stopped—"

"Don't. Please don't say another word. I can't bear it."

Without further acknowledgement, she took off in a run towards the doors.

The time had come.

CHAPTER TWO

Austin

What the fuck was that? Out of all the people in the world, Claire was the last person he expected to see his first day back in town. He had planned to avoid her at all costs. He figured out she was back in Springridge when his friend Michael showed him her painting a few months ago. He'd mentioned he bought them off some artist in a farmers' market in the town he grew up in, and Austin wasted no time in convincing his friend to buy all the paintings she had. Austin knew he sounded crazy, but didn't give a shit as long as he owned a piece of her. They held pride of place on the walls of his living room in New York.

He flopped himself down on the king-size bed, draping his arm across his face, suddenly plagued by exhaustion. The energy he'd used to keep his hands to himself in the lobby was strenuous work. At the sight of Claire, his heart had jumped back to life. He hadn't seen her in six years, but everything he'd felt for her suddenly surfaced. He'd forgotten for a few minutes he was supposed to hate her. She was gorgeous. A little fuller, he noticed, but gorgeous nonetheless. He dropped

17

his arm to the bed, letting out a long, ragged breath.

She mentioned she'd signed a contract with the hotel. He looked around the suite he was in and wondered how her paintings would fit into the modernized rooms. She was classical. She was unique. In his Manhattan brownstone, he would stare at her paintings every night, lately with a tumbler full of amber.

Those damned paintings were the inspiration for the band's current album. He'd shed a few tears looking at them, even drank himself to a numbing stupor one night after throwing his tumbler of bourbon at one of the paintings—of course, he had regretted it instantly. He'd wiped it clean, hoped and prayed the paint didn't run, ruining one of the few things he had of her. Whatever she'd felt in that moment was reflected in those paintings. There were messages in them, and he had yet to decipher them.

He rubbed his face hard, wincing with regret at the things he'd said to her in the lobby. He reminded himself that she'd broken his fucking heart, but the shit he spurted was uncalled for. It was like a force had urged him to go to her, to say something, anything. He just hadn't expected to be such an asshole. How could he say those things to her? She wasn't the kind of girl that one frolicked under a willow or otherwise. She was his Claire, would always be his.

Singing in front of thousands had taught him to hide his emotions—his poker face was legendary among his band members. No one messed with him. He kept to himself, wrote the saddest fucking songs, and moved on. The wretched pain that singing those songs caused was something he'd learned to hide well.

While his bandmates loved to party, he went to his hotel. He wasn't into the groupies—he got with a few in the beginning of course. He was a guy, after all. But he didn't like how easy the conquest was. There was no respect for these girls, and he didn't want to be associated with any of them. Reminded of the piece of paper in his pocket, he reached for it, looked at it, and tossed it across the room. The concierge had given him her number, had hoped to have an opportunity to go to his room. He never took numbers from girls, but he knew Claire's eyes were on him—that was the only reason he'd done it. He never flirted with chicks either; they always got the wrong idea. The fact that he turned and smiled at the chick was all to piss Claire off. He wasn't into one-night stands. He'd been in two serious relationships—the first broke his heart into a million pieces, and the second never lived up to the first.

He groaned out loud. He had a couple of interviews in an hour, not enough time for a good nap. He needed to get his shit together. Rick would be banging on his door any second to prep him. The questions were always predetermined. He didn't like being blindsided. He was a private person—his past wasn't up for discussion, mainly because he didn't want anyone loitering in his little town searching for answers. It was his way of protecting his family, of protecting Claire, to an extent. She hadn't wanted a part of this lifestyle, had made it clear to him the day she broke up with him, but damn him if he didn't miss her.

After their first big show he had wanted to call her, went as far as scrolling through his contacts, searching for her number. He wanted to tell her what had happened, how fun and exciting it had been. He'd been alone in his room, his finger hovering over her number, but it had hit him in one fell swoop that he had no right to call her, and that she didn't want him to. The anger had overwhelmed him, the excitement and novelty of the night forgotten as he threw his phone across the room with so much force it shattered. He'd never let himself reflect too much on his situation or given in to the frustration he'd felt when she'd left him. He'd never cried so hard in his life as he did that night when reality set in. And after that night, he never cried again. Austin closed himself off and concentrated on the only thing that would keep him going, his music.

The pounding on the door made him jump from his bed. He'd been so lost in his thoughts that even though he knew the banging was coming, he hadn't been ready for it.

"You better not be sleeping, McKinley," yelled Rick, always a subtle son of a bitch.

He could never do anything quietly, and he was starting to get on Austin's nerves. God, he was looking forward to this break. Two months. The band needed it because lately they'd been at each other's throats. Austin was losing steam. He'd begun to drink heavily again and was spiraling into a black hole he was finding difficult to climb out of. This time off was to figure out what they were going to do. Once tight as any five friends could be, they were now at odds over every little detail. Right down to the music, which Austin always wrote.

He was the lead singer, mastermind of the band. Without him, they were doomed. Despite their differences, those guys meant a lot to him, and he couldn't just walk away. But he honestly didn't know if he had it in him anymore.

Two hundred nights of the year were spent on a tour bus, city after city, arena after arena. After a while, he didn't bother to find out where he was. Usually, someone would remind him just before he got on stage. Last thing he wanted to do was give a shout out to Buffalo when he was in Detroit. Shit, he'd been to Paris eight times and had yet to see the Eiffel Tower from the ground. It looked magnificent from the air.

Watching his muse staring at him, glassy-eyed, and then seeing her disappear from his view once the elevator door closed, he wondered how much more he had in him. He had exhausted every word to describe love and hate. The knocking got louder. He ran his hands over his face, the scratch of stubble reminding him he needed to shave. Roughly, he dragged his fingers through his hair as he made his way to the door.

"Okay, so the car will be here in ten to take you to the studio. The interview is one segment, so you shouldn't be there for more than half an hour. Then at..." Rick stopped to look at his watch like he hadn't just checked it two minutes ago, "three, you have an interview with the magazine. That should also be no more than half an hour. They want to interview the whole band individually, probably trying to get some dirt on you guys. Everyone is getting suspicious about the amount of time you're all taking off. You're going first, and then you're free to figure your shit out."

21

Austin let out the breath he hadn't realize he was holding. Ten minutes, he thought. Not enough time to shave or take that shower he wanted so badly.

"Where are the questions they're going to ask?" he asked his manager.

"Oh, well. The show is on the fly. They want your genuine reaction."

"That's not the deal. You know that. My contract states that in interviews my questions are to be predetermined. You're in breach, Rick," he said, his temper boiling to the surface.

The fucker had caught him at a bad time; he wasn't in the mood for surprises.

"Come on, Austin. A few questions on the fly aren't going to hurt your delicate reputation. Everyone knows you don't screw around. Your privacy is legendary, man. No one has ever been able to dig one clump of dirt on you in years. You'll be fine."

"I don't like it."

"Shit, man. What the hell's got you so on edge? I saw the chick behind the counter slide her number towards you. Maybe you should give her a call, let off some steam."

"I don't do that shit, Rick. You know that."

"I'm just saying. You were fine in the limo ride over here. Was it that sweet piece of ass in the lobby I saw you talking to? Maybe you should—"

Austin caught him by his blue designer tie and pushed him against the wall.

"Don't even finish what you were about to say," he said through clenched teeth.

"All right, relax man. It's just that I saw you tense up after you spoke to her."

"She's none of your concern, Rick. Just drop it."

Rick looked at him knowingly. Austin rubbed his face hard again, a sure sign he was about to lose his cool.

"That's her, isn't it?" Rick asked.

"What?"

"Don't play dumb with me. She's the one. The girl you sing about." Austin stared at his manager and friend and nodded.

"Yeah," he breathed out.

Rick nodded in understanding. He'd been the one to rescue Austin's phone from the mangled mess he'd left it in after his first concert. Austin confided in him that night, told him all about Claire because he needed someone to talk to about her. His band members knew her well, and he didn't want to discuss her with guys who had once been her friends too.

"Think things through, Austin. I know you've been struggling this past year, and I want you to have a level head when you make whatever decision you make about the band. I'm your friend, man, and I want you to be happy. This doesn't make you happy anymore. I don't think it ever has."

"Thanks," was all he said before turning to the bathroom and shutting the door.

He leaned against the white marble counter on his elbows, the heel of his hands digging into his eye sockets, trying to keep his fucking tears at bay. Seeing her had done a number on him. She'd been nervous, Alexa's hand the only thing keeping her standing. He couldn't help but think that there was more to her reaction. She was too on edge, too guarded, almost incoherent when she talked. She had very little makeup on, and that white dress she wore showed off her smooth, tanned skin. Those heels enhancing her mile-long legs.

He loved those legs—they were the first thing he'd noticed about her, and those cheekbones, so high and defined, flanked by her curly chestnut hair. He stretched his arms up high, swinging his neck from side to side in an effort to shake off the vision.

He turned on the water, let it run cold, and splashed his face several times. He ran his wet hands through his hair to tame it, dried his face a little too roughly, threw the towel into a corner on the bathroom floor, and walked out with renewed purpose.

"Come on, Romeo. We need to head out," Rick yelled from the living room.

"Coming, asshat," he said as he pulled his shirt over his head.

He searched for his toiletries, rolled on some deodorant,

24

and dug through his suitcase for a clean shirt. He found a white button-down dress shirt—one of the few clean shirts he had packed. None of the guys had time to do any laundry after their last show. The band packed what they had and hopped on a plane home from L.A. He stared at himself in the mirror as he buttoned up his shirt and rolled up the sleeves to his elbow, watching his tattoo appear beneath the sleeve. Hidden in the curves of the colorful ink was her name—a secret he'd never revealed to anyone. Unless he pointed it out, no one could see it.

"Ready?" asked Rick, poking his head into the bedroom.

"Yeah, let's go," he said, striding out into the living room.

He grabbed his black leather jacket, expertly swinging it on as he followed Rick out the door.

They drove into the CBC studios in Toronto through a small gate twenty minutes later. The parking garage was a public one—this always freaked Austin out, because fans had places to hide. As he looked around for surprise jumpers, they were led into an elevator, up to the main lobby and another set of elevators. He continued to inspect his surroundings as he followed what he assumed was one of the production assistants. The guy had introduced himself, but Austin hadn't been paying attention. They were asked to wait in a green room that was actually red and were offered beverages and pastries. He served himself some coffee and walked to a window that faced the Rogers Center. He'd never been in a green room with a window before. Looking out at the stadium, he thought it might be a good idea for him and his dad to attend a Jays' game. It'd been years since he'd seen a live baseball game.

Rick mumbled into his phone, trying to make arrangements for his other clients, making notes on a pad with efficient ease. The guy was a complete pain in the ass. He did good work, but Austin often wondered what his intentions were. The paparazzi had published some photos of Austin a year ago, and he often suspected Rick had something to do with it. The location of his vacation had been, like most things in his life lately, a secret. The only people who knew where he'd be were his parents and Rick. He knew for a fact that his parents would never rat him out. He could never prove it, and he didn't have the energy to confront the man. He just wanted to get over this last matter of business and take the next two months to himself.

As he sat across from the host, he thought about how much he hated interviews. They weren't overly hard, just really fucking tedious. The same pointless, intrusive questions. Strangers sitting across from him thinking they knew him, or at least acting like it. This George dude wasn't any different. He played it cool, leaned in when a question got too personal like the answer would stay between them.

"These songs you write, dude, they are profound. Are they about someone you know, or knew?"

Austin had been asked this question a hundred million times, and the answer was always the same. Although he pretended to put thought into his answer, he knew exactly what his response would be. This asshole was going fishing, and

Austin wasn't taking the bait.

"No, man, I just write about experiences, things that everyone goes through. A lot of people relate to those songs, and that gives me great pleasure. It makes me proud of our work."

"So there's no inspiration?"

"No. It's all in my head."

"It's no secret that you're a very private person. Does it take a great deal of work to keep your private life private?"

"Not so much work. I don't put myself in situations that might make the gossip columns. I'm actually quite boring. I don't party like most in the industry. The press and paparazzi learned that after a couple of years, I think. They pretty much leave me alone."

"You've achieved the impossible, man, for someone of your caliber."

"Yeah, so I've been told," said Austin, laughing that laugh that most people used for effect. "But my privacy somehow still manages to be invaded…"

Nothing he did was sincere anymore. With the exception of the last sentence, the whole damned interview was a lie. What did they expect from him, to spill his guts out on the shiny red leather chair he sat on? Not happening.

"There are rumors out there that there's some tension in the band, hence this long hiatus you're all taking."

"No, we just need a break. We're exhausted. We've been

touring for five years straight with a week or two to chill. Some of the guys in the band have families, girlfriends. At some point that needs to take priority. It's just a break; time out to write a little and just relax. Get our heads back in the game for the fall."

"What about you? Taking time out for your girl?" George asked. The question took Austin by surprise. So much so that he didn't even have time to hide his reaction.

"Nah, man, no girl. I'm single. I live a pretty solitary life. I like it that way."

"So will there be a new album and a tour come fall?"

"Possibly. I will write some stuff, then we'll record and see where it takes us."

"That's awesome, man. I can't wait to hear what you come up with. Well kids, give our hometown boy a round of applause. Thanks for stopping by, Austin."

"Yeah, thank you."

They broke to commercial, and both men shook hands.

"Sorry about the chick question, but I had to get it in there."

"Yeah, whatever, man. You gotta ask what you gotta ask for the show."

"Well, it was nice meeting you."

"You too," Austin said, not meaning a word.

He rushed off the stage and to the elevators that would

take him back to the garage. A horde of fans waited in the underground, crowding around him as he exited. He hated this, the groping and the hair pulling. Why did chicks have to pull your fucking hair? He had his Bubba Gump hat in his jacket and pulled it on in an effort to keep his hair on his head. Girls started reaching for him the second he walked out. His security team started pushing them back. Someone grabbed his jacket, he turned, and his temper reached a boiling point.

"Don't fucking pull at my clothes," he yelled and moved out of the death grip of a girl with a heavily made-up face. "Go, go. I'm not stopping," he yelled to Tiny, his head of security.

The guy was massive. He even scared Austin sometimes. Fans didn't mess with him, and neither did his staff. He was tough, honest, and a friend.

"Open the car door," Tiny yelled to his partner, Mike.

He could hear the name-calling as he passed the group of girls, some of which didn't look old enough to even know who he was. Someone threw a marker, hitting him in the nape of his neck.

"Jesus. What the fuck?" he said, rubbing the back of his neck.

Mike pushed him into the car, where he leaned back against the headrest and breathed a sigh of relief. He hated when the fans got aggressive; it was the one thing he would never get used to. Most felt they had some right to him. It was like a thousand jealous girlfriends in one place. He'd seen chicks get into fights when approaching him or any of the

29

other guys. Austin and Jackson were the only single ones in the band. Their lead bassist, Mark, had a girlfriend, but the guy took whatever he could get on the road. Simon, their pianist, had a wife and kid he loved more than anything, but he had his faults and never passed up easy pussy when it was offered. Austin hated that about him. Jackson was more discreet, but a slut like the rest of them. That was a pattern Austin had never been interested in following. Not at that rate anyway.

He hadn't exactly been a monk on the road. He had needs, but those needs were met on rare occasions. The chicks were usually respectable, not the high traffic zones his dumbass bandmates ripped through. Those chicks would give it up to anyone on the path to get to one of them, and some had. It disgusted him.

"You all right, Austin?"

"Yeah, just get me out of here."

He stared up at the CN Tower as they drove onto Front Street. How long had it been since he'd gone up there? How long since he'd done something as mundane as taken a walk down the street, sat outside on a patio to have a meal or coffee? Everything about his life in the past five years had been rushed. He was looking forward to some down time. Hanging out by his parents' pool, seeing his sister, who had been worried about him the last time he'd seen her three months ago. He reassured Analia and her husband Trevor that he was just tired—not a total lie. The truth was he was lonely. He needed to have something aside from music to connect to, to look forward to. He needed his family. His older sister had gotten married three years ago, and now he had a two-year-old hell-raiser of a niece. He wanted to spend time getting to know Sydney. Hell, he wanted to take the time to find himself once again.

He reached into his pocket for his phone, scrolled through his contacts, and called his mom—the one solid, honest thing in his life. She was the one who kept him humble, and to a certain extent, sane. He could tell her anything, trusted her with every fiber in his being. She was his only true friend.

"Sweetheart!" she greeted on the first ring.

"Hi, Mom. How are you?"

"I'm doing good, honey. How about you? You sound tired."

"I am tired, Mom, so tired."

"When are you coming home?"

"Later today. I have a magazine interview now, and then I'm coming home. I need to come home."

"What time did you get in?" she asked.

"A couple of hours ago," he said, the exasperation evident in his voice.

"Is everything all right, Austin?" He should have known his mom would pick up on his mood. She'd always been the more perceptive one in the family—a mom thing, he supposed.

"I saw Claire, Mom. She looked…so beautiful. It was…it just…well, I…" he trailed off.

"Austin," she whispered.

"I missed her, Mom. Seeing her made me realize how much I need her. None of this is worth a thing without her. I should have fought harder for her. I should have stayed."

"It might not have changed a thing, Austin. You could have missed out on all your success."

"I don't want any more success, Mom. I'm so fucking tired," he said, catching himself after dropping the f-bomb. "Sorry."

"Oh, sweetie. Just come home. Sleep, relax, and think things through."

"I wasn't very nice her."

"What did you do?"

"I didn't do anything. It's what I said. I might have implied she was…easy."

"I've raised you better than that, Austin. I know you're angry, but she had her reasons, and I think the time has come for the two of you to hash things out."

"What aren't you telling me, Mom?"

"I saw her a couple of days ago…on Main Street. She didn't notice me. She wasn't alone, Austin," she said.

"Was she with…a man?"

"You could say that. Just come home, son. Find her, talk to her." There was a brief moment of silence—in the background he could hear laughter and shouting.

"What's all that ruckus? Having a party without me?"

"It's just your dad with Analia and Sydney out by the pool."

The thought of his sister and her daughter enjoying the day at his parents' filled him with envy. Although he cared deeply about his family, he craved normalcy and something of his own. Nostalgia had plagued him the past few months. Memories from the past and dreams for the future were part of his daily train of thought. He was lonely, so fucking lonely it hurt. He rubbed his face, surprised to feel tears in his eyes.

"Sounds like Dad's having a blast. I can't wait to see him."

"Yeah, he is." She laughed.

"I can't wait to see everyone. I'll let you go. I'll see you in a couple hours."

"So soon? I thought you were coming home tomorrow," she said.

"I changed my mind. I need to come home sooner."

"I can't wait to see you." He heard her intake of breath.

"Everything okay, Mom?"

"Yes, everything is fine, darling. I'll see you later."

"I love you."

"I love you, too, Austin."

Austin dropped his head onto the headrest and wondered what she wasn't telling him. Maybe it was because he was tired, but he swore he heard nervousness in his mother's voice.

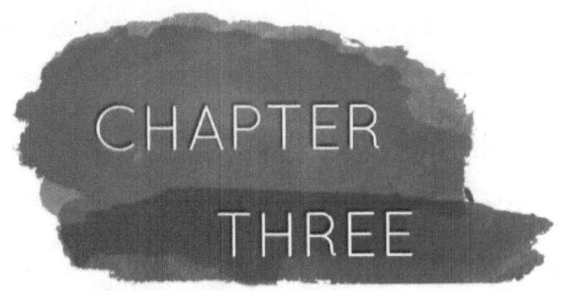

CHAPTER THREE

Claire

The drive to Springridge was a hideous one, with cottagers clogging the roads on their way to their sanctuaries by the lake—a sure sign summer was underway. Cars were slowing down traffic to stare at an accident. The freeway was at a standstill, and Claire looked around desperately for the nearest exit. She glanced at the clock on her dash and wondered why people left the city so early in the day when it wasn't much of a quicker option. The only thing on her mind was getting to her son.

Eventually the rubberneckers of Southern Ontario began to move. In her peripheral vision, she could see the big red trucks and flashing lights, but she could care less whether or not the car everyone slowed to look at was a mangled mess. With her exit now in view, she let out the breath she'd been holding from the second she looked up to see Austin McKinley walking towards her and Alexa. Stunning was the word that stuck out in her mind as he neared them in rugged, faded jeans, a perfect fitted T-shirt, and that damn cap. Of all things, he had to be wearing that cap.

She had searched the ends of the Internet looking for that baseball hat. After a weekend spent watching Oscar-winning films, Forest Gump had stood out for all the wrong reasons. He'd gotten it into his head that he needed to have a Bubba Gump cap. After an extensive search and seven years after the release of the movie, Claire had found it for sale on eBay. Seeing it on his head six years later was as much of a shock as seeing him—she couldn't believe he still had it. That night, she gave him a lot more than that damned baseball hat. She gave him everything—her body, her soul, and her heart. He took it all and gave the same things right back to her.

Did he think of her every time he put it on? Did it have some sentimental value for him? Is that why he still had it and wore it?

These thoughts were jumbling her brain as she sped down the two-lane country road that would lead to her parents' house. Although she'd been friends with Austin since the sixth grade, it wasn't until they both turned fourteen that things began to change between them. She had spent so much time at his house growing up—she knew the way there by heart. Since her parents were rarely around, the McKinleys were the only stable thing she and Hunter had known. She'd had a kind of freedom she despised, but most of her friends envied. She wanted nothing more than to have parents who cared enough to ground her for coming home after midnight, parents who would give a damn if she failed her math tests. Since she had none of that, she relied on Austin for all of it. He gave her stability, love, and in some admirable way, he understood how to give her all that without demanding a thing.

36

Letting him go was like letting go of a piece of herself, and despite her own pain, she took solace in the fact that inside her, a piece of him would always be with her. He had been her rock, her best friend, and she'd had to save him from the confinement of young parenthood. Over the years she'd bought his albums, although she never listened to any of them. They were stored in a box in her closet, still sealed. She'd also ordered a concert T-shirt or two. She told herself those things were for his son, but she had to admit, they were for her too. She was proud of him and loved him just as much as she did the day she said good-bye. Talent like his needed to be shared, and she needed to share him.

Turning onto the long driveway, she took several deep breaths to calm her nerves before coming to a stop on the circular driveway of her parents' home. Several minutes later, she was leaning against the steering wheel, her face in her hands, the car still running. A knock on her window made her jump. Her mother, Angie, stood on the other side of the glass, a somber smile on her lovely, ageless face. In the past few years, she and Claire had become close. It'd been a long road for them all, but she finally had her parents back, so to speak. She turned the ignition off and opened the door. Angie stepped back, giving her the necessary space to get out of the car and gain back some of her composure.

"He's here. In Toronto. I saw him."

"I know. Alexa just called and told me. She was worried about you, said you were a little shaken."

"He wasn't very nice." In fact, he was cruel, calm, and

collected.

"Are you okay?"

"No, I'm scared, worried..." she trailed off. "Did you know his parents were back in town?"

"No, I had no idea."

"What if they've seen us, Mom? Charlie and I spend a lot of time walking up and down Main Street."

"She would have approached you."

"Maybe," she whispered and looked right at her mother. "It's time, then?"

"Yes, sweetheart, it's time. Claire, we'll be here for you, with you, whatever you want. We won't push you, but I think now will be your best chance. From what Alexa said, it sounds like he'll be here all summer. That's a lot of time for him to get to know his son."

"I need to get Charlie."

"We figured you'd want to take him home right away. He's ready. A little disappointed, though," said Angie, giving Claire an understanding smile.

"He's got baseball this evening. You'll come?"

"Of course. You know we don't miss a game. Six thirty, right?"

"Yes."

"Okay. Come on. Let's go get our boy. He's had a big lunch, finished about a half hour ago, so he should be okay for

38

a little bit." She winked, knowing a little bit meant he would be asking for food in the next hour.

Her son was a bottomless pit, and nothing seemed to satisfy his growing-boy appetite. At five years old, he was giving her wallet a run for its money, literally. It seemed the only time Charlie wasn't eating was when he was sleeping, but even then, Claire swore he dreamed about food.

"Thank you."

"Anytime, Claire."

"No, I mean with everything. I know I haven't made things easy, and you didn't agree with my choices."

"No, we didn't. But you're our daughter and we support you. Maybe you didn't go about things the right way, but I understand why you did it. You love Austin, Claire. I see it every time you look at Charlie. We all wanted him to succeed, you more than any of us. Things will turn out. You'll see."

"I hope you're right."

"He's going to be angry. Most of that anger will be directed at you. You have to be prepared for that. Your father and I made a lot of mistakes when you were little. We were selfish and irresponsible, but you, my sweet girl, you inherited none of that selfishness. I'm proud of you. You're a great mother, Claire. Don't ever let anyone tell you any different."

"Oh, Mama," she said and threw herself at Angie.

She'd prided herself on being the independent person she'd grown into. At twenty-three, she'd lived through so much, had endured a life away from all that was comfortable and familiar. She was in the process of raising a fantastic human being, and now she was about to face the biggest obstacle of her life.

In the family room, her son was leaning against the large brown leather sectional, his face twisted as he and his grandpa played an intense game of hockey on the X-Box. The large French doors let in sunlight, brightening up the space nicely and providing a direct view of the Escarpment and the backfields she loved to take in on lazy afternoons by the pool. It all seemed very intimidating all of a sudden, a sort of finality settling in the pit of her stomach. She and Austin had spent so many days at her house out by the pool, under that damned willow where they'd kissed until their lips hurt. With him so close, memories flooded her mind. Claire wanted nothing more than to get the hell out of there. The heavy sickness was a direct line to her intuition—Austin would show up at her door sooner rather than later.

"Would you like something to drink, Claire?" Angie asked from the kitchen, snapping Claire from her thoughts.

"No, I'm good. We really should get going. I've got some grocery shopping to do and, well..." She was babbling again.

"I understand. Charlie, Bruce, finish up," Angie said, her voice authoritative.

Claire couldn't help but smile at the tone she used on her husband. It was a familiar one—one she herself had adopted with her own son. She guessed women were born with it. As time passed, they perfected it with the menacing tone that made kids and husbands jump to attention.

A resounding "aww" came from the area directly in front of the large flat screen. Claire had always loved this room. It was homey; a place for gathering. No matter how beautifully the rest of the house was set up for any Monroe party, no one ever left the kitchen. During family dinners, which were rare, everyone moved the few feet from the kitchen to the living room area. The flat-screen TV had replaced the stand-alone plasma that had been all the rage thirteen years ago. It was now the ultimate entertaining area, with surround sound and, much to her son's delight, the ultimate gaming equipment. Although the house had a completely finished basement, no one ever went down there. She was certain she and Austin were the only two people that ever took advantage of the privacy it offered.

Those memories were blush worthy. Nights spent curled up in each other's arms on the sofa, sometimes naked. If those walls could talk, the things they would reveal. She smiled to herself as she watched Charlie dutifully put away the gaming controllers, not before making sure they saved the game, of course. How things changed.

She looked through the big sliding doors, swaying in the light breeze; Claire spotted the giant willow they'd spent countless hours beneath. Just thinking of his comment made her angry. How could he? How could he say something like that about moments that meant everything to her?

"You ready, buddy? We have to go grocery shopping, and you've got baseball."

"Do I have to go grocery shopping? Why can't I stay

here?" asked Charlie.

"If you stay, I buy what I want and you don't get the cereal you want."

"Okay, fine. You guys coming to my game?" he asked his grandparents.

"What kind of a question is that? Of course we'll be there. Have we missed a game yet?" asked Bruce.

"Nope."

"Nope, that's right. Now let's go get your things before these two gang up on us and take away our privileges."

"You're right, Grandpa. Last thing I need is my pool time provoked," said Charlie convincingly.

"Revoked, Charlie. The word is revoked, not provoked," corrected Claire.

"Well, as long as you know what I mean," he said and turned towards the laundry room in search of his things.

Out in the car, Charlie insisted on buckling his own seatbelt. A month after his fifth birthday, and he insisted on being treated like a bigger kid.

They drove in silence. Claire too absorbed in her thoughts, and Charlie focused on his new iPod, a birthday gift from Hunter. The kid was spoiled rotten—his grandparents had mastered the art, and his uncle Hunter was no better. Claire's job had always been to keep him humble. He knew his grandparents had lots of money. At five years old, he was anything but dense. It was all around him when he visited their home. What he didn't know was how much money they themselves had.

Claire had been given access to a very generous trust fund when she turned twenty-one. Despite that, she drove a vintage 1988 Land Rover in safari green. She lived on what she made; every penny was saved, and she even used coupons at the supermarket. Her parents never taught her humility; that was something she developed on her own, and something she intended to pass on to her son.

The supermarket was a breeze, thankfully. She picked up snacks for Charlie's baseball team, settling on tube yogurt and apple slices, certain she would get moans from the team. She wasn't in the mood to think of something more exciting, too preoccupied with the events of earlier in the afternoon. She couldn't even manage to remember what it was she needed to stock her own fridge, let alone what a little league team preferred to eat. She picked up what she needed to make a decent stir-fry and the essentials: bread, milk, and eggs. She would make a list and go back sometime during the weekend. Hopefully by then her nerves would be back to something resembling normal.

Once at the house, she had no choice but to put her thoughts aside and urge her son to do his chores. One other thing her parents never encouraged. When she moved out, she had no clue how to do laundry, cook, or use a dishwasher. She felt stupid, and at times, useless. It was at those times when she wondered how she was going to take care of a child. She'd managed, though. She stocked up on cookbooks and baby books, and she learned. She'd become quite domesticated, and was surprised at times at how far she had come. Charlie was well-rounded, respectful, smart, and a joy to have around. There were times when she could barely remember her life before him because, before him, there was only Austin. Now, she had Austin's much shorter, energetic replica.

"Charlie!" she yelled from the driveway.

"Yeah?" he yelled back from the porch.

"I need you to help me, buddy."

"Oh, okay." He jumped the four steps from the recently renovated front porch and ran to the back of the car where Claire was gathering the shopping bags.

"Grab these. They're not so heavy. Leave them on the porch and come get your backpack."

He moaned and grumbled under his breath, but did as he was told. Nearly knocking her over, he ran back to the car and grabbed his backpack from the back seat. Claire fumbled with her keys on a door lock that had seen better days. Although her parents had taken care of the inside of the house, the outside needed some fixing. The old sagging porch had been recently given a facelift. Now the locks on the doors needed to be changed. The upstairs windows also needed replacing. That was something she would have to do before winter rolled in.

"I thought you were going to change that?"

"I will. Maybe we can go to the hardware store this weekend. You can help pick something nice."

"Can I help you change it?"

"You have to help me. You're the man of the house."

"I am?"

"You're the only man that lives here."

"Okay then, I'll help," he said with a smug smile so much like his father's.

After struggling a few more seconds, the lock finally gave way and the door unexpectedly swung open, bouncing off the wall. Both she and Charlie cringed at the sound of the glass insert clattering from the impact.

"Did it break?" he asked, his eyes closed.

"No." She laughed. "I'm not sure what it would take for it to break."

"Maybe we should get a new door too, so we don't have to find out."

"Maybe. Come on. Let's get this stuff put away. I need you to clean your room and find your baseball uniform."

"I don't know where it is."

"Find it."

"Can I watch some TV first?"

"No. Room and uniform first, then you can watch TV if we have time."

Sulking, he dragged the shopping bags into the kitchen. Although he tried, chores weren't his favorite thing to do. Her mother always pestered her for making him do things. In Angie's eyes, he was still a baby. She argued that she felt it necessary to not only teach him some independence but routine and discipline. Structure and stability were things she and Hunter grew up without, and it was something she craved as a child. She wanted Charlie to have a sense of normalcy that her parents never bothered with, and she'd be damned if anyone was going to change the way she raised her son. She and Hunter had turned out okay; the damage had been repaired, to a certain extent.

As her son pouted his way up to his room, she began the mundane task of putting their meager groceries away. As she placed the milk in the refrigerator, she realized she already had two cartons. How in hell were they going to drink four liters of milk? She only used it in her coffee. Her son drank more, but there was no way they would drink the older cartons before they expired. She wondered briefly if she should go return them. Putting that thought aside, she grabbed the necessary ingredients for chicken stir-fry as she put away the rest of the groceries.

She looked up at the large clock over the fireplace mantel and was relieved to see that for once she wasn't running late. The meeting in Toronto had gone on longer than she expected, but she was home in time to prepare dinner and get Charlie ready for his game. Thanks to Alexa, the deal was practically in the bag. She just needed to sign the contract Rae was going to courier over, and then she'd put her creative mind to work. As her agent, friend, and hotel manager talked, Claire got a good idea of what she wanted to paint. Still, she wanted to take a look at the room designs; she didn't want to paint anything classical if the rooms were going to have a more contemporary feel. Two months, three paintings. She could do it. It was her job, after all. The one thing besides spending time with her son that she loved to do.

She also wondered what Austin's reappearance was going to do to her creativity. He'd always been her inspiration, brought the best artist she could be out of her. His support and enthusiasm for her art was unwavering, and his encouragement was everything to her. Every brush stroke and color combination was for him, even in the years they'd been apart. The thought of the possibility that he might see her paintings on a wall somewhere always excited her. She also wondered if he would know that she was the artist. Her ringing cell phone snapped her out of her thoughts. She walked to her purse and dug through it for the phone, but didn't get to it in time. She checked the call log—it was a number she didn't recognize.

She turned to the kitchen island and began the task of chopping vegetables and chicken for their dinner. She put the wok on the stove and waited for the oil to heat. In a separate pot, she cooked some rice and, as she always did, no matter the dinner theme, she put together a Caesar salad for no other reason than because her son loved it. The sizzling of the chicken was a comforting sound. She loved to cook for Charlie—he ate everything and anything put in front of him and tried everything at least once. It was imperative that he eat at least a good two hours before the game. She'd made the mistake once of taking him to a game on a full stomach, and she spent a whole evening cleaning vomit off the floor of her car.

"Charlie!" she yelled as she set two places on the island.

"Yes, Mom!"

"Did you find your uniform?" she yelled again, only to have the last word catch in her throat at the sight of her child in the doorway.

"Yep, and that jock thing too. I don't need to put it on yet, do I?"

"No, not yet. Dinner should be ready shortly. Did you tidy up your room?"

"Sort of."

"Sort of? Buddy, bedroom, now."

"Fine."

She toasted some garlic bread, which they both loved, gave the chicken one last stir, added the vegetables and soy sauce, and let it sit. Her phone began to ring again, and she picked it up from the coffee table. She saw that it was the same number as a few minutes ago, and let the call go to voicemail. The ringing stopped, only to start up again. She turned the volume off, not in the mood to speak to anyone really, let alone a stranger. She added the dressing to the salad, put apple juice on the table, and yelled for her son to come to dinner.

CHAPTER FOUR

Austin

From the second he saw her at the hotel, he had no clue what had propelled him toward her. And just like at the hotel, his battered heart had taken over his cluttered brain and once again pushed him in her direction. All it took was some calls, and within minutes of being home, he had her address.

His mother had insisted he call her first, not just show up unexpected. She'd seemed nervous and asked him to wait a day or so. He couldn't though; if he waited another night, he would lose his nerve.

It had taken everything he had to not go after her earlier. God, he loved her so much. He missed her like crazy over the years, but she'd made her choice. A choice he questioned every day for the last six years. He tapped one of the handlebars of his bike with his fingers to an invisible tune as he pulled up to the curb—he was nervous as hell. The last time he'd been this nervous was when he played their first show at Madison Square Garden. Claire was the only woman in the world that could bring him to his fucking weak knees. He took a deep breath and walked up the path leading to her porch.

The house was large. Three floors of red brick seemed to tower over him. He looked around the well-tended garden, full of color. He wouldn't have expected less from her. Her attention to detail, right down to the green shrubbery, was strategic. He ran his hand over his hair as he stood in front of the door and heard her yell.

"Charlie, dinner!"

What? Who the hell was Charlie?

Shit. What if that was the man his mom mentioned? He hadn't seen a ring on her finger. Then again, he hadn't really looked away from her face.

"Charlie!" she called out again, but he couldn't hear any response. The thought that she was involved with another man grated at his every nerve.

He never imagined she'd move on from him. There was more to their breakup; he was certain of it. No chick cried as hard as she had after breaking up with a guy because she didn't love him. He'd seen the torment in her eyes, no matter how hard she tried to hide it. He didn't want her to be with anyone else. He knew that made him a hypocrite, but this was Claire. His Claire. The fist of jealousy had him by the throat, and without further thought, he reached for the doorknob. When it turned, he let out a breath, and then quickly held it again when the door swung open like it had been pulled from the other side. He reached out to grab it before it rammed against the wall. He'd have to talk to her about locking her door. Sure, Springridge wasn't the break-in capital of the world, but you never know. She lived alone, or so he thought. She needed to be more careful.

"Charlie, dinner!" she yelled again, her irritation barely masked.

Who the hell was this dude? She'd called him three times now. He looked around her living room to see if this Charlie character was around. The last thing he needed was some dude blindsiding him. He walked quietly past the dining room and stood in a large archway that gave way to a kitchen and family room. She was standing on her tiptoes, reaching for bowls, her sweet ass perfectly displayed in the white dress she still wore. The large kitchen island was set for two in front of white wooden bar stools. He looked around. For an artist, the kitchen was boring and sterile-looking, with white walls and off-white cupboards. The dark island in the middle of the room was the only thing that stood out.

"Baby, you need to...Jesus!" she shrieked at the sight of Austin standing in her kitchen doorway.

He watched her reach out for the fridge handle for support. Her breath caught, and he wondered for a moment if she was going to pass out.

"You scared the shit out of me. Don't you knock?"

"Don't you lock your door?"

"It's my house."

"Yes, and the door was unlocked. You need to lock it. Anyone can walk in."

"Clearly. What are you doing here?" she asked, sounding annoyed he'd shown up.

Okay, so maybe he should have knocked, but damn it, she was here with another guy, and he didn't like it. He didn't like that one bit.

"I finished early, so I thought I'd come home. Who the hell is Charlie?" he asked, trying to reel in the caveman act.

"How did you get my address?"

"I called around. Now, who the hell is Charlie?"

She brought her hand to her chest, and he could see the pulse at the base of her neck beating frantically. Why was she so nervous? If his heart was beating a million miles an hour, he could only imagine what hers was doing. They'd been in love once. They'd been best friends. There wasn't another soul who knew him the way she knew him, and vice versa. At least he thought that was still the case.

He watched her lovely chest rise and fall as she tried to even out her breathing. His eyes focused on her breasts; she'd filled out there too. He'd always loved her breasts. Hell, he'd loved every part of her, had devoured every patch of skin he could reach. He watched her, her eyes darting from him to something behind him, and he fought the urge to turn around.

"Mom? I can't find my socks or my..." he heard from behind him, turning at the sound of a child's voice, unable to mask the surprise at him calling her mom.

She had a son.

The kid couldn't have been more than five or six. Austin watched him walk down the stairs and stop talking suddenly. The boy's face went from one of confusion to one of recognition, then awe. Something about the child seemed familiar to him. He could sense Claire's eyes on him. Austin turned to ask her who he was, but something deep in his battered soul told him he knew even before the kid spoke the word.

"Daddy!" he screeched. "You're home! I can't believe you're finally home."

Austin saw rather than heard Charlie's little footsteps as he ran towards him. On instinct, he bent at the knees and put out his arms to catch the little fireball throwing himself at him. He heard the intake of breath from Claire. Austin's only response was to wrap the beautiful boy in his arms. His scent was all he could register as he held his son—there was no doubt as to who the child was as he held him. He fell to his knees and turned in Claire's direction. She had covered her mouth to keep the sobs from escaping as tears streamed down her face. She wasn't a crier. The first time he'd ever seen her cry was the day she broke up with him. Austin too had tears in his eyes. The questions swimming in his head were endless. All of a sudden that anger he had suppressed towards her had surfaced with a vengeance.

"I've missed you," said Charlie, the comment taking Austin aback. It was as if this child had known him forever, as if Austin had left for work a day ago and just got back.

Austin didn't respond. Instead he pulled away from

Charlie, keeping him at arm's length as he inspected the miniature version of himself. Those eyes, so much like his own. He had his mother's mouth, but the dirty blond hair was Austin's. Austin touched his face, ran his hand over Charlie's head and shoulders, until he reached his little hands and held them. He wanted to commit this moment to memory. He was beautiful, more beautiful than anything he'd ever seen.

"Let me look at you," he said, his voice catching.

"Mommy says I look just like you."

"You do," he agreed, not hiding the emotion in his voice.

"I have pictures of you in my room. One of you and Mommy before you had to leave for work. One of you when you were by yourself that she took when you weren't looking and one when you played baseball," he told him excitedly and then stopped suddenly. His eyes grew big and round as an idea formed in his little head. "Oh my God! I have baseball today. Can you come? And dinner. We were about to eat dinner. Can you stay? Mom, is it okay if he stays? Why am I asking? Of course you can stay. You're my dad. I can't believe you're home," he said at the end of a long exhale. Charlie turned and stared at Claire. "Why are you crying, Mom? You never cry."

"I'm just happy."

"Me too," he said. He turned towards the door and back to Austin. "Where are your bags?"

"My bags?"

"Yeah, your bags. Where are they?"

"I...uh...I..."

"They're at Grandma's," said Claire, saving Austin from any more awkwardness.

"Oh, okay. Maybe we can go get them after the game and I can finally meet them."

"Yeah, that's a great idea, buddy. Why don't you go wash up before dinner," Austin told him.

He reluctantly let Charlie go. He turned to Claire, observing her as she watched her son skip towards the stairs. The child started singing a song he couldn't quite make out.

"Well, that's a surprise," said Austin, his tone dry, anger simmering at the edges. "I was all prepared to apologize for the way I spoke to you at the hotel. Looks like our frolicking under the willow had consequences. I would question his paternity, but a blind man would be able to see the resemblance."

"Don't be a jerk, Austin. I'm not in the mood for your insinuations."

"You're not in the mood. Well, I have a dozen or so questions, Claire, so you better get in the mood real quick." Tears filled her eyes. He was being an ass, but he honestly couldn't help himself now. How could she keep something like this from him? "You know what's funny? I thought that look on your face at the hotel was from the shock of seeing me. Now I see I had nothing to do with it, and that it had everything to do with what you were hiding from me."

"I wasn't hiding—"

"Oh no? Then why not call me, give me a heads-up about my new status?" he said, teeth clenched.

"I can explain."

"I don't want your explanations, Claire," he said through gritted teeth. "What time is his game at?"

"Austin…"

"What time, Claire?"

"Six thirty," she said, staring down at the dish towel she was wringing the shit out of in her hands.

He stared at the clock, then at the two place settings on the island.

"Should you set another spot?"

"You're staying?"

"Of course I'm staying, he's expecting me to. I won't disappoint him."

He watched as she turned to the first drawer in the cupboard next to the fridge and took out some silverware. She didn't say a word to him, just went through the motions of setting his place next to theirs. He could see her hands were shaking, and her face was a little pale and devoid of any emotion.

"Charlie, come and eat!" she called out.

"Why Charlie?" he asked.

"What?"

"Why did you name him Charlie?"

Neither one of them heard him enter the kitchen. "It's your middle name, Daddy. Mommy named me Charles Monroe McKinley. Monroe is my middle name," he explained proudly.

He looked up at Claire. Why, after everything she said to him six years ago, did she name her child after him?

He'd been right. There was more to their breakup than she let on, but he couldn't process the questions regarding that right now.

"I like it. It has a nice ring to it."

"Ha! That's what Mommy says all the time. Everyone calls me Charlie, though."

"How old are you, Charlie?"

"Five. My birthday was in May."

He looked at Claire as he ran the numbers in his head and closed his eyes. It had been six years since she broke up with him. She stood wide-eyed and let her shoulders drop. She'd been in the early stages of pregnancy when she ended things. Had she been further along, he would have been able to tell. He knew her body by heart.

He'd left her pregnant. That thought killed him a little more inside.

CHAPTER FIVE

Claire

She saw his eyes close as he nodded to himself, coming to his conclusion. She watched his face, stared into the bottomless green of his eyes the second he opened them. There was no spark in them. When he spoke to Charlie he smiled, but the smile didn't reach his beautiful eyes.

Charlie's enthusiastic chatter filled the awkwardness between his parents as they sat down for dinner. Claire watched Austin as he listened to his son talk about everything from school to video games to baseball. He hadn't touched his food, in awe of the little boy who couldn't stop filling him in on all the aspects of his life. Every so often, Austin would caress Charlie's face. The affection she saw in his eyes was overwhelming. Along with that affection, she also saw his exhaustion. There were dark circles under his eyes, and a weariness she'd never seen in them before. Day-old stubble coated his face still, and crow's feet appeared at the corners of his eyes when he smiled, making him look older than his twenty-three years. He'd been successful, but at what cost? What toll had it taken on his life, his health?

Like Austin, she hadn't touched her food—for different reasons of course. While he was mesmerized, she was a nervous wreck. At least her hands had finally stopped shaking.

After their meal, Charlie dragged Austin up to his room, insisting he help with his uniform. She took advantage of the alone time to calm her rattled nerves. If only the knot in her throat would lighten up. Instead, it became heavier while the two people she loved most in the world bonded up in Charlie's room, laughing. There was no comfort in knowing they were together. She felt his anger and she knew the second they were alone, he would unleash it on her. She continued to move around the kitchen, not wanting to stop. She dried and put the dishes away, something she never did since she'd gotten a top of the line dishwasher. She gathered the snacks she was required to take to baseball and walked to the garage to look for Charlie's bat, glove, and shoes. Suddenly at a loss for what else to do, she sat down on one of the steps that led to the garage.

She covered her face with her hands and let the tears that rarely saw the light of day fall. One minute was all she needed to let a fraction of her emotions out and compose herself before they came looking for her. She jumped when the door opened. Austin stood in the doorway, looking down at her with a flash of sympathy that was quickly replaced with furrowed brows and a terse tone.

"It's a quarter after six. Where does he play?"

"Rotary."

"We should get going then. Need help with anything?"

"Can you take his bag to the car? I need to fill his water bottle and get the snacks for the team."

"I rode my motorcycle over here. We'll need to take your car."

"That's fine, it's unlocked. I need to change. I'll be out in a minute."

He walked away, letting the heavy door practically shut in her face when he let go of it.

Outside, he and Charlie were playing catch. Austin was giving him pointers, and Charlie listened to every word. Tears filled her eyes again, and both looked up at her when she stepped out of the shadows of the porch. She wiped under her eyes and walked towards her car—Jesus, once the dam opened it flowed hard. She walked towards the back of the car and put the cooler in the trunk.

"Come on, Charlie. In you go," she said.

She helped Charlie into the car and reached for the seat belt to buckle him in. "I got it, Mommy," he said, smiling up at her, proud of himself. She leaned in, giving him a kiss that he wiped off his face just as fast.

"I'll do that when I want, remember that," she whispered and kissed him again.

This time he wrapped his arms around her neck. "Thanks, Mommy."

She leaned back and stared at him, and for the first time since dinner, she saw tears in her son's eyes. It took everything she had to not unbuckle him and hold him in her arms.

"I love you, baby."

She walked towards the front of the car.

"I'll drive," Austin said.

"It's fine, I can drive."

"I'll drive," he repeated.

Claire stared at him with an incredulous look. The way he talked to her was really starting to irritate her. She reached into her back pocket for the keys and slammed them into his hand.

"You don't get to be angry here," he said to her, grabbing her hand.

Neither one of them expected the shock when they touched. Claire pulled away abruptly, the keys falling to the ground. She started to bend down to pick them up, but Austin's voice stopped her.

"I've got it."

She nodded and walked around to the passenger side and hopped in. She buckled her seat belt, but not before moving as close to the door as possible. The space was too small for the both of them. The physical distance was not far enough. The emotional distance, on the other hand, was unreachable. She turned briefly to look at Charlie.

"Don't fall asleep, baby. It's not a long drive," she said, smiling at her son.

"I won't, Mommy."

They drove in silence. Charlie concentrated on some game on his iPod, a smile playing on his sweet face, unaware of the tension between his parents. Claire rubbed her forehead, urging the headache looming at her temples away. All of a sudden, the soft orange of the early evening sun was too bright, and the events of the last couple of hours was too much. One of them would cave sooner rather than later. Might as well be her.

"There's going to be a lot of people at the game. A few people we grew up with whose kids play as well. My parents come to every game too."

"Who else knows about Charlie?" he whispered.

"Everyone knows about him, Austin. If you're asking who knows he's yours, well, like you said, a blind man would know who the father is." She stopped to take a breath.

"I'm sorry I said that. I shouldn't have spoken to you like that."

"Maybe I deserved it."

"You didn't. So no one has ever asked you?"

"No. People are just discreet enough not to ask for confirmation. Those that know us suspect, though."

"With me there today, there won't be any doubt," he said, more to himself.

She turned to the window and stared at the century-old houses they passed. Her nerves were even more on edge now that she thought of what people were going to say. Sure, she'd never come out and said Charlie was Austin's son, but the people she knew had always assumed.

"Why are we driving to the field when it's five minutes away?" he asked, breaking into her thoughts.

"I have the cooler," she said simply.

She didn't mention that she wished she'd walked, or that the drive had been the longest five minutes of her life. He expertly made his way down Main Street, down the back streets, and into the driveway that led to Rotary Park. She took several deep breaths as a dozen familiar faces greeted each other. This was going to be a nightmare. The parking lot was packed. Older kids from a previous game loitered near their cars, having the traditional after-game drink. She didn't want to explain things, or worse, put Austin in a situation where he might feel obligated to explain his absence. He hadn't been exactly kind with his words, but she wouldn't wish any awkwardness for him. He was fiercely private. Very little was written about him in the tabloids. Only once had she seen a picture of him with another woman. It broke her heart to see it, but he wasn't hers anymore; she had made sure of it. This would be putting everything he tried so hard to protect out in the open for people to scrutinize and question.

Once Austin parked the car, Claire practically ran to the back to grab her son's equipment and the cooler of snacks. Before she could get a handle on either item, Austin grabbed his son's baseball bag, swung it over his shoulder, and then grabbed the cooler. He called out for Charlie to follow him and left Claire standing by her car.

"Who coaches the team?" he asked over his shoulder.

"Do you remember Jim Bryant?"

"Yeah, I remember him."

"Mary got pregnant around the same time I did. They have twin boys."

"You don't say. Twins. Can't say I envy the guy."

"You shouldn't. We got the angel. Mason and Max are hell-raisers."

With an amused smile, he turned to Charlie. Done with her for the moment, she supposed.

"Do you know what field you're on?" he asked his son.

"Over there, by the hill. The blue team."

"Lead the way, my man," he said.

Charlie looked up at him with the biggest smile on his face. Austin reached out and rubbed his head before putting his baseball cap on.

Claire watched father and son walk together. She noticed some similarities as she walked behind them. Austin's head always tilted a fraction to the right when he walked—she recently noticed that Charlie did the same. Side by side, the resemblance was unbelievable. She pulled out her cell phone, and before she could second-guess what she was doing, she snapped a picture of the two. Once the camera was ready for the next shot, she lifted it and snapped another one. This time Austin was looking down at Charlie; both were laughing at something the other said. They had the same smile. It was new for her to be on the outside watching her son. She'd always been witness to his remarks, funny or not. To watch them bond was impossible to come to terms with. Charlie acted as if they'd been in each other's lives since he was born. He knew a lot about him, of course. Claire made sure to answer any questions her son had: who his father was, where he was, what he did. She never lied to him. The only fact she ever kept from him was that Austin didn't know about him.

He rarely spoke about his father to people. Claire had tried to explain as best she could that Austin didn't like it when he was talked about, and Charlie respected that. For someone so young, he understood the need for privacy. She supposed that in his mind, Austin wasn't real until a few hours ago. Even Charlie doubted whether he would ever meet the man.

Despite the eighty-degree weather, Claire pulled the cardigan she wore to keep mosquitoes off her skin closer to her as a sudden chill reached her bones. The nerves had gotten the better of her, and she realized the heaviness in her chest hadn't subsided a bit since seeing Austin.

She finally looked up to see her son running towards the outfield.

"Grandma, look, my dad's here!" he yelled, the joy evident in his voice.

Charlie's words caught the attention of some onlookers. Claire noticed people whispering and beginning to point in their direction.

"Hey, big guy, I see that. Must be nice to have your old man home," her dad said, looking right at her. In that moment, she felt every bit the little girl. For the first time in her life, she saw something she hadn't seen in her dad's eyes before— sanctuary.

"Good to have you home, son," Bruce said to Austin, giving him an awkward man hug.

"Thanks, Bruce. It's good to be home, surprises and all."

"He's quite the firecracker, that one. Been looking forward to meeting you for a long time. Don't disappoint him." Claire rolled her eyes. The sentiment grated at her nerves, especially coming from a man who preferred his social life over his children while they were growing up.

"I won't. I promise," Austin assured Bruce and turned to greet Angie. "Hi, Angie."

"Hello, Austin," she said.

Like her father, she kept an eye on Claire, aware of the emotional toll this reunion must be taking on her. Her mom walked towards her and gave her a gentle, reassuring hug.

"How you holding up?"

"I'm fine, Mom."

Charlie called out loudly to Austin, waving him over to the outfield. Claire followed—not wanting to be too far from her son as she noticed all the stirring going on around them. People had begun to take pictures, and the situation didn't make her entirely comfortable as she remembered the fans at the hotel. Would this turn into that?

When she looked back to where her son was, Claire was

surprised to see his parents walking down the hill towards them. When had Austin called them?

She watched Austin greet them and introduce them to his son, and Marcia wasted no time in pulling Charlie into her arms. There was no hesitation as her son willingly wrapped his arms around his grandma's neck.

"Son," Ben said in way of greeting.

She noticed Austin's jaw tense as he gave both his parents a stern look. His chest rose high and he quickly let out a long, frustrated breath.

"I don't know what to say, I'm so angry. I'm trying to figure it all out, trying to find it in me to understand, and I don't know if I ever will. Did you know?"

"No, we didn't. Your mother had her suspicions, though."

"What? How?"

"I saw you," said Marcia, turning to Claire. "A couple of days ago. I didn't approach you...I just watched the two of you."

"You should have. I wouldn't have run," said Claire guiltily.

"I know. I just didn't know what I would have said, or how much Charlie knew. I suppose I didn't want to...I don't know, shock him," she said, laughing nervously.

"Well, it's all clear now."

"Mom, when you told me Claire wasn't alone, you meant..." Austin said, pointing at Charlie.

68

"Yes, Austin."

"You should have told me. I would have been prepared...I feel so betrayed. Hurt. If you had your suspicions, you should have said something, Mom."

"What difference would it have made? It's been years since you left. Obviously Claire had her reasons. You can both talk about that later. Now is not the place. You have a crowd gathering, Austin," she said, speaking to both of them as Marcia surveyed the assembly of people all around them.

"Shit," Austin exclaimed. He walked away, urging Charlie to follow him into the dugout.

Claire watched him go, people stopping him for pictures on his way. He signed a few autographs and smiled that smile that didn't quite reach his face for pictures. Clearly annoyed by the attention, he politely asked to be left alone. It shocked her to see his fans oblige.

Well, the hardest part was done. She turned to his parents.

"I'm sorry," she whispered, her voice cracking as the words barely passed her lips. "It seemed like the best thing to do...I...he would have stayed," she stammered.

She felt the tears pricking at the backs of her eyes. She hadn't cried in years, hell, she didn't think she had any tears left. At some point during Charlie's first year, she was sure her tears had run dry. She looked at her father. The look on his face was one she'd never seen before. She swore he was on the verge of tears himself. He opened his arms to her, and she ran towards him.

There was the comfort and support she'd longed for as a little girl.

"You have nothing to be sorry about, Claire. We weren't there for you when you needed us most, and I will regret that for the rest of my days. I am sorry. You're a wonderful parent, better than your mother and I ever were. I admire you. Your strength, your dedication, and most of all, the love you show that little guy every day," said her father.

"Oh, Daddy." She tightened her arms around his waist.

"You did what you felt was best at the time. Best for who, I can't say," Marcia said as she reached out her hand to her. "But I don't think it was the best decision for you. He's hurt. In time he'll get over it because it's obvious to me that you haven't. Regardless, that's something you and Austin have to work out. I just hope you'll let us get to know Charlie. He seems like a great kid," said Marcia, tilting her head in the direction where Charlie and Austin chatted and laughed up a storm in the dugout.

"He's amazing, Marcia, and I can't wait for you to get to know your grandson."

"Thank you," Marcia said and pulled Claire into her arms.

Everything she'd done, she'd done for Austin. And she took great solace in the fact that the four adults in front of her understood her reason for her actions six years ago. Austin should be angry, deserved to be angry, but she'd be damned if she was going to let him bring her down. At some point during his visit, they would have to sit down and talk it out. She would explain, make him understand her reasoning for doing what she did. He had to know it had nearly killed her to let him go.

"Now come on, let's go see my grandson hit a couple of home runs. I bet him ice cream if he hit three home runs," said her father.

"How could you? I've asked you countless times not to gamble with him."

"It's just a friendly, innocent wager, Claire. We haven't asked for his piggy bank. Yet."

"You too?" she said, looking at Austin's father. "Unbelievable. May I ask at what point in the day you made this wager with Charlie?"

"I talked to him earlier, when Austin called while at your house."

"Don't let him corrupt you," she said, pointing at her father.

"It means ice cream with my grandson." Ben shrugged.

"This is little league, for crying out loud. I want him to have fun. What if he doesn't hit three home runs, huh? What then? He hates disappointing you, Dad. So you better have a backup plan and make him feel like a winner."

Both his grandfathers looked at her sheepishly and then at each other as the realization of their actions dawned on them. "Yeah, that's what I thought."

She let out a long, relieved breath and laughed at Ben and Bruce's reaction. Nothing like the joy of scolding two grown men to get her through the rest of the day.

CHAPTER SIX

Austin

Austin watched from the dugout as Claire walked towards the bleachers with their parents. How his parents could accept her deceit was beyond him. Then again, his mom always did have a soft spot for her. Behind him, he could hear whispers, giggling, and the never-ending sound of pictures being taken. To his surprise, Charlie ignored the whole annoying scene. You'd think the kid had been around it his whole life.

His attention, on the other hand, was on Claire. She'd changed into a pair of skinny jeans and tank top, with a light pink cardigan held tight over her chest. She said something to his father and laughed as she walked away from them. Both men looked like they'd gotten in trouble. He wondered, smiling to himself, what she might have said to them. All three women smiled at each other and continued walking. She looked more relaxed, happy, that hurt look he'd put on her face gone. He was so angry with her, and it pissed him off even more that he periodically forgot his anger when he watched her. He turned his attention to Charlie, who was struggling to get his cleats on.

"Let me help you with that."

"Not too tight. Mommy always does it too tight and it hurts my feet after."

"That's because girls don't know anything about baseball."

"Don't let her hear you say that. I said that once and she got really mad at me. Started telling me how she went to all of your games and knew more about baseball than anyone because you explained things to her. She said you even taught her how to bat. Is that true?"

He looked at Charlie wistfully. "Did Mommy talk about me a lot?"

"All the time. At least, anytime I asked. Sometimes she would tell me stories about when you were little. Is it true you climbed that big willow in Grandpa's backyard and couldn't get down?"

"Yeah, buddy, that's true," he said and laughed at the memory.

He climbed that damned tree because she'd dared him to. He'd wanted to impress her; instead, he embarrassed the shit out of himself. He looked up then, only to see their friend John circle his fucking arms around Claire's waist. He swung her around like a rag doll and had her squealing and laughing. They were close enough to the dugout that he could hear them talk.

"John Deere, put me down," she yelled.

"Aw, come on, sweets. Where's your sense of fun, and why are you calling me John Deere? I thought we were over that."

"It's the only name that gets your attention. Besides, as long you work on that farm and drive that green and yellow tractor, you'll always be John Deere to me."

"Oh, yeah? I could be a lot more if you let me. You still coming next Friday?" he said, as one of his hands traveled down her arm to her hips.

Austin watched in horror as John's face came down towards hers, his lips lightly brushing her cheek. They were making plans. No way. No damned way she was going anywhere with him or any man while he was around. He wouldn't be able to stand it.

"I wouldn't miss it. I haven't told Hunter, though. He'd love to hang out at the farm."

"No worries, sweets. I'll give him a shout at some point in the next few days."

Mine, he thought as his caveman instinct kicked in. He rose from his crouch, not taking his eyes off John and Claire.

"Shoes good, buddy?"

"Yep."

"Good. Now go on the field and practice with your team."

Austin was incensed at the display on the field, and before he could process what he was doing, he made his way out of the dugout. He hated how comfortable she looked in his arms, hated the way his hands held her hips like they belonged there, and he hated how she let him. It was obvious they were friendly; how friendly remained to be seen, and he would demand an explanation. The second John pulled away from her, Claire lifted her head and caught sight of Austin heading her way. He saw her body stiffen. Her eyes went wide as he approached them.

"What is it?" he heard John say as she put her hands on his forearm to push him away. "Sweets, what's going on?"

Austin hated that he called her sweets. How fucking pathetic. She wasn't sweets. Sweetheart, maybe, or even baby (that's what he'd called her). But sweets? It sounded so juvenile.

"Something I need to know about here?" asked Austin, his hands fisted at his sides.

John's head moved slightly to the side. His eyes darted to Austin and then back to Claire. He saw John's shoulders slump.

That's right, asshole. I'm back. Hands off my girl. He wanted to yell it as he stared at the man who had once been his good friend.

"Maybe I should be the one asking that question," said John, directing the question to Claire.

"John I...he showed up today...I didn't know...I'm..."

"You don't owe him explanations," said Austin, cutting her off, indignation in his voice.

How dare this fucker demand any explanations from her? He was here, that was enough. To top it off, John still hadn't let go of her. He was giving him ten seconds—which was too much time, in his opinion—for him to let go of her. John slowly faced him.

"You've been gone a while to be so demanding, McKinley."

"Gone for work and kept in the dark is more like it."

"I was just saying hi to a friend, okay. Chill out, there are kids around."

"Is that how you greet all your friends? I don't see you hugging me and making me squeal."

"Staking some sort of claim, Austin?"

"Damn right I am. This is my family, John. Make sure you know the boundaries, or I'll remind you."

"Get off your goddamned high horse, will you. There isn't anything here you need to question. We're friends, have been since we were kids. So tone it down," John told him.

"I'll call you later, sweets. We need to talk," John whispered, loud enough for him to hear. "I'm going to go tell Charlie that I'm sorry I can't stay."

Austin continued to clench his fists as John walked past him towards the outfield. He gave Charlie a high five, bent to speak to him, and ruffled his hair. John looked up in his direction and left. There was no way he was going to allow that idiot to hijack his family. He looked over at Claire, who was frowning at him. Okay, so he didn't know he had a family of his own a few hours ago, but he knew now, and he was keeping them.

"What the hell is wrong with you? You come into my home, disrespect me in it, and now you do the same in front of our friend and family? If you have questions, ask me, in private, and I'll be more than happy to answer them for you. All I ask is that while we're in public, you have the decency to keep your temper in check," she said.

"Oh, of course. Wouldn't want to cause you any awkwardness, now would we?" he antagonized.

"Not for me, you jackass. For your son. Don't embarrass Charlie. It's not always about me or you," she finished and walked past him, bumping him hard on the shoulder.

He ran his hands through his hair roughly and looked for his son, who was happily tossing a ball back and forth with a teammate, oblivious to the encounter his parents just had. When he looked up at the stands, however, it was a different story. Everyone was staring at him, giving him the wrong kind of attention. He hoped to God no one had recorded their exchange.

What was wrong with him?

He walked back to the dugout and put Charlie's running shoes away. He grabbed the cooler he'd carried from the car and took out his son's water bottle and put it on the bench. The umpire yelled for the teams to get in position, and Austin watched as all the kids ran to their coaches. Too embarrassed to join his parents, Austin stood behind the dugout, his fingers gripping the chain-link fence with fierce anger. How in God's name was he going to forgive her, he wondered for the hundredth time in the past few hours.

Once the game started, he shouted instructions out to the team. This calmed him—it was familiar territory. He even went as far as to step on the field and help the kids run the bases. He yelled, cheered, and jumped up and down when Charlie hit his third home run. He gave his son a high five as he rounded third base and urged him to keep running. He acted every bit the proud dad. The action seemed so easy for him like he'd waited his whole life for a son, and this opportunity.

Charlie was red-faced and panting when the game finally ended. Austin rounded the fence and sat beside him, giving him a congratulatory hug before he bent down on one knee to take his shoes off.

"Drink your water, Charlie. You need to stay hydrated."

"What does hyrated mean?"

"Hydrated," he repeated slowly, making sure to pronounce every letter. "It means you have to drink a lot of water because you sweat so much when you play."

"Oh, yeah. Mommy says that to me too."

"Does she?"

"Yep."

Austin put Charlie's baseball equipment away while Claire handed out the snacks. He watched as she greeted some of the parents, laughing and hanging on to their every word. A few of the moms leaned, and whispered to her as they pointed to him. Claire smiled, looking embarrassed by the attention because of him. Not once did she acknowledge his presence or introduce him. He'd never felt like such an outsider.

"Come on, son. We're heading out for ice cream. Your mother and me want to get to know your son," his father told him, tapping him on the shoulder.

"I'm not sure I want to go, Dad. I need to talk to…"

"There's time for that, Austin. Give her a break," he said sternly. "Besides, Bruce and I made a bet with your son. If he hit three home runs, we'd take him out. He gets a double scoop on a waffle cone."

"You're making bets with him? Dad, I want him to enjoy the game, not be disappointed every time he doesn't come through," he told his father.

"That's what your gir...I mean, Claire said. She already gave us heck for it, but I don't want to disappoint my grandson, so we're taking him for ice cream," he said. He yelled back to his grandson, "Charlie, you coming?"

"Yeah, hold on," Charlie yelled back.

Austin watched as he ran back to Claire, spoke to her, and pointed at them. He smiled up at her and gave her a hug. She brushed his hair back and kissed him on the forehead. He smiled when he noticed Charlie attempting to wipe the kiss away, only to have Claire stop him. She pointed her finger at him and he leaned in to kiss her on the cheek before he started running in their direction. Austin held his hand out for him and they both began walking behind Ben and Bruce.

"Is she coming?" Austin asked, unable to keep the hope out of his voice.

"Nah. She said she's heading home and will see us there. You remember the way right?"

"Yeah, I remember the way."

It was nearly dark when they got back. Charlie had complained halfway home that his legs hurt. Austin gave him a piggyback ride but let him down once they reached the house. The two-block walk wasn't much to complain about. Charlie ran up the porch steps, went straight for the door, and swung it open. He cringed when he heard the loud bang as it hit the wall.

"Charlie, how many times do I have to tell you to watch it when you swing that door," he heard Claire say.

"Sorry, Mom," Charlie said through a long yawn.

"Where's your father?"

"Right here," said Austin as he walked through the door.

"Can I take a shower tomorrow? I'm really tired, Mommy."

"Sure. One night going to bed all sweaty can't hurt."

"Yay!"

"But you need to wash your hands, face, and teeth, please."

"Okay," he said, too tired to fight her on it.

She completely ignored him as she followed Charlie up the stairs. She heard them talking and laughing. He heard the sound of water running and Charlie complaining it was too hot. Austin stood immobile in the entryway as he followed the sounds of their footsteps on the ceiling. He debated whether or not to interrupt their nightly ritual, wondering if he'd be welcomed. More by Claire than by Charlie—he knew his son wouldn't object. He walked up the stairs, and he could hear voices coming from one of the bedrooms. He peeked through the open door. Seeing Claire lying next to their son reading him a story pulled at his heartstrings.

The one word circling his mind all day was why. Why did she not tell him? The hurt that all of a sudden engulfed him mixed with the anger he was trying to control. In the seconds he watched his son drift off to sleep, he envied her. He envied her for lying next to him, and all the bedtime stories he'd missed out on. Had he known, he would have taken care of them. He should have been there for them all these years. Hell, he would have been. Of that he had no doubt.

He would have wanted to see her grow full with the life he'd fallen in love with the second he heard that one word that would do any man in when he heard it for the first time. Daddy. He would have wanted to see and hear his son let out his first cry. Hear him say his first word, take his first steps. It should have been Austin who taught him how to ride a bike and throw and catch a baseball. She had taken so many firsts away from him. He was caught off guard at the resentment that was slowly crawling up his bones. Tears stung his eyes. Why? He asked himself again. He didn't want to be angry with her. He'd spent too many years with those emotions wrapped around his heart.

What was her reasoning for keeping his son from him? He'd done nothing but love her; shown her a hundred times over. Surely she didn't think he'd leave her alone to deal with the pregnancy? No, she knew him better than that. He would have done anything for her, still would. At the ice cream shop, the three men talked things out. He hadn't been able to hide his irritation when Bruce told him that she had struggled financially after his birth. Considering the wealth her family possessed—he couldn't wrap his mind around that fact. When he'd asked why, Bruce said she'd insisted on doing things on her own. She moved away, started a new life with their son in Ottawa.

He couldn't understand her need for such independence when she had a life depending on her. She'd always been stubborn, but never selfish or irresponsible. Despite her upbringing, she'd never been spoiled. So why had she kept his son from him? The whys were never ending. She owed him an explanation. He didn't want to hate her, but by God if he wasn't close.

He turned abruptly from the door and went in search of something to drink. He needed something strong, something to take the edge off, and something to ease his rising temper. It was so damn frustrating to be on the outside looking in. In the kitchen, he opened cupboards, looking for glasses. Then he ruffled through more cupboards looking for a drink. All she kept was wine and beer. He didn't like the first, so he settled for a beer, which he walked out to the back porch to drink.

He wanted some air. He wanted to think and figure out what the hell he was going to do with a life that had stopped satisfying him long ago. Leaving Springridge now without Charlie was not an option. Now that he knew of him, he couldn't imagine his life without his son. The unconditional love he felt for him was instant and overwhelming. Was that what it was like when a child was born, he wondered? Was the love that instantaneous? Claire had taken away the opportunity for that theory to be proven. He ran his hand roughly down his face, took a long pull of his beer to calm down. Tears he'd been holding back since seeing his son for the first time streamed down his face. Now those tears were not only laced with love but astounding fear at not knowing what the future held. What was worse, he realized every tear he'd ever shed had been for her or because of her. He wiped at them angrily with the back of his hand in an effort to gain some semblance of control. He needed to clear his head and think. He didn't want to do anything irrational.

He turned suddenly at the sound of the squeaking hinges of the storm door Claire had walked through.

"What are you doing out here?" she asked, her voice soft.

"I needed some air and a drink," he answered, his voice harsher than he intended.

"Are you okay?" she asked. He could hear the worry in her voice.

"No, actually, I'm not."

"We need to talk. I've never thought of what I would say to you when you found out. I've always dealt with things

84

alone."

That last word opened the can of worms they'd been avoiding.

"You didn't have to be alone. That was a choice you made, and one I'm trying to come to terms with at the moment," he said, keeping his eyes on her face.

"There's nothing to come to terms with, Austin."

"Oh no? The fact that I have a son that everyone but me knows about isn't something I should come to terms with?" he asked incredulously.

"Austin, I can explain."

"Explain what? That you're a selfish bit—" his words were halted the second Claire's hand connected with his face.

"How dare you? You have no idea what it was like for me. How I felt, what I felt. I'd never in my life been so scared. What I did wasn't selfish, despite what you might think."

"I'm so angry with you," he said through clenched teeth. He ran his hands roughly through his hair. "Just tell me this. Did you know you were pregnant when you broke up with me?"

She stared at him blankly. She nodded, tears welling up in her eyes as she fidgeted with her hands. A nervous gesture he remembered her doing the day she told him she didn't love him.

"It's late, Austin. We can discuss this in the morning."

"No. We'll discuss this now, damn it!"

"I need to think," she said and turned to walk back into the house.

"Don't you dare walk away from me!" he sneered, placing his hand on the screen door. "I need to know why you did it. Why did you break up with me when you knew you were pregnant with my child?" He grabbed her by the arms, forcing her to look at him. "I would have done anything for you. You had to have known that."

She raised her arms, effectively dislodging his hold on her. She walked towards the porch banister where his beer sat, grabbed it, took a long, fortifying pull, and turned to face him.

"Of course I knew that. It's why I had to let you go," she admitted.

"I don't understand."

"Austin, I struggled with telling you for days. We were in your car when I'd finally gotten the nerve to tell you. Just as I was going to get the words out, your song came on the radio. You went crazy because someone had requested it. You pulled me out of the car and we danced in the dirt and you exclaimed how big you guys were going to be. You looked so happy. So excited and relieved that all your hard work had paid off."

"You should have told me!" he yelled.

"I couldn't. I knew that if I told you, you wouldn't have left. You would have let the band down, given up on your dreams. I couldn't let you do that. You'd worked too hard."

"Damn you, Claire. That wasn't your decision to make. You told me you didn't love me. You said it would be best for the both of us if we made a clean break. Well, you were wrong. Our break-up wasn't good for either of us."

"Yes it was," she contradicted. "Look at you; you're one of the biggest bands in the world. How could you say it wasn't good? You wouldn't have any of this if you'd known about the pregnancy. You would have resented me if you'd missed out."

"Resented you? Fuck, Claire, I resent you now. I resent you for letting me go that night six years ago, I resent you for lying to me, and I loathe the fact that you kept my son from me," he said, watching her expression.

She took a step back—the fury in his face was not something she'd witnessed before. Austin knew that everything he'd been holding in for the past few hours, not to mention the past few years, showed in the tilt of his head, the clenching of his jaw, and the look of disgusted anger on his face.

"I couldn't let you abandon your dream. You would have stayed. Me and Charlie would have turned into an obligation."

"An obligation I would have welcomed. I would have taken you both with me."

"I'm sorry," she whispered.

"No, I am sorry for believing you when you told me you didn't love me anymore. You broke my fucking heart. Losing you gutted me. Damn it, Claire, I went along with the record for the band because I couldn't let them down, because when all was said and done, the only obligation I felt was to them. I didn't want any of it without you. After a while, it was all I had to keep me sane, the only way of expressing what I was going through. Every song I ever wrote and sang was about you. About missing you, about losing you, about having you. How much I loved you, how much I hated you. How your lips felt against mine, how your tongue tasted, the curves of your body. I've spilt my guts out on those albums. Have you listened to any of them?"

"No," she said, not looking at him. Tears streaming down her face.

"We'll, you should have, because then you would have known how much I loved you, how much I still love you," he said, bringing his fists down hard on the rickety white banister of the back deck. "I'm so angry with you. What pisses me off even more is that you didn't even give us a chance. I missed out on so much because you decided it was what I needed. It wasn't you that was alone all these years. It was the other way around, and for that I resent you more." He was done talking. He turned, walked through the house, and out the front door.

CHAPTER SEVEN

Claire

She stood on the deck with her hands braced on the railing, frustrated with the situation she had put herself in. Had she made a mistake? Of course she had.

Austin hadn't been the only one missing out. She'd taken the opportunity of a family away from Charlie as well. That guilt, along with lying to Austin, had burdened her for years. In the process of saving him from the obligations of a family, she had cheated her son out of a father. She'd always known that, of course, tried to prepare herself for this confrontation, but no amount of time was enough for the lash of his wrath. She'd stayed away from social media and forbade her parents and brother to post any pictures of her or Charlie on social media. She lived like a goddamned criminal. The only time she accessed the Internet was for work, and she never let herself stray to the gossip sites.

Until she moved back to Springridge, she never had a TV either. She'd stayed away for a reason. Whether it was a good one or not, it didn't matter. She knew deep down that she had no right to be angry with him, but she couldn't help but feel a little hurt by his bitterness. In the back of her mind, she knew she wasn't going to make Austin understand why she'd made the decisions she had. At the time, it all made sense—she was giving him a chance at a life and a career. In the process of achieving success, he'd missed out on a life-altering event, one of the most important in a man's life. And it was her fault.

She stared at the clear night sky and asked for guidance from whatever God would listen. It was a rare evening to be able to bask in the shining glory of distant and ancient lights in the sky reflecting on the calm water of Mill Pond—a welcomed extension of her backyard. The tranquility of the water brought her little comfort tonight. She shivered suddenly. That chill that had seeped into her bones at the game had her tightening her cardigan around her chest again. She took one of many fortifying breaths and walked back into the house.

Inside the dim kitchen, she realized she hadn't heard the rumble of Austin's motorcycle after he'd walked out and wondered briefly where he could have gone. He was "The Austin McKinley" after all. How far could he get before he was recognized and hounded for an autograph or picture was anyone's guess. Although Springridge was a small town, there was no shortage of nightlife. The Ivy Arms was around the corner from her house, and people staggered out of the pub well-fed and thirst-quenched at all hours. They weren't closed off from the rest of the world. Besides, no one forgot the success of their residents. This town was the home of a rock star, an Olympian, and an astronaut—all of which had a street, a school, or a sports complex named after them.

No, people didn't forget. If anything, they rubbed it in your face. Claire had never heard the end of the success of Yellow Scarlet. She never went anywhere without bumping into someone who knew her or had known them as a couple. People asked questions. They asked her how he was doing, where he was playing, and the best one, the one that would be the answer to that burning question; they asked if she'd talked to him recently. Her only response was "not lately." It was the best she had. She didn't admit they never spoke, would never put Charlie in a position where he had to explain why he didn't see his father. No one asked him anything, of course. It was an unspoken agreement between her and the people who knew her.

In the years she and Austin had been together, whenever they argued—which wasn't often—he would go for long walks. Sometimes he would return, and sometimes she wouldn't see him until the following day, but he always texted to let her know he would see her then. She unconsciously picked up her phone from the counter where she'd left it and brought the screen to life. It dawned on her suddenly that he didn't have her number. On the other hand, maybe he did. She had never changed it, but there was no way that he would know that. There was never any reason for him to call her—she'd made sure of that. When she let him go, he let her go just as easily, without a fight. She wondered sometimes if deep down he'd known that every word that passed her lips that night was a lie. She'd maintained eye contact, and although she cried while she broke up with him, her voice only wavered slightly.

She put the phone down, shook off the sudden wishful thought that he would call, and turned to shut the door to the deck.

There was no doubt in her mind that Austin would return. She busied herself preparing coffee. The task took her mind off of the impending discussion. She would need the energy in order to continue the conversation, and for rehashing a past that wasn't so distant. She stared at the coffee pot, the sound of it percolating a strange comfort as it filled the decanter with the dark liquid. She had zoned out and startled when the beeping from the coffee maker announced its completion. She filled a cup to the brim and relished a rare cup of strong, black coffee, which she took with her to the large gray sofa. Staring at the stone fireplace in the living room adjacent to the kitchen, she took careful sips.

The open floor plan was one of the things she loved most about her house. The idea that conversation could flow freely from the kitchen to the living room when she had people over appealed to her. Although in the months she'd been back, there hadn't been time or reasons for any sort of gathering. Who was she kidding; there was no one she wanted to have over aside from family. Most of her friends had moved away, and those that were still around were more interested in her "connection" to Austin than in her. With the exception of the two times she'd gone out to dinner with John, her social life was at a standstill.

Now that Austin was back, any dinner dates would be extinct. She wouldn't dare go anywhere with John after the pissing contest she'd witnessed at the game. Maybe they could plan something together. This Sunday's barbecue could be at her house instead of at her parents'. She would mention it to them, and have the whole family over. A McKinley-Monroe reunion was a necessary step to put her little family together.

She loved to cook, and as she stared out the big picture window, she planned on what she would make them all for dinner. She thought of Austin's face when he watched her cook. He had already seen her put a meal together, even ate it, but anyone could make stir-fry. She wanted to make something wholesome and delicious. Something that would blow his mind away. She would even bake a cake. Yeah, she thought to herself, smiling. That would surprise him for sure. They would plan and put it all together as a family. She pictured him sitting on the other side of the island as she chopped and sliced vegetables. He would pick at them, giving her his advice on how she should chop. They would argue playfully. She sighed. The idea seemed crazy. Something a normal couple would do. Except, they weren't a couple. With any luck, they'd become a family.

At that thought, her smile faded. Family was the farthest thing from what the three of them were. Who was she kidding? She'd be lucky if Austin wanted to be friends after everything was hashed out. She leaned back on the sofa and closed her eyes, hoping to rid her mind of her wishful thoughts—family.

The thought that she had refused Charlie the opportunity at a loving family had her sitting up all of a sudden. She was struck with the fact that in some ways, she was no different from her own parents. As a child, she'd been deprived of the chance to a normal, stable family, and she was now depriving her son of the same. For Charlie's sake, Austin had to be in his life—there were no ifs, ands, or buts about it. She had many

93

insecurities growing up, wondering often if maybe she'd done something wrong, and that was the reason her parents abandoned her and Hunter so often. The ironic thing was that it had taken Austin to convince her that neither she nor Hunter had done anything wrong.

Claire would make it her mission to ensure her son never had those doubts. They would be the family Charlie deserved, no matter what. It wasn't about her anymore—it stopped being about her the second she held her child in her arms. Reflecting on her parents' past mistakes and the road she'd been heading in with her own child was a beacon she hadn't noticed flashing in her direction.

With the events of the day on replay in her head, she was exhausted. Her eyes began to droop. Despite the large mug of coffee, sleep slowly overtook her. She laid her cup down and swung her feet up on the sofa, telling herself it would only be for a few minutes. She raised her head, looked at her front door to ensure it was unlocked for when Austin got back, and lay back.

Claire woke suddenly, the sounds of clanking ceramic and pots too loud for her to sleep through. She resisted the urge to sit up when she heard her son talking.

"Mommy never lets me put chocolate syrup in my cereal."

"I won't tell if you don't," said Austin.

"Never. We'd both get a time-out."

She had to smile at the thought that anyone could give

94

Austin a time-out. She could hear the amusement in his voice.

"I'd like to see her try," he mumbled.

"Yeah, you are kind of old for a time-out."

"Not that old."

Not wanting to interrupt their little breakfast conspiracy, she lay still on the couch, her body protesting from the pain of sleeping on the lumpy sofa. They stopped talking, the crunching sound of their cereal filling the silence.

"What was your favorite cereal when you were little?" Charlie asked through a mouthful.

"Captain Crunch."

"Really? That's Mommy's favorite too."

"I know. When we were younger, we would take a box each into your grandma Marcia's backyard and eat it by the pool."

"No milk?"

"No milk."

"That's gross."

She remembered those days. Some of their friends would head out for pizza or ice cream, but she and Austin would stay back and indulge in cereal by the pool. They would talk for hours about everything and nothing. Life seemed to stand still when they were together. At some point during those nights, he would pull her lounger over, slip his arm around her, and let her head rest on his shoulders.

Those were the moments she cherished the most. They both knew she would be walking into an empty house, so she stayed as long as possible. He hated that she was always alone. Hunter would spend the weekend at his friend's house, but no matter how close they got, she rarely spent the night with Austin. Even though her parents weren't around much, there was always a sense of respect. Something deep down told Claire her parents wouldn't approve of Austin staying over.

"Something's burning, Daddy."

"Oh shit!"

"You're not allowed to say shit, Daddy."

"Sorry."

"You're lucky Mommy didn't hear you. She would have made you eat hot sauce."

"Hot sauce?" he asked.

"Yep. I had to eat it once."

"Hot sauce..." Austin repeated, as if to himself.

She could imagine him shaking his head in disbelief.

Claire closed her eyes briefly, willing the headache looming in the back of her eyes away. The light streaming in from the insert on her front door was a laser beam directed at the pulsing pain. She stretched out her arms, her legs tangling in a thick blanket. She grabbed it, rubbing the fabric tenderly and touched by the realization that he'd covered her.

She hadn't planned on spending the night in her living room. She sat up slowly and watched her son. Charlie sat on one of the bar stools, his hands bracing his face, elbows on the granite, his bowl of cereal forgotten as he looked in the direction of the stove in complete awe and admiration. She followed his gaze. Her breath caught in her throat at the sight of Austin—he was stunning, tall. So much taller than she remembered. Or maybe it was just his body. It had been transformed, every muscle defined.

Austin stood at the stove, stirring what she assumed were eggs. His back was to her in a gray T-shirt, dark blue cargo shorts, and flip-flops—an Austin McKinley staple. He pulled the look off effortlessly. His shirt stretched over taut, muscular shoulders. The intricate sleeve tattoo changed with each movement, the feathers fanning out, going from deep blue to green, almost in a lenticular motion.

She took the opportunity to take in the subtle differences. His hair was darker than she remembered, curling at the nape of his neck. She looked over at her son, still staring, mesmerized by his father. Charlie had the same curls on his unusually long hair, a shade lighter than Austin's. The matted, tangled mess was a nightmare to brush through. Charlie had, months ago, decided that he wanted to let his hair grow a bit. She'd conceded on the condition that he washed it regularly— a nightly fight between the two of them.

"Mommy!" Charlie yelled. "You're awake."

"Good morning, baby."

"Daddy's making breakfast for us."

She looked at her son, trying and probably failing at putting on an excited face. Her nerves were still rattled. She

97

had no idea what time he'd returned, hadn't heard the door open at all.

"I see that. Smells good."

"I made coffee. Charlie wanted eggs and pancakes. I made lots," said Austin, not bothering to look at her while he spoke. "The pancakes are fresh, and there are bagels in the

toaster. I know you—" he stopped himself. "Anyway, they're in the toaster." Bagels were her favorite. It was a staple on her grocery list.

Back in high school, Austin would pick her up every morning with an extra toasted bagel with butter, and a coffee with milk. She was glad his back was to her. She hadn't wanted to see his face as the memory that slipped through his angry, foggy mind surfaced. It didn't escape her that he hadn't bothered to actually offer her any food; he'd just let her know what was available.

"Thanks. What time did you get back?"

"Late," he simply said.

She looked up at him and rolled her eyes at his curt response.

"Did you brush your teeth, Charlie?"

"Yep. Look, I'm dressed too."

"To what do we owe that miracle?"

"Daddy told me to. We're going to the market. He said there's nothing to eat here."

"Oh, really. Well, had I known we would have company, I would have stocked up," she said sarcastically.

"You wanna come with us, Mommy?"

"I was hoping it could be just us guys, buddy," said Austin, cutting off her response.

"Oh, okay. Sorry, Mommy, it's a guy thing. I promise we won't buy junk, and we'll get you the stuff you like. Right, Daddy?"

"Eat up, Charlie," he said, ignoring his son's request. He tossed a few words her way. "You joining us?"

She noticed then he hadn't bothered to set a place for her at the island. The urge to tell him to shove his pancakes up his pissy ass was at the tip of her tongue. She only stayed quiet because Charlie was in the room. If Austin was going to be around, then she would do what she could to keep the peace. But she planned to have a few words with him about respecting her in her home. She took a deep breath. As much as it would break her heart, she would deny Austin's unenthusiastic breakfast invitation. She didn't think he would care much if she joined them or not; however, this would be the first time since Charlie was born that she wouldn't have breakfast with him. That thought saddened her.

"Thanks, but I'm going to go take a shower."

"You're skipping breakfast?" Charlie asked, concern edging his beautiful eyes.

"I'll eat after. Don't worry."

"But what if..." he began, but Claire quickly cut him off

"I'll be fine. I promise I'll eat something after my shower."

"Will you?" he asked.

Claire's gaze darted briefly to Austin, who was witnessing the exchange with apt attention. She could see his curiosity in his facial expression. She wanted to avoid divulging her medical history to the man, who had, since the second she'd seen him, been a total ass towards her. She knew his attitude was validated, but she wasn't going to pretend it didn't bother her. Also, the fact that he felt he could plan out their day without consulting her was one more thing that grated at her nerves. Everyone else in the family asked to spend time with Charlie. Why she expected this from him was something she questioned. He was his father; she shouldn't expect anything less, but she felt a sort of loss all of a sudden.

Charlie had been hers and only hers for the past five years. She'd shared him with grandparents and an uncle, not out of obligation, but because she wanted him to connect with all of them. This, however, was something entirely different. There was a deeper connection, one that ran through their veins, and she didn't want Charlie getting hurt. There was no doubt by the way her son watched and listened to every word out of his father's mouth that he was already as madly in love with Austin as she was. Love like that always let you down, and she didn't want that for Charlie. She didn't want anyone he cared about to disappoint him in any way.

Austin couldn't just come into their lives and take charge.

There were rules that applied, even for her, that he had to be made aware of. Even though he was Charlie's father, they were strangers, and they still needed to get to know each other. Charlie wasn't a difficult child by any means, but this was new to Austin, and he couldn't pretend to be Charlie's friend to win him over. He needed to set his own set of rules and let Charlie know that he was an authority figure.

"What's the big deal if she doesn't eat?" Austin asked.

"Mommy was sick when I was in her belly, and she's still not better."

"Charlie!" she admonished.

"What? If something happens, Daddy needs to know what to do."

"No, he doesn't. Now eat your breakfast."

"Need to know what?" he asked, staring at both her and Charlie. "Will someone tell me what the hell you're talking about, please?"

"You said what the hell, Daddy," Charlie said. Austin looked at him, questioning. "You can't say what the hell. That will get you hot sauce in your mouth too."

"Then we'll have to stock up," he said drily. "So what do I need to know?"

"It's nothing. Don't worry about it," she said, using the same clipped tone he'd used on her.

"No, it's something," Charlie started, looking in her direction with trepidation before continuing. "Mommy has to make sure she eats or her sugar falls down and she gets really sick. Last time I had to call nine-one-one, and we spent a whole night in the hospital. It was scary."

"You have diabetes?" Austin asked. It was the first time he'd directed a question her way since last night.

"I had gestational diabetes. It was under control. Now I get dizzy sometimes and faint. I just have to make sure I eat, that's all. My body hasn't been the same since Charlie's birth."

"She gets tired a lot too."

"Why do you get tired?" Austin asked.

"Low iron. I take supplements," she told him as she looked over at her son. "Really, kid. Are you going to just blurt out all my medical problems to everybody?" she asked her son.

"No not everybody, just Daddy," he said. Charlie looked down at his plate, playing around with his soaking cereal before looking at her with worry in his eyes. "I don't want you to get sick again. I didn't like spending the night in the hospital."

"What does he mean he didn't like spending the night in the hospital?"

She looked up at Austin, knowing he wasn't going to like her answer, and braced herself for his reaction.

"We were in Ottawa...alone. It happened a year ago. Charlie stayed with me. I had nowhere to leave him."

"Jesus, Claire..." he started but stopped himself. He

gritted his teeth and ran his hand over his face in frustration.

She knew what he was thinking. She didn't have to be alone—she chose that and put herself and Charlie at risk. It wasn't something she hadn't already heard from her parents. That incident had been the main reason her parents insisted she move back to Springridge. When Austin looked at her, all the anger he'd shown was replaced with something else. Helplessness, sadness—she couldn't tell which.

CHAPTER EIGHT

Austin

God, he was an asshole. Too absorbed in his anger, he hadn't stopped to think what it had been like for her during the pregnancy or after Charlie was born. His sister had mentioned that she moved away shortly after he left town. He hadn't requested any more information. He hadn't known she had moved so far away from everyone. The thought of her being sick and alone pissed him off. She was so damned stubborn he wanted to shake her.

"I'll grab you a plate," he said and walked to the stove.

"That's not necess—"

"Sit," he said, cutting her off.

He filled the white ceramic plate with eggs, bacon, and the pancakes he made from scratch. The two of them sat in silence, listening to Charlie's chatter. His son who barely stopped to take a breath between words and bites of food. He talked about baseball practice, school, his friends—he wanted to fill Austin in on every aspect of his life. He even told him stories of when he was a baby that Claire had shared with him.

Like the time he peed on himself while Claire changed his diaper.

"He tells that story to everyone. He can't believe he did that to himself," she said, filling in the blanks.

"Good thing you learned how to use the potty, huh?" said Austin.

"Oh, I have to tell you. One time..."

"Charlie, please, can we keep the potty stories for after we're done eating?"

"I guess, but it's not that gross, Daddy. Some of the stories are kind of funny. Like the time the toilet paper roll was empty and it was like the second or third time Mommy put me on the potty. She had to run to the pantry in the basement for some toilet paper. When she came back, I fell in the toilet butt first with p—"

"Okay, I get the picture. No need to go into details," Austin told him, laughing.

"There's no way you remember that," Claire told Charlie.

"I do remember, I swear." He laughed.

Charlie's laugh was contagious, and neither of them could help joining him. Austin stared at both at of them in wonder. Identical dimples to his indented the skin just below Charlie's cheekbones. His cheekbones were high, like hers. Charlie had Austin's eye color, but their shape was all Claire. She looked up suddenly. He caught her hazel gaze. The shade of her eyes was lighter in summer months, closer to a moss green. When he smiled at her, she turned away, a light blush tinting her face. He noticed her slight shiver.

Her body actually fucking shook. If one look could do that to her, what would a touch do? Austin had to shift in his seat to alleviate the discomfort he felt all of a sudden in the vicinity of his crotch. He was mesmerized by her reaction. In the back of his brain, he could hear his son talking, but the thoughts of Claire shaking under him clogged his mind. He was so fucked.

"Right, Daddy?"

The tug on his shirt brought his attention back to the one other person who was quickly filling the other half of his heart. Charlie stared at him, a light in his eyes so genuine, only a child could pull it off.

"What's that, buddy?"

"Aren't you listening? I just told Mommy you said you were going to teach me how to play guitar."

"Oh, right. Yes I am. And we're going to make a lot of noise together."

"Goodie," Claire mumbled.

"You done, Charlie?" asked Austin.

"Yep."

"Great. Go and brush your teeth so we can leave."

"I already brushed my teeth."

"Do it again. You have food between them."

Charlie jumped off his seat without a fight. Austin saw

Claire's mouth hang open in disbelief as she watched her son run out of the kitchen.

"I assume it takes a few tries to get him to brush his teeth?" he asked, smirking.

"It takes me a few tries to get him to do anything. Shower, get dressed...you name it."

They both laughed as they gathered the dirty dishes. While she put them in the dishwasher, Austin busied himself cleaning the countertop. Mainly the mess left behind by his son. He wondered how much the kid actually got in his mouth, considering half his food was on the counter. He turned back to the sink in time to watch Claire stretch her arms high over her head. Her shirt lifted a couple of inches, giving him a glimpse of the soft, tanned skin of her stomach. There was muscle definition. She'd always been fit, he remembered. He wondered what fad she followed these days. She'd been big on Pilates when he left. Did she still do that? Did she still run? All of a sudden it hit him; he didn't know this Claire. Did she still make cookie dough and stick it in her ice cream? Did she still shower with scorching hot water? Did she still twist her hair around her index finger when she stared at a blank canvas?

Something in him shifted at the thought that he didn't know the little things anymore. Although he was still questioning her relationship to John, he wondered whose hands had had the pleasure of discovering the planes of her body, the newly formed curves, and her full breasts. Who had experienced the pleasure of listening to the sounds she made when she came? Just thinking about someone else coming anywhere near his girl had him clenching his teeth. His girl. Damn, he was barely back twenty-four hours and he was already staking his claim. Albeit a mental one, but a claim nonetheless. Charlie had him in knots, and Claire could have him falling to his fucking knees in seconds if she let him. But he knew that wouldn't happen, at least not yet. He needed to tread carefully if he wanted to get her back, get his family back. He couldn't dwell on the fact that she'd taken away any chance of them being together as a family from the start. No, he had to concentrate on what they could build now and hope for the future he'd always wanted with her.

He took his fill of her as she turned to the sink and wiped it down. There were some significant changes. He understood now where her curves had come from. If this was the transformation she took, he would keep her pregnant. Her body was more curvaceous, fuller. Those long, toned legs had been his undoing once. Her long wavy hair was pulled up in a messy bun on the top of her head. He'd noticed her eye makeup was smudged under her eyes while they ate, her clothes wrinkled from what he assumed was a restless night's sleep on the sofa. Yet, none of it made her look one bit less attractive. She was as beautiful as she'd been when he first laid eyes on her, and even then he wasn't old enough to understand the impact she would have on him—hell, the impact she would have on his life.

Her phone rang on the coffee table. She turned quickly, catching him watching her. She smiled at him, a light blush coloring her cheeks. She bent at the waist, giving him a delectable view of her ass.

"Hey, Mom…We're good, you? We just finished breakfast…"

He didn't miss the use of "we" in her sentences. He liked the way it sounded. He knew he was standing there like an idiot, listening and watching her, but he couldn't bring himself to move.

"Yeah about that. I was thinking maybe we can do it here…I know, but since Austin's back, I think it would be nice to have everyone over. I want Charlie to get to know his grandparents and aunt. He's going to be excited when we tell him he's got a cousin…"

Another "we." He loved it.

"… Awesome. I'll get Austin to tell his parents and sister…No, don't worry about anything, I'm cooking…Thanks for the confidence, Mom…I know you're joking…Okay, I'll see you then…I promise I'll call if I need anything…Love you too."

She hung up and turned to him. "We're having a barbecue here at the house on Sunday." She shrugged as if expecting him to give her the go-ahead.

"Cool. What do I need to get?"

"Oh, don't worry about that. I can go to the market tomorrow."

"I'm going there now. It'll save you the trip. I don't mean…I mean, since we're hosting…" he paused and stared at her. She bit her lip, her eyes starting to brim with tears as she nodded.

He reached for her bare arm, couldn't keep himself from touching her for another second. Her skin was soft, warm under his fingertips, and it took him a second to speak. His thumb caressed her small but muscular bicep.

"I'm sorry," he said, enjoying the look of surprise on her face.

"For what? You have nothing to be sorry about, Austin."

"I've been an ass to you since I got here. Look, I know you keeping your pregnancy from me wasn't easy. Do I wish you had told me? Yes. Do I think we could have made it work? I don't know, but I wish you'd given us the chance to find out. What I do know, though, is that I'm here now, and I want us to be friends. I want to get to know my son, and I want us to get to know each other again."

"I did it for you," she whispered, tears catching in her throat.

"I know," he said, sliding his hand from her arm to her shoulder, up her slender neck, and finally cupping her face.

He watched in awe as she closed her eyes and leaned into his touch. One lonely tear escaped from the corner of her eye onto his thumb. He wiped it, leaned in, and kissed her forehead. Never again did he want to see her cry. A small gasp from the doorway had them both turning. Charlie stood there with tears in his own eyes as he watched his parents.

"I can't believe you're really here, Daddy. I wished so hard you would come back," he said and ran towards them, hugging them as if his life depended on it.

"Oh, Charlie," he whispered.

He fell to his knees, grabbed his son by the shoulders, and hugged him tight. His emotions had been all over the place since he saw her at the hotel. His throat closed in on him, tears and a desperation he couldn't understand gripped him. He needed to make things good because the little person in his arms made all the pain worth it. With his free hand, he reached for Claire's hips, pulled her to him, and with his son's face buried in the crook of his neck, he buried his face into the tiny bump below her navel and cried.

He let it all go, cleansing his heart of the anger that had settled there overnight. He'd been angry for so long, he was determined to show he could be something else. Something better. Her fingers brushing back his hair was an intimate act, yet unbelievably reassuring. He was finally home. Claire and Charlie were his home. All these years he'd been going through the motions, surviving, trying to find the place where he belonged. Looking for the person he belonged with, when deep down, he had always known where to find it all.

"I'm so sorry," she said so softly he wasn't sure he was meant to hear.

A minute later, Austin reluctantly separated himself from her. He hadn't realized the intensity of his feelings for her, how much he'd missed her, missed talking to her and holding her. He knew he had always cared, but nothing had prepared him for the rush of desire that coursed through his body when he held her and felt her warmth. If it wasn't for Charlie urging him, he wouldn't have gone anywhere. His son had other ideas, and spending time with him or Claire held equal pull.

After some back and forth, searching for shoes and keys, and waiting for Claire's list, he and Charlie were out the door. The supermarket was a nightmare—there was no other way to explain it. Charlie walked him through the aisles, putting things in the cart Austin wasn't sure Claire would appreciate. They were in the cereal aisle when Austin finally stopped, looked at the items in the cart, and noticed that aside from tangerines, there were no other fruits or vegetables.

"Hold up, buddy. What's all the shi...stuff you're putting in here?" he asked.

"Let's see. There's bacon bits, hot dog buns, chocolate croissants, those round cheese thingies for a snack," Charlie explained as he moved things around for inspection. "There's also Lucky Charms, juice boxes, Nutella—"

"Junk," Austin cut him off.

"Not really. There's no cookies or chips in there yet."

"Yet? Tell me this, Charlie. What things does Mom usually get?"

The sour look had Austin smiling down at him—the twist of his mouth and scrunched brow was all Claire. Then it happened. He saw it coming the second Charlie's eyelids closed, leaving a tiny slit where he watched his son's eyes reach up to the ceiling as he rolled them. Of all of Claire's gestures, the eye roll was not one he wanted his son to inherit. He hated it when she did that.

"I suppose we should get some more fruits and

113

vegetables," he finally said.

"Let's call Mom and find out what she needs," he said. Saying the words caused him to smile, thinking it was something he'd heard his father say. He watched his son's shoulders drop in defeat. "Maybe if you help me out, we'll pick up some chips and cookies."

"All right," he conceded, letting out an exasperated breath. "We should probably take the Lucky Charms out and switch it for something else. Mommy doesn't like buying it for me because she says I only eat the marshmallows."

They went back through the aisles, putting things back where they belonged, and decided to start over. Austin took a chance and texted Claire, realizing after he hit send that she might have changed her number.

Austin: Anything specific you need me to buy?

He waited with bated breath for a response. Charlie in the meantime filled a bag with red apples, and when Austin felt the phone vibrate in his hands, he nearly jumped.

Claire: I'm not picky. Buy whatever you want; we need a little bit of everything. Don't let Charlie talk you into buying any junk. Oh and don't forget the Captain Crunch.

Austin: Never, one box for each.

Claire: Glad you remember.

Austin: I remember a lot...

He could see the message bubble on the screen, and he wondered if she was going to respond at all. Might as well put shit out there—he'd never forgotten a damned thing they'd shared, food or anything else.

Claire: And no Lucky Charms, that stuff is lethal for him and gives him a wicked stomach-ache every time he eats it.

Austin: You could've warned me. We just emptied out the cart to start over. Lucky Charms was the first thing that went back on the shelf.

Claire: Sorry, learn as you go is the name of the game. He didn't come with warning labels or instructions. Besides, what's the fun in warnings...

Austin: A little guidance then?

Claire: Just set the rules, you're the dad, the boss...He'll listen. He's a smart kid, he's not about to let you down.

Austin: I won't let him down either...

Another long pause, he watched the bubble blink, waiting for her response. Then ping. His heart sped up; he couldn't help but laugh at himself. When he read the words she wrote, his heart leaped.

Claire: I can't believe you still have my

number...

Removing it from his contacts was never a question. It was those times when he wanted to press call that he questioned everything. Although he knew there was a possibility she might've changed it, having it gave him a sense of comfort and made him feel close to her. He had stared at the picture attached to her contact information countless times, rubbed his fingers over her face, had a few drinks with it staring back on the worst of nights.

Austin: I couldn't bring myself to erase it. It was all I had of you...

His finger hovered over the send button in debate. He wanted to be honest with her. Lies weren't something he wanted to continue with if he was going to rebuild their relationship—no matter what direction it took. He was going to give clear and brutal honesty a shot. It was naive of him to think it was going to be smooth sailing from here on out. If anything, it was going to get tough.

Claire: I still have your old one.

Well then.

Austin: Now you have my new one. BTW, are twenty apples too much?

He tried to ease the awkwardness they couldn't escape even in text. He could already see her reaction—her eyes going wide, her mouth opening in alarm.

Claire: What? Yes it's too much. God, six is good.

Austin: Oh, okay. I should tell Charlie to take some out of the bag then...

Claire: Uh...yeah. Don't forget what's on my list. Get meat and chicken too, breasts preferably. I didn't put it on the list.

Austin: Hmm, it's on my list. I like breasts, too. I'm quite partial to them actually.

Claire: Austin!

Austin: LOL! I better go; our son thinks we need thirty peaches.

Claire: Oh, God, I'm worried. I don't think I'll have the room for the things he'll talk you into.

Austin: I've got this, Claire...

Claire: I trust you...Talk to you when you get home.

Home. Would it be his one day as well?

He didn't respond to her. He simply put the phone in his back pocket and went to reduce the amount of fruit Charlie was collecting. He hadn't been exaggerating about the thirty peaches.

CHAPTER NINE

Claire

Claire read and reread the texts between her and Austin twenty times, at least. Their playful banter had been interrupted by a bout or two of reality that made her think.

How long would he stay? Now that he knew about Charlie, how would they work the whole business of dividing the time? She didn't want her son bouncing back and forth from house to house, or worse, from city to city. The whole every other weekend thing wasn't an acceptable option.

Exhausting the scenarios, she sat staring blankly at the white canvas in front of her. In the background the radio was set to a local radio station, the DJ announcing a contest in which listeners could win tickets to a music festival she'd never heard of. She rarely turned the radio on while in her studio, preferring to work in silence. In fact, she'd rarely listened to the radio at all in the past few years, preferring to stick to the safety of her CDs. She'd always been afraid of hearing one of Austin's songs, or worse, an interview. After hearing his words the night before, she'd unconsciously walked to the shelf that was littered with paint jars and turned on a clock radio that had seen better days. Had he really written those songs about her? It terrified her to listen to the lyrics; writing a song had always been a personal journey for him. He told stories and felt everything deeply.

So much had changed in the last few hours. Charlie was not hers anymore—he was theirs, and she really liked the sound of that. Despite the tension that simmered when he arrived, she felt a lightness she hadn't experienced in quite a while—her conscience no longer weighed her down. Her not so big secret had revealed itself with a giant hug to the one person it should have never been kept from. So she thought it would be nice to change her routine a bit.

The radio was at a decent volume, not exactly background music, but not blaring either. Song after song played on, and she had yet to put the brush to the canvas. Clear conscience and all, she couldn't help but feel off-kilter. Austin had always managed to throw her off. If it wasn't something he said, it was something he did. Like the day he held her hand for the first time. She felt his fingers entwined with hers long after he'd dropped her off at home. Like a fool, she'd stared at her hand, flexing her fingers. She remembered vividly the day he'd kissed her for the first time. Instead of studying for her history test, she'd lain on her bed recounting the entire moment. She had gently rubbed her fingers against her lips, trying to hold on to the sensation of his soft mouth against hers.

The next day, she couldn't bring herself to face him. Embarrassed by the whole situation, she avoided him for two days until he cornered her and demanded an explanation. She didn't know what to say to him. She'd barely passed the history test, and with his body so close to hers, she couldn't think. To make a point, he kissed her again and promised that it wouldn't be the last time he did it.

Just like those days long ago, she could still feel his arm around her waist, the warmth of his breath as he cried against her hip after breakfast, mourning the loss of time. He had insinuated that she hadn't been the one to be alone these past few years. What must it have been like out on the road? Was he lonely? Maybe at times, she thought. There was no deluding the fact that he was Austin McKinley—he must have had his share of women throwing themselves at him. Surely he'd given in to some of them. What hot-blooded man wouldn't?

The thought of him being with anyone else grated at her nerves. She'd never been a jealous person, but until that moment, she'd never let herself truly entertain the thought of Austin with someone else. It was in the back of her mind, however. She avoided glancing at magazines at the supermarket checkout for fear she would see him with someone else. It was as if she'd tried to fool herself that he was alone. She never Googled him or the band, and never, ever did she let a conversation go far enough for anyone to divulge information she didn't want to hear.

Like a horse right out of the gateway, she'd worn blinders for the past five years. She would have to be delusional to think he'd spent all this time they'd been apart celibate. She, on the other hand, well, she could never see herself with anyone else. Although she tried to date, she never met anyone she wanted to give that part of herself to again. John had tried, and yes, she'd entertained the idea a couple of times, had gone out to dinner with him. He was her friend, but it was obvious to everyone he wanted more. One evening, she'd felt compelled to be honest with him, and she made it clear that friendship was all she could offer him. He wasn't thrilled, but he also knew it was that or nothing. Nevertheless, his flirting never ceased.

Once she cleared her mind, she focused back on the still blank canvas, and out of nowhere, it happened. That one moment she'd avoided for five years. There was no interlude, no introduction—the songs just seamlessly faded from one to the other. There was nothing to indicate what she was listening to, just his voice, a cappella at first. The sound of his voice was husky, breathy, and pained. Claire couldn't help but tune in to the lyrics. He sang about being kicked out of "her" heart, about being left with the memory of a touch, a last painful kiss. He sang about his pain, how much he wished "she" hadn't walked into his life, how he wished he hadn't walked into "hers." He described her dress—the red flowers in strategic places, legs he remembered wrapped around him on display in strappy sandals and lightly painted toes nails. The things most men never notice, he always did. He sang about loving her for the first time, and on and on, one heartbreaking word after another.

You've held my heart in a grip

Nothing I do takes away the pain, the loss

I loved you and you didn't love me enough

You took me on a wild trip

How could I go on, how am I supposed to go on...

She remembered that dress. She wore it on the first day of their senior year. By then, they had been together for two years. Their relationship was still innocent, the sexual tension high and frustrating the hell out of both of them. He'd always said that dress did him in. She still had it. She could never bring herself to get rid of it.

One particular weekend he had requested that she wear the dress. He took her out and surprised her with dinner and a walk around the pond at the foot of her backyard. She remembered him slipping the dress over her head, careful not to wrinkle it. Her parents, no surprise to either, were out of town, and Hunter had gone away on a camping trip with his friend Mackenzie and her parents.

Her room had been transformed—candles were lit on every surface, and a vase with two dozen roses sat on her dresser. He made the moment memorable and romantic. She was surprised to realize she wasn't nervous at all. In fact, she looked forward to the moment when he would truly make her his. She loved him so much, trusted him with everything she was. He was gentle with her, whispering sweet words to her as they lost their virginity together. He loved her so softly—he made sure he was tender, worried he would hurt her. Then, while caressing her from shoulder to hip, he told her he loved her for the first time.

Claire's vision blurred as she stared at the blank canvas. How many more firsts would they share now that he was back? She couldn't bear to listen to any more of the song. To hear the pain of loss in his voice was enough to let the tears fall in an unstoppable stream down her face. She managed to block out the words, but the music still penetrated her wall. Music without words was even more devastating. She tried to focus on the canvas in front her. She took a deep breath to refocus, trying but failing miserably at keeping a sob from escaping. The next verse was about still loving her. About how there would never be another. She dropped her brush and covered her face, crying into hands stained from mixing paint, feeling his pain.

Then there was silence. It took her a moment to realize there was no music through the sound of her sobs.

"You really never heard any of our songs before?"

She jumped and roughly wiped at her tears. "No," she whispered.

"Did you like it?"

"No. It was so sad," she told him, a sob catching in her voice.

"Most of them are. A broken heart is kind of a great muse, although depressing as hell." He grunted out a laugh.

"I don't know what to say."

"You don't have to say anything. I just wrote what I was feeling."

"You hated me," she pointed out.

"A little, yes. Mostly, though, I hated the way you made me feel."

"You were sad..."

"And hurt, and angry, and so fucking confused."

"I'm sorry," she told him again for what was probably not the last time.

She noticed then that his hand was stretched out. He was standing beside the radio, his hand on the power button.

"Why did you turn it off?"

"It was making you cry."

"I don't think I can bear to hear another one of your songs if that's how sad they are."

"We'll just have to listen to other stuff then..."

She didn't miss the "we'll" in his statement. They watched each other. She looked at his hands, clenching and unclenching at his sides. His forearms flexed, lines of defined muscle tightening every time he formed a fist. She wanted to go to him, to comfort him, to have him comfort her. She wanted to do something that would take the pain she saw in his eyes away. Pain she had caused. How, she wondered, were they going to put things back together? Did he even want to put things back together? Did she?

They could be just friends; they had to be, for Charlie's sake. So far today, they'd been civil. She was stunned as he started to walk towards her, stopping suddenly at a loud crashing from the main floor.

"Charlie," he whispered, and turned to run downstairs, Claire right behind him.

He skipped several of the metal steps as he hurried down

the spiral stairs that led to her studio. She'd fallen once before, slipping on the hard black metal, so she took her time. She knew from experience that if there wasn't a frantic scream of pain or crying, Charlie probably wasn't hurt. Sure, her heart skipped several beats, but she never worried as much as when he was smaller. Austin, on the other hand, might need a defibrillator by the time the week was through.

He ran towards the kitchen, Claire a few steps behind. There was a broken jar of jelly on the kitchen floor—its red contents splashed across her white tiles. Some had even made it onto the lower cupboard doors. Charlie was on the counter getting ready to jump off when Austin yelled for him to stop. Startled, Charlie fell back on his bum and looked at Austin with terrified eyes.

"Sorry, I didn't mean to drop it. I was trying to put it away and it slipped."

"It's okay, buddy. I'm sorry I yelled," Austin said as he skipped over the splattered jelly. "Are you okay?"

Claire watched as he patted their son down, checking for cuts and other injuries. She refrained from pointing out that Charlie was nowhere near the broken glass. She put her hand over her mouth to stifle the laugh that was bubbling in her chest. It was going to be fun, she thought, to watch Austin become a father. She could see his overprotectiveness was something that was going to drive her indestructible son nuts.

"I'm fine, Daddy. I wasn't near it when it broke," he told Austin, a questioning scowl on his face as his father continued to inspect every part of him.

126

"Jesus, you scared the sh...heck out of me."

"You can't say heck either."

"Well what word can I use then?" he asked, irritated.

"Just leave it out. That's what Mommy always says."

Austin looked over at her and shook his head. She knew what had crossed his mind—she'd been quite the potty mouth, could put any trucker to shame. He turned to smile up at his son right before pulling him off the counter and hugging him fiercely. Charlie looked at his mother, his eyebrows scrunched in question. She shrugged and let out the laugh she'd been holding in.

"What's so funny?" Austin asked her.

"You're smothering your son," she told him.

"I am not, am I?" he asked Charlie.

"I don't know what that even means, Daddy."

"Good, I'm not telling you," he said and hugged his son against him.

Claire stood just outside the kitchen, watching her two men. She wanted to leave them. She felt like an intruder, but she couldn't bring herself to move. She realized in that moment that she didn't want to miss a second of Charlie and Austin getting to know each other. She didn't want to miss a moment, in fact, of Austin falling in love with their son. She looked down at the mess, dreading the cleanup. Before she could turn to walk toward the small closet that housed all her cleaning supplies, Austin was giving Charlie instructions on the cleaning process.

"You go on back upstairs, Claire. Charlie and I've got this."

"I don't mind helping."

"You've got work to do, don't worry about it. We're going to make dinner too. Right, buddy?"

"Yep, and it's a surprise," he sang.

"I really don't mind. Today's a bit of a write-off."

Austin walked up to her and held her by the shoulders. His touch was like a lightning bolt striking right in the center of her heart.

"Really, babe. We've got this."

She stared at him, dumbfounded. Had he just called her "babe"? Did he even realize he'd said it? It had come out so naturally. Tears sprang to her eyes, and she couldn't hold them back. God, she hadn't cried in years, and in the past hours the floodgates had failed.

"What is it?" he asked, concerned.

"Nothing, I'm fine."

"Babe—" he started. He let his shoulders fall as he caught himself. "I hadn't realized I said that. I'm sorry...I—"

"I should try and get some work done."

"Claire…"

"I'm fine."

He nodded. "We'll call you when dinner's ready."

She turned as fast as she could and ran up the stairs to get away from him. Everything she'd ever felt for him, with him, resurfaced with that one word. At the top of the stairs, she covered her mouth to stifle the sob that had risen in her throat. What the hell was she going to do? How were she and Charlie going to move on once he left? Because he was going to leave. This wasn't his life, his home—he had a career away from them. Not only was her son going to fall in love with him, but she was going to fall deeper.

At the top of the stairs, she listened to Austin give instructions. This dad thing might not be so hard for him to get into. He was good at it, patient. She was going to have to help him reel in his holy-shit-Charlie's-bleeding-to-death reaction, but it was going to be fun watching his paternal side unfold. They would work through any obstacles. It all came down to Charlie, no other reason, no other choice. He was their number-one priority.

CHAPTER TEN

Austin

Austin sat on the back deck with his laptop, staring into the pond, trying to come up with the words to the email he was about to construct to his manager, lawyers, publicists, and band. There were several things he needed to put in order. First was adding both Claire and Charlie to his will.

Whether things worked out between the two of them or not, he was going to make sure they were both taken care of. If he knew Harry at all, his lawyer would demand proof, ask a million questions, and would go as far as to confront Claire. Austin would do all he could to keep that heartless shark away from her. The man was loyal to a fault, but harassing his family wasn't one of his job requirements.

He heard her rummaging in the kitchen. An array of bowls and trays were set up on one side of the counter. She'd been preparing for the family barbecue for hours. Vegetables had been chopped, salads put together. Claire managed to create quite the feast, and she enjoyed every second of it. He looked down at his watch—the whole family would be there any minute. He closed his laptop and was about to head inside to offer his assistance when she came bouncing out in a short floral dress. The floral dress.

She was humming a popular song he'd heard a million times on the radio. Her hips were swinging back and forth, that damned dress hugging every luscious curve. It was shorter than he remembered, and although she looked beautiful in it, he couldn't believe that one: she still had it, and two: it fit her...nicely. He leaned forward on his elbows, resting his face on his hands, and watched her for a few more seconds. Her feet were bare, and her legs moved, bending at the knees to the tune she continued to hum.

"That's not one of my songs. My ego is wounded."

She jumped, letting out a squeak as she brought her hand to her chest. He smiled at her reaction. Her cheeks flushed, and her eyes sparked with something he couldn't quite identify.

She laughed. "I'm sure your ego can take it."

"I don't know about that," he said, and before he could think it through, he was on his feet.

"I didn't know you were out here," she said as she swallowed and took a step back.

"I was trying to write an email to my lawyer. Nice dress, by the way," he said as he inched closer to her.

"This old thing," she said, running her hands down and over her hips.

Mischief. That's what the look in her eyes was.

132

The little tease knew exactly what she was doing the second she put that damned dress on. This would be the beginning of his torture. He took his sweet time perusing her body, from her bare feet to the slope of her cleavage. He followed the flush that started there and traveled onto her face as he got closer.

The distance wasn't far, three feet maybe, but he took his sweet time. When he stood in front of her, he reached for her. It was the natural thing to do; he didn't have to think about it. Not where he was going to put his hands or whether or not he was going to slide them north or south. He looked into her eyes and opted to rest them on her hips. Pulling her towards him, a desperate need to touch her, feel her, to hold her overwhelmed him. Claire's breath hitched. Her chest rose and fell, giving him an excellent view of her cleavage. Six foot three had its advantages.

"It's tight," he said as he slid his hands to her waist.

"A little." She shrugged.

A little. The damned thing looked like it had been painted. If it had been anyone else but family coming over, he would have her back in the house changing out of it. Hell, he was still debating it. It was tight in all the right places, too short and sexy for public consumption—he suddenly wondered if she'd ever worn it out. He hoped not. He couldn't even imagine the heads she'd turn walking down Main Street. She'd driven him mad the first time he'd seen her in it, and his reaction was no different now.

"Can I remind you what happened the last time you wore

this dress?"

"No need. I remember perfectly."

"I'm glad. Why then?"

"Why what?"

"Don't play coy with me, Claire. I see you in this dress and I can't…"

"Can't what?" she breathed out.

His hand slid down past her hips to her thigh. He felt her quiver beneath his touch. He smirked, loving how she reacted to him. He felt the goose bumps rise one by one as his calloused fingers made contact with her skin.

"Jesus, Claire," he whispered into her neck.

Her hands were around his biceps, her nails digging into his skin. Her scent, which he remembered vividly, drove him nuts—the citrus mixed with a hint of coconut was something that had embedded itself into his own pores. As his hand reached just below the curve of her ass, he ran his nose down her neck. He wanted to rip any barrier between them right then and there, forgetting for those seconds as he reveled in her that they were having people over.

"Hello, McKinleys," Alexa's booming voice interrupted their trip down memory lane. "Hope I'm not interrupting anything…"

Austin growled against her neck, gave her ass a squeeze, confirming she was wearing a thong. Claire flexed in his hands, and he couldn't help but chuckle. He held her in place, willing his erection into submission before he turned to greet the first ill-timed guest.

"Later," he whispered, and kissed her neck.

He stared right at her and watched with amusement as she blew out her breath, the blush on her cheeks glowing. He put that color there. He made her breath hitch, made her skin rise in tiny bumps, and he'd enjoyed every second of it.

Alexa had come in through the side gate and made her not so subtle way up the stairs to the deck. A snide remark on the tip of her tongue no doubt, from the way she was biting her lip and smirking. She wouldn't let what she'd witnessed slide if her life depended on it. Her sarcasm and sense of humor, Austin realized, was something he'd missed. She'd been as much a part of his life as Claire was—not in the same capacity, of course, but she'd been important. They'd all been great friends.

"Well, I see we've been working on the bonding part of this reunion..."

"Weren't you supposed to be in Cabo?" asked Claire.

"Nah. The project has been pushed back a few weeks. Mr. Swimming-in-dough can't make his mind up about what flooring he wants. I gave him two choices. Two. And he can't make up his rich freaking mind. These spoiled billionaire types are all the same. They think people are at their beck and call."

"Who's the client?" asked Austin, angling Claire in front of him to cover his defiant cock.

"Patrick Pemberton."

He whistled. "Wow, that's quite the client."

"So I've been told."

"I met him once at a fundraiser. Quite the uptight fucker. Have you met him?"

"Haven't had the displeasure. Don't think I ever will, to be honest. He prefers to deal through email or through his assistant. It's not easy to work with him."

"You should Google him. He's very good looking, just your type."

"I don't Google my clients. Besides, spoiled billionaires aren't my type at all. You could always give him a shot though," she yelled from the kitchen.

"No, I prefer the lying curvaceous type." He felt Claire stiffen next to him the second the words crossed his mouth, and he regretted it instantly.

"Do you want anything to drink, Alex?"

"I'm good for now," she replied, looking straight at him as she popped a carrot drenched in dip into her mouth.

"Okay. Well, I'm going to pull the steaks and chicken out of the fridge," said Claire as she turned and flipped the lever behind the barbecue to turn it on. "Make sure Charlie doesn't get near that," she said to no one in particular.

Now who was the fucker. He looked over at Alexa, who was shaking her head, a smug look on her face. Claire closed the top to the barbecue and then walked into the house. He looked up to the sky and let out a frustrated breath.

"Way to go, genius."

"Don't say a word." He pointed at Alexa.

"Oh no, I will not say how you should keep your mouth shut or that you should think before you speak. Men, I've learned, have no clue what 'thinking before' means," she said, making exaggerated air quotes. "I will not point out that you had her back in your spell when I walked in. I will not in any way, shape, or form highlight the fact that you had her ass, as well as her little lonely heart, in the palm of your hand, but you ruined it by the stupidity you so intelligently articulated. Idiot."

"Are you done?" he asked and watched as she looked to the sky, twisting her mouth in thought. He really hoped she was done.

"Yes…for now." She popped another carrot in her mouth.

"Auntie Alex!" Charlie's excitement interrupted his rebuttal.

"Hey, little man. I've missed you," she told him as he jumped into her arms.

"Daddy's mom and dad are coming, and so is his sister. I have a cousin. Can you believe it?"

"That's exciting, buddy."

"I can't wait to meet them. Daddy, do you know when they'll get here?"

"Soon. They should be here soon."

"Okay. I need to change my shirt. I don't like this one."

137

He jumped out of Alexa's arms and ran back inside. He was nervous. The shirt he had on was perfectly fine, and in the few days Austin had been home…back rather, he'd never seen Charlie worry much about what he wore.

"You know, if you reel in your antagonism and give her a break, this might work really well. You have a son, Austin. A beautiful, charming, funny, and smart as hell son who has loved you since he could remember, even though he didn't know you. I'd give anything for my dad to show up and love me the way I see you love that child," she said, pointing towards the house. "Remember that. Remember everything you have and cherish it."

"I should go apologize."

"Good luck with that…"

When Austin walked into the house, the kitchen was empty. A dish towel had been thrown on the counter next to an abandoned knife and cutting board full of chives that had been half chopped. A pot had come to a rolling boil on the stove. Austin walked to it and turned it off.

He found Claire in an emotional embrace with his sister Analia in the front hall. Her two-year-old daughter Sydney and Charlie were between them, and his niece was struggling to get out of the group hug she'd been pulled into. Although he couldn't hear what Claire had said, he heard his sister clearly say, "It's okay. You're all together now."

He looked to his mother, who was standing behind Claire and Analia, tears swimming in her as eyes as she stared at him. He felt it then, Claire's regret, her pain, and weight of her decision as she apologized over and over. Why it sank in at that moment, he didn't know. They'd have a long road to travel to get to where they used to be. He loved her, and he hoped that she loved him enough to put up with the shit that he might spurt out. He wasn't perfect by any means, but he wasn't entirely whole yet—not until he had her completely.

The next morning, Austin once again found himself out on the deck. He stared out to the pond, watching joggers run around its perimeter. He hit send on a very specific, very extensive email to his lawyer and team at 3 a.m. He hadn't been able to sleep, the day with his family and Claire's family playing in his head. They'd laughed a lot. Claire told stories about Charlie, starting from his birth. She filled everyone in on his life. Analia would high-five her every once in a while when Claire mentioned a specific event she could relate to. Mostly the cry-it-out method, which he didn't agree with and said as much.

"Well you weren't there, so you wouldn't understand what it's like..." Yeah, that grated at a couple of nerves, but after his comment about her being the lying type, he kept his mouth shut. His mother had given him a sympathetic look, and he'd had enough. That's when he grabbed a couple of gloves and a baseball. He and Charlie had spent a good part of the afternoon teaching Sydney how to catch.

"Oh, I didn't realize you were here," Claire said, bringing him back to his hopeless reality. "Alexa, I gotta go, I'll call you later...oh, okay. I'll sign the contract and send it to you tomorrow...I won't forget, I promise...Bye." Claire dropped the phone on the island. "Sorry, it was Alexa; I have to sign the contract for the paintings the King Edward commissioned..."

"You should get on that."

"I will. I thought you were going home?" she asked as she poured herself some iced tea.

"I am home," he said. He watched her as she lifted her head to look at him, that little wrinkle in the middle of her forehead making its recurring appearance.

She cleared her throat. "I meant your parents' house."

"I got back about an hour ago. I didn't want to disturb you. Charlie at art camp?"

"Yep, which reminds me, I have to go get him. He's off in fifteen minutes."

"Dressed like that?" he asked, waving his hand up and down at her appearance. He didn't bother to hide his disapproval.

If he had anything to do with it, there was no way she was going out in that poor excuse for a dress. The damn thing looked like a nightie. Who the hell was she trying to impress? Was there someone she was trying to impress? Charlie's instructor perhaps, or worse, one of the other fathers? Hell no—she could just turn around and walk right back into her tower where he could lock the door and keep her away from prying eyes.

"What's wrong with what I'm wearing?"

"It looks like lingerie," he told her.

"It does not. It's a dress. I've worn it tons of times."

"Outside of the house?" he asked, the incredulity in his tone was unmistakable.

"Yes. What is wrong with you?"

"You're not going out in that dress," he told her, pointing at her in disapproval.

She looked at him like he'd lost his ever-loving mind. He didn't think she was far off. This whole situation, Claire, the way she looked, had thrown him off like nothing else—and not just today, but from the second he walked into her house. He'd wondered for years what she would look like if he saw her again. Nothing prepared him for the vision he saw when he walked into that hotel lobby. She was beautiful, absolutely fucking breathtaking. He wanted to protect her. No, scratch that, he wanted to keep her hidden. Guys would ogle. Did she not realize that, for Christ's sake. Did she have any idea how gorgeous she was? How desirable she looked? If the wind blew in any direction, some fucker would get a delightful view of the firm, round ass he wanted so badly to put his hands on.

"Okay, why don't you and your little caveman act take it somewhere else? I have to go get Charlie."

"Like hell you are," he argued, standing up so fast he knocked the chair over as he followed her back into the house.

She was slinging her purse over her shoulder, her hand on the doorknob when he reached her. He nearly jumped on her when she opened the door. He could see the puzzlement on her face when he leaned over to take the car keys from her other hand. They engaged in a brief tug of war, grunting and twisting in the process. The whole thing was utterly ridiculous, but he couldn't help it. Unless she put on those ugly overalls she used for painting, she wasn't setting foot outside the house.

"Austin…what the…Let me go. I have to go get Charlie."

"No. I'll go," he said as he backed her up against the wall.

Her breathing came out in sharp, shallow gasps, her breasts pressed against him. The thin strap of her dress slipped off her shoulder, revealing the swell of one of her breasts. She was braless. No way could she make things easy on him. No, he had to endure an endless case of blue balls. He started to wonder if she did that shit on purpose. Without meaning to, he moaned. He had one leg between hers; his cock nestled right in her center. Her eyes widened as his cock twitched against her. Her breathing got heavier, and the keys hit the ground as her hands gripped his arms. Whether it was to push him away or bring him closer, he couldn't tell.

"Let me go, Austin," she said in a ragged whisper.

He ran his hand up her arm, to her shoulder, and back down to play with the strap of her yellow dress. He gripped it and pulled, ripping it from the seam in the back effortlessly. The front fell, revealing more of her breast. The only thing keeping the damn thing from completely slipping off was her nipple.

"Go change. I'm going to pick up Charlie," he said, fighting to keep it together, his mouth inches from hers.

God, he wanted her.

He bent down to pick up the keys and wordlessly walked out of the house, giving the door a frustrated slam.

When he got back from picking up Charlie, he would go for a jog, take an ice cold shower, and reel in his goddamned possessive stand on her. What the fuck had come over him? He hadn't seen her in six years, and in eight days she'd managed to unravel him. He ripped her dress, for crying out loud.

His phone pinged with a text message.

Claire: I thought you should know that Charlie's at the Performing Arts Center. I called, told them you were coming to pick him up. Just give them your name.

He made a U-turn and started to drive back to Main Street where he made a left towards the center. He reached up to position his cap lower on his head, only to realize he wasn't wearing it. In his haste to get away from Claire, he hadn't bothered to grab it. Now not only were his nerves on edge because of Claire but also because of the slight anxiousness he felt when out in public. He was picking up his son— he wanted that moment to be just theirs, no interruptions. He figured if he got recognized, he'd have to deal with it, but he wouldn't hesitate to decline an autograph or picture. The last thing he wanted was Charlie thrust into the spotlight. He had no doubt that any picture of him with his son would hit the Internet before they got back in the car to drive home.

He parked the car as close to the entrance as he possibly

could, contemplating how he was going to get past the people loitering at the entrance to the building. Chances were no one would recognize him at all, but he couldn't risk it. He searched the back seat for a cap, something that would hide his face. He reached for the glove compartment and was relieved to see that Claire's obsession with aviators hadn't waned. Three pairs sat neatly on a car manual. He grabbed the first pair he saw and slipped them on.

Trying to look inconspicuous, he walked to the main entrance with his head down. A couple of kids ran into him, and he put out his hands to stop one of them from falling. The place was packed. He'd forgotten that attached to the center was the town's library. He looked around, having no idea where he was supposed to go. Spotting the information desk, he walked in that direction. He'd rather face the possibility of recognition than text Claire. He looked around for clues as to where he might have to go, wanting to get the hell out of there fast. As if she could read his mind from a mile away, his phone pinged again with a text from Claire.

Claire: He's in the Robert Bateman Art Studio. Go through the set of doors to the right of the entrance to the theater. It's the third door on the right.

Austin: Thanks.

The room was nearly empty. Aside from Charlie, only three other kids remained. Charlie saw him the instant he pulled the door open.

"Daddy!" he yelled, breaking into a mad run and jumping

into his arms. There was no way in the world he would ever get tired of his son calling out to him.

"Hey, my man, how was class?"

"Good. Want to see what I'm working on?"

"Sure."

Charlie pulled him further into the room, towards an area lined with easels. An older lady sat at a desk fiddling through some paperwork. She gave him a kind smile as Charlie pulled him in front of his masterpiece. He had to remind himself the kid was only five. He wasn't sure what Charlie had inherited from him, but he certainly didn't inherit his talent for art from his mother. He hoped to God the kid stuck to baseball.

"What do you think?"

"It's something else, buddy. I'm impressed."

"I'm not finished yet. Hopefully by the end of the week."

"I can't wait to see it finished. Come on, Mom's waiting."

He watched Charlie go to a rack and grab a backpack and a light jacket. While he waited, he looked at the art on the other easels—no Picassos in this bunch. He laughed to himself. He figured if Charlie was having fun, there was no harm done. The second he brought his painting home, however, Austin was going to frame it, take it to New York, and hang it right next to Claire's true masterpieces.

"Mr. McKinley? Hi, I'm Rebecca, the art teacher."

"Nice to meet you."

"Can you please have Miss Monroe fill out this paperwork for our files? Although she called, it is our policy that anyone who can pick up Charlie be registered," she informed.

"Certainly. I'll give it to her to sign."

"Perfect, thank you. Please sign out on the sheet by the door."

"Will do. Come on, Charlie."

"Bye, Miss Rebecca," Charlie called back.

"Bye, Charlie. See you tomorrow."

The drive back to the house consisted of Charlie recapping his morning to Austin. He mentioned something about his friend Robby getting into a fight with another kid in class over red paint, which was a shock to Charlie because Robby never fought. Charlie informed Austin that he had stayed out of it. Good thing, because he didn't know what he would do if someone laid a hand on his son.

"I'm glad you stayed out of it. I never want to hear you were fighting."

"Okay. Don't worry."

He looked at Charlie through the rear view mirror. His son was quiet, a thoughtful expression on his face as he stared out the window. He wondered what things worried him, what he was most scared of, what his favorite color was, his favorite food. He wanted to know everything. And from his actions today, he was glad to realize that Claire had raised a kind child.

146

CHAPTER ELEVEN

Claire

It couldn't have been better timing if she'd planned it. Just as she made her way past the neighbor's house, Austin drove the Rover onto the driveway. The look on his face when he saw her still wearing the yellow dress was priceless. His mouth hung open, and the white-knuckle grip he had on the steering wheel told her she'd gotten the reaction she hoped for. Sashaying up the walkway, she lifted her arm to give her boys a wave that hiked up her dress significantly.

After he'd left, Hunter called to say he was in town and coming over. As a treat for both Charlie and her brother, she headed out to grab wings for dinner. She thought about changing after Austin had so passionately ripped her strap. Instead, with a vindictive smile, she ripped the other strap and tied it behind her neck—a little halter never hurt anyone.

"What's in the bags, Mom?"

"Wings. Uncle Hunter's in town. He wants to come over and see you and your dad."

"Awesome," said Charlie, fisting the air.

147

"Charlie, why don't you go wash up," said Austin as he walked towards her with purpose.

She had to fight the urge to step back; she refused to be intimidated by him. She had to admit that she'd been quite turned on earlier—it had been a while since she'd felt her body heat the way it had. The swarm of butterflies fighting to take flight in her belly hadn't ceased. He stared at her chest, the dress dipping enough to show a good amount of cleavage.

"You didn't," he said through clenched teeth.

"I did, and it felt good, liberating, sexy..."

"Men probably looked at you."

"Probably." She shrugged.

He reached down for her hand, grabbing hold of the bags and making a point to grind against her. His face inches from hers, it took everything in her not to move the inch it would take for their lips to connect.

"Go change."

"Or what?" she countered.

"Don't test me, Claire."

"You have no say in what I do, what I say, or what I wear."

His jaw clenched, and with a subtle force, he took the bags from her hand and walked into the house. She let out the breath she'd been holding and took a few minutes to calm herself before she followed him into the house. She would change eventually, only because Hunter was coming over. Despite the fact that he was her little brother, he'd have something to say about her dress as well. The last thing she wanted was for both men to gang up on her.

Inside, she heard Austin and Charlie talking in the kitchen. Silverware clinked, plates clattered, and the plastic bags containing their dinner filled the house with the unmistakable smell of chicken.

"Daddy, can I ask you something?"

"Of course, bud, you can ask me anything."

She heard Charlie clear his throat. A tense silence fell over them, and she couldn't help but move closer.

"When are you going back?"

"Back where?"

"Home."

And there it was—the question she hadn't been able to ask.

The man he'd waited so long to meet was with them on what could possibly be borrowed time. He'd have to go. At some point he needed to go back to his life, his career, his responsibilities. It's why his next words had her gasping, not in disbelief, but in fear that her son would take his declaration to heart.

"I am home, Charlie. I don't plan on going anywhere."

"But you have a house somewhere else, right?"

"Yes, I have a house in New York City. It's where I've been living all these years."

"So while you're here, you're living with us…"

"Yes," was his simple answer.

"Awesome!" The word of the day.

Claire heard Charlie's footsteps out on the deck. She moved so Austin could see her. Her eyes burned with the need to cry.

"Please don't hurt him," she told him.

"I won't. I promise."

Claire simply nodded.

"I'm going to change," she announced.

"Why? You look pretty. Doesn't she look pretty, Daddy?" Charlie said from the doorway.

Austin looked at her, his gaze traveling up and then down, his face showing no signs of the frustration he'd expressed earlier. His eyes softened as he looked at her face.

"She's looks beautiful, buddy," he said, the sincerity in his eyes reaching a place she thought dead.

"Thank you," she said and walked away.

In her room, she rummaged through drawers that were in desperate need of a summer cleaning. Every top she picked out was wrinkled beyond any help an iron could provide. She settled on a pink tank top and navy shorts. She slipped her feet into the flip-flops she'd been wearing and made her way back down.

Austin was on the phone, a dish towel thrown over his

shoulder, shaking a bottle of salad dressing. On the deck, the table had been set for four. With no sign of Charlie, she ventured out to look for him. Her son was bent over her garden, picking out flowers and putting them into a mason jar. As if sensing her eyes on him, he looked up and waved at her. Austin's laughter had her turning.

"No way…dude, we have to get together, shoot the shit sans wives…right." She didn't miss the plural in his statement. "I'll be there, man, but let's keep it on the down low. I don't want the kid's game to turn into a fan event…Perfect. Six thirty, got it. See you then." He turned to look at her, took his fill, and walked right past her onto the deck. "It's a done deal, buddy," he yelled down to Charlie, who ran up the stairs.

"What's a done deal?" she asked.

"Daddy's coaching!" Charlie cheered. He did what was quickly becoming the customary jumping into Austin's arms.

She watched them high-five each other and do some funny dance they invented the day before. In the past few days, she had gotten to see a hundred different sides to Austin—angry, sad, and the one he bestowed upon his child in that moment: unconditional love. This was it, the dream she'd had a while ago, waking her with an ache in her heart when she realized it was still just her and Charlie. The guilt she felt when she saw them together continued to eat at her slowly. Austin wasn't just a part of her son; he was an essential part of both their lives.

"Hey, what's up? Why're you crying?" asked Austin.

She hadn't realized she'd been crying. "Happy tears, I

promise."

"I'm helping coach the team," he repeated with a smile a mile wide.

The look of joy had undone her. Her lips quivered, and as hard as she tried to keep any more tears from spilling, she failed.

"Babe, what is it?" he asked as he pulled her into his arms.

"Thank you for making him so happy. Thank you for coming back when I know you didn't want to."

"I wanted to. You have no idea how much I wanted to. I was just afraid."

"You don't have to be. As much as I hate to admit it, Charlie needs you."

"And you, do you need me?"

She only nodded before he engulfed her in his arms. Who was she kidding? She'd missed him like crazy, and she had feared and wished for this moment for years, never imagining what it would actually do to her. She loved him, had loved him for the past ten years. She could go back to that love so easily it scared the shit out of her.

"Why do you do that?"

"What, honey?" he asked. She loved when the endearments spilled so naturally from his mouth.

"Act like such a brute one minute and then go do something as benign as agreeing to coach a baseball team and break my heart."

"Break your heart in a good or bad way?" he asked, pulling back from her and smiling.

"Good way."

"If you promise to stop wearing miniature clothing, I promise to stop being a brute."

"My clothes aren't miniature, and I doubt you'll ever stop being a brute."

"You're probably right. Now, what time is that ingrate of a brother of yours getting here?"

"Not too soon for you, asshole," came Hunter's voice from the kitchen.

Both she and Austin turned to look at him. Hunter took in her appearance, his brows furrowing as anger replaced his expression. He looked at her and then at Austin with his hands on her waist, paying close attention to the tear streak down her face.

"Did he make you cry?" he asked, his tone harsh.

"No. Well yes, but in a good way."

"I'm keeping a close watch on you, McKinley. One wrong move and your pretty face is history."

"Threaten me all you want. I have a partner now. Right, Charlie?"

"Yeah, Uncle Hunter. You just try."

Austin high-fived his son, both laughing at the action that, despite the short amount of time they'd been bonding, came naturally.

"Traitor," Hunter mumbled and turned to his sister. "You good?"

"A little overwhelmed."

"You glad he's here?" he whispered.

"For Charlie, yes."

"For you?

"It'll take a long time to get there, Hunter. I hurt him."

"If that look on his face when I walked in is any indication, he's already forgiven you," Hunter told her before he drew her into his arms.

"I don't know. He seems fine one moment, but then he doesn't hesitate to throw it in my face. I know he wants to do the right thing by Charlie, but he's still angry with me."

"He'll get over it."

Claire held him tight as she nodded. They'd spent so much time together growing up, their bond unbreakable. She wasn't sure what she would do without him. Hunter kept her strong. He was the reason she went home every day when all she wanted was to stay away from the lifeless house. She couldn't stand the thought of him alone in that big house. Sure, they had housekeepers and cooks, but nothing ever beat being there for each other.

"Guess what, Uncle Hunter."

"What, little man?"

"Daddy's going to help coach my team."

"You don't say." He smirked. "Coaching baseball. Have you cooked dinner yet? Gone to the supermarket?"

"We did those things the other day, Uncle Hunter."

Hunter's laugh matched his voice, deep and clear. He was tall, and he had the same color hair, eyes, and skin tone as Claire. Had it not been for the two-year age difference, they could be twins.

"My sister must work some magic if she's managed to domesticate the big rock star."

"Fuck you."

"You first, bitch."

"Guys! For heaven's sake, Charlie's here," she reprimanded.

"I got an idea," Charlie announced.

He bounced down the stairs of the deck to the garden and into the shed that housed all of their garden tools. They all looked at each other as they heard him rummage through whatever mess he was making. He ran out of the shed and back up.

"What you got there, little man?" asked Hunter.

"A bad word jar. Matthew says his mom has one in the kitchen, and every time someone says a bad word, they have to put a dollar in there. So you two owe me…" He stopped as he ticked off his fingers. "Three bucks."

"You'll get rich with these two," Claire told him.

"I know," he said, making a lame attempt at wiggling his eyebrows.

Both Austin and Hunter reached into their back pockets, pulled out their wallets, and fished out six twenties between them and put it in the jar.

"There," Austin said. "That should cover it for the rest of the day."

"Holy cow!" Charlie yelled.

They broke into harmonious laughter at her son's reaction. For the rest of their meal, Charlie filled them all in on the shenanigans of his friend Matthew's family life. She had to admit that they were quite comical. It appeared no topic of conversation was off limits in that household, and he enjoyed retelling the stories he heard. Her son had no filter. Charlie knew right from wrong, but like his father, he didn't care what he said, who he said it to, or how much he said. Claire's only advice to him was that he ensured his words didn't hurt anyone's feelings.

She sat back and watched three of the most important men in her life exchange baseball advice. At times the conversation became heated. Her son, never one to back down, put his two cents in when he had the men's attention.

As she licked barbecue sauce off her fingers, she saw Austin's eyes were captivated by the simple action. And because she enjoyed tormenting him, she took advantage of his interest in her mouth and finger. Claire met his gaze and seductively sucked, pulling her finger out and then back into her mouth with excruciating slowness. Austin's open-mouthed response encouraged her. She spread her lips in a seductive smile. He licked his lips and reached down, trying but failing to be inconspicuous as he adjusted himself. Knowing what she did to him had her shifting in her seat, Austin's own vindicated smile spread across his face, that damn dimple making a rare and gorgeous appearance.

"At least have the decency to get a fucking room." Claire lifted her head suddenly at the sound of her brother's voice. She looked around the table and noticed Charlie was no longer in his chair.

"Where's Charlie?" she asked.

"Kid got grossed out watching his parents devour themselves with their eyes. Said something about having a game. You two done?" asked Hunter, staring from her to Austin.

"He went to the game?"

"No, he didn't go to the game. What's the matter with you? Get your damn mind out of your sexually frustrated gutter. He asked twice what the time was, but you two were too busy. He went to change."

She stared at him and couldn't help the flush in her face. She chanced a glance at Austin and was furious to see his checkmate smile on his stunning face.

CHAPTER TWELVE

Austin

He knew Claire and her brother had been close growing up, and it didn't seem like much had changed in that respect. He watched Claire and Hunter walk up the bleachers as he shook hands with Jim, who was delighted to have him on board. Jim had been trying to get one of the other parents to assist him, but none had accepted the challenge. He turned to his old friend, excited to be part of his son's team.

Austin heard Claire call Charlie over, and he watched her bend down in front of him, beaming a glorious smile at their son. She tucked in Charlie's shirt, handed him his water, and re-tied his laces. Claire framed Charlie's head with her hands, taking in every little inch of the face so much like Austin's. He saw her expression change—the way she looked at Charlie, the way her eyes saddened all of a sudden. As much as he wanted to be angry at her all the time, he couldn't be. Her worries were his worries, her fears were his fears. Austin walked towards her. Charlie must have noticed the change and realized that she wasn't herself in that moment. He put his own hands over hers.

159

"You okay, Mommy?" he asked, so in tune with her.

"Yeah, sweetheart, I am," she said and leaned in to kiss his face. "Good luck, baby, and…"

"I know, I know. Have fun," he said, interrupting her mid-sentence.

"You all right?" Austin asked as he closed the distance.

"Yes," she whispered, still on her knees, watching her baby run to the outfield to do some practice throws.

He wished in that moment he could get inside her head. To know what she was thinking, what she was feeling. And then he blurted, "Where's mine?"

She looked up, her mouth dropping open as she eyed him from head to toe.

"When did you change?"

"Just now."

"You look…" she began but stopped herself.

"Like when I was seventeen?" he asked, smirking down at her.

He knew what was going through her mind. Hell, the same things were going through his mind. Not the games she used to sit through and cheer him on, but what happened afterward. She let out a short breath and straightened out of the crouch she'd been in. Her hands on her hips, her head tilted to the side, she stared at him like she was calling his bullshit. Yep, she was back to herself. Phew, crisis averted. He smiled at her and the attitude she loved to project.

160

"So, where's mine?" he repeated.

"Your what, exactly?"

"My good luck kiss?"

"I..." she started, and before he could process the ramifications of the PDA he was going to demonstrate, he cut her off. He stepped into her space, curled his hand around the back of her neck, and pulled her to him. He was determined. The foreplay at the table had been torturous and had him reeling. He wanted her to respond. It wasn't a brush of the lips; it wasn't gentle. It was a crash of flesh that had her bunching his shirt in her hands. He grasped her neck and hip, holding on for dear life. He was demanding, possessing her, making a point to her and everyone else who was seeing the display. The message was crystal clear: mine. He released her with a satisfied smirk, leaving her dumbfounded.

"Thanks," he said over his shoulder as he made his way to the dugout.

He looked up at Hunter at the same time she did. Her brother shrugged and looked away. This reunion might not be pretty, but damn, it felt good for a few, glorious seconds.

Charlie was still wound up by the 4-1 win. Claire had a hard time getting him in the shower. All the kid wanted to do was talk about the game. Typical, Austin thought. All athletes want to talk about the game, the plays, the score, the saves, and in this case, a significant home run his son had hit. It was exciting; his first day as coach and he was proud of the outcome.

The walk home had been awkward. Claire had been quiet—even Hunter seemed to be a bit uncomfortable in their presence. He shouldn't have kissed her, but after the display at the dinner table, all he'd thought about was putting his lips on hers. Hunter and Charlie had walked ahead of him and Claire. Even walking side by side, she made no attempt to speak or to look at him. In the past few days, every time he said anything to her, she buckled. He wasn't immune to her tears—he noticed when they pooled in her eyes at his sometimes harsh words. If Claire didn't want him around, he wished she would just say so. He hated the idea that she tolerated his presence for Charlie's sake. She was torn about him, he could see it. Every thought and feeling showed on her face. Austin knew her better than he knew anyone, and she couldn't hide from him. He knew she hurt. She had regrets, and he wanted badly to relieve her of them. He also knew she was scared. Scared of what she did, scared of what she felt, and scared of what was to come. They had led very different lives in the time they'd been apart. He committed himself to the band, and she to her art and their son. Austin's obligations would haunt them for the next few weeks. The future of their little family hung in the balance of his decisions about his band. These thoughts had plagued him daily since he'd walked into her kitchen a week ago.

Out on the deck nursing a beer with Hunter, Austin could hear his son's happy chatter as he bathed in Claire's master bath. It donned on him that in the days he'd been there he had yet to set foot in her bedroom. Every night before heading in to his appointed bedroom, he stared hungrily at her door. The sound of Hunter's phone ringing snapped him back to the present.

"Hey, what's up...yes, we're all here...That would be great...Just for tonight. I'll talk to Claire and Austin and give you a shout back...Oh, she hadn't mentioned anything...Okay, perfect. I'll tell them. Later, man."

"What's going on?"

"That was John. They're having a party at the farm tonight. Apparently he mentioned it to Claire last week. We should go. We could all use the load off..." he said, gesturing up to the ceiling.

"What could you possibly off-load?" Austin asked.

"You don't wanna know, man."

"Women trouble?"

"One woman in particular..." he admitted, letting his sentence hang.

Austin nodded in understanding. "Still hung up on Mack."

"She's been gone for years, man. We text, email, and she manages to grip me every time. She's coming home at the end of the summer."

"What does she look like now?" Austin asked.

He remembered Mackenzie. She was a pretty girl, if not a little scrawny. From his experiences, he knew women only got better with age.

"I've um…only ever seen parts of her body…"

"Oh, wow. Do those parts look good?"

"Yeah, they look real good. She's been fucking teasing me for years."

"And she's coming home?"

"Yep. I don't know what the hell I'm gonna do when I see her."

"Self-control, my man. It's a virtue, trust me. I've been testing it out for a week."

Seeing the love of your life for the first time in years wasn't something you could prepare for. Hunter had confided in him about his feelings for the girl right after she'd left to study music in France. Hunter hadn't admitted his feelings to her, and he regretted it the second he let her go at the airport. They'd been young, yet so had he and Claire. Love didn't ever just die, it lingered. Your soul was never able to rid your body of the feeling. It was pain in the worst way.

"How'd you handle being away from Claire all these years?" Hunter asked after a moment of both men being lost in their thoughts.

"I didn't," he responded honestly.

"I think I know what you mean. We totally need to go to John's place tonight. It might be fun."

"We'll have to find someone to watch Charlie," said Austin.

"Already on it, bro," said Hunter, waving his phone

briefly before finishing off a text.

Hunter's phone pinged almost immediately, indicating an incoming text. He wasn't sure how he felt about going to John's place after how he'd reacted at the field his first day back. He hadn't seen the man since, but really had no reason to. Hunter was right, though. It might be a good thing to get out and chill for an evening.

He was surprised minutes later when Claire agreed to go to the party, although it was only after she ensured that her brother would be there as well. He scowled at her. What was the problem if it was just the two of them? It's not like they haven't spent time together lately. They had, in fact, spent quite a few summer nights sitting around the large bond fires at the very farm they were headed to. Most nights they would sneak away into the cornfield that made up part of the Lowes' extensive backyard. Austin would give anything to get those days back now.

Austin fidgeted in the small foyer and started up the stairs anxiously. In the hour since Hunter left with Charlie to his parents' place, Claire had locked herself in her room, claiming to be getting ready. She'd avoided him since they'd gotten back from the game. It was just a kiss, damn it. He decided the he would take his bike, forcing her to get up close and very personal as she held on to him.

"Let's go!" he yelled up to her.

He heard her footsteps and tried to ignore the buzz that

seemed to always gravitate through his body when she was around. Austin could smell her perfume; her scent assaulted him. He closed his eyes and inhaled it. He wanted to remember that smell, wanted to bury himself in it. When he finally turned, he was mesmerized. Her hair was fixed in an intricate braid. Her makeup was seductive yet subtle, making her light caramel-colored eyes stand out. She wore skinny jeans that complimented her long, lean legs. Her top was high at the neckline; no cleavage, he thought with disappointment. She had great cleavage. The halter angled loosely at the waist. He took in her whole appearance, right down to the short booties on her feet.

"Are we taking the bike?" she asked as she struggled to put on a bracelet, not bothering to look at him.

"Yes," he croaked out, his throat suddenly dry.

"Can you help me with this, please," she asked, extending her arm to him.

He walked over, and with shaky fingers, grabbed hold of both ends of the bracelet. It took a second before he realized the piece of jewelry he was fastening on her wrist had been a gift from him. It was the first thing he'd ever bought her, the first thing he'd ever bought any girl. Austin ran his fingers over it, remembering her reaction when he'd handed her the light-blue box. He'd promised to love her, to care for her, and he told her that he would never leave her. She cried, of course, and in turn, made him cry.

"You still have this?" he asked.

"Hmm, I didn't realize I'd..." she began but stopped

herself.

What would she say? he wondered. What excuse would she make?

"I gave this to you," he stated, reminding her of what the gift had meant.

"Oh, right," was all she said as if the significance mattered little.

What the fuck was she playing at? Angrily, he fastened the clasp. As soon as the bracelet was in place, she moved away. He didn't miss when she let out her breath. He watched as she ran her finger over the bracelet, a sad look crossing her face. She remembered. He affected her then, and he affected her now. He wasn't a fool; he never missed her reactions. In the past few days, he'd wished often that he was immune to her, but the time had only shown that he was just as addicted to her as he'd been at seventeen. He had to admit that he felt lighter, that raw pain he'd felt over the years easing with every minute he spent in her presence. Maybe he needed to see her to get closure. Nah, he would never get her out if his system. Not now that he knew he had a son. They'd always had a connection, but now there was something tangible keeping them together. Not just memories or song lyrics.

Without another word, he turned and walked out the door. He waited patiently on his bike, taking several deep breaths to calm himself down. Being around her day after day was one thing, but to have her wrapped around him on his motorcycle was something else. He needed to relax if he was going to drive without killing them. If that damned bracelet opened the

167

floods for memories, riding with her would fucking engulf him. He stood abruptly, the bike between his legs, and adjusted himself—he'd been doing that a lot lately. He sat back down and rubbed his face furiously, then ran his fingers through his hair.

"You okay?"

"No. Now get on," he said, his voice harsher than he'd intended.

Her arms came around his waist, her fingers fumbling with his shirt, just like she used to do. Despite the years, some things were just habit. He let an array of curse words run through his mind as he pulled out of the driveway. The damned bike ride was going to be the longest ten minutes of his life. Should have taken the car. Idiot.

The party was in full swing when they drove up the long winding driveway. People were milling around with red solo cups in hand. Claire jumped off the bike before he had a chance to put down the kickstand. What the fuck was her hurry? He pulled off his helmet and picked hers up off the ground—the least she could have done was leave it on the seat. Completely pissed, he made his way towards the party. Passing the wraparound porch of the old white Victorian brought more memories to the surface. God, he wished he could forget some things.

There was a large white tent to the right of the house. Tables lined up with more red cups led the way to a large bar set up in one corner of the tent. He looked around and was impressed by the way the Lowes put together a party—it was all out or nothing. At the sight of Claire, Austin stopped dead in his tracks. Her pretty little head was thrown back in laughter next to John. His hand was on the small of her back, her hand squeezing his bicep as she laughed at what was most likely one of his lame jokes.

He took a step towards them, intent on two things: one, taking his hands off her, and two, ripping his fucking arms from their sockets. A hand on his shoulder stopped him. Austin turned, ready to sock whoever dared to put a hand on him.

"Whoa there, cowboy. I thought you could use one of these," said Hunter, handing him a plastic tumbler of whiskey.

"Thanks," he said, taking it and throwing back its contents in one big gulp.

"You need to tone it down, man. Remember that no matter what happened all those years ago, you've both moved on."

"Has she...moved on with him?"

"Nah. I don't think so. She doesn't talk about her dating life...to anyone."

Austin leaned back on a strategically placed barrel, replacing his empty glass for a full bottle of beer a waiter carried, not taking his eyes off Claire.

After he downed his first beer, which was quickly replaced, people started to approach him. He hadn't factored in that he could be recognized when he'd decided to come to the party. People asked for autographs and pictures, to which he kindly obliged. It was either give in to the fandom for the evening or watch Claire obsessively. He'd just finished taking what felt like the hundredth picture when bright red manicured nails slid down his arm. When he looked at the body attached to them, he couldn't help but be impressed. Austin's eyes traveled slowly from the red cowboy boots, to the daisy duke shorts, to the clichéd red and white checkered shirt tied at her belly. His eyes continued to travel up to an overly made-up face and exaggerated blonde curly hair that fell over one shoulder. He realized that people really didn't change very much—no matter how much time passed.

"Myra," he simply said by way of greeting.

"It's been a while, Austin."

"It has." Not long enough. She was the source of his greatest mistake.

He'd like to not think about the one drunken night she'd filled the doorway to Yellow Scarlet's dressing room. He hadn't even remembered what city he'd been in, just that Myra Hernandez was there. Not exactly the right place at the right time kind of thing. More like the right place, wrong time, and too drunk to think, let alone function with any amount of common sense. The only reason he remembered that the woman had gotten to her knees on the dirty dressing room floor and sucked him off was because she'd been kind enough to send him a picture. Yes, a picture of her with his cock in her mouth, his head thrown back in drunken ecstasy, and those same red nails holding on to his shaft. If she only knew that it wasn't her mouth he was picturing.

"Are you here alone?"

"No," he simply said.

"With Claire?" she asked, pouting as she waited for his response.

"Yes."

She leaned into him and whispered in what could have been a seductive voice if he'd been into her, "What would she say if I gave her my phone to scroll through my pictures?"

His head snapped up, his eyes piercing hers as he clenched his teeth and said, "You do that and I will have my lawyer on your ass so fast, you won't know what hit you. Give me your phone."

"What?"

"Your phone, now!"

She reached into her back pocket and slipped her pink shiny iPhone case into his hand. He swiped the screen and handed it back to her, silently requesting that she put in her password. Myra let out a loud sigh and leaned on the barrel next to him as he searched for the pictures she'd taken. He'd meant to do that years ago, and quite frankly, he couldn't believe she still had them. Who had she shown them to? He closed his eyes at the thought of Claire seeing them.

"That's my favorite one," she said when he came across one taken from below them. His cock was halfway in her mouth as he stared down, leaving no doubt as to who was in her mouth. He went through the pictures one by one and erased them. She'd had them long enough. He wasn't stupid enough to think these were her only copies, but he'd scare her enough to erase any copies she did have.

A gasp from behind them had them both turning as Austin hit delete on the second to last picture. Claire stood with her hand over her mouth, her face losing all color as she stared at the last picture. His gaze was locked on Claire's face. He chanced a glare at Myra, who was smirking in triumph as she looked down at the phone in his hands. When he finally got the nerve to look down, he was shocked at what he saw. Myra was on all fours, her mouth on him, with Jackson ramming her from behind.

"Jesus," he whispered. How could he not remember any of this? Worse, who the fuck took the picture?

"Can I keep that one?" asked Myra with a triumphant smile on her face.

"You're fucking dirty and crazy," he told her before he hit the delete button.

"Clearly, you all enjoyed the crazy and dirty that night, Austin."

"I wasn't thinking…" he said, mostly to himself as he watched Claire slip through the crowd.

CHAPTER THIRTEEN

Claire

She was going to be sick. Claire ran towards the house, clutching her stomach in search of the bathroom. Why? Out of all the women, why did it have to be Myra? The woman didn't have an ounce of dignity. Was it desperation that drove him to her? Loneliness? Did he like her? Did they date? For how long? These questions would plague her.

She reached the back porch and took the steps two a time in an effort to get away from Austin. Despite the pounding in her ears, she heard the crunch of gravel behind her. He'd called her name several times, but she couldn't acknowledge his plea for her to stop. She didn't want for him to see the tears streaming down her face. All the pain, disappointment, and guilt that had taken root years ago had been front and center since he arrived. She'd done that. She'd pushed him towards that woman. Towards so many women.

In the house, Claire made a beeline for the small bathroom just outside the kitchen. She turned the water on, letting it run, desperate for it—she wanted it freezing, to numb her. She splashed some on her face, not caring if her makeup left a black trail under her eyes. Bending over the sink, she took long slurps of water right from the tap to try and ease the queasiness in her stomach. She shook her head, snapping out of her bewilderment, fixed her makeup as best she could, and leaned against the counter. She breathed deep and slow in order to keep the alcohol and what she'd eaten down. She took one last look in the mirror, ran her index finger under her eyes, and opened the door.

Austin was standing just outside the door, leaning against the wall. The look on his face mirroring her own. What could he say? What could she? He straightened to his full height. He was so tall, so handsome. His eyes showed uncertainty.

"I'm sorry," he whispered, his hands deep in his pocket. "You weren't supposed to see that picture. I was erasing them."

"You think she doesn't have copies?" she asked sardonically.

"I don't know."

"Well, it doesn't matter. It's your life. Do what you want with it."

She stormed past him and back to the party.

Screw this!

They were free. He didn't owe her explanations, and she didn't owe him any. Sniffing out the tequila like it was her last meal, she made her way to the bar. Alexa was laughing loudly at something her friend and co-worker, Abby, had said. Claire reached for the small shot glass in Alexa's hand and downed the potent liquid. She let out a long hiss before turning to Alexa.

"Claire!" Alexa cheered, holding up her phone. "I Googled him."

"Googled who?" she asked as she tried to grasp the phone from Alexa's hand, which swayed drunkenly along with the rest of her body.

"How many shots have you guys had?"

"Lots!" yelled Abby. She tapped the bar, signaling to the bartender for more.

"Wow. This is the elusive Patrick Pemberton?" asked Claire when she finally got Alexa to let go of her phone.

"I know right? He looks like…like Teen Wolf. Yeah, that's it," kindly supplied Abby.

She wasn't far off. The man in the picture looked scruffy. A heavy beard covered most of his face, and his hair was long and dirty looking. Not at all the picture Austin had painted. There was nothing attractive about this man.

"That beard is disgusting. God only knows what lives in that thing…" said Alexa.

"He looks mean," said Claire.

"He is…" Alexa hiccupped.

Claire handed Alexa back her phone and took the shot she held out for her. She watched her and Abby as they slammed down each of their empty shot glasses. Abby and Alexa were

175

the same height, same hair color, and even their eyes were the same. They worked together at Fielding Designs, a firm owned by Abby's father for the past four years. The more Claire saw the two women together, the more she found they resembled each other. Abby was quite the character. It took energy just to keep up with her jubilant personality. Claire liked her very much—she was funny, outgoing, and unbelievably ambitious. She and Alexa had that at least in common.

"Drink up, sis." Alexa pointed to the drink in Claire's hand.

She did. Then she slammed the glass like her friends had and let out in a loud cry, "Another!"

Yes, this would work. A few drinks to drown out her conscience, to forget her mistakes, her fears, and for a couple of hours, ignore her wounded pride.

"So when do you leave?" asked Claire.

"Not sure. First the flooring, and now we have an issue with the electrical. It's fucking ancient and needs to be completely redone. That alone will take at least two weeks. This job is going to take forever," vented Alexa, the frustration evident in her voice.

"We could be in Cabo for a month. It's going to be awesome!"

"You're going too?" asked Alexa.

"I'm supervising," Abby said, her words slurred. "The tequila is to get us in the mood... arriba! Drink. We have Mexico to get ready for," yelled Abby, passing more shots to each of them.

They raised the small shot glasses, and the three of them drank in unison. Abby tapped the bar and the bartender dutifully put down three glasses of water. The three women pouted, then laughed boisterously.

Claire caught a glimpse of Austin's gaze. Scowl away, big boy, she thought. Quite frankly, she didn't care. Determined to have a great time, she let Abby and Alexa pull her onto the dance floor for an impromptu line dance. Only at John "Deere's" would she do this and laugh at herself as she tried to keep up. A tap on her shoulder had her turning. John stood there with a wide grin, tipping his cowboy hat that had seen better days towards her in greeting. He was so handsome. If her mind hadn't been so tied up in Austin, she might have given him a shot. How would his lips feel on hers? She thought of his big, overworked hands on her, over her, in her... she swayed, reached for his arm, and had no idea if the misstep was because of the alcohol or her wayward thoughts about the man in front of her—no doubt a combination.

He caught her by the elbow, smiled down at her, and directed her to the middle of the dance floor. He guided her through a few steps, his hands resting helpfully on her hips as he showed her the steps to the country song blaring through the big speakers. She stumbled several times, John's strong arms quick to wrap around her waist. Turning in his arms, she placed her hands on his chest, stared into eyes that showed more than she was prepared to handle. Claire took a quick step back, scanned the room, and once again caught the scowl on Austin's face. He pushed away from the barrel he was leaning against and walked towards her with purpose, a possessive look in his eyes. She had enough sense to push away from John, saving him from the confrontation she could see coming from the look on Austin's face. She sidestepped John, walking on wobbly feet to the bar, where she ordered a beer. Claire didn't see Austin approach the bar—his hand shot out, reaching for the bottle and handing it back to the bartender.

"Get rid of that," he said, not hiding his annoyance.

"What the hell do you think you're doing?" she slurred.

"Cutting you off."

"I wanted to finish that."

"Too bad. You've had enough."

"Who the hell do you think you are?" she sneered at him, jabbing her finger into his chest.

She turned and leaped onto the bar, making a lame attempt to reach for a bottle of vodka. Austin grabbed her by the waist, pulled her off, and sat her forcefully on the stool.

"We are leaving," he told her.

"What the f...You can't make me," she spat, her words running together as she spoke.

Screeching sounds from the dance floor made her turn and smile. Her friends stumbled their way back in her direction. Abby ordered three more shots, sneaking one over to her. Austin was busy texting and didn't notice the drink conspiracy taking place under his nose.

"Claire, please stop. You'll regret this in the morning;

believe me," he scorned as he turned just in time to see her stuffing a lime wedge in her mouth.

"You would know, wouldn't you? I read all those stories of you drunk and high in clubs. Tell me, were they true?"

"Claire…"

"Austin," she mocked, using the same tone.

He ran his fingers through his hair, a sign of frustration she couldn't help but enjoy. She loved when he got upset, passionate, unwavering.

"What is it?" Claire heard her brother's voice.

"Really, you called him?" she slurred.

"What the hell, Claire?" asked Hunter.

"What the hell, Hunter? Can't a girl have any fun around here? Austin was. Just ask Myra over there." She pointed to the dance floor, where Myra swayed provocatively.

"What is she talking about?" Hunter asked Austin.

Claire watched Austin roll his eyes, her anger reaching a new high at his nonchalance.

"Go ahead, Austin. Tell him. Tell my brother how you let that slut suck your—"

"Claire!" he sneered, halting her words. He turned to Hunter and said, "It was a long time ago. While I was on the road. It was a stupid mistake."

"Dude, that's a new low, even for you."

"Well, she did go very low…" Claire muttered under her

breath.

"I hope you got tested after bagging it," Hunter told Austin.

A gagging sound escaped from Claire's mouth. All eyes turned to her.

"What? We all know Myra has no standards, clearly," she said, waving her hand at Austin. "Sloppy seconds are her only options."

To her right, Alexa and Abby giggled, too drunk to pay close attention to them. She watched with a smirk as Alexa slowly slid another shot glass her way. All three women laughed, and once again Austin's hand beat her to her drink.

"I gotta get her out of here before she gets alcohol poisoning."

"Pfft! You're so dramatic, McKinley," said Claire

Austin looked at her with disapproval and turned to speak to Hunter. "You still ride?"

"Yep."

"I need to take your car. There's no way I can put her on the back of a motorcycle."

"She better not puke in it."

"I'll get a bag or something from John."

"She's a lightweight, man. You of all people should know that," her brother pointed out.

"Right, because I let her get this drunk?"

"Yo! I'm right here. Although I did wish I was blind for a second earlier…" She gave a drunken giggle.

Both men stared at her and reached out for her when she swayed in her stool.

"This is your fault," said Hunter, waving his hand at Austin.

"How so?" he asked, indignant.

"If you'd kept it in your pants…"

"Hey! Bad judgement call, okay? I was—"

"Desperate?" Claire chimed in.

"Angry," Austin corrected. "Now give me your keys."

Claire watched in a blur as they exchanged keys. Austin grabbed her by the elbow, not so gently pulling her to the makeshift parking lot. She twisted and jerked, trying to pull away from his grip on her arm.

"Let go of me. You're hurting me," she yelled, digging her heels into the gravel.

She beat on his arm, even going as far as to pinch him, all with little effect. She went in for seconds but was cut off at the pass by his free hand.

"Try that again, and I swear I will—"

"What. What will you do? Hit me? Pinch me back?"

"Damn you, Claire. I would never hit you, but holy shit do I want to shake you right now," he said, grabbing both her arms and turning her to face him.

181

"Fuck you!" she sneered.

She took a step back—as far as she could go with the iron grip wrapped around her arms. Her words had startled her. She'd never spoken to him like that. He was the one person she'd always respected, but in that moment, she'd been so angry with him. He let go of her suddenly. She was certain he was going to leave her standing in the middle of the dirt driveway. Instead, he bent down, grabbed her by the knees, and tossed her over his shoulder.

"What…Austin, put me down."

"Shut up, Claire," he said and spanked her ass.

"Ouch!" She was sure she would have his handprint on her ass in the morning. It wasn't a playful smack; it was angry, frustrated. The sting brought with it a surge of desire she hadn't felt in years. That alone surprised her. Her hands were on his firm ass, and she had to fight the urge to caress it, to slip her hands into the waistband of his pants. Even in her drunken haze, she felt the familiar stir he caused within her. She let her head fall to his back, resting it there until they reached the car.

Austin let her down slowly, his hands sliding up her body as he did so. She shivered in his arms, her body responding of its own volition. She could blame it on the alcohol, but all the liquor in the world couldn't keep her from feeling, wanting. He held the door open, waited until she was seated, and leaned in to buckle her seat belt.

"Let me know if you need to throw up," he said.

"Are you going to hold my hair back like the old days…"

she mocked.

"Yeah, like the old days," he whispered. She was not sure if she was meant to hear him.

As teenagers, she'd only ever gotten drunk once. Austin stayed up most of the night with her, holding her hair as she and the toilet became acquainted. He let out a ragged breath before starting the car. They drove down the long, winding driveway in silence, the music blaring in the party tent as Austin cautiously prepared to turn onto the main road that would take them home.

The night was clear, the country air crisp as Claire practically hung her head out the window, allowing the breeze to clear her muddled, drunk mind. See stretched out her hand, moving it in an up and down motion. She chanced a peek at Austin, who was lost in his thoughts, his thumbnail on its way to nonexistence as he chewed on it— a clear sign he was pondering something.

Once in their driveway...their? Where did that come from? The only thing that was theirs was Charlie, and she had to admit she was hesitant to relinquish part of her proprietorship, for lack of a better word, to Austin. This was, after all, a temporary trip for him. Momentarily lost in her alcohol-induced thoughts, she hadn't heard Austin get out.

"You getting out?" he said angrily.

She looked up at him suddenly, thinking for a moment that he had no right to be angry with her. She'd done nothing wrong. Then, as if a switch had turned on in her brain, she wondered why he brought her home. She'd been having a great time, laughing, dancing, and maybe drinking a little too much. But damn it, it had been a long time since she'd been out and enjoyed her friends' company with that much abandon.

"Why did you bring me home?" she asked.

"You were drunk."

"So."

"So?" he echoed.

"Yeah, so. I was having fun, and you and your damned caveman act decided to make an appearance."

"Oh please, Claire. You could barely stand."

"I was standing just fine."

He scoffed. A smirk, although small, made its rare appearance.

"What?" she asked.

"Get inside, Claire."

"This is such a double standard, you know?" she said as she made her way up to her porch. "You partied yourself into oblivion, drinking and getting high on God knows what, but I can't have one drink?"

"You didn't have just one drink, and you're not used to drinking like that. Besides, John was all over you."

"Maybe I like him all over me. At least he didn't go down on me in a room full of people!"

"Claire!"

"What? Is that what's got you so upset, that I haven't thrown myself at you like you're used to? Or maybe it upsets you that I haven't dropped to my knees and sucked you off," she shouted, her face inches from his. "You're such a hypocrite. This is my life you're disrupting here, my life you're trying to dictate, and I don't appreciate it."

"Get inside, Claire. You're making a scene."

"There's no one around. Besides, you're the one who enjoys an audience. Come on, baby. My claws aren't bright red or anything, but I can still suck..."

"Stop it!" he gritted through his teeth.

She stepped back, the tone in his voice not one she'd ever heard before. He looked disappointed, and she wasn't entirely sure if it was with her.

"Go to hell, Austin," she said, unable to hide the hurt in her voice. "And leave me alone."

"Is that what you want?" he asked. She stopped as she reached the door. "Do you want me to leave you alone?"

No, I need you. You can't leave me. Please don't ever leave me. Love me, Austin. Love me like you used to. She couldn't bring herself to say any of it. She was a coward, and even in her drunken state, she knew there was a great possibility she could lose him. She unlocked the door, unable to give an answer at all.

She ran up the stairs, taking the steps two at a time, praying she didn't fall. The last thing she needed was for him to have one more thing to criticize her about. He was right behind her of course. There was no way he would just let it go.

"Claire. Babe, stop."

"Don't call me babe. You can't do what you did with that slut and then call me babe. What was wrong with you? What were you thinking? Were you even coherent?" she said, her anger too powerful to keep in.

"No, I wasn't coherent. I was hurt, angry, and all I wanted was to forget the fucking heartache for one second."

"An orgy will sure help with that..." she said with acerbity. He had the decency to look shocked.

She waved her hand dismissively in his direction and turned to walk into her room. His hand on the door stopped it from slamming in his face. She took several steps back, the back of her knees hitting her bed. She reached out, catching her balance—she needed to remain standing for this confrontation.

"I had to forget you. I missed you so much. I didn't know how to get you out of my system. Don't you get it?"

She did get it; she hurt too, but she didn't go screw everything in sight. How many times did he try to get her out of his system? she wondered. The thought sobered her enough to want him out of her room.

"Thank you for enlightening me, Austin." Her voice was dripping with sarcasm.

"Damn it, Claire...it wasn't her mouth I was picturing on my cock. In my mind, I was never inside anyone else. Don't you get it? It was always you!" he yelled.

Now she was really going to throw up. She turned her back to him. She couldn't stand to look at him in that moment. Not after that profound confession...

"That's disgusting," she whispered.

Not caring that he was still in the room, she reached for the hem of her shirt and pulled it over her head and held it to her chest. She hadn't worn a bra, and she didn't miss the small gasp that came from the doorway.

"While you were living your life the way you wanted, I was merely surviving. I'm not naïve to think you were all alone all these years. The thought of another man touching you grates at my every nerve. I know that makes me a hypocrite, but I felt alone and I needed something—whether it was alcohol, drugs, or women."

There was a long silence in the room. She reached under her pillow for the tank and shorts she slept in, and as she pulled on the shirt, she heard the soft click of the door. Austin's footsteps faded down the hall, along with her will to do anything about it. She'd done this. She'd pushed him.

CHAPTER FOURTEEN

Austin

Awkward. That was the word of the year and the current state of their...what could he call it? Relationship? Association? He should be more technical and call it an affiliation. What the hell was a guy to do? The damned days felt eternal, and he should be concentrating on practice, not her.

He and Claire had barely uttered a word to each other—except where Charlie was concerned. Even then, most answers were a simple yes or no. She had been avoiding him since the party, and she was good at it too. She had never joined him for breakfast the following day. She'd gotten dressed and left the house. An hour and a half later, he'd found her chugging a large glass of water in the kitchen after a run. She looked incredible. Sweat trickled between her cleavage, her chest rising and falling from exertion. He would've given anything to have been the one to have left her that breathless. He missed talking to her. Being away from her was one thing, but living in the same house, so close and yet so far away, was torture.

From the second they'd reached the baseball field for practice, he hadn't been able to take his eyes off her. He reached down and alleviated some of the pressure on his jock. Thinking of her sweaty and breathless was torturous. He shook his head, frustrated, and concentrated on the task at hand. He yelled instructions at his son, running drills in the outfield. As assistant coach, he was expected to help out. He enjoyed his summer job. Jim didn't treat him any differently than he had when they were younger, and Austin appreciated it. They'd managed to somehow keep the fans away. Aside from some parents, who simply greeted him, no one hounded him for an autograph or picture—it was refreshing.

The last time they'd been at the field, he'd kissed Claire. They'd had an audience, and the selfish prick in him didn't care that he embarrassed her. He wanted her so badly. He wanted to feel more of her, and it was driving him fucking mad. The best part of fighting with her was always making up—he craved to make up with her. He was acting like a puberty-ridden, frustrated, moody teen. His hand was on the verge of tendonitis, doing overtime to relieve his frustration. Not to mention the fact that he would have to cover the water bill. Contrary to what some might think, cold showers do jack shit for calming arousals.

"Austin?"

"What?" he snapped. He looked up at the source of his shitty mood to see her snap her head back at his response. "Sorry."

"You okay?"

190

"Yeah. What is it?" he asked, unable to tone down his irritation.

"Jim's calling you," she said, tipping her head towards the head coach, who was standing at second base.

He looked over to where his friend stood, waving at him to move his groups to the next drill. He felt pride as he watched Charlie run to the dugout for a drink. He had wished on many occasions that he and Claire would someday find their way back to each other. That ship seemed to sail further away with each year that passed. Now those dreams and wishes were within his reach. He couldn't get over the fact that he was at a little league practice yelling instructions to his son, his girl sitting in the bleachers, angry, but there nonetheless.

He looked over at Charlie. He watched in horror as his son walked past a teammate who was swinging a bat, nearly missing Charlie's head. He winced, preparing himself to jump to his feet from the crouch he'd been in near the dugout.

"Shit," he hissed through clenched teeth.

"He's fine," Claire chimed in from her perch on the bleachers.

"What, you're talking to me now?" he retorted as he snapped his head to look at her.

"I was always talking to you." She smirked.

"Right, excuse me, but the silent treatment doesn't exactly compel me to have a conversation, dear."

She threw her head back and laughed, loud and sexy.

She'd been sitting on the bleachers for the past hour, looking so relaxed, her nose deep in a book.

He stood, fidgeting, slamming the ball into his glove and baseball. His right leg bounced nonstop, itching to go and have a talk with Charlie about safety on the field to keep his son from a bat-induced concussion. It irritated the shit out of him that it didn't seem to faze Claire that their son had walked inches from a swinging bat.

"Look at that kid swinging that bat. Charlie was nearly hit."

"He's on first base, Austin. I don't see a bat near him."

"He was just at home plate," he said, frustrated.

"Austin, relax. Charlie's five. He's going to get hurt. Hell, he's going to bleed, have bumps and bruises. We won't be able to protect him from all of that."

"I can try."

"You will smother him."

"I just want to keep him safe. Is that so bad?"

"No, it's not, but you'll age a hundred years in trying. He's a smart kid. He knows better than to get near a swinging bat. He's been there, done that."

"He has?"

"Yep. Left one hell of a goose egg on his forehead. Things happen. You kiss it better and move on," she said, a smirk playing on her lips, mocking him.

192

Damn her. How could she be so calm, only glancing up occasionally to watch Charlie? It was instinctual too; her head rose at the exact moment Charlie had the ball or was up at bat. Once the ball left his hand, she turned back to her book. Austin watched her, her eyes going bright at one point as Charlie slid into third. The bright smile and thumbs-up he gave her made him a tad envious. They had this connection, this friendship that had been established the second he was born. He wondered, idly, if Charlie would get to that point with him. He was well on his way; there was no denying that fact.

Almost fourteen days into his new status and he still couldn't believe the little boy running like mad to home plate was his. Two weeks ago, even one week ago, he'd felt lost. His life had been the band, his home, a luxury tour bus where he spent most of his time holed up in the master suite. He had started drinking again to keep the loneliness that had taken root at bay. Now, he had it all, the girl (well almost), the kid, and maybe a dog—he would look into the dog. All this time he'd had a family he wasn't aware of. A family that, to some extent, still wasn't quite his. He was determined to change that.

He didn't doubt that Claire cared for him. He fucking sensed it. He knew the exact moment she was looking at him. He'd caught her a time or four in the past few days—she could try her damnedest to ignore him, but he knew. The light blush that rose up her face was endearing, giving her away. How deep those feelings ran, he'd yet to find out, but he wasn't going to sit back and wait and see. He was going to get his family.

He'd been so out of it during practice that when Jim called

it a day, he nearly cheered. He looked at Claire, gathering her things on the bleachers. When she bent over, he nearly ran to cover her up. The shorts she had on barely covered her, and he hated them…well, not really. He just hated her wearing them in public. He did his best to keep his opinions with regards to her wardrobe to himself, but fuck him if the shit she wore didn't drive him to the brink of explosion. See, horny teenager. There was no other word for what he was going through. She had the same effect she'd had on him from the second he laid eyes on her.

"So what's the deal?" asked Jim.

"What do you mean?"

"With Claire…"

"There's no deal."

"You keep telling yourself that, my man. You watch her like a hawk. Gotta get your mind in the game, brother. You've got it just as bad as you did in high school. And just like in school, she's fucking ignoring you," he said with a laugh.

"Except this time, I almost believe she wants nothing to do with me."

"That's not how I see it. I see her look at you. I don't know what happened between you two, but she still loves you. In all this time, she's never had one bad thing to say about you. Also, since she's been back, I've never seen or heard of her dating anyone."

He didn't say a word to his friend. He simply stared at the object of his intense attraction and affection, hoping with all his might that Jim was right. He gathered his and Charlie's things and met Claire. They both reached for Charlie's hand at the same time, and they laughed at the natural gesture. They walked quietly for a good while. Practice had been a bloody heart attack waiting to happen. He figured it would be a while before he mastered the art of laying off the overprotective-dad bit.

Walking back to the house on the trail that ran along Mill Pond, Charlie swung his legs up in the air between Austin and Claire, laughing his little ass off. Austin was lost in his never-ending train of thought about the future he wanted with Claire and Charlie. He watched as she looked out into the pond, smiling at one thing or another. He couldn't pinpoint what— her painter's eye was probably creating her next masterpiece. Neither one of them were prepared for when their son swung himself so high, it pulled Austin and Claire towards each other at an awkward angle, making them both lose their balance. Claire stumbled, reached out to get a hold of Charlie, and a high-pitched squeal followed. Expletives that could overflow the bad word jar left her mouth.

Everything happened fast. Charlie's legs went flying, Claire's other hand went up to grab high up on his arm, and Austin did the same. In the process, all three of them tumbled to the ground. Austin somehow managed to get himself under Claire and Charlie. Both who landed with a dull thud on his chest. His back hit the wet grass, the weight on his chest knocking the breath out of him. He let out a pained groan, his shirt soaked from the damp grass as Charlie's laughter penetrated the air and the ringing in his ears. Claire moaned.

Her arm caught underneath Austin.

"You said shit, Mommy."

"It was warranted," she said as she tried to free her arm. "Get off your father. My arm is caught under him."

Charlie moved and lay beside Austin, still laughing. His hands grabbed his belly as tears streamed down his dirty face. "I'm gonna pee my pants," he said.

"Please don't," grunted Austin.

"You have to move, Austin. I need to get my arm out."

"I kind of like it there," he told her.

He felt her fingers flex against his ass. Did she want to cop a feel? But as soon as the stupid smile transformed his mouth, she rolled her eyes. He released her arm but moved so that he ended up on top of her.

"Austin," she admonished.

"What? It's not fair only I get wet." He wiggled over her, the uncomfortable bulge in his pants nestled right at her center. Her eyes nearly bugged out before she tried to squirm from beneath him, making him groan from the contact. Never in his life had he wanted to kiss her more than he wanted to in that moment. Her mouth parted and her breath came out ragged, clearly waiting for the kiss. Okay, so that might be all in his head, but did she want to kiss him? He wanted her to want to kiss him, because if she wanted him as badly as he wanted her, there was hope.

When they first got together, their relationship hadn't only been sexual. But he'd be an idiot to think the physical aspect wasn't what he looked forward to. He was seventeen. He lived for sex at that age, and so did she. They were young, but that hadn't stopped them from experimenting. A lot. And he hoped to God she was still as adventurous. Just thinking of some of their trysts made him harder. She put her hands on his chest to push him off.

"Cool it."

"Don't move yet. I can't stand, not like this. I won't be able to walk," he confessed, tightening his arms around her.

"I don't think this position is going to ease your…discomfort. You should control your hormones."

"I can't. Never could with you around." He didn't miss the tiny glimpse of a smile that threatened the edges of her mouth.

"What are hormones?" Charlie asked, loud enough for a couple walking past them to look over.

"Nothing you need to know about just yet, buddy," Austin told him.

"Is it grown up stuff, like kissing?" asked Charlie.

"What do you know about kissing?" asked Claire.

"Matthew says his parents do grown-up stuff a lot. One time he walked into their bedroom and he…"

"Okay. I don't want to know," said Claire, pushing Austin off her.

Austin landed on his back again. The cold mud seeping

through his clothes was enough to cool his very grown-up problem for the moment. He got up quickly, grabbed Charlie's baseball bag, and crossed it over his chest, strategically placing it to cover his bulge. He made an unflattering move to alleviate the discomfort against his jock, catching Claire's eye. She smiled that mischievous smile he knew too well. He watched suspiciously as she grabbed Charlie's hand to continue on their way. Her teeth scraped over her bottom lip, trapping it as she approached him. Evil—that's what that look was. Pure fucking evil. He loved it, and he should have been prepared. Hell, he should have known placing his son's bag where he did was a bad idea. He had zero seconds to react when she pulled the bag away from his body and then let it drop. He let out a loud groan, bent over, and put his hand on his knees to ease some of the dull pain on his dick. He took several deep breaths through his teeth and wished she had balls so he could inflict the same cruel, vindictive pain on her.

"That," he said, pointing at her, "was uncalled for."

"That will teach you to keep it in your pants," she told him.

"It is in my pants. I can't help it if it has a mind of its own. You did that. You woke him up."

"Oh, I did that."

"Yes," he said through gritted teeth. "Come on, Charlie. I need to get home and check on my jewels."

"Your penis?" he asked.

Austin looked at Claire, who looked up to the heavens for

guidance.

"How do you know that's what I meant?" asked Austin.

"Matthew says that's what his dad calls it. Always tells his mom that he'll be waiting in the bedroom for her to shine the jewels."

"That's it," Claire declared from behind them. "You are not to speak or play with Matthew again."

"Why? He's funny. He's full of stories."

"I don't want to hear any of them, Charlie. Ever."

"See what I mean?" Charlie told his father.

"Yeah, I get it now."

"What are you two talking about? Charlie, have you been talking about me?"

"A little, but only because Daddy asked."

"Oh, really?"

"You don't talk to me. I had to go to my best source." Austin shrugged.

"Best easy-to-manipulate source. You could ask me. I've got nothing to hide."

"Not anymore, you don't," said Austin.

Her eyes widened and her face reddened. He sensed the wrath of her anger—not a good place to put her if he wanted to get lucky. Her eyes started to water, instantly making him feel like shit for saying what he did. What did she expect? Shit was going to come flying out of his mouth whether he meant for it to or not.

"Charlie, come on. You need to change before Grandpa comes to get you," she said, reaching for Charlie's hand and walking past him.

"Claire, I'm sorry."

"Don't worry about it."

They walked in awkward silence, Austin a few feet behind her.

At the house, Austin's father was sitting on the porch waiting to take Charlie to the movies. Claire gave Ben a curt hello and walked with Charlie into the house, Austin right on her heel.

"Claire?"

"I'm going to get Charlie some clothes. Tell your father he'll be out in fifteen," she said on her way up the stairs.

He stood at the bottom of the stairs, staring up to where she had disappeared. Things couldn't always be like this, he thought. At some point they would have to get past the crap.

Back out on the porch, his father sat, examining the porch swing lying on the floor. Austin sat on the steps. A motorcycle speeding by caught his attention, reminding him he needed to go get his own bike back.

"In the doghouse, son?" asked Ben, moving to sit next to him.

"You could say that."

"I know the feeling. Was just in there this morning."

"What did you do?"

"Nothing, as usual. You?"

"My brain-to-mouth filter failed."

"Happens to the best of us. By the way, Hunter dropped off the bike," said his father, pulling the keys out of his pocket.

"Why didn't he drop the bike here?"

"Not sure. Said something about getting back to the city. He also said to keep the truck for the week, figured you'd need it."

"Then what is he driving?" asked Austin.

"Not sure, I didn't see."

"I know you're going the opposite way, but can you take me home? I want to pick it up."

"We've got some time before the movie."

"Thanks, Dad. I'm going to change."

Claire's fifteen minutes turned into thirty minutes. When Austin came back out, he sat on the porch with his father, and they stared out at the traffic, waiting. From the open window above, Charlie's laughter filled the silence between him and his father. How the hell did he get so lucky? Great kid, great girl, and a great life. He would make it his mission to spend that life with the two people upstairs.

He should have known going to his parents alone was a bad idea. An hour later, Austin was stuck, literally stuck, at his mother's house. The second he walked through the door, she put her motherly claws into him and tortured him into confession with the best pie he'd ever tasted. His father dropped him off in front of the door and sped off without a second look down the driveway. It started with a simple "how are you doing, how's Claire and Charlie?" and then without warning, she jumped right into the nitty-gritty.

"So, any progress with Claire?"

"I am not talking to you about me and Claire, Mom."

"I'll take that as a no. Are you going to make a play for her? She is still kind of yours, you know."

"Mom!"

"What? I want you to be happy, and I love her for you, always have. Besides, I want more grandkids, more Charlies. So get to it."

He rolled his eyes at her, her smirk never faltering, and he knew she was completely serious.

"She needs time, Mom. I need time. Things are okay, but there's a lot we still need to work through."

"Oh, please get over yourself. She had her reasons. Has she told you what they were?"

"Yes."

"She wanted the best for you, which is what we all wanted for you. She did what she thought was right at the time. Was it? Maybe not. But you have a healthy son, and he has an amazing mother. Anything she did back then, she did for the both of you."

"Yeah well, she went about it the wrong way," he said, unable to keep his anger from seeping through.

"But you're here now, son. You stop sulking and help raise Charlie. He needs his father, has talked about you for years apparently, and has wanted nothing more than to meet you. He loves you."

"I love him too. Is that weird? I mean, I've only known him for a couple of weeks, and I can't imagine my life without him."

"It's the way any father feels after meeting their child. It's how your father felt the second he laid eyes on you."

Austin looked up at his mother, wondering once again what it would have been like to see Claire grow big with their child inside her. What would it have been like to be present when he was born, to be the first to hold him? He wasn't angry that she'd made the decision to keep the pregnancy from him, he realized. He was angry that he'd missed it all, that he'd missed so much.

"I wish she'd given me the chance to experience it with her," he whispered.

"Has she told you that she was afraid you wouldn't believe her?"

"No, she didn't. Questioning his paternity hasn't even crossed my mind. I mean, you could see it, he looks just like me."

"And acts like you sometimes, too, it's quite irritating. Now go home and make things right."

"It's not my home, Mom. It's theirs." Another thing that grated at him.

"Make it yours, Austin. Claire might have made a hasty decision about the two of you, but you two created something beautiful together. I need you to remind yourself of how lucky you are to have that. It's not and never will be about you ever again."

He nodded, letting the words his mother spoke sink in. He got up from the stool, went around the counter, and wrapped her in a tight hug. She had always been his rock. She was the driving force behind his success with the band. When he'd wanted to give it all up, she convinced him to stay. She was the one who made him realize how hard he'd worked to get to where he was.

The sound of the mudroom door had them both looking up to see Analia walking in, Sydney in her arms. She looked flustered.

"I need help. I've created a monster that doesn't sleep or eat," she said. Despite her words, she stared lovingly at her daughter.

"I'm gonna head out. Leave you two to love this monster," he said and snuggled into Sydney's neck, making her laugh and wiggle in her mother's arms.

"Please drive carefully. You know how much I hate that bike," said his mother.

"I'm gonna sell it. I need to get a car. Can't very well tug a family around on a bike," he said, smiling at her. "And I plan to get a dog. A boy needs a dog."

"I suggest you discuss it with Claire first." He looked at her quizzically. Like he needed Claire's permission. "Don't look at me like that, Austin. If you want to get on a woman's good side and stay there, you ask first."

"Like she asked me, right?"

"Don't do that. What's past is past, look forward, Austin."

He was looking forward, years into the future. He just didn't know how he was going to get there. He hopped on his motorcycle, and the rumble of the machine soothed him. He couldn't wait to get home.

CHAPTER FIFTEEN

Claire

Claire was standing at the kitchen sink, cleaning up from breakfast. As usual, the morning had been a hectic one. They'd left in a rush for practice, leaving their mess piled in the sink. She had just put the last plate on the drying rack when she heard the front door. Assuming it was Austin, she made no effort to greet him.

Just when she was getting over her irritation, he'd gone and pissed her off. She'd had enough of his bitterness and mood swings, and she decided that she would face him head on, tell him how she felt, and worse, how he made her feel. She hated feeling as if she'd done a horrible, horrible thing. She hadn't. Her intentions were never to hurt him, and he needed to understand that. His steps sounded determined. He was probably upset because nothing grated at his nerves more than when she didn't lock the front door. He hated that she took her and Charlie's security for granted. She wasn't in the mood to argue.

"I know what you are going to say," she called out. "But

you don't have a key, and I was going to head upstairs…" She turned to face him and was surprised to see John.

There was the oddest look on his face. You'd think he was about to cry. His usually tanned skin looked pale, and she quickly walked towards him, drying her hands on a dish towel.

"John, what's the matter? Is everything okay?" she asked, concerned.

"Is he here?"

"Austin? No he's…" she began but stopped herself when he walked up to her, grabbed her waist, and pulled her towards him, his lips on hers with a fierce passion she hadn't experienced in years.

The kiss not only caught her off guard, but she was surprised to find herself giving in to his touch. His lips were soft, his tongue insistent. He kissed her with so much desire that she wondered suddenly if she wanted him to stop at all. When the dish towel she was holding hit the floor, her hands found their way into his hair. Her fingers tangled and pulled, holding him against her. Her back hit the counter. She hadn't realized they'd moved. He grabbed her hips, lifting her onto the cold granite. His hands traveled up her legs, under the hem of the long, pink dress she'd changed into, his mouth never leaving hers. She wouldn't have let him move away even if he tried. Claire wrapped her legs around his hips, wanting suddenly to feel more. He tried to pull away, and she tightened her grip around his neck, kissing him with the same desire he had just displayed. But she sensed his resistance.

"What is it?" she asked.

"I know that I don't have a chance now that he's back. I'm not sure I ever did, but I needed to taste you at least once."

"Don't stop," she whispered.

"I don't want to, sweetness, but I have to. We can't do this. It's not what you want."

"No it's not, it's what I need," she whispered against his lips.

It must've been depravation. There was no other explanation for her actions. She should stop, she knew that much, but damned if the logical part of her brain had shut down. She couldn't think with his soft, insistent tongue in her mouth. All she knew was that in that moment, she wanted him badly, and she was willing to deal with the consequences later.

John moved back and stared at her, questions swimming in his dark eyes. She brought him down to her mouth, savoring every inch of his. He moaned against her, the vibration reverberating right down to her core. She wanted him to make her feel like a woman again. She wanted him to make her feel wanted.

"Jesus, Claire...stop. This isn't why I came here."

"Why did you come here?"

"I don't know...I had to see you. I had to know," John said.

"Know what?"

"Nothing. You're not thinking clearly, Claire. I should leave."

"Shh...just this once, John. Stay."

She held on to him, not wanting him to move away. She kissed him some more. She felt his body relax. Claire moved her fingers to his chest, unbuttoning his plaid shirt—a John Deere staple. Her fingers ran over his impressive six-pack. She wanted to feel his skin under her fingertips, wanted to ogle his tanned chest. John's fingers started to glide from her thigh to her hips, up her sides, resting just below her full, aching breasts. His thumb caressing the underside of her breast brought with it a sting of desire she had forgotten could be felt. The type of longing that could only be brought on by the touch of a man.

In the back of her mind, she knew this wasn't the man she wanted—it wasn't his hands she wanted on her. Despite that, she couldn't bring herself to stop any of it. It had been so long since someone had made her want like this. She had always known John was willing to offer her much more than she could ever offer him. She made note of it, kept her feelings strictly platonic, and purposely kept him in the friend zone. That thought should have been the bucket of cold water she needed to stop.

"John," she whispered.

"What?"

"If we...just this once..." she said between breaths. "Take me to bed, John," she urged.

"Are you sure?"

"No, but I need more, please." Without further protest,

John slid his hands under her thighs, just below her bottom, urging her to remain wrapped around his waist. He picked her up off the countertop and turned to walk away as she excitedly kissed his neck and chest. She felt him stiffen, stopping all of a sudden mid-step.

"What's wrong?" she complained.

He slid his hands to her waist, her legs sliding off him without his support. Her weak knees had her losing her balance, and she grabbed the counter to catch herself. He placed his hands on her shoulders and turned her around to face the one person that could tamp out whatever flames their brief tryst had ignited.

Austin stood in the kitchen doorway, glaring at them. His fists were clenching and unclenching at his sides, one of those "if looks could kill" expressions on his very menacing face. They'd been so engrossed in the moment that neither of them heard the front door open. Claire was stunned. She wondered how long he had been standing there; she was appalled at the thought that they had an audience.

"Jesus, Austin?" she shrieked.

"What the fuck is this? I asked you two point blank if there was anything between you, yet you lied to me. Again," he sneered through clenched teeth.

"Calm down, Austin. I just came over to talk to her," said John.

"Do you talk to all girls with your tongue down their throats? A bit difficult to get a word in, don't you think?"

"Austin!"

"What, Claire? Something you need to clear up? Something I'm disrupting? Because I can just take my son and give you—"

"No!"

"Man, now you're just talking shit. She has a right to a life. What did you expect, for her to be pining over you all these years?"

"Who the fuck asked you for an opinion? Get out of my face before I rearrange it."

"I don't want any problems with you, man."

"You should have thought of that before you went behind my back." He turned to Claire. "And you, you're full of lies."

John stepped forward, but Claire put her hands on his arm to stop him. She watched Austin prepare himself for battle.

"Leave us alone for a minute, Austin," Claire said, not taking her eyes off him.

"I'll be on the porch. Get rid of him," said Austin, pointing a firm finger in John's direction.

Claire stood, dumbfounded. It took a moment for her to gather her thoughts. She closed her eyes briefly and let out the breath she'd been holding. When she turned to face John, he was wearing the same expression he had when he initially walked in the house.

"I'm sorry," she said. "I shouldn't have—"

"Don't…you don't have to apologize to me. I shouldn't have come. I just…I needed to see. I didn't believe Hunter when he told me Austin was living here."

"His son is here."

"I didn't ask for a reason."

"No, but your face says it all. What do you want me to tell you, John? It's not like I have a choice. I can't very well kick him out."

"You always have a choice." With those words, his face softened, and it was in that moment that she understood the urgency in his kiss—he was giving her a choice.

"You knew he was coming home?" she accused, her voice sounding hoarse.

"Oh, so it's home now for all of you?"

"Answer me."

"Yes. Mark and I saw him drive up his parents' driveway," he said, referring to his brother, who had been part of the band for a while but decided on college instead.

"And you came right over to complicate things," she said, her voice condescending.

"I just wanted to talk. We've been out a couple of times, and we had a great time at the cookout, too. You know how I feel. When I got here and saw you…I couldn't…I um…got scared," he admitted.

"Scared of what?" she asked, afraid she already knew the answer.

"Look, I had no idea he would be home so soon. Just go talk to him, sort things out. I didn't mean to cause any trouble for you," he said, not answering her question.

"But..."

"It's fine, Claire, really, I understand." He leaned in and kissed her on the forehead.

"I'm sorry, John."

"You have nothing to be sorry about. I didn't mean to put you on the spot, I just...I needed to make sure it wasn't just because of Charlie."

"It's never been because of Charlie," she admitted.

"I know. I can tell every time you look at Charlie that you weren't just looking at your son. You were seeing him too."

Claire shook her head. He brought his hand up to her face and caressed it.

"You'll have to talk to him eventually," he said. "This was bound to happen sooner or later. Clear shit up, sweetness. We'll talk soon."

"What about you?"

"Don't worry about me. What happened just now was a one off." He shrugged.

"How can you say that?" she said, his comment wounding her more than it should.

"Claire, let's face it. If I hadn't come in here and kissed you so unexpectedly, you would have never voluntarily done

WHEN HE CAME BACK

it," he said, almost accusingly. "I don't know what happened between the two of you all those years ago. I, like everyone else, had my suspicions, but I think I was wrong. Whatever you two have is unfinished."

"I don't know how to finish it…"

"Yes you do. I can't understand the love you two share, but I know it's big, all-consuming, and to my regret, impenetrable."

He was right. John had always known where things stood. He tried to test the waters many times, only to come to the same conclusion. He grabbed her hand, and they walked out together. Austin was right where he said he would be—his elbows on his fidgeting knees and his face in his hands. She hesitated a moment, feeling John's hand tighten on hers in reassurance. In the months since she moved back, he had been an incredible source of support, Charlie's honorary uncle, and most of all, a great friend. She didn't deserve him.

He kissed her on the face and walked down the porch steps past Austin, who mumbled something she didn't hear. The next thing she saw was John's fist hitting Austin's face with so much force, she was certain he had broken his nose.

"You have no right to have an opinion, do you hear me? She relieved you of that right years ago!" John pointed out as he slowly released his hand from Austin's shirt.

"You don't know shit."

Austin jumped to his feet and swung his arm around, catching John in the side of the head. If the hit didn't hurt John, who barely stumbled, it must have hurt Austin.

"Stop. Both of you stop!" Claire yelled.

The two men grunted. Shirts were torn and more fists flew. Claire ran around the house and grabbed the garden hose. She twisted the faucet, letting the water run. She knew it would be cold—if they wanted to act like rabid animals, then she would treat them as such. She pointed the hose in their direction, pushed down on the nozzle, and doused them with cold water.

"Ah! Stop, that's cold!" yelled Austin.

"What was that for?" both men said at the same time.

"What the hell are you two thinking? If you're going to kill each other, go do it somewhere else. You're animals, and I'm not some prize," she scolded.

She'd never been this angry, at them or at herself. She was also embarrassed and scared at the damage they were causing each other and their friendship—they'd been close once. She stared from Austin to John, both bleeding from various parts of their faces. She had caused this, she decided and felt the tears pool in her eyes. Before Austin arrived, her life had been simple. Her only fear had been confronting Austin about Charlie. Once he found out, she'd almost managed to convince herself that things would be fine. She never once stopped to question Austin when he moved his things into the guest room. Why would she? It was where he belonged. He needed to be near his son. Charlie needed him. They could live their lives the way they had been for the past couple of weeks in relative peace. Besides the occasional rebuke Austin threw at her, they'd been getting along. Some friendly banter, the rare moment she would be caught in his stare, the unintentional touch. And the tension. She couldn't forget the conflict she felt at being around him. She just wanted Austin to stop blaming her.

"I'm sorry," she said. She turned and ran into the house, leaving both men lying on her front lawn.

She ran up to the only place she ever felt at peace—the only room in the house that was hers. She wanted to cry. She could feel the knot in her throat, but no tears came. She just wanted it all to go away and live happily ever after, but she wasn't that naïve. Happily ever after took time, patience, and a hell of a lot of forgiveness.

CHAPTER SIXTEEN

Austin

"Shit," Austin said as he dropped his head back on the grass. He covered his face with his arm, letting out a long, ragged breath, wincing at the pain the action produced in his chest. "I don't know how I'm ever going to get this right," he mumbled.

He peeked at John from under his arm, not really waiting for an answer, but suspecting his long-ago friend was dying to say something. John lay next to him, feeling his face for the bruises that were slowly surfacing. His left eye was in the process of swelling. Austin felt a sense of satisfaction that he'd gotten him good. Fucker deserved it. How dare he kiss his girl?

"Look at us, all bruised up like a couple of high school hooligans, and she's the one apologizing. Why?"

"Because she feels guilty—for everything. Charlie, you, me. I want..." Austin started but stopped himself. John was not the person he wanted to talk about Claire with.

"Want what?" John asked, his voice slow.

Austin stared at him, debating whether he should confide in him like he once had. He thought back to what he'd said about Claire pining for him. Now that he knew she let him go on purpose, he wondered if she had. But the thought of John's filthy mouth on hers grated at his every nerve. She was his, and it was about time he showed her and every asshat who dare lay eyes on her who she belonged to, starting with the one next to him.

"I want to make things right with her. I want her back."

"What the hell took you so long?"

"My pride was a little hurt, okay? The prettiest girl in school made me fall in love with her and then dumped my ass."

"Not because she didn't love you, man. We all knew that."

"Yet you still went after her and put your filthy mouth on her."

"Can you blame me? I'm sure you've noticed what she looks like now..." Austin's fist came down hard on John's chest, making him grunt loudly. "For fuck's sake, man, ease off. I was just making an observation. And if this shiner is the consequence, it was worth it." John moved before Austin could get at him again.

"Don't ever try it again."

"Let me ask you something," John said, turning to look at him. "If you want to fix this up so bad, why in God's name are you spilling your guts on the front lawn like a little a pussy? Go get your girl."

He couldn't help but laugh at that. Then he grunted. Damn, his body hurt. You'd think playing the guitar while running up and down a stage kept you in shape, but none of that exercise could prepare you for a John "Deere" Lowe beating. He went to get up, winced again, and quickly lay back down, holding on to his ribs as if they were going to fall out of him. He reached into his back pocket, hoping to God his cell phone wasn't broken. He looked over at John, who was stretching his arms over his head. Austin winced as he heard John's bones popping—probably putting his spine back into place. He dialed his dad's number, waiting to leave a message. The phone rang four times before he picked up.

"Dad, it's me. Why'd you pick up?"

"Because it rang."

"I mean, aren't you in the theater?"

"We were, but your son decided to chug a large drink in six seconds and now he's emptying his bladder and we're missing half the movie," he said, raising his voice for Charlie to hear, no doubt.

"Dad, can you please take Charlie tonight? I need to work some things out with Claire."

"Still in doghouse, Son?"

"Is there a place worse than the doghouse?" he asked, hearing John laugh next to him.

"Yes. It's called the couch for a week. Bad place to sleep let me tell you."

221

"Can you take him?"

"Of course I can. Oh look at that, the prince is off his throne," his father said. "You know, Austin, someone needs to teach this boy to pee like a man and not a girl sitting down. Why don't you mention it to Claire while discussing whatever it is you're going to discuss."

Austin laughed. There was so much he still needed to learn about his son, and pissing sitting down was the first thing he was going to fix.

"I don't think it's a good time to bring that up. But I'll work on it with him."

"Good luck, Son."

"Thanks."

He watched his phone screen until it went black, preparing for the pain getting up would trigger. He took a long, fortifying breath, turned on all fours, and pushed himself off the grass. John still lay deep in thought next to him. Austin stood carefully. His arms had started to ache, and so had his face. The adrenaline that had rushed through his body minutes ago was slowly winding down, and he felt it. He looked down once more at John and walked away—leaving him to his own defenses and hoping the bastard went home soon. He heard the grunting from behind him but didn't bother to look back to see if his friend gotten to his feet. Yeah, he could still call him a friend.

"You better not hurt her, asshole," said John.

Austin gave him the one-finger salute and walked into the

house.

The silence inside was unsettling. He realized that without Charlie home, the house felt empty. He walked towards the kitchen, desperate for a glass of water. Although Claire would have a conniption if she had seen it, he washed his face in the sink. He made sure the water was cold, certain his battered face would welcome it. He watched the water flow down the drain, stained with his blood. He wondered where he was cut, hoping he didn't require stitches—a trip to the hospital would certainly make the papers, and so far, he'd managed to keep a low profile. He grabbed some paper towel, patted his face dry, and threw the bloodstained paper in the trash. Slowly and painfully, he headed up the stairs. There was only one place she could be. The only place she ever went when she was upset—her studio.

When they were younger and her parents left her and Hunter alone to go globe-trotting, it was where he always found her in that big, old mansion. He used to hate it, seeing her so alone and sad. He was happy to know things had changed, that she and her parents had a relationship now, but he couldn't help resenting them still. Who did that to their kids? Leaving for days on end to enjoy the world?

He walked slowly up the metal spiral stairs and wished that just for that one day she'd been in the kitchen. He hurt; his muscles would surely protest in the morning. He tried to make as little noise as possible, not wanting to disturb her if she was painting. When he peeked through the door, she was sitting on her stool in front of an easel, an unfinished painting staring back at her. She sat with her face resting in her hands, elbows on her knees, taking deep breaths. He could hear the inhale and exhale as her back rose and fell with each attempt.

"Hey," he said uncertainly.

She turned slightly and took a long look at him.

"Your shirt is ripped," she said, disgusted. She quickly turned back to the painting.

He silently walked down to his room to change. That was another thing he was determined to change—their sleeping arrangements. He hated the fact that although he'd settled in with her and Charlie, he was still a guest. He detoured on the way back to her studio and stopped in the bathroom in search of some painkillers. A white bottle with green letters advertising its strength stared back at him from the medicine cabinet. He twisted the cap off, popped three green gel pills in his mouth, and bent towards the sink to drink the water that had pooled in his hands. He took that opportunity to assess the damage. Yep, just as he thought. One cut brow that would possibly need four or more stitches, but he'd live. The bleeding had stopped, but fuck did the open wound look nasty—the flesh raw and the edges white. He wondered if he pressed both edges together like they do to boxers, would it close the wound? He did just that and carefully taped a butterfly bandage over it. He ran wet fingers through his hair, brushing the grass from its ends before turning to face Claire's wrath.

She was in the same position he'd left her in. He didn't know what to say, how to re-break the already too fragile ice without hurting her. Although he tried, he never seemed to do or say the right thing.

224

"I'm sorry," he simply said.

She straightened her back but didn't turn to look at him.

"Is this how it's always going to be? You apologizing to me, me apologizing to you? Because let me tell you, Austin, I can't live like this. I can't walk on eggs shells around you, wondering if something I say will have you throwing your pain and anger in my face."

"What do you want me to do?"

"Move on. I'm sorry I lied, I'm sorry I hurt you, but I'm not going to spend the rest of my life letting you make me feel guilty over it. I did what I thought was right. I've lived all these years doubting and regretting my decisions, but I had a child and I needed to move on, so I did. I never forgot you, but I couldn't sit and dwell on my choices either. Charlie needed me."

"Is John a result of you moving on? Is he who you want?" he asked, angry now.

"What happened today with John was a one off," she told him. "That's never happened before with him."

"So there've been others?"

"You have no right to ask me that. Especially when you hardly lived the life of a monk," she said, turning towards the window.

"I have every right to ask you that," he said, indignant. "Any man that comes into your life comes into Charlie's."

"Charlie and I have done just fine. He's my first and only

priority. Nothing will ever change that. I think you need to move out," she blurted the last part out.

"My son is here."

"Yes, and you can see him whenever you want. I won't keep you away from each other."

"No!" He was not going to move out. He ran his hands through his hair, accidently brushing his cut, which made him wince. No way was he going to leave them; he did that once already. He walked away never fighting for her.

"I'm not leaving."

"I don't want him to see the lifestyle you lead."

"And what lifestyle is that? You don't even know me anymore."

"The kind of lifestyle where you think you can beat a man because he's in my life. Besides, I've read enough about you and your bandmates to know I don't want your bad habits influencing my son," she said, finally turning to look at him.

"Our son. And I don't have any bad habits."

"What about all the women?"

"What women? You are not doing this to me again, Claire. You forced me to walk away once. I am not walking away again without a fight."

"Fight for what?"

"My family, damn it!" he yelled, his jaw set, readying for the fight of his life. "Is this your solution to everything? Talk

226

some sweet bullshit and hope the people you're spurting it to buy it? We loved and trusted each other once, and you broke that," he said, pointing a shaky finger at her.

He wasn't sure if it was his anger, nerves, or fear that she would let him walk, but he couldn't stop his body from shaking. As always, he regretted the damned words the second they left his mouth when he saw her take a couple of steps back, gasping. He had thought them often in the past few days but never wanted to really say them, because he too wanted to stop blaming her.

"Don't you think I know that," she whispered, her head bent. "But right now, I need you to go. I don't want you here."

"Liar!"

She looked at him, her face devoid of any emotion, but he could see the tears swimming at the rims of her eyes.

She kept her eyes and body still. Her lips, pressed in a tight line, gave away little aside from the tears she was trying like hell to not let spill.

"I don't want you going near John again." He took a step closer to her.

He knew he could never intimidate her, but in that moment, there was significant purpose in his short, determined stride, and he was sure she could see it. No one read him better. The pulse at the base of her neck beat rapidly. Her face flushed, and he hoped to God it was his presence and not the leftover desire from kissing John.

"Oh, please. I just told you what happened with John had

never happened before," she said calmly, too calmly.

"Why the hell did you kiss him then? You let him touch you. Why did you let him fucking touch you?"

"I..." she began but stopped herself.

"Tell me," he repeated, his voice softer this time.

"I needed it."

"You needed it?" he asked dubiously.

"Yes. I wanted to feel something."

"Feel what?"

"Anything that could fill this void and ease this need that I've been feeling all of a sudden."

"Void? Need? For a man or affection?" he questioned.

"Both..."

She was a beautiful woman. Surely she must have had her share of affairs in the past few years. She was insatiable, loved making love, enjoyed his explorations, and she was adventurous. The thought of her going on any of those adventures with another man pissed him off, and he wanted to run out after John again and finish the job he'd started. He couldn't imagine her being alone all this time. What if she had been alone all this time? What if she'd never...His heart beat a rapid, expectant beat at the possible conclusion he'd come to. He took another step toward her, and his movement was met with a retreat that brought her smack against the wall—he was getting sick of this dance.

"I've been here all these days. You could have gotten whatever you needed from me," he whispered in her ear, his hands braced at either side of her face.

"Contracting an STD wasn't on my agenda," she said sharply.

"For your information, I've had a physical every year. I'm clean. I was never stupid or careless."

"Right, never…"

"Now, you're being the hypocrite, you know that? You moved on while I was stuck in a life you wanted for me," he growled. "I was barely living, Claire." His voice rose with every word as he took a step back. "I had my share of women. Meaningless nights drunk out of my fucking mind in the arms of another!"

"Don't…" she whispered, her voice barely audible.

"Don't what, tell you my truth? I didn't ask you to hide yours. You want the gory details, here they are. I went through women like they were nothing. I never got their names, couldn't even remember their faces. Half the time I was too high or drunk and out of my mind in love with you. I missed you, I wanted you, and I needed you. I never slept with any of them; I slept with you. It was your face I saw every single time. Then a year into this adventure you sent me on, I stopped. I started hating you, and I stopped hating myself."

That she had driven him to that state was what he despised the most about his first year away. He was a fucking rock star. Chicks wanted bragging rights, and they got them. Didn't matter that it wasn't their names he called out when he came. His behavior earned him a reputation. Girls lined up for him. Marijuana was set out on silver trays for him because high was the only way he got through the lay. Then one day, he woke up and didn't feel so empty. He couldn't explain it then. Suddenly, it was like a light went off in his head. It was Charlie. Austin took a few steps back, staring at the floor as he came to the only explanation that made sense. Everything stopped right around the time Charlie was born: the partying, the drugs, and until recently, the drinking.

He met her eyes and watched in despair as she began to tremble, dropping her face into her hand, sobbing.

"I can't believe you said those things to me," she cried. "I can't believe you did all those things. I would've never...I didn't...Oh, God." Her shoulders shook, the pain in her voice was his undoing.

"Babe, I'm sorry...I just...You destroyed me. You destroyed us, what we had. We were young, but it was so good, it was real. Damn it, Claire, you make me crazy...please stop crying. I can't stand to see you like this. Talk to me." He wanted to take her pain away. He wanted to give her everything.

"I've never...There's never been anyone else. I didn't want anyone else," she said through her sobs.

"Since me?"

She nodded.

"I never so much as looked at another man. I couldn't."

"Then why now? Why John?"

"I'm just so tired of not feeling connected. I miss the desire, the euphoria of…sex. I know you think that because I had Charlie I was never alone. It may be like that now because he's older, but when he was a baby, I was alone. Those first few months after he was born were terribly lonely. The late-night feedings were a killer; I would cry through the whole thing. I was exhausted. My body had morphed into something I didn't recognize, I was emotional, I couldn't sleep, and I couldn't eat. Charlie would cry for hours, and I would cry with him," she said, tears streaming down her face. "I thought maybe he needed you. I mean, I know I did. I started talking to him about you. I put pictures of you in his room. I would point at your image, tell him stories. Believe it or not, it helped. Both of us. He calmed down, and I fell deeper in love…with the both you."

"Today with John…"

"Today I wanted to see if it was still possible to feel passion—something I hadn't had in years. For the first time in so long, I felt something else, and I wanted more of it."

"Claire…" He pulled her to him, held her while she cried. He wished for the umpteenth time that he'd been around. That she'd trusted him to make the best decision for them.

Maybe he wouldn't have gone with the band, or maybe he would have. They could have compromised. The road wasn't a place for a baby, at least not in those early days—they were brutal for him. He saw the grief on her face, the regret, the pain and emptiness he'd felt. Not even their son had been able to

231

fill it.

"I'm here now, babe."   He framed her face, tilting it. "Look at me,"

Her puffy lids lifted, her bloodshot eyes killing him a little more inside. Her lips were swollen from the crying, and he couldn't stop himself from taking her face in his hands and lowering his head, crashing his mouth to hers. He wanted to erase any mark left by John.

He licked her warm lips, tasted her tears. He kissed her tenderly, waiting for her to respond, to feel whatever it was she wanted to feel, and to want everything only from him.

"I want to make you feel, Claire," he whispered seductively against her lips.

"Now, Austin. Make me feel now." He brushed back her hair, his gaze capturing hers.

CHAPTER SEVENTEEN

Claire

Claire watched him reel back, looking at her in complete awe and uncertainty. The darkening of his intense green eyes proved his words weren't uttered in vain. She closed hers, savoring the feel of his hands brushing her hair back, his callused fingers running down her face as he wiped away the trail her tears had left. She watched him, his eyes following the path of his hands from her face to her shoulders and down her arms, leaving a trail of goose bumps. His hands were on her hips, and he fell to his knees, tightening his grip.

Unable to resist touching him, she brushed her fingers through his hair and watched lovingly as Austin closed his eyes. Judging by the soft hum coming from him, he was basking in the feel of her nails massaging his scalp. He ran his nose over her belly and leaned his forehead against her.

"I wish..." he began, his voice hoarse with emotion. "I wish I'd seen you grow big and round with our son inside you. I wish I'd been able to sleep next to you with my hand here, feeling his movements, and I wish I'd been there when he let out his first cry," he said, laying his hand flat on her belly. "I understand why you did what you did now. Thank you for giving me the life I had, but most of all, thank you for giving me a beautiful, healthy son."

"Oh, Austin. I'm so sorry I took that from you," she said between sobs.

"Shh, don't cry, baby. I don't want you to cry ever again. I don't want you to feel guilty anymore. I don't want you to be alone ever again. I'm here and I'm not going anywhere, but I can't give you what you want right now, Claire. I've dreamed about you, of having you again, almost every night since you sent me away," he said, taking deep breaths. "Since I've been back, you're all I think about, and you're here, so close. You have no idea what you're asking of me. I wouldn't...I couldn't be gentle."

She stared down at him, her hair a curtain of chestnut waves falling to frame her face. Austin reached up to brush the hair behind her ears, his hand lingering there. She turned her face, grabbed his hand, and pressed long, tender kisses across his palm. He entwined his callused fingers in hers. She'd always loved the roughness of his hands, the size, how strong they were and how gentle they'd always felt on her body. She remembered what it was like to be taken hard and fast by him. She remembered what it was like to be taken slow and gentle. She didn't want the latter. No. She needed hard, fast, and whatever roughness he promised. She needed to be reminded of what they once were. She needed him, had always needed him—had waited for him. She swallowed hard, gathering all her courage to say the words that were about to leave her mouth. She put her hands on his strong jaw and turned his face up to her.

"I don't want you to be gentle."

He leaned back on his haunches, mouth open as he stared at her in complete and utter amazement. She smiled at him, leaned against the wall, and began to gather her long dress in her hands. Getting a hold of the hem, she slowly revealed her body to him, inch by painstaking inch. She pulled it over her head, laughing at the sharp intake of breath she heard from the man at her feet, and dropped the dress in his lap.

"Jesus, Claire, you're not wearing any underwear." He grabbed the dress that had landed on his thigh and bunched the fabric in his hands.

"Hmm, another one off," she said, smirking.

"He touched you. He would have known. Damn it, Claire, he could have taken you so easily," he said, his eyes on hers, his voice laced with anger.

"He didn't get that far. But you, you'll get somewhere far and deep, baby," she said mischievously.

"Fuck," he hissed. His eyes started the slow, heated perusal down her body, stopping halfway.

She watched, eager to see what he would do, what he would say. Since Charlie's birth, she'd felt a tad insecure about her body. Although she ran often, she'd never managed to get her body back to the shape it once was. Her belly had an eternal bulge. Although small, it was there. Her hips were rounder and her breasts fuller—she didn't mind that part. From the way Austin was devouring her with his eyes, he didn't mind any of it.

"Austin," she whispered.

Seeing him on the floor in front of her, on his knees, not doing anything was driving her mad.

"What, baby?"

"Please..." she begged, yes begged. She couldn't just stand there naked as he leaned forward and rubbed his nose down her belly, stopping at her pubis, lingering there for too long. She felt his hot breath against her, the rasp of day-old stubble rubbing against skin that was too sensitive at that moment.

"I like this," he said, swiping his tongue over the area she'd waxed a few days ago.

"Good, now enjoy it," she dared.

He leaned back to look up at her, a roguish smile on his face. He threw the dress over his shoulder, grabbed her hips, and pushed her against the wall.

"Hold on," was all he said before he lifted one of her legs over his shoulder, and without preamble, slid his tongue through her sensitive flesh at the same time he slid first one, then two fingers into her. She bit her lip as she rocked against his hand.

"Austin," she cried out, her body shaking from the sensation of him devouring her.

She gasped, filling her lungs with the air she let out in a

ragged breath seconds later. She reached out instinctively to a shelf on her right for support. She rolled her head back against the wall, taking and feeling everything. Her whole body drummed with renewed vitality. He hummed against her folds and she reached down, pulling at his hair with her free hand to hold him against her. This is what she'd held out for. John made her feel good, but Austin made her feel exquisite.

She realized through her muddled senses that he'd moved his other hand to her breasts. He pushed against her, holding her, grabbing, pinching, and driving her to the brink of heaven. Her nipples ached deliciously, whether it was from arousal or his manipulations, she couldn't tell. All that was on her mind was the feel of his tongue and fingers inside her. She made incoherent noises—whimpers, gasping, and moans—all jumbled together in her foggy state. She felt a rush of cold air as he moved away from her. She looked at him staring up at her, his lips swollen and wet with her juices.

"I want to watch you come," he told her. "Now!"

As if on command, she began to writhe against the wall, his fingers manipulating her, the stirring starting at her thighs, climbing up in a flash of glorious lights behind eyelids she could no longer keep open. A loud, victorious groan from deep within her chest made its way past her mouth. Her body trembled in his arms as he kissed his way up to her neck, to her mouth, ravaging her lips, taking with him the last remnants of her orgasm.

He drew a gasp from her as he roughly pulled her to him, her hands landing on his chest. She felt the frantic beat of his heart through his shirt and gripped it in her fist, holding him in place. In a slow, torturous motion, he continued to kiss her with an infuriating, insistent want, tangling his tongue with hers. She tasted herself and trembled in his arms. Her hands slid up his chest to hold on to his neck. The soft curls at his nape tickling her knuckles called to her. She sunk her fingers into his soft hair, pulling. She never wanted him to leave her mouth. She never wanted him to leave her again. The thought drew her own soft moan from her lips.

He reached down to cup her ass, lifting her. She wrapped her arms and legs around him, holding on for the ride he was about to take her on. The friction of his shorts against her bare, sensitive center made her gasp. He shifted her slightly and pressed her back to the wall. With his hands free, he ventured over her ribs, stopping just below her breasts to run callused thumbs over each sensitive, pebbled tip. She arched her hips, putting her in direct contact with his rigid erection. She ground against him, making him groan, ending their torrid kiss.

No! She wanted to yell and beg him for more, but before she could voice her protest, he went to work on her neck, licking and nibbling a particularly sensitive spot just below her ear, knowing damn well what it would do to her. He kneaded her breasts as his lips inched closer, leaving hot, wet kisses on her collarbone, her sternum, the soft swell of her breasts, and finally, taking one compliant nipple in his mouth. She gasped again, and he laughed against her breast as his lips continued their ministrations. She tilted her head back, her whole body arching towards him, wanting more friction. Again was all she thought as her hands reached for him, frantically scratching, wanting more. So much more. He lifted his head. She leaned into him, gripping his bottom lip between her teeth. She licked the indent her teeth left when she let go.

"Austin?"

"Yes?"

"You're wearing too much clothing," she said.

"We should do something about that."

"Yes, we should..."

Austin quickly set her down. Without wasting another second, Claire reached for the hem of his shirt and clumsily pulled it off. She took her fill—she'd only sneaked glimpses of him in the last couple of weeks, never daring to linger and examine the changes his body had gone through. In that moment, she was seeing him for the first time as the man he'd become. Her eyes roamed over every inch of his hard, defined chest, his tattooed arm. She ran her fingers over it, thinking it gave him that edgy look a rock star owned.

"I like this," she told him as she ran a finger over the design.

She was dying to study it more closely, but later. Her concentration at the moment was focused on getting him naked.

"There's a story behind it."

"Will you tell me what it is?"

"Later..."

He smiled at her as her eyes finished their leisurely perusal. He was beautifully built. She wanted to run her tongue over all the crevices of his muscles that hadn't been there at eighteen. She ran her hands over his pecs, his abs, following the V at his hips into the waistband of his shorts. She curled her fingers into the belt loops and tugged. She peeked down at the considerable gap between his skin and the waistband—the belt doing very little to keep the low-slung shorts on his waist. She followed the trail of light blond hair past his hips and noticed she wasn't the only one going commando.

She looked at him, questioning. He shrugged. "Too hot for underwear."

Claire slipped her fingers in his shorts, making him gasp. He leaned his forehead against hers, breathing hard, making a considerable effort to control himself. Determined to bring him to his knees, she wrapped her fingers around his cock and felt it grow harder in her hand. She wanted him to lose the sweet control he thought he'd gained with those few deep breaths. She made quick work of his belt, cursing when she couldn't loosen the button of his shorts.

"Austin, help me!" she whined.

The sweet sound of his laughter both irritated and delighted her—she wondered how he could stand with her naked in his arms while she was barely holding it together. She was so turned on her whole body buzzed and ached with desire. She ventured further into his shorts, the head of his penis skimming her wrist, making every single nerve ending in her arm sing in harmony. He sucked in another deep, ragged breath, putting his hand on her wrist, effectively halting her exploration. She smiled at him and watched, mesmerized, as he bit into his bottom lip, a smile tugging at his delicious mouth.

"Shit, Claire, wait," he whispered, the muscles on his pecs shaking with the little bit of restraint he exercised.

"I've waited long enough."

"I know, baby, I know," he said. Claire reached down, her hands pulling on the zipper while he worked on the button. His shorts hit the hardwood with a thud.

He lifted his right foot to step out of his shorts. Unable to dislodge them from his ankles, he nearly lost his balance. His hands moved quickly to her bottom, holding her against him. She let out a shriek and wrapped her hands around his neck. She moved slightly, her lips brushing his, unable to keep from kissing him.

"Shit. Fuck, babe. I'm stuck," he said against her lips, frustrated.

Claire let out a long, exasperated breath. She got on her knees, looking up at him mischievously.

"Don't. Even. Fucking think about it, babe, or this will be over way too fast."

"I thought we were going for fast?"

"Not that kind of fast, sweetheart," he said as he leaned his hand on the wall for support.

She slid her hands from his thigh, down to his calf, to his

ankle. She took great satisfaction in feeling his muscles quiver and strain under her touch. She could see his chest rising and falling when he leaned his head back. Swallowing hard, his Adam's apple bobbled in his neck with the effort. She wrapped her hand around his ankle, lifting and helping him out of the puddle of clothing at his feet. He was stuck on his worn rubber flip-flops, and they both laughed at the absurdity of their situation. She grabbed the shoes, put them together, and tossed them out the open window.

"Hey!" he protested.

"We'll get you new ones."

"We are one hot fucking mess, babe," he said, laughing.

"Yeah," she simply said. She looked up at him coquettishly, determined to emphasize the "hot" in the mess he mentioned.

At eye level with his impressive erection, Claire ran her nose up the thick column of his cock from tip to base, then back down with her tongue. As if he'd been struck by a bolt of lightning, he stepped back, his hands holding her shoulders at arm's length.

"What did I do wrong?" she asked, feigning innocence.

"Not a damn thing and you know it. Are you trying to kill me?"

"It wouldn't be a bad way to go."

He looked down at her; lust filled his moss-colored eyes. Still holding on to her shoulders, he lifted her to her feet. He slid his hand up her thigh, to her ass, up her back. She could feel his erection pulsing against her belly. He swallowed once more and leaned his face against her shoulder.

"Please tell me you have condoms in the house."

"I don't," she said, putting her hands on his chest, his heart beating so hard she was sure it would end up in her hands.

"Fuck," he hissed.

"I'm on the pill."

"I thought you've never…"

"I haven't. Irregular periods after Charlie," she said.

"Shit, babe. I'm clean. I haven't been with anyone in a…"

"I believe you. I believe you. Now please just—" Her sentence halted when he assaulted her mouth with his. He suddenly grabbed her hips, lifting her and impaling her with his cock.

"Ah!" she cried out in part pleasure, part pain as her inner muscles protested the sweet invasion of his hardness.

"Holy fuck, you're tight. Am I hurting you?" he asked between breaths.

"No, no…shit…oh…shit…" she whispered, but he slowed his movements anyway.

He framed her face in his hands, urging her to look at him. She tried to move away, she didn't want him to see the emotion in her eyes. Not because she didn't want this, but because she missed it. She missed him so much that nothing could ever replace the way he made her feel. She knew with every fiber of her being that he loved her. Tears welled in her eyes, and she tried her best to keep them from spilling, but all the emotions, the love, and the completeness she felt in that instant overwhelmed her.

"Am I hurting you, Claire?" he asked again, his own features scrunching with worry.

"No, not at all. This feels so good, so right. Like…" she started but couldn't think of the right word.

"Home," he said, finishing the sentence for her.

She nodded. That was exactly what it was. They'd finally come home to each other. Austin brushed her hair back, caressed her lips with his fingertips. She licked them and tasted her essence on his fingers. His breathing was heavy on her neck as he moved his face to lean on her shoulders. Only then did she realize he'd stopped moving, giving her the time to adjust to him.

"I need to move, babe," he breathed out.

"Yes, please…" Whatever words she was going to say were swallowed up when he started to move slowly, her body taking every inch of him, becoming accustomed to him again, and surrounding him with her heat.

She recognized the quickening starting at her thighs, and she tightened her legs around his hips. So fast, she thought. He brought her to climax so fast.

"Fuck, I can't be gentle, baby. I need this too. I don't want to hurt you."

"You won't hurt me, Austin. Take it, take what you need. Take everything."

He rammed into her harder than she thought possible. She let out a rough "Oh God" as he moved nearly all the way out of her, only to push back in until he was buried to the hilt. His hand protectively held her head to keep it from hitting the wall. His other hand held tight to her ass as he continued ramming into her. Their sweat-slicked bodies gave an erotic twist to an already hot encounter. She lifted her head, her lips colliding with his as she ravaged his mouth, biting into his bottom lip as she came again—the tendons in her neck stiffening with the force of her orgasm.

"Oh, God…Austin," she screeched through clenched teeth.

She leaned back and watched as Austin's face took on the look of a man in the process of stunning release. He thrust hard one last time before stilling, his dark eyes rolling back as he came with a grunt, followed by his usual array of expletives.

"Fuckshitfuck…FUCKINGMOTHERFUCKER!" he yelled as his body vibrated against hers.

He once again grabbed her face and kissed her. She felt the passion, the desire, and most of all, the love that had never died between them. Three words lingered at the tip of her tongue, but in spite of what they just experienced, she was not ready to say them out loud. Home echoed in her head as he turned them around so his back was against the wall. He was still inside her as he slid down to the floor.

CHAPTER EIGHTEEN

Austin

Claire was right—it wouldn't have been a bad way to go. If he died, he would have died a happy man. He was the happiest he'd been in years, as close to death as he was. Her breathing had slowed significantly in the few minutes since positioning her comfortably against him. Her breasts were deliciously pressed against his chest, her legs astride his semi-hard cock still inside her. If she moved any which way, he would be ready to take her again in no time. He needed to be careful with her. She'd been as tight as any virgin, and he didn't want to hurt her. But damn if he could help or control himself. The second his cock slipped into her sweet heat, he was a goner. She felt amazing. Aside from her, he'd never entered a woman without a condom. He wasn't lying when he told her he'd never been careless. She'd been the only one because he trusted her. That trust had led to Charlie, and he'd never regret that one slip. They hadn't talked about when he was conceived, but he had a good idea.

He didn't want to think about any of that now. He just wanted to enjoy the feel of her wrapped around him. This is

247

the way he wanted to go to bed with her every night and wake every morning. His hands slid easily up and down her sweat-slicked back, up her neck, moving her hair to one side to help cool her. He could feel his own hair stuck to his neck and forehead, but he couldn't bring himself to move a muscle. He didn't want to miss a minute with her in his arms.

Eventually they would have to move. The light she relied on for painting was fading quickly, the sky becoming dark on the other side of the wall of windows leading to the terrace. Not wanting to move even his head, he turned only his eyes in that direction. He knew it wasn't late enough for the sun to completely disappear. A loud clap of thunder in the far distance and the distinct smell of rain indicated a looming rainstorm. He continued to caress her up and down, stopping to draw circles at the small of her back.

"You still with me, babe?"

"Hmm."

"Feeling okay?"

"I feel amazing," she mumbled into his chest.

"That was pretty fucking incredible."

"Do you have money in your pocket?"

"I don't have any pockets at the moment, why?"

She let out a short laugh. "I was going to charge you five bucks for every F-bomb you dropped."

"Baby, I have fucking millions in the bank. I would fucking gladly give you all of it if I could fucking experience what we just did again. How's that for filling the jar?"

"You have such a way with words, Austin McKinley. Now I know how you come up with all those hits."

"You've always been my only source of inspiration. So, yeah, it's obvious where those hits came from. Right here. From you."

"In that case, I should sue for royalties."

"If this is the way you'll sue me, me and the appendage currently inside you will take you on anytime."

"Such a class act," she said and gave him a weak smack on the chest.

"I've been called worse."

She laughed, and every damn muscle in her body contracted, stirring his dick back to life. He brought his hands to her hips to keep her still. He didn't want to take her again just yet. He wanted to take her to bed, make love to her, slow and soft.

"Don't laugh, babe," he said with a groan.

She laughed again and wiggled her hips.

"Claire, shit. Don't move."

"Such a way with words," she repeated as she peppered his neck with kisses.

She braced her hands on his chest and pushed herself back slightly to look at him. Her brows furrowed, and he wondered if she was rethinking "suing" him.

"Your cut is bleeding," she pointed out. She leaned over to pick up one of the clean rags she kept in a basket and dabbed the cut.

"It'll be fine."

"It's deep. You might need stitches."

"There's no way I'm moving a muscle right now to go get stitched up," he said as he moved his hips towards her and smiled his devilish smile. "Well, maybe one muscle…"

"Like I said, class act…" She laughed, again her center tightening around him.

She lowered her face, pulling his bottom lip between her teeth, licking the sting away. Smiling mischievously, her face barely an inch from his, she slowly—so fucking torturously slowly—began to grind against him. Yep, he thought. This is it—she was going to be the death of him. She sat up straighter, her movements harder, quicker.

"Claire, please. Baby, I want to take you to bed."

"We don't have time to get to a bed, Austin. I'm almost there."

He watched in wonder as she swung her head back, her hair tickling his thighs. She was completely lost in the moment. Her hands slid from his chest to her thighs, continued to glide up her torso to her breasts. The second her hands closed around her fabulous tits, he growled like a damned animal. She pinched her nipple between her index finger and thumb; he was certain he came just a little right in that second. She moved her hand up her sternum to her neck, and like a dream, gathered her hair as she rocked against him. She moved with such vigor, driving him mad with each swing of her luscious, round hips. She was mesmerizing.

Her mouth was slightly open, losing all her inhibitions as she let go, murmuring his name as her inner muscles squeezed the life out of him. He wasn't prepared for the tension that gathered in his gut, ready to follow her into whatever paradise she had just taken them. Taking her against the wall had been nothing compared to what it was like to watch and feel her take him, to possess him. She owned him, had always owned his body, heart, and soul. Entranced, he watched a bead of sweat run between her breasts just before his eyes rolled back. That, he thought a moment before he let go, had been his undoing.

"Babe, Ah! Jesus..." he managed just before she collapsed on him.

She sucked the breath right out of him, literally. He was having a hell of a time trying to fill his lungs with the precious air he needed to survive at the moment.

"What are you doing to me?" she mumbled, her breath hot against his neck.

"What am I doing to you? What are you doing to me?"

"Loving you. Making up for lost time."

Those words had him falling a little more in love with her. Although he wasn't naïve to think that things would be smooth sailing after this, he wanted to work through everything right then and there. He wanted to raise their boy with her, love them, take care of them, and in the near future, fill their house with more children. He wanted the future he'd always envisioned with her, and by God, he was going to get it.

"I want to get a dog for Charlie," he blurted.

She lifted her head, her body slipping a little, and he grabbed for her. He let out a small groan when he slipped out of her, feeling strangely bereft without her warmth. She leaned into him and kissed him, a smile playing on her delightful lips.

"I just had two of the best orgasms of my life, and you want to talk about getting a dog?" she asked, her face flushed, her pupils still dilated as she looked at him. "Which we aren't getting, by the way."

"We aren't. I am. For us."

"A dog is so…permanent," she said.

"I'm not going anywhere," he told her, suddenly annoyed.

He wanted to get back to their flirty banter. Nothing turned him on like a feisty Claire, but he didn't want to turn her off or make her question his intentions. Although in his mind, shit should have been pretty clear by now.

"Is…" she began, stopping as she contemplated her next words. He could feel her thinking. "Is all this for real?"

"It doesn't get more real than this, sweetheart. This is us. Everything we weren't while apart and everything we are when we're together," he cleared his throat. "I love you, Claire. I've loved you since I was fourteen years old. No matter what I do, I can't get you out of my system—believe me, I tried. You're not only a part of my heart, you are my

252

soul."

There. That was the honest-to-God truth. His new vow was to always tell her the truth about everything, how he felt about her, even the nitty-gritty parts of the past five years. He told her the truth about his promiscuity. He hated that part, but they'd kept enough shit from each other. That stopped now.

She lay back down on his chest, letting out a long, shaky breath. He wanted to put her at ease, convince her that he wasn't going anywhere. Somehow he knew that it was going to take a lot more work to reassure her that he was as permanent as any pet they could get. There was no way after what they had just experienced that he'd leave her. Not after seeing her again, and definitely not after meeting and falling in love with Charlie. The kid was amazing—he was funny, smart, kind, and so full of love for the both of them. The responsibility he felt to not disappoint his son was overwhelming. Hurting either one of them was not in the cards. Decisions had to be made, contracts would be broken, and people would be let down. In the end, a guy's gotta do what a guy's gotta do. The reward was in his arms, and it far outweighed the consequences.

"We should get up," she whispered, snapping him out of his thoughts.

"Why?"

"Your father's going to drop Charlie off soon."

"No he's not. I told him to take him home because you and I had some things to sort out."

"Did we…sort things out?"

"I may be far off, but I don't believe we're done sorting through things just yet."

"Oh really?"

"Yes really. But first I need a gallon of water and some food if I'm going to keep up with you."

She laughed. The sound was like heaven to his ears.

Although he truly was starving, he couldn't find the will to move. So much dreaming of this moment made him weaker than he'd like to admit. He could put on a good face, a brave face, but the thought of losing this newfound connection with Claire scared the shit out of him. Despite the age he fell in love with Claire, he'd never had any doubt she was "the one"—it was why the break-up had hurt so much. There was so much at stake now; losing her and Charlie would tear him to pieces. He knew this time he would not come out of that loss whole. He took a deep breath and let it out slow and loud. Claire's hand moved up to his face.

"I'm not going anywhere either, you know."

"You can't, I couldn't bear it. I only just made it through these years."

"I'm sorry."

"Stop apologizing. I don't ever want to hear you say you're sorry again. You did what you felt you had to. We're here now, and I will do everything I can to make this work, to make it last. You and Charlie are my family, and I will walk over hot coals for either one of you."

Her breath on his chest came out harsh and shaky. Yes, this was going to take time, but he would get the girl and the kid. He raised his hand, gave her ass a swift slap in an effort to get them both moving. His body was starting to hurt again from lying against the hardwood floor. She took his cue and slithered down his body. Her lips left a trail of kisses down his neck to his chest, stopping at one of his nipples and biting down, making him gasp. There was no way they were ever going to get out of her studio at this rate. Her hand moved back up his chest, to his face, inserting one finger into his mouth. Damn. She was hot and sexy and just as insatiable as he was. She moved lower. He had a pretty good idea where she was headed.

"Claire, stop. This isn't what it's about," he told her.

"This is what it's all about and more, so much more."

For the brief second before her tongue snaked out to taste the tip of his cock, he thought of stopping her.

"Jesus…" he whispered as his hips surged up to meet her hot mouth.

Without any teasing or warning, she took his entire length into her mouth, enveloping him. Her head moved slowly up, then back down, driving him mad when her tongue and teeth guided him right to the back of her throat. She let a soft moan that vibrated through him, and not all the fucking cold water in the world could stop him from releasing his orgasm into her mouth. He was lost to the sensation of the delicious heat of her mouth.

The last time he'd come that fast, he was fifteen, and she was at the helm. The only woman to go down on him in the past five years was Myra, and he'd regretted it. He'd never let anyone go down on him since. There'd been plenty of volunteers, but he couldn't bring himself to let anyone near him like that again. Austin knew how crazy that sounded, hypocritical even, but in a way, he felt that the privilege had always belonged to Claire. He closed his eyes, waiting for the blood that had rushed down to his groin to make its way back up to his satiated brain.

"I've been thinking of doing that for days," she said, surprising him with her statement. She'd been very good at hiding her desires.

She was sitting back on his legs, her breasts on display, enticing him.

"All that thinking really must have been something, baby. I haven't come that quick since I was fifteen when this sweet-ass brunette surprised me in my truck."

"Oh yeah? Was she good at it?"

"Yeah, she was good at it. I'm afraid to ask how she's gotten better at it, though."

"Toys," she said.

"Toys?"

"Yep. Big toys, small toys, vibrating toys…"

"Baby, please tell me you're kidding?" he asked, sitting up to be at eye level with her.

256

She shook her head. "If you're good, maybe I'll let you play…"

With that, he watched her get up, swaying her saucy ass to where her dress lay. She half turned to look at him, her middle finger wiping at the corner of her lips for any remnants of him. It was by far the sexiest thing he'd ever seen. She stretched like a fucking goddess, her arms in the air as the dress slowly covered her curves. She slipped her toe under his shorts and kicked them to him. She waited for him by the door as he put them on. Her mouth pulled slightly at the corners, not quite a smile, and he wondered what had crossed her mind.

"What is it?" he asked because he just couldn't stand not knowing what she was thinking.

"You're just so different. Your body—it's changed."

"It's called a grueling workout schedule," he attempted to joke.

"It's not just that. I let go of a boy, and let a man back in. I know you feel that you missed out, but so did I. I missed watching you change, mature…" she said, her words stalling as her eyes welled.

"Don't," he said and rushed to her side. "Please don't cry, I can't stand it. Let's just concentrate on now and tomorrow and the day after. Forget the past; let's create a future. I love you. There isn't enough time in the world to show you how much. You make me want things, Claire. You make me want everything, and giving me Charlie is a pretty great start."

Suspecting that she wasn't ready to admit how she felt, he

257

didn't protest when her delicate hands framed his jaw, her mouth closing in on his. She softly rained kisses over every inch of his face.

"Be patient with me, Austin."

"Don't feel you have to reciprocate, baby. I have nothing but patience."

"Thank you."

"I'm starving, and you need to eat. Charlie's orders," he said.

"Lucky for you I'm famished. Although I just had dessert…" She winked.

"I'll give you more after I feed you a meal." He smirked and grabbed her hand. With his other hand, he reached into his pocket for his phone and dialed for a pizza.

CHAPTER NINETEEN

Claire

She felt exquisite, loved, satiated; she could go on and on. He loved her, and although she couldn't find it in her to say the words back, she felt the same. This wasn't his life, after all. He had obligations elsewhere, a life elsewhere. Her eyes were engrossed in Austin as he paced the kitchen and ordered their dinner. He was comfortable in their home, despite some tense moments between the two of them.

She watched as he flicked each finger, calling out the toppings without missing a beat. She listened to him rattle off the strange combination—broccoli, olives, green and red peppers, red onions, chicken, and her favorite, salami. Not pepperoni. He remembered every single ingredient, right down to the feta.

She watched him grab an old gas bill from her magnet board by the fridge and rattle off the address. He'd left his shirt off, and she relished the fact that his incredible torso was on display for her to ogle. She again admired the tattoo running up his shoulder. The high of the orgasms he'd coaxed out of her may have been clouding her brain, but she was certain there was writing within the curves of the design. She was certain the tattoo was a replica of the painting she'd made him.

Claire walked to the French doors leading out to the deck and stared out at the pond that always seemed to calm her frazzled nerves. The tranquil familiarity of the water grounded her.

"Okay, the pizza should be here in a half hour," Austin announced.

She turned. He stood in front of the island. The tilt of his head and the crooked, boyish smile were just like his son's. Tears pooled in her eyes. Her brain and her emotions were a mess. She couldn't seem to bring herself under control. She was on overdrive, feeling anything and everything all at once. Overwhelmed wasn't a strong enough word to describe what she was feeling.

"You look just like Charlie when you do that," she said, trying to keep any emotion from showing in her voice.

"When I do what?" he asked.

"When you bend your head to the side and smile like you are."

The boyish smile turned roguish and predatory as he walked toward her. He reached for her waist, his fingers slipping but recovering quickly by pulling on her dress. He pulled the clingy pink fabric far enough away from her body that he got an eyeful of her breasts. His smile widened, and he trapped his bottom lip between his teeth. He brushed back her hair, again running his hands down her face, his fingers over her lips, watching her, absorbing every inch of her, and she did the same. She committed the arch of each eyebrow, the movement of his eyes as they roamed over her face, and the gentle slide of his hands over her arms to memory. She knew those gestures; she knew them well, had stored them deep in her mind for the occasional walk down memory lane. When she was alone, wondering about him, it was those very recollections that kept her heart beating for him. His face was harder, his features more defined, but he was still her Austin. He was her dream, her ideal, her love. He was her everything and anything, and he made her feel and want and hope.

She felt the tears again—there was nothing she could do that would stop them from surfacing. She leaned into him, sinking her face in his neck and holding him. That's all she wanted in that moment, to hold him and be held tight against him. His arms came around her, and for what seemed like an eternity, neither one of them spoke. His hands slid up and down her back, and Claire moved her fingers over his hard muscles. He knew her so well, she thought. He knew just when to give her a minute to breathe. He had always known to do that for her. They both looked up at the sound of Austin's cell phone.

He reached for it and shrugged apologetically. "I need to get this. It's my manager. It could be important—he never calls me when I'm off."

"The Imperial March?" she asked, referring to the ringtone.

261

"Although he rarely calls, he never has anything good to say when he does."

Without letting go of her, he answered. He kept her pressed against his chest. She could hear his heartbeat and his deep voice through his chest as he spoke.

"You're bugging me, Rick. This better be good...I'm good, you?" he asked, his hands drawing circles on her back. She could hear the other man clearly as he asked Austin if he was busy. "I'm just chillin'. Did you get my email?" he asked. Rick's next question drew a gasp from Claire. She lifted her head and attempted to move away, but Austin's grip on her waist kept her from doing so. She knew the question would come up, but she hadn't considered how someone questioning her son's paternity would make her feel. With his eyes locked on hers, he answered. "I don't need to, I'm sure. Don't ask me that again...I know you have my best interest in mind, and I appreciate it. But I'm positive we don't need proof."

Saved by the doorbell, Claire was relieved for the opportunity to step away. She reached for her purse. He placed his hand on her arm to stop her and handed her a fifty-dollar bill.

"That's all I have," he mouthed.

"Thanks."

She could hear him still talking. "We haven't signed a new contract, Rick...There's nothing to discuss. Besides, I was under the impression this would be me stepping completely off the grid for the summer. I need this time away, man. I have a ton of things to consider," he said, his tone becoming more

262

irritated as the conversation progressed. "When?" he asked, his tone harsh. "Change it to Tuesday. I need to be back by Thursday afternoon at the latest. My son has a game and I'm helping coach...baseball...Fuck you, Rick. Laugh all you want, but I need to be back by Thursday..."

He was going to leave. The fact that he'd insisted on being back by Charlie's game didn't register. He was leaving. Her hands began to shake, nearly dropping the pizza box as she walked back to the kitchen. Putting the pizza down, she never looked at him. Instead, she walked straight back out to the deck. The early evening air was humid, the wood wet from the storm that they'd completely blocked out as it passed. The willow at the edge of the water swayed, its long branches stroking the water bellow it. She concentrated on its movements, desperate to force down the fear of being left alone, of abandonment, of knowing that if it came down to it, Austin could very well choose his career over them. Although she'd forced him to make that choice before, she wouldn't be able to bear it a second time, and she wished with all her might that karma didn't come back and bite her in the ass.

What would she do about Charlie? If Austin left, he would be heartbroken. He'd waited so long to meet his father, had dreamed of the moment when the man whose pictures he stared at before bedtime would come to him. Her son's hopes were elevated to a point of no return. She knew that in his mind, his father was here to stay. That knowledge practically bowled her over. What had she done?

Every decision she had made before and after he was born would ultimately affect him. Austin wasn't going to be responsible for breaking his heart; she was. She heard the door open but didn't turn. Tears were streaming down her face uncontrollably.

"Claire," Austin whispered, his voice cautious.

She took a deep breath but was unable to keep her sobs from escaping when she spoke.

"You can't leave. If you go you'll break his heart. He thinks you're going to stay… forever. You can't leave, please don't leave. You can't hurt him. Hurt me, but not Charlie, I deserve it," she rambled.

"Babe, no, no. Please stop. Stop letting the guilt eat at you. I forgive you, Claire. Please don't think I would do anything to hurt you or Charlie. Not intentionally at least," he told her, practically on the verge of begging her to believe him. "Besides, I can't leave. Not after meeting Charlie and not after what we just shared. You and I…we're it, babe, always have been."

She turned then and nearly winced at the pained look on his face. Her son was her whole life. Charlie's pain would always be hers, and she would never be able to forgive herself for causing that.

"You have obligations…"

"That I'm trying to get out of. Look, the band hasn't signed anything yet. Without me, there's no Yellow Scarlet. I write the songs, most of the music. I made them," he said, tipping her face up so that her gaze met his. "Look at me, Claire. I have never been able to be without you. All these years, I've been merely existing, going through the motions and doing it all because it's what you wanted for me. I have always known that."

"How?"

"Because no girl breaks up with a guy and cries like the world is ending if she didn't love him."

"But Austin, the phone call…"

"We have a meeting with the record company on Tuesday. A few details need to be panned out. It's no secret we haven't been getting along. It's not a recent development. This unease within the group has been going on for years."

"You can't break up the band, Austin."

"You don't get it, do you?" he asked, both hands on her face, forcing her to keep her eyes on him. "I don't love the band. I love you. And this, right here, is where I want to be. It's where I've always wanted to be. You are my life, Claire, and now Charlie."

"I don't…" she started, her mouth opening and closing, choosing her words.

"What? Tell me," he said. Her eyes blurred as the tears continued to flow. "I need you to talk to me, Claire."

"I don't know what I'm supposed to feel. How much I need to feel."

"Feel everything, all of it, with me."

She could do that, so easily. He was the only person aside from her son who she would and could give herself to. But the

265

fear, it paralyzed her. Austin being back was just too good to be true. Nothing stayed this perfect, she was sure of it. Maybe the novelty of their reunion had more power over him than he thought. As she looked into his eyes, there was no way any of it was new. It was the same old feeling that had never left either one of them. When he declared his love to her, she believed him. How could she not when she felt the same?

"Okay," she whispered after a long silence because she wanted to feel it all, with him and only him.

"Thank you. I won't let you down, I promise."

"I'm going to hold you to that."

"I expect you to. Now come on. Let's go eat that pizza so I can take you to bed."

"We could eat it in bed," she said, dabbing at her eyes.

"Sounds awesome," he said, grabbing the pizza box and walking towards the stairs.

"I'll grab the beer."

He waited for her at the bottom of the stairs. Switching the pizza box to one hand, he smacked her ass and ran past her up the stairs. She couldn't help but laugh at his playfulness. He'd always managed to make her smile. Growing up, her sadness over always being left behind by her parents was forgotten the second she heard his voice.

She nearly dropped the beer bottles when she walked into her bedroom. Austin was lying in bed, the sheets covering him to the hips, the pizza next to him on the bed. He'd turned up her side of the bed, ready for her to slide in.

"You work fast. Comfy?"

"Not yet. Ever eaten in bed, naked?"

"Not in about six years…"

His smile faded instantly, his face serious. "Was that when…"

"Yes," she whispered. "We ran out of condoms and risked it."

"It does only take once," he said, smiling.

"Well, it was one of the times that night," she responded and shrugged.

They'd been desperate that night. The staff had gone. Since she was seventeen, she didn't need them around. She'd proved time and again that she was responsible enough to take care of herself. Getting pregnant was her first lapse, and she would never be sorry for that.

Putting the bottles down on the dresser, she lifted her dress up and over her head. With the confidence he always brought out in her, she walked to the bed and into his arms. Dinner would have to wait. She walked to his side of the bed.

"You need to eat. I don't want you getting sick on me."

"I'm okay, Austin. A few more minutes won't make a difference."

"I don't know how to say no to you."

"Then don't…"

Austin ran his hand up one of her legs, grabbing it and pulling her onto the bed. She kneeled, straddling his thighs. She watched his face, the way he bit his lip as he looked at her. His gaze traveled from the apex of her thighs to her face. Her eyes never wavered from his face as she reached for his shoulders and held on, preparing herself for his delicious assault on her body.

He kissed her. No, not just kissed her; he possessed her and every part of her with just that kiss. The combination of lips, tongue, and teeth gave way to pleading moans and blistering desire. The connection was there. The love, the past, the present, and the future all became one perfect mixture of who they were. He brushed back her hair, his kiss slowing without warning. His hands slid down her neck, to her shoulder, stopping in the valley between her breasts as he left a trail of kisses down her throat to the swell of her aching breasts, stopping to tease her nipples.

"I've always loved dessert," he said as he pushed her back to lie on the bed. He kissed her on his way down her belly, moving further down the bed, his shoulders parting her legs, opening her to his ministrations. "I missed this. I missed the taste, the feel." She shivered when she felt his warm breath on her.

She arched against him, the stubble on his face scraping against the sensitive skin of her inner thighs. She tunneled her fingers in his hair, holding, urging him as he nipped, sucked, and kissed her to the best fourth orgasm of her life—not that she was counting. Claire sunk back into the bed, beads of sweat gathering on her overheated skin. Her breath came in shallow gasps, and her body quivered as she came down from her release. He moved back up her body, reaching her lips and taking them in a kiss that bore into her essence.

"I'm ready for the main course now," he spoke against her lips.

"So am I," she told him, taking him in her hand and gripping him hard.

He hissed, putting his hand over hers to stop her from sliding it up his cock.

She bit her bottom lip, knowing that action drove him crazy. She knew his weaknesses, his faults, his strengths, and he loved that she did. She loved that despite his public persona, no one else knew the things about him she did.

"Easy, babe. I want to go slow this time. I want to savor you."

"You already savored me." She laughed, and he joined her.

"I did, but I've waited what seems like an eternity to be with you like this again. I really want to make love with you," he told her, his voice full of emotion, cracking as he said the last words.

She, on the other hand, was speechless. She knew that if she did try to say anything, nothing would come out clearly with the tears that clogged her throat. Several seconds later, she had to say what was on hr mind.

"When you say things like that...I..."

"What?"

"I wonder if I hadn't…"

"Don't," he said, sitting up and bringing her with him. "From now on, no more wondering, no more what ifs, okay?"

She nodded, the tears she failed to keep at bay trickling down the side of her face. Austin kissed them away, his fingers tracing their path as he raised her hips. He lowered her ever so slowly onto him. They moved in unison, face to face, making slow, sensual love.

Claire woke a while later, half draped over Austin, the blanket tangled around their bodies. She propped herself up with one elbow, resting her head on her hand as she watched him sleep. He seemed calm in sleep, peaceful, a slight smile on his luscious mouth. She shifted slightly, and he woke with a start, grabbing for her, panic on his face, his breathing heavy.

"Hey, you all right?" she asked.

"Yeah, I just…I felt you move. I thought…"

"I'm not going anywhere, Austin. I promise."

Claire grabbed the warm beer still sitting on the dresser and handed it to Austin in the hopes that a sip would calm him. She reached for hers, took a long, fortifying pull, and nearly dropped it as she moved to put it on the nightstand. Austin instinctively reached for it, and they both laughed as beer splashed over his arm. With a seductive smile, she brought his arm to her mouth and licked up the beer with her tongue. She loved beer. Her fridge was always stocked with it but never did she like it as much as she did in that moment. She reached for one of the bottles, straddled his lap, and let the amber liquid drip over his abs, gathering in each crease of his muscles. Bending forward, she licked every last drop of beer from his body. He sat up suddenly, startling her into laughter. His crooked smile did her in every time.

"Stop. We need to eat if you want to keep up this…this…" Words failed him.

"Game, lovefest, fuc…"

"Lovefest. Let's say lovefest," he said, cutting her off.

"The pizza is cold now."

"There's no way I'm leaving this room. So if you don't mind eating it cold, I don't."

"I'm not moving either." With her in his arms he stood, walked the short distance to the dresser, and retrieved their dinner.

CHAPTER TWENTY

Austin

"Do you and Charlie have passports?" asked Austin, catching Claire with a mouth full of pizza.

She nodded as she wiped her mouth. They'd settled comfortably on her bed to eat. She'd pulled up her white sheet to cover her breasts and tucked it under her arms to keep it in place. One slight tug and the thin fabric would fall away from her body. After what they'd just done, he'd found her attempt at modesty amusing. Still, he'd humored her by covering part of his groin. His right leg swung over the bed, his foot tapping away to a rhythm in his head as his muse eyed him warily.

"Yes. Why?" she asked as she chewed.

"I want the two of you to come with me to New York. I would love to show you where I live, and after what you said, I don't want Charlie thinking I'm leaving him. Besides, I don't think I can handle being away from either of you."

"People will see us."

"So."

"Are you ready to be outed as a father?"

"I sent an email to my manager, assistant, lawyer, publicists, and the band. They all know about you and Charlie. My lawyer and publicist are putting a statement together. I also advised that they not release your names. I'm afraid of the gong show this will cause. I don't think you're ready for that."

"Are you ready?"

"I've been part of it. But I need you two to be only mine for a while longer. I'm not ready to share you with the world."

He stared at her, hoping he was being clear. He hadn't been fucking around when he told her she was his everything—and Charlie was too. He was prepared to do whatever it took to keep them safe from the incessant paparazzi and overzealous fans.

"When will this statement be released?"

"When I give them the go-ahead. I need you to be prepared, Claire. The paparazzi are crazy. They will follow you everywhere, and your picture will be everywhere. Things will be written about you. It won't be easy."

"Will Charlie and I need protection?"

"I wouldn't rule it out if it means keeping you both safe."

Her life would change. Her privacy would be invaded, and he was scared shitless it would all be too much. After all the years he'd spent in the business, he still wasn't used to the attention from the media. He was prepared to face anything that was thrown at him, but he would never be able to stand it if the attention drove her away.

"I'm sure we'll be fine. You'll be with us through it all, right?"

"Of course. I've made lots of changes in the last few days. One of them is to my will," he informed her, watching for her reaction.

She looked up at him, her face neutral. "You added Charlie?"

"And you," he told her.

He had debated sharing that latest development with her until he was sure they could work things out. He figured they'd have to work out visitation times and such, and although he wanted things to progress between them as a couple, he hadn't expected it to happen this seamlessly.

"Me?" she asked, surprised by his admission. "Why? You don't need to do that."

"Sure I do. You're the mother of my child. If anything ever happened, I'd want you both taken care of. I need that peace of mind, Claire. I hope you don't mind."

"I don't. I just wasn't expecting that. I was fully expecting you to question whether Charlie is really your son, though."

"The only lie you've ever told me was that you didn't love me. Although, I had my doubts about that. But with Charlie, I knew the second he called me Daddy, the second I held him. I loved him instantly; everything in me told me he was mine. There was never a doubt," he said as he crawled from the foot

275

of the bed to where she sat crossed-legged against a small mountain of pillows. "Besides, he looks just like me."

"He does."

"Tell me about him. How was he as a baby?"

He took her plate and his and put it on the nightstand. Austin lay next her, waiting for her to recount every second of their son's life. Her face split into a huge, infectious smile. She looked up to the ceiling and let out a soft laugh. She turned on her belly, her arms wrapped around a pillow, and she started from the very beginning. How he moved all the time inside her, especially at night, making it difficult for her to sleep. She felt her skin stretch, and she couldn't get enough of his bumpy movements. Austin wished again he'd been able to see that, to feel it. He asked if she'd been sick, and was relieved to hear she hadn't. The thought of her being alone and pregnant was bad enough. He didn't think he would have been able to bear knowing she'd been sick too. She briefly touched on the twenty-seven-hour labor, saying only that it was hard and took days to recover from the sleepless night she spent suffering through the mind-blowing contractions. Although most of the time Charlie was a good baby, there were the odd times when he would cry nonstop. At her worst, she cried with him. That alone broke his heart, and he wished he'd fought for her. Had he come back just once during the first few months, he would have known she was pregnant.

"Can I ask you a question?"

"Of course."

"Why Ottawa?"

276

"It was far enough away and…" she trailed off.

"It's okay, I can take it," he reassured, wanting her to go on. Needing to hear this confession.

"It was the one place you wouldn't look for me. I moved there a month after you left. I planned letting you go for weeks, the move, everything. By the time I got to Ottawa, I had an apartment, a doctor, and I got a job at a local art gallery. I taught and painted." He hadn't expected her to open up like she had, and he was grateful. He had so many questions. "My parents didn't want me to leave. We argued about it, but I really wanted to be left alone." She looked up at him then. "There's a difference, you see, between wanting to be alone and feeling lonely. I needed time to think, to get my life together for the baby. Anyway, Alexa's mom had just died, and she needed them more than I did."

"So no one ever came to stay with you?"

"Alexa would come every weekend—she too needed to be left alone. We'd always been close, but over those years, we became sisters. She didn't approve of me keeping the pregnancy from you, by the way."

"I knew I liked her for a reason." He smiled. "What was his first word?" he asked, changing the subject.

She laughed then. "Every night I would show him a picture of you. I would repeat the word daddy and point at you. One night, I was rocking him to sleep, and he tilted his head back and pointed to the picture and called out daddy."

"No way!" he said, astounded.

Shit. He was going to cry. He felt his eyes fill with tears, and as much as he tried not to shed them, he couldn't contain his emotions.

"I'm not kidding. For the next twenty minutes as I rocked him to sleep, I cried."

He reached out and brushed a strand of her brown hair away from her face. He let his hand linger, wondering what that moment must have been like for her, to know that despite his absence, Charlie knew who he was. In fact, his son had always known who he was. It comforted him to know that she included him in his son's life.

"When did he take his first step?" he asked, wiping away his tears.

"He was ten months old. We were in my mom's backyard, and Sandy walked past us and he watched her intently. He had a death grip on my finger, and then all of a sudden, he let go. He followed the dog further into the yard, and that was the end of any control I would have over him."

"Your mom still has that dog?"

"Yes, but she's so old now. What else do you want to know?"

"Gosh, so much. I can't think of anything else right now."

"When are we leaving for New York?"

"Monday morning."

"We almost went a couple of years ago. One of my paintings was auctioned at a charity event I was invited to, and

I wanted to be there so badly."

He looked at her, shocked at the possibility that he could have seen her that night.

He'd gone at the urgency of his agent. The charity gala was for a children's hospital his record company supported, and various contracted artists had attended. When her painting went up, he couldn't hide his surprise. He remembered the tears that pooled in his eyes and the way his heartbeat picked up. One of her paintings was as good as having her back. The bidding went on for longer than he'd liked, but he didn't care how much he paid for it. He was determined to get that painting.

"Bid until we get it, no matter the cost," he'd told his assistant.

Fifteen thousand dollars later, he was the proud owner of a Claire Monroe original. He would have paid anything for a piece of her. He wondered what her reaction would be when she saw the painting over his mantel.

"Why didn't you go?"

"It was right around the time I ended up in the hospital," she said with a shrug.

"Do you know who bought it?"

"No, but I was told by my agent that the buyer was relentless. Paid a fortune for it, more than it was worth, that's for sure."

"Your work is beautiful. Don't underestimate your

talent."

He scooted down to lie on his side, and they stared at each other for an endless amount of time. She was so beautiful, her hair all mussed up, her cheeks flushed, and her eyes glowing. For the first time in days, he could see in those eyes that she was happy. He never wanted that glow to go away.

Austin closed his eyes. Taking in a deep breath, he succumbed to the exhaustion of the last couple of weeks—hell, the last few years. Every emotion, every sleepless night knowing she was down the hall was catching up to him— seeing her prance around in her tiny dresses, form-fitting jeans, and short shorts had been torture. Not all the cold showers in the world could have eased the hard-on he sported daily.

"I love you," he told her.

"I know," she said, and he knew without a doubt she did.

He leaned in and kissed her. He was gentle; he needed to be gentle.

"I'm so tired, Claire," he told her, his words holding more meaning than she could imagine.

He'd lived a hard life, a busy, nonstop life, and he knew it would someday catch up with him. But this was different. His exhaustion was emotional—the worst kind. Now, finally, he felt at peace and whole for the first time in years. Most of all, he was happy.

"Sleep, baby," she whispered to him.

He closed his eyes, clasping one of Claire's hands against his chest. He relished the feel of Claire combing her fingers through his hair, down the back of his head, to his neck, and to his shoulder. God, he loved her hands on him. He opened his eyes slightly, only to find he barely had the strength to keep them open anymore. He was vaguely aware of her finger tracing his tattoo.

"Is this the painting I gave you?"

"Yes."

"You still have it?"

"Yes." And others, he wanted to tell her.

He was certain she would see it—if she looked close enough, she would see it entwined in the curves and edges of the design he used to hide it. Her name.

"Is that my..." she began as she traced the letters with her finger.

"Yes," he managed.

"When did you get it?"

"Five years ago. Claire?"

"Yes"

"Please don't ever leave me again. Don't go anywhere," he mumbled.

"No other place I'd rather be."

"Promise?" he asked her, squeezing her hand tighter.

"I promise." He was in her bed, her scent surrounding

281

him. It was heaven. It was home, he thought, as sleep enveloped him.

CHAPTER
TWENTY-ONE

Claire

Claire jolted awake. She had tears on her face, and a light sheen of cold sweat coated her skin as she looked around furiously, panicked. Her breathing was heavy as she looked over at the pillow next to her. It was dented, an obvious sign someone had slept there. Where was he?

Deep in her unconscious mind, she remembered he was leaving. Sure, they'd decided she and Charlie would go with him, but the dream had been so vivid—he'd left without them, and waking alone only added to the unnecessary anxiety. Her heart hammered in her chest, so she lay back down, closing her eyes for a few seconds to try and calm her rattled brain.

Her mind slowly cleared. Her breathing got back to normal as her ears tuned in to the sounds drifting from downstairs. Music was playing, disrupted by the clinking of dishes and silverware. She took a deep breath, her nostrils filling with the scent of bacon—he was making breakfast. She looked around for her silk robe, a short nude piece of fabric she'd indulged in a year ago. She loved pretty things, lingerie being one of them. Tying the silk belt, she walked to the bathroom to take care of necessities before making her way down to the kitchen.

Austin was singing along to a popular hit that played at least a hundred times an hour. She was sick of it but found she didn't mind it so much when he sang it. It struck her in that instant that it had been a long time since she'd heard him sing. His back was to her as he stirred something in a pan, his muscles in his arm flexing with the movement. He was shirtless. His body was tanned, his back smooth, and his shoulders broad. She approached him slowly, snaking her arms around his waist.

"Good morning," she whispered against his neck.

She leaned her face against him, loving the feel of his smooth, warm skin. He turned, his arms coming around her shoulders.

"Good morning. Sleep well?"

"Hmm, better than well. It was the best sleep I've had in a really long time."

"Me too. The first full night's sleep I've had in years."

"Do you have trouble?"

He leaned in and whispered in her ear, "Not anymore."

She watched him for a few seconds—he looked more rested than when he first arrived. The dark circles under his eyes less pronounced. He also didn't look so stressed, she noticed. There'd been a lot of tension in the last two weeks.

He had been easily irritated—by her, anyway. His patience with Charlie had never wavered.

"Well, you look more relaxed," she pointed out.

"I feel like I'm on cloud nine. I have you, Charlie, our home...can I call this ours?" he asked, looking around the large kitchen.

"Yes, Austin, if you want it to be yours, you can."

"I want it like you wouldn't believe."

"It's ours."

Never since she left him did she think of how saying those words would feel. The weight of her secrets lifted with every second he was around. The weight of her guilt, however, would take time to alleviate. She'd hurt him after all, and she'd never been able to forgive herself for that.

"I love that," he said and framed her face with his hands, kissing her thoroughly. "Good morning."

"You already said that."

"But I didn't kiss you." He smiled a wide, genuinely happy smile.

She smiled back, her hands moving up and down his back—she couldn't get enough of him under her fingers. She moved away suddenly, startling Austin, who looked at her, a question in his expression. She sniffed the air and gasped as she realized something was burning.

"Our breakfast!" she yelled.

"Oh shit," Austin exclaimed and turned quickly to try and save their scrambled eggs.

He picked up the pan and turned to look at her. He looked down at the deep brown mush their eggs had become, not one bit of it salvageable. In fact, neither was the pan. They were lucky the thing didn't set fire. She walked back to the fridge and retrieved more eggs.

"Throw that out…the pan too. It's ruined," she told him.

He dutifully scraped as much as he could into the compost bin under the sink. She had yelled at him a few times about the amount of garbage he threw out when most of it was compostable or recyclable. It made her smile to see the small things he did to please her. She bent over to retrieve a new pan and heard an audible gasp from behind her.

"Jesus, Claire…" he whispered as she felt his hand on her exposed behind.

She stood up. His hand tightened on her ass while his free hand held her hips in place and moved her to face the counter. His lips were on her neck, his tongue snaking out to lick over every bump his touch resurrected. She bent her head to the side, giving him access to more of her. There were no words spoken. Gentle moans begging for more escaped from her. His breathing was harsh, demanding, wanting—a discussion only their bodies could relate to.

There was rustling of clothes, metal scraping against metal as he worked his zipper down, and at last she felt his shorts sliding down his legs against her skin. His hand slid to her front, testing her readiness. With fingers slicked with her

286

wetness, he grasped her chin, turning her mouth for the delicious invasion of his tongue. Foreplay be damned. He slid into her, moving slowly at first, but she had different ideas. She pushed back, urging him to take her harder. His groan was the only indication that he got her drift. She gripped the pan in one hand and held on to the counter for support with the other. Neither one of them spoke. With every thrust, he groaned. With every kiss to her neck, she gasped. When they both climaxed, it was silent. It was hot and so fast, and she loved every second of it.

Both their bodies quaked with the intensity of their release. If it wasn't for Austin's hand on her hips, she was sure her legs would've given out on her. She laid her face on the cold granite counter. Her robe had slipped to the side, exposing her breast, which now rested against the cold marble of the kitchen island. Her skin was scorching, the cold stone only minimally easing her heated skin. It was another hot day, and even that early in the morning, sweat trickled down between her breasts and back.

"Austin," she whispered.

"Just give me a minute," he told her, his voice hoarse with emotion.

He was still inside her, throbbing as she tried to catch her breath. It was so intense. He'd caught her off guard; she liked that about him—he always surprised her. However, his silence concerned her. The man who had always spoken his mind in the last few days remained quiet.

"Are you all right?" she asked, her face still pressed

287

against the counter, his face pressed against her back. She could feel his hot breath on her skin.

"In the last hours…every time I'm inside you, I wonder how I made it through the past few years without you. How I lived without feeling you, without kissing you, without you, period. I can't get enough, Claire. I honestly think I never will," he said, kissing the back of her neck as he spoke. He took a long, ragged breath and continued. "I know we're young still. I know that from the beginning everyone doubted what we felt for each other, but I feel like I've lived half a life with something always missing."

"Babe…" she whispered.

"Wait, let me finish," he rasped out. He pulled out of her slowly and she whimpered, feeling the emptiness all of sudden. He leaned heavily against her, his body heat comforting her as he chuckled softly at her reaction.

He slid his hand down her arm and reached for the pan she still held. "Look at me," he said as he turned her to face him. "What I feel for you is inexplicable. I could always find the words for the pain, but the love, the words for the love always eluded me. That love I have for you carries with it this need to show you. A need to take you, to feel you and make you feel everything that I am. You're the only one who can see, Claire. You're the only one who has ever been able to see me, see my truth. You're it, babe, you're everything to me, for me, and with me. Forever."

She reached up, brushed the hair away from his face, caressed it, and traced the creases that the emotion of his words had created. She loved this man, loved him more than she herself could ever express to him. His words had reached a place deep inside her, a place she'd closed off for so long. The day she let him go, he took with her the key to that place. The key to her heart, and most of all, the key to her soul.

"Well, I'd say you said that quite easily just now, my love."

"Everything is easier with you, Claire. Everything. Life, love—even the pain is more tolerable."

"No more pain, Austin. I can't stand it. But now that you've gotten that off your chest," she said in an effort to lighten the mood. "I'm starving."

"If you hadn't distracted me, we would've eaten by now," he said as he pinched her behind.

"My fault is it? If you could control yourself, we'd…"

"No," he said, interrupting her midsentence. "I can't, I won't. Not with you. I told you that."

He tidied himself, reached out for her and retied the belt of her robe. Claire watched his chest rising and falling as he still tried to catch his breath. She leaned into him and kissed him. He ran his hand down her face, the look in his eyes turning heated, so she turned him towards the stove.

Resuming his position and setting to the task of finishing their breakfast, she leaned against the kitchen island and watched him, a smile playing on his lips as he stirred quietly. She liked the idea of spending many more mornings like this with him. She loved the idea of waking next to him even more, so she brought up the fact that waking alone had bothered her.

"I'm sorry," he said. "I wanted to surprise you with breakfast in bed."

"I appreciate it, but I've woken alone more times than I care to think about. Don't ever   leave our bed before I wake up ever again."

"Noted," he said, smiling at her over his shoulder.

Claire gathered the silverware and plates Austin had set on the counter. She placed them next to each other on the patio table. She raised her face to the sun, already high in the sky. The air smelled of rain and the wood below her bare feet was still damp from the storms that passed through the night. They'd been exhausted and hadn't heard a thing.

Around the pond, canoers lingered on the shore, preparing to get their morning exercise. The trails were littered with joggers pounding the rough terrain, trying and sometimes failing to avoid the frantic cyclists. The mornings were peaceful near her home. Life had become easy to build a routine around busy schedules. Baseball, hiking, swimming— all things she and Charlie had fit in and some of which they did together. The simplicity worked for her, and she hoped more than anything that it would work for Austin. He seemed, she thought as she turned to look at him, to be quite comfortable in the domestic surroundings. Not only did he fit in perfectly, he also adapted to domesticity effortlessly. Would it have been that easy, that simple, had he stayed?

"Okay, all ready. Sorry it took so long. I know you're hungry."

"Well, it was my fault, as you said." She smiled at him mischievously, sat down, and seductively raised one leg to rest her foot on the chair.

"Don't," he told her, his own face transformed by a gorgeous smile. "I need to eat, babe. You're wearing me out."

She threw her head back and laughed. He could say what he wanted, but it was both their doing. They had years to make up for, after all.

"Come here," she said, patting the chair next to her. "Sit next to me and feed me."

He put down the tray on which he'd gathered their coffee, eggs, fruit, toast, and an assortment of spreads. He leaned down, his hand wrapping tightly around the nape of her neck, and kissed her. She loved the way he kissed her.

They ate in relative silence, sneaking glances at each other every few minutes. He fed her fruit, she buttered his toast—all wordless conversation she would cherish. She turned on her chair, her back to his front, and leaned on him as she wrapped her hands tightly around a cup of steaming coffee. Austin's hands ran up and down her arms, his callused fingers playing a silent tune on her skin.

"You know that swing I have on the porch?" she asked suddenly.

"The one that should be hanging, you mean?"

She laughed at his sarcasm. "Yeah. We had to take it down when we redid the porch. I want to hang it on the willow by the water."

"That would be a great spot. I'll help you. We can see about doing it sometime this week."

She stared at the tree. This would have some significance. Their first kiss was under a willow, their first date was a picnic under the same willow, and they were going to hang a swing on a new willow. Their very own willow.

"Are we making plans?" she asked.

"Yes, I suppose we are."

She turned enough to wrap her arms around his waist and closed her eyes.

"I love you," she told him.

"I love you…so much. Let's clean up here and go take a nap before Charlie gets home." He smacked her hip.

They worked quickly in unison as they washed and dried dishes. Once finished, they raced up to her bedroom and scrambled onto the bed. They were both exhausted. Not bothering to undress, they slipped under the blankets and fell asleep almost instantly in each other's arms.

CHAPTER
TWENTY-TWO

Austin

As Austin neared the house, he couldn't believe how hard and fast his heart beat with anticipation. In the past few days, his heart leaped every time when he was closer to seeing Claire. It didn't matter that he'd only seen her a half hour before.

He dropped Charlie off at his parents, at which point, his mom urged him to stay for a snack. He should have known better.

It was no secret she wanted them together. It was also no secret she wanted more grandchildren. There were no signs his sister Analia was even close to granting her another. He blamed the fresh scone and cream for his lapse in judgment. Although he gave her few clues as to their status, it was enough to give her hope. And when Marcia McKinley hoped, disappointing her was not an option. He prayed to God things worked, because if they didn't, he wouldn't see the end of his mother's wrath.

He smiled, thinking of when he'd opened his eyes to find

293

Claire wrapped around him that morning. He'd awakened with her legs tangled in his, her arms holding on tight, afraid he would disappear during the night. He'd kept his promise to never leave her to wake alone. After dressing and breakfast, they'd had little time together. He'd been on the phone all morning, setting up meetings. He planned to make the most of his trip to New York. There were some major kinks he had to work through if he wanted to be completely hers.

He took a deep breath, nervousness he couldn't explain enveloping him. He needed to see her, to ensure himself that all the progress they'd made in the last few days wasn't just in his head. He raised his hand to his chest and felt a sense of dread that came along with the feeling. Hell, he couldn't stand to be away from Claire for more than five seconds. He was obsessed, in love, completely fucking smitten. He parked the car and got out quickly, leaping onto the porch. Austin gripped the doorknob and was annoyed to realize the damned door was unlocked. He swore she did careless shit like that on purpose.

"Claire?" he called out.

The house was empty, silent. As much as he looked forward to time alone with Claire, Charlie's absence was noticeable, and he missed him. He'd grown incredibly attached to his son, couldn't fathom a life without him.

He understood that his reaction to Charlie was normal, the kind of reaction any father would have when meeting his son. He may not have changed his diapers, held him while he cried, or taught him the many things that up until now, Claire had a hand in. Things like riding a bike, throwing a ball—dad things that would have meant the world to Austin. He'd come to terms with all he'd missed. He was with him now, and he was going to try his damnedest to never disappoint him. Both Claire and Charlie completed him in every way. They were his home, they were his heart and soul, and he was going to do everything humanly possible to keep his home, heart, and soul intact.

"Claire?" he called again, looking up the stairs, assuming she was in her studio.

He walked up quietly, not wanting to disturb her if she was working. He wasn't sure he was going to let her work, however—he needed her. In that moment, he wanted nothing more than to hold her, to feel her and have her feel him. He knew without entering the studio that she wasn't in there. Every time she worked, there was this energy he couldn't explain when she was engrossed in her art. On the easel sat a finished painting. From the paint smell in the room, he knew she'd finished it not too long ago. Its vibrancy was stunning. Blues, browns, light greens, and dark mossy greens depicted the pond and the weeping willow she'd inserted into the canvas with magnificent detail—its branches brushing the water at the edge where its roots were buried. He walked to the window and looked at her subject—the aging willow was something she'd been obsessed with for days. He couldn't pinpoint exactly what the allure was. Within its long branches, he saw movement.

"What the hell?" he whispered to himself as he watched Claire step from the curtain of green.

She walked to the shed, only to walk out seconds later with a ladder. He wondered once more what in hell she was doing. She wasn't dressed to be climbing anything. The long green, blue, and white striped dress she wore wasn't what he would call gardening attire. He turned from the window and hastily made his way down to the backyard.

"What the hell are you doing, Claire?" he asked from the bottom of the ladder.

"Oh, Jesus. Don't sneak up on me like that. I could have fallen."

"You might have fallen without my assistance. Get down."

"Just a second, I need to weave these ropes over this branch."

Austin let out and exasperated sigh. "For what?"

"For the swing," said Claire, as if he should know just what the damned ropes were for and what swing she was referring to.

He looked around to see the porch swing lying on its side next to the tree. He looked up at her once more. That love he felt for her was quickly turning into anger. Not for her as much as for himself. For giving her years to decide she didn't need assistance in anything she put her mind to.

"You dragged the swing all the way down here? I was only gone for a half hour. You couldn't have waited for me?"

"What for?" she asked, the nonchalance in her tone

annoying him further.

"Get down, Claire. Now!" he said, his tone giving no reason for her to think he wouldn't climb that ladder and drag her down.

"Geesh, calm down. No need to get all pissy on me."

"I'm here now, you know. You could ask for help. It drives me crazy to know you're used to doing things for yourself. I won't allow for you to do something as stupid as climb a twelve-foot ladder on unsteady ground. And in a dress...that specific dress no less," he said, pointing up to her.

"What's wrong with my dress?"

"Really? You're asking me that?"

"Yeah I am. I happen to love this dress."

"The dress looks fantastic. It's what you're wearing it for that's bothering me."

"Maybe I knew you'd come along sooner or later and..." she began, halting her words with a mischievous smirk on her face.

"Get down here. Now."

She laughed as she carefully made her way down the ladder. He watched as she hiked up the fabric around her thighs, giving him a good glimpse of her toned legs. He was certain she'd purposely given him a quick flash of the silky skin of her ass. He felt his cock stir at the thought of removing her underwear and getting a full view.

"There, on solid ground. Happy?" she said as she swung

her arms around his neck.

"Yes, very."

"Charlie was okay when you left him?"

"Yes. My parents are dropping him off later."

"So we've got, what, four hours to kill?"

"Yep," Austin nodded, his annoyance forgotten the instant her arms came around him, unable to keep the amusement from his face. "Shouldn't you be packing, not hanging porch swings on trees?"

"All packed and ready."

"Yeah?"

"Yeah," she repeated.

"Then let's kill some time."

"Let's," she whispered, reaching for his head and pulling his face toward her for a kiss she took no time in deepening.

He pulled away from her, let out his breath, but couldn't convey the exasperation he felt at seeing her up on that damned ladder—not after that damn kiss, anyway. God, what if she'd fallen? He shivered at the thought of something happening to her. He pulled her to him, his lips crashing with fierce feeling against hers, terrified for the first time in a long time of fucking up and losing the two people that had come to mean the world to him. It had only been a short time, but the love he felt for them was like no other, and he knew with immense certainty that he would never love another the way he loved Claire. He let his hand roam down and around her body, feeling and

298

grabbing her ass, pulling her towards him. The gasp she let out against his lips was what he lived for. That he did this to her, made her feel like just touching wasn't enough, was his fucking undoing. He felt the lines of the poor excuse for panties she wore, the fabric barely covering her firm, round ass. He turned her, walking her backward toward the thick trunk of the massive willow and began to pull up her dress.

He ran his hand up her leg, exploring the defined curves of her calves. He grasped the crook behind her knee, pulling her center even closer to him.

"Jesus, Claire. You're so soft, so warm. Just thinking of the feel of you in my hands drives me crazy."

"I like you crazy."

"I'll never be able to contain myself around you. It's never enough," he admitted.

Her head tilted back. "Austin…"

"Hmm," was all he could manage as his mouth busied itself at the base of her neck.

"Hurry…"

"Not out here," he whispered into her shoulder.

He lifted his eyes to the shore of the large pond, noticed the branches of the tree reached the water, giving them some privacy. The thought that there could be a photographer lurking in the woods on the other side of the pond sickened him. It wouldn't be the first time it happened to him, but not with Claire. No, he wouldn't let that happen ever. He'd taken great lengths to ensure his stay in Springridge was kept secret. He lifted his head and looked around anyway; he liked to think he could spot those giant lenses a mile away. It was a scary thought to have to even think of that sort of violation. Paranoia struck him all of a sudden, and he pulled away abruptly.

"What is it?" asked Claire.

"Let's go inside," he told her.

"I think we'll be okay."

"Maybe, but I don't want to risk it. Not with you." She raised a brow, a question in her expressive eyes. "I mean...damn it. I've had pictures taken of me from miles away. I know what that invasion feels like. I don't want you to experience that sort of exposure. "

He saw the disappointment on her face. He felt her pull away then, wrapping her hands around his wrists and pushing his hands away. He hated upsetting her. He hated reminding her that the years spent apart had rendered them completely different experiences. The thought that she might've walked past a magazine stand and seen the paparazzi shots of him and a well-known British actress frolicking naked on a supposed private beach pissed him off. The damned pictures were taken from a boat miles away. Even if they'd concentrated on the open ocean, they wouldn't have spotted the intruder floating, clicking away at his money shot. It'd been embarrassing, for both him and Kayla. He'd cared about her, had made a significant effort to make the relationship work. That trip had been planned with the intention of salvaging a union that had little hope to begin with.

He looked at Claire in panic as she bent down to gather her tools. There was no hope for him and Kayla. No matter how much he tried, the situation and the effort was hopeless. His heart wasn't in it because his heart was right in front of him—it had always belonged to Claire.

"I'm sorry, I just…please, Claire. Don't be angry with me."

"I'm not angry with you. Don't you see?" she asked. "I look at you, Austin, and I don't see the man most times. I don't see the rock star. Every time you smile, I see the boy I fell in love with when I was fourteen. I missed him, I miss him now. I know I tore us apart, but I can't help wanting back some of that normalcy. I want to sneak off and make love on your bike. Remember those times?"

He nodded. He remembered every single second he spent with her. He remembered every place, every detail, and every fucking noise she made. He looked around once more. He wanted to give her a little bit of normal. He wanted to give her the world. In that moment, he realized he wouldn't stop until he handed it to her on a silver platter. He reached out for her, wrapping his hand around the nape of her neck, pulling her towards him, crashing his mouth to hers. Her response was instant, insanely hot, and so damned delicious.

He walked her back once more, pressing her against the tree. She lifted her leg, wrapping it around his, and he fucking lost it. Their hands tangled in the fabric of her long dress as they both started to pull it up. Her hands reached for his shorts, fumbling as she desperately tried to unbutton and unzip. They laughed against each other's mouths. Austin reached for her hand and pushed it out of the way in order to finish undoing his shorts just enough to free himself.

"Hurry," she repeated.

"Fuck," he groaned, pausing to lean his forehead against her shoulder to catch his breath.

He tried to push away the doubt of the idea of taking her out in the open—in the middle of the day, no less. Although control was something he had no concept of when he was around her, he had more to think about than what would certainly be a very satisfying quickie. She'd put some sort of fucking spell on him, he thought as he continued to breathe against her shoulder. Her hand was comforting as she caressed the back of his neck. He felt her fingers gently massage his suddenly tense muscles, and memories swarmed him. Her scent had always been the same, her hair always long, and he remembered with such clarity the time she walked through the door of Springridge District High looking every bit the woman.

The tomboy he'd fallen for had disappeared overnight. Waves of chestnut hair tumbled over tanned shoulders, and the white dress with red flowers he once wrote a song about swayed along with her as she walked towards him. She was athletic—slim, but not skinny. And until that day, he'd never seen her in a dress.

"Hi, baby," she said, and for the first time in his life, he was speechless.

If he hadn't already been in love with her, he would have

fallen then. Instead, he fell further, and he knew, even at sixteen, that he would never love another. Without speaking, he grabbed her hand, dragging her through the halls past their peers. He turned several corners before stopping in front of a utility closet door. He then pulled her in it. Austin closed the door behind them, turned her, pushed her against the door, and kissed her like his fucking life depended on it.

"When the time comes," he whispered against her lips, "I'm gonna fuck you in this dress." His hands kneaded her round, heavy breasts. He didn't have time to think about the words that he'd blurted. He just needed to tell her how much he wanted her.

"Now, Austin. Do it now," she begged.

"No way, babe, not here. I'll find us a place. Right now I just needed to kiss you in this dress." He smirked and kissed her once more before he reached for her hand and walked back out into the hall.

He let out the breath he hadn't realized he'd been holding as the slide show of memories engulfed him. He gripped her hips, trying to control the flood of emotions the memory of that day brought forth. He wanted to cry. He loved her so much, even then.

"Hey, you okay?" she asked, kissing his temple.

"Yeah. I was just remembering the first time I kissed you like this."

"The utility room…"

"Yeah…"

"We'd done a lot of hot things by then, but that was the hottest thing you'd ever done."

"Seeing you in that dress did it for me. You'd never worn one before that day."

She laughed. "That, and it was the key to getting you to finally take the next step. Right now, though, I need you to take the final step to this little encounter."

In answer to her comment, Austin gripped her panties, gave a rough tug, and ripped them off her. Claire let out a small grunt but smiled.

"Sorry." He laughed, putting the mangled piece of fabric in his pocket.

"It's fine, just..."

He grabbed her legs, lifting her completely off the ground, and slid inside her effortlessly, not letting her finish whatever she was going to say. Heaven. Her moans, her movements, her kisses, her urgency, all fucking heaven. She gripped his hair at the nape of his neck, holding on, pulling herself closer. She knew what drove him to the brink, and she dragged him right along with her, always had. He met her thrust for thrust, gasp for gasp, feeling her tighten around him as her body pleaded for release. Austin gripped her ass with one hand, afraid he'd lose his balance. He leaned his other hand against the tree. Breathing hard, letting her lead as he buried his face once again in her neck, and bringing them both to completion. He would never, could never get enough of her—this wanting was like an addiction. Coming down from his orgasm was as disappointing as coming down from any high.

With weak legs, he pulled out of her. His lips traced the trail of sweat down her neck. She smelled fantastic—coconut and sex were quickly becoming his favorite scent. They briefly pulled apart, straightening their clothes. He watched her for any signs of discomfort. Instead, he was dumbfounded by the smile that transformed her beautiful face. She let out her breath through grinning lips and looked up at him bashfully. She reached out her hand and caressed his face gently. He then reached out for her hand, needing to feel her. He pulled her down to sit with him on the ground. He sat against the tree and Claire naturally lay down with her head on his thighs. He ran his hands through her hair, brushing the strands that stuck to her temple.

"Are you okay?" he asked as he stared down at her.

"Hmm, fantastic. Why do you ask?"

"I've been taking you so roughly. I wonder sometimes if maybe...I don't want to hurt you."

"You didn't hurt me, Austin. You never do."

"You'd tell if I did, right?"

"Of course. But if you feel so bad about the way you just took me, you can make it up to me later and make love to me slow and sweet," she said, laughing.

"I might just do that. I want to always be gentle with you, but you drive me crazy, Claire. I can't seem to control myself."

"Don't ever control yourself with me. Even when you take me like you just did, you're not...well, it's...I don't feel like you're taking advantage. I feel loved, I feel cherished, and

I feel needed."

"And I need you so bad, Claire." hHs voice caught on his words.

"Oh, Austin," she said, raising her head from his lap. "You'll never have to find out what it's like to never be without me. Besides, I don't think I could survive it."

"I'm gonna hold you to that."

"I expect you to," she said, smiling up at him.

Once again the force of his love for her felt like his heart would burst. He continued to run his fingers through her hair. Her eyes closed, and within minutes, there was no doubt she'd fallen asleep. The day was hot, but the branches of the massive willow blocked out the sun, the shade cooling them down significantly. He thought briefly of closing his own eyes, but he couldn't bring himself to stop looking at her. The way her chest rose and fell with each relaxed breath, the faint smile that formed on her lips. In the time he sat with her head on his lap, he thought of the decisions he'd have to make.

He wanted to give her normal—he wanted to give her the chance at a family. A stable environment for their son and any other children they may have together to grow up in. He didn't want them subjected to the circus his life had become in the last few years. He didn't want that anymore, and the more time he spent with Claire and his son, the more he felt the decisions taking root in his head. His future was no longer his job, his future was his family—his son and his future wife (there was absolutely no doubt he would make her his wife). He smiled at that thought. The idea of seeing her walking towards him in a white dress brought a pang to his heart and tears to his eyes.

In hindsight, that's all he'd ever wanted. Not just any wife, but Claire. She had the power to break him like no other, and he could either fear that realization or make it so he'd never have to know what being broken by Claire Monroe felt like ever again. He'd been leaning against the tree, the trunk digging into his back. He tried to move to a more comfortable position and felt his body protest. Their activities, as well as the fight with John, were taking a toll on his body. He maneuvered them so he could get his hands beneath her. Despite his aching muscles, he lifted her off the hard ground. Careful not to trip on her toolbox and ropes she'd brought down to the shore for her project, he walked with her in his arms towards the house. Inside, he put her down on the sofa, reached for a blanket, and lay next to her.

CHAPTER
TWENTY-THREE

Claire

Her body felt heavy. She'd had the craziest dream. She reached down and felt her flat belly and was disappointed to realize that no matter how vivid the picture her subconscious painted, it had only been a dream. She turned her head, listening to the sounds of her son's happy, giggling screams out in the yard.

"Hey, you're awake."

She looked up to see Austin leaning over the couch. "How long was I asleep?"

"Just over three hours. You must have been exhausted."

"I've been kept up late these past few days…"

"I can't say I'm sorry." Austin smirked.

"Neither am I."

He leaned down closer to her, framed her face in one of his large hands, and kissed her. She couldn't complain about waking to that every day. If he's not careful, she thought, he might just spoil her.

"Who's Charlie with?" she asked.

"Your dad. He's teaching Charlie how to kick a soccer ball. Says the boy should be interested in more than one sport," he said with a hint of annoyance.

"You aren't joining in the teachings?"

"I was, but I came in to check on you. You've been asleep for quite some time. I was worried. You feel okay?"

"I'm fine, but I had the weirdest dream."

"Want to talk about it?"

"I dreamed I was pregnant," she told him and watched for his reaction.

"You think you…you might be?" he stammered.

"No."

"Well, I wouldn't mind if you were. We could try. You can get off the pill and…"

"Making plans, are you?"

"Tons of plans, baby. I want our family to grow. Think of all the fun we'll have making the perfect baby."

"I love you, Austin, but we already made the perfect baby…"

"Yes, we did."

She smirked at him. "So you came up here to get away from my dad?"

He shook his head. Austin had made no secret of the fact that he had little respect for Bruce Monroe. He resented him for the way he'd treated his children—abandoning Claire and Hunter when they most needed their parents. Although Bruce had expressed his regrets over his choices to his children in the past few years, and now most recently to Austin, he was still a little wary of Bruce. Claire knew he only put up with her father for hers and Charlie's sake. She hoped in the future the two men would be friends.

Claire did what she could to keep the peace, but she'd lived in relative calm and didn't have the energy to deal with any of it. She knew that what irritated him the most was that since Austin had been back, he really had nothing bad to say about her father. The man was the perfect, doting grandpa. He enjoyed every second he spent with Charlie, and not because he wanted to make up for past mistakes. He genuinely enjoyed being with him. Her father had changed a thousand percent. Charlie, of course, had a lot to do with that change. Alexa losing her mother and the trust Stephanie had put in them to care for her daughter had made a significant impact on both her parents. The turnaround had practically happened overnight.

Their lives changed that summer in more ways than they could have ever imagined. While Stephanie was losing her life, one was growing strong in her womb. It's a wonder sometimes that Claire even made it through that year unscathed. Her heart, of course, had been shattered, but she'd done that to herself. To think that at the time she felt letting Austin go was the right thing to do was mind-boggling to her now. How the hell had she managed without him? Her son gave her unconditional love and reason, but Austin gave her life, energy, safety, and the happiness she'd only ever experienced with him.

Still on the couch, Austin had come around to sit at her feet, lifting them onto his lap. She was so lost in thought she hadn't realized he'd moved until she felt his finger skim the bottom of her feet. She was incredibly ticklish there, and her foot flinched. His hands ran up her leg; she knew he wasn't trying to seduce her, but it didn't matter how he touched her, he had her wanting more. Always more.

"You sure you're okay?" he asked, the concern in his voice unwarranted.

"I'm fine. I promise."

"Your dad wants to take us out to dinner." The lack of enthusiasm made her laugh.

"Where to?"

"Charlie wants to go to that gourmet burger place on Main Street."

"Of course he does. Why even bother asking him," she said. "I love you for putting up with me and my crazy family. I know spending time with my parents isn't on your favorites list, but I appreciate it."

"Only for you do I put up with this much," he said, smiling at her in the way that let her know he was teasing.

His mouth curved up in a crooked tilt, the mischievous

312

glint in his eyes wasn't lost on her. It had taken two weeks to experience the peace they now felt. There was no other direction to go but forward. The past was a not so distant memory, their love enduring, and their friendship the most important aspect of their lives. She sat up abruptly and crawled to straddle his lap. As if she hadn't done it in days, she kissed him deeply, passionately, overlooking for just a few seconds the fact that her son and father were a few feet away in the backyard.

"Babe," he whispered, his plea ragged against her lips.

She ignored his protest, quieting him with her mouth. The need to feel him in that moment had trumped all reason. She loved him; she loved him more than she could ever express to him. He and Charlie were everything. She smiled against his lips at the knowledge that they could start to plan their future. Marriage, more kids, and the dog he so badly wanted for Charlie. They could have it all—together.

"Maybe if you stopped ravishing my daughter, she wouldn't be so exhausted," Bruce accused from the doorway to the deck.

"Dad!" shrieked Claire, making no attempt to move from her position on Austin's lap.

"Why are you ravishing Mom?" asked Charlie.

"Oh God," she groaned.

"Because I love her, and when a boy loves a girl, he ravishes her…"

"Austin!" she said, smacking him on the shoulder. "You

313

can't say things like that to him."

"Sure I can. He needs to know because there's going to be a lot more ravishing going on around here."

"All right," Bruce said. "Sorry I brought it up. You two ready to go?"

"I just need to change," she told him.

"You look fine, sweetheart," he told his daughter.

"Yeah, sweetheart, you look ravishing," mocked Austin.

"Stop it. Charlie, come on. Let's at least change your shirt and try to tame that hair."

She slipped off Austin's lap, righted her dress, and reached for her son. Together they ran up the stairs, a race to the second floor she always let him win.

The restaurant was dim, the exposed brick walls and makeshift electricity poles giving the impression you were eating dinner in a city alley. Claire was not at all surprised Austin had enjoyed himself, laughing with their son and her father. They'd spent almost two hours devouring burgers and fries, and consuming massive milkshakes she had no desire to try. She stuck to her normal pint of beer. Austin and her father were having an amicable conversation about motorcycles. She only interrupted briefly when Austin had mentioned he wanted to sell the bike that to her, held so many memories.

"You can't sell that bike. I love that bike," she said.

"I have no real use for it anymore. I can't very well put my family on it. I need to get rid of it."

"We can ride it on weekends, and in the summer. I love that bike," she repeated.

Austin simply nodded, and she abandoned the discussion when Charlie pulled on her hand to accompany him to relieve himself.

Tucked into a small booth in a far corner of the restaurant, they didn't realize when Claire was approaching the table after the potty break. She noticed Austin and her father's conversation had changed significantly. She didn't want to eavesdrop, didn't want to know what topic had gotten the men so serious and speaking in low voices.

"You'll take care of them?" asked her father.

"Of course I will."

"Love her, Austin. Love her with all your heart. Charlie too. Be the father he deserves, the father I never was."

"You don't have to say anything, Bruce. I'll take care of them, always."

"I don't want her..." he began but stopped the second he saw her.

Austin shifted in his seat, visibly uncomfortable. She could tell from looking at him that he was hiding something. Her father stared at her, gauging her reaction. She'd overheard part of an intense discussion. Isn't this what she wanted—for the two men in her life to be civilized, to be friends? But curiosity got the better of her; the topic they'd been discussing wasn't about riding motorcycles. That much she knew.

"What's going on?" she couldn't help but ask.

"Nothing," Austin answered, all of a sudden concentrating on playing around with his fries.

"Are you sure?"

"Of course, sweetheart. Austin and I were discussing your trip to New York," said her father.

She looked from her father to her boyfriend, who had still yet to look at her. Lying bastard. For now she would let whatever it was they were talking about slide. Soon, though, she'd get it out of him. They'd promised each other honesty, no lies. She wouldn't stand for it.

The walk home was a quiet one. Aside from a smile and "hmm" of acknowledgement to something Charlie said, she and Austin didn't say one word to each other. Her father had hugged her good-bye outside the restaurant where he'd parked the car. He made a big deal of her mom waiting for him at home. Something was definitely wrong. Her father had never been one to give explanations, not when they were kids, and not now—that's one of the things that hadn't changed about him.

At the house, there was more silence. Claire untied Charlie's running shoes and instructed him to head up to the bathroom for a shower. She walked to the coat closet, deposited their shoes, and walked barefoot back towards the stairs to follow her son. Austin hadn't moved from the entryway. He simply watched her, his eyes following her every move.

"Hey," he said, reaching out to grab her arm. "We okay?"

"Whatever it is between you and my father is fine with me," she stated. "I like to think that if your discussion affected me and Charlie, you'd let me know."

"Of course I would."

"Okay," was all she said before sliding her arm out of his light grip and walking up the stairs.

She knew she'd put him in a rough spot. The last thing she wanted was to be kept in the dark. Things were great between them, better than she'd first thought. What scared her most was that whatever he and her father had been discussing would change everything. Ignorance sometimes truly was bliss. She'd heard the resigned rush of air that traveled past his lips. He knew that she was aware he was keeping something from her. Perhaps his fear was the same as hers. If he told her, everything would change...

CHAPTER TWENTY-FOUR

Austin

He lay awake most of the night. For the first time in the last four days, Claire had gone to bed without him. After she'd gotten Charlie ready for bed, she hadn't come back down. He listened for signs she might awake next to him, but all he heard was the soft, relaxed sound of her breathing. The space between them in the king-size bed was maybe a couple of feet, but it seemed like miles. He felt desperate, helpless, and he couldn't stand it. He reached for his phone to check the time; it was 5:00 a.m. He noticed several missed calls and messages. Both voice and texts. All from Rick, who was probably wondering if he was going to make the meeting the next day. Although he'd made plans to travel with his family, he'd never confirmed. He could picture the guy panicking, his blood pressure rising to dangerous levels. The man really needed a vacation, and maybe after this gathering, he would get just that.

Austin shut his eyes tight at the thought that he would have to deal with his manager and band on an hour of sleep. He realized then that he didn't want to leave the sanctuary

319

Springridge had become—it provided the security and privacy he'd craved for years. Did no one think to look for him there? The whole town knew he was home; someone must have tipped off the press. Or, he thought, these people were very protective of their own. He liked that idea. That he could walk down the street and no one would look twice. In the weeks he'd been home, only a handful of people had stopped him for pictures and an autograph. There were no out-of-towners hanging around for a glimpse, which further cemented the fact that Springridge was quite possibly a safe haven for him.

He couldn't lose what he'd found there. He couldn't get on a plane and wonder if what he and Claire had shared was just passing the time. No, there was no way. Not the way she looked at him. Not the way she made love with him. The way they'd become a family, the closeness he felt with her and Charlie. No, he wouldn't lose that. He knew what being without her felt like—he had no desire to feel that empty ever again. He needed to feel her, to feel the newfound connection. It wasn't just about sex; it had never been about that between them. From the second he'd realized he loved her and that she loved him, the connection had been deeper. All consuming.

He turned to reach for her, noticing that aside from sleeping with her back to him, she had also worn a tank top to bed. They'd been sleeping nude, wrapped in each other. They'd held on, breathed each other's air, and fell asleep to the rhythm of each other's heartbeats. Of course his boxers and her robe were always nearby in the event that Charlie walked in the room—which happened often. He loved his son, but the kid had terrible timing.

He turned onto his back, let out his breath, and wondered once again if telling her what her father had told him would make it all better. He put his arm over his eyes, trying to reign in his own frustration at being put in a position that, no matter the consequences, would hurt her.

Austin couldn't help but resent her father just a little more than normal. The man had an impeccable way of delivering news and putting him in a position where he had to keep things from Claire. They'd kept enough shit from each other already. Austin didn't need to add to that pile.

With his free arm, he once again reached for her, startled to find bare skin below the hem of her shirt. He sat up, pulled the blankets away from her, watching his hand travel up and down her naked hip. He bit his lip and shook his head as the realization that she'd been fucking torturing him dawned on him.

"You're evil," he whispered in her ear.

"And you took your sweet time."

He laughed then, his relief clear. Damn, he loved her.

"I'm sorry," he told her.

"I know. My father has a way of putting people in awkward positions. I'm sorry you had to be a casualty."

"I don't know if I can keep my promise I made him not to tell you."

"Is he going to tell me?"

"Yes, after we get back. He didn't want to ruin our trip."

"Then I'll wait."

"Babe…"

"No, Austin. I don't want anything to ruin this trip either. This trip is huge for us as a family. I know it's an awful thing to say because he's my father. But I can't worry about him. I need to concentrate on us."

"I'm glad you feel that way, but this is big, Claire," he said, feeling the weight of her father's revelation, fearing the distance that it could create between him and Claire.

"My whole life I've felt like I've been in search of more. I found more the day I found you, Austin. Although things are good with my parents now, more was not something they'd given Hunter and me. Our whole lives were spent trying to make them notice us. It was hardest on Hunter. He needed his father, needed that male influence and role model. He rarely comes around anymore. I worry about him. When he does come home, he stays with me—the only reason he didn't this time is because you were here."

"He never visits with your parents?"

"He does, but his limit is a couple of hours. They can't seem to make amends with him."

"Your parents fucked up, babe."

"They know that and I know that, but I blame myself for his distance. When I broke…well, when I let you go, I didn't think of him. I took away his one role model. You weren't the only one that was angry with me…"

322

"I didn't know."

"We worked it out; he understood my reasons. Didn't agree with them, but he stood by me. We still felt we only had each other, even though our parents were on their way back, so to speak."

He just stared at her, wondering why he hadn't listened to his instincts and stayed. He could have been there for her, for Hunter. She'd been pushing for him to make a significant effort with Bruce for weeks, and yet she still held some resentment. How alone had she felt? He closed his eyes and rubbed his hand down his face in frustration. Her stubbornness had been a turn-on at times, but it had also been his biggest rival.

"You and Bruce seem close, though. I've seen the two of you together. He loves you."

"It took a long time to get where we are. In the end, it was him making the effort, not me. I'm just now getting what I'd wanted so badly as a little girl. I have my parents back, but something in me is always waiting for the rug to be pulled out from under me."

"I'll take care of you, Claire. You've spent enough time looking out for yourself. I'm here now," he said and bent down to kiss her. "You don't have to do things alone."

"Why don't you start with taking care of me right now," she smiled up at him.

"You need taking care of?" he teased.

"Yes. Right now, right here," she said, pulling his hand

towards her.

"Let me see what I can do."

He crawled over her at the same time she reached for him.

She moved slightly up to meet him, and he sucked in his breath as the head of his cock met her entrance. He needed her like he needed to breathe in that moment, and he had to fight for control not to drive into her. This was different. Every single time was different and meant more. One inch at a time he slid into her, and her legs came around his hips, lifting herself off the bed, urging him, taking him deeper.

"Ahh." She sighed as Austin began to slowly move in and out of her.

He couldn't take his eyes off her—he never thought he would find his way back to her again. Never imagined in the time they'd been apart that he could feel this much love still. She had his soul, had guarded and kept it safe all that time. He thrust into her, softly at first, until he felt her body tighten around him. He wanted to go slow, but she had different ideas as she tightened her legs around his hips, pulling him towards hers. He could never last with her, and he felt himself go under, the current dragging her with him as the pleasure shuddered through them.

Their bodies shook in the aftermath, and she continued to grind against him, chasing her release. He felt her tighten around him and felt himself getting hard again. He let go then, buried himself in her and pulled out, quickly pushing back into her again and again. She met him thrust for slow, sensuous thrust. She came fast and hard, clenching around him, and with

324

her head thrown back, milked him for all he was worth.

Austin knew he was crushing her, knew he should get his hands under him and pull himself from her body, but damned if he could get his body to comply. As if sensing his little turmoil, she wrapped her legs and arms around him, holding him to her. Her soft, warm curves were everything he'd missed when he wasn't in her arms. He smiled against her neck—he was still lodged inside her warmth. Just as he'd made the decision to move, they heard footsteps down the hall seconds before their bedroom door flew open.

"I can't believe you two are still in bed. Let's go. We need to get to the airport and I need breakfast."

Claire growled against his chest, and he couldn't help the laugh that escaped. He tried to move away from her, but once again she held him to her—her legs a vice around his thighs.

"Babe..." he whispered, thankful they had the covers over them.

"Give us a minute, Charlie," she said as her hips continued to move.

He lifted his head and looked at her, shocked that she was still seeking release. The insatiability wasn't a surprise. Hell, half the time he was right there with her. But he was only human, for fuck's sake, and he'd just had the most explosive orgasm of his life. He needed a break, his dick needed a break, not to mention the fact that their son was in the room. Austin looked over his shoulder to make sure the covers hadn't slipped off them.

"No way," said Charlie. "If I leave, you two will go back to sleep and I don't want to miss our flight."

"We won't, buddy. It's a private jet, they'll wait for…" He stopped midsentence on a grunt, took a breath, and looked down at Claire. He whispered, "You need to stop that. Now."

"You're no fun," she complained.

"We just had our fun, baby…" He winced as he pulled out of her.

"Okay, Charlie. Give me a few minutes to get dressed and I'll come down to get your breakfast," she said to her son, smiling as he came to her with open arms.

"I can't wait to see Daddy's other house," he said in what Austin was certain was supposed to be a whisper.

"Come on, buddy. Let's get breakfast while Mommy gets dressed," he said as he pulled on a pair of sweat pants. He looked around for his shirt. Once he found it, he grabbed his son by the arms, flipping him over his shoulders, and turned to look at Claire. "That's my baby you're talking to, buster. Ain't no one gonna make a move on her but me." With his laughing child hanging upside down, he bent to kiss the love of his life.

As usual, the morning was crazy. At exactly 8 a.m., all three of them were hurrying to get their things together. Austin had already put their suitcases in Claire's beat-up Land Rover, but Charlie had to go back in the house for the fifth time to retrieve something he forgot. As he stared at what she called a vintage, he vowed to buy her a new one the moment they got back from New York. She had complete faith in the old piece of tin, but he wasn't going to chance her safety or that of his son to the safari-green Rover. He wanted her in something reliable, definitely newer, and with a lot less rust and mileage.

He walked back up the porch steps to hurry everyone up.

"Let's go, family," he yelled, suddenly caught off guard by his statement. Family. His very own family. Life was great.

He'd told Claire he would wait awhile before outing them, but damn it if he could wait to show them off. He wanted to hop on every New York rooftop and scream of the love he had for Claire and Charlie at the top of his lungs. He was a shit load of nerves. Paparazzi were staking out his place. According to Rick, word had gotten around that he was coming back to town. He lived in a four-story brownstone in the West Village—far enough away from the ritz and glamor associated with the Upper East Side. The nineteenth-century building where he lived was his pride and joy. He liked to think of himself as traditional when he thought of his home. It was the feel of family and tradition that had appealed to him when he first walked into the house. He'd felt instantly at home. Claire would be surprised by his choice, he thought. His tastes, despite his financial means, were simple.

Claire and Charlie came bounding down the stairs, snapping him out of his thoughts. Their laughter was infectious, and their excitement palpable. Claire walked past him in the entryway and leaned in for a kiss.

"Let's go, babe," she whispered against his lips.

He had no words for her actions. It was simple, natural,

yet it was those little things that floored him. A knot formed in his throat as he watched her help Charlie into the car. They were his—a thought that took a lot to wrap his mind around even after weeks with them. It was something that comforted him, and at the same time, terrified him. It was a simple explanation, really. For the first time in his life, he had something he could lose that meant everything to him. The sound of the horn jolted him into action. He locked up, jumped off the porch, and ran to the car.

CHAPTER TWENTY-FIVE

Claire

Charlie was nervous, and nothing Claire said or did seemed to relax the kid. His thumb was in his mouth, and he chewed manically on his nail. She reached over to pull his hand away. Now sitting across from him and Austin, she noticed for the first time that her son was chewing the inside of his mouth. Looking at Austin sitting beside him, she had to laugh as she noticed he was doing the exact same thing. God, they were so much alike.

On more than one occasion, she would sit back and just watch them. When they lay on the floor creating some superhero city with Charlie's beloved Legos, or when they worked on a word search with their heads bent together staring at the page, she saw the resemblance. Each day they spent in each other's company, she noticed the similarities right down to the hand and facial gestures when they spoke. Both furrowed their brows when they spoke of a particularly passionate subject. She'd realized early on that Charlie had Austin's mannerisms, but all those traits had become more prominent in the days since Austin came home.

329

They spent a lot of time together, had gotten very close very quickly, and she enjoyed every second of them getting to know each other. It was also a relief to have Austin around and to realize that she didn't have to do it all on her own anymore. Aside from watching them bond, she liked the companionship, working as a team, and taking turns carpooling Charlie around to his various activities. She'd gotten a lot of work done—two of the four paintings that had been commissioned by The King Edward Hotel were finished. Austin brought out the best in her, always had. Over the years, she'd sold well over a hundred paintings, but none of them had been created with such love and devotion.

"Shit!" Austin whispered through clenched teeth.

"You're not allowed to say that word, Daddy."

"Sorry, buddy."

"What is it?" she asked.

"Charlie, why don't you go to the bathroom quickly before we take off?" said Austin as he unbuckled his son and pointed him in the direction of the bathroom. He turned to Claire, the concern on his face worrying her.

"Babe?"

"I just got a text from Rick. The paparazzi are everywhere. Apparently one of the gossip magazines published a picture of you and me."

"So."

"It was from…"

330

"Oh God!" She brought her hand to her chest. "Please don't tell me it was from yesterday."

"No. It was taken last Thursday at Charlie's baseball game."

"Is Charlie in the picture?"

"No, it's just you and me. Here, look," he said, handing her his phone.

Despite the invasion, she couldn't help but smile at the picture. They'd been lying on the grass, under the shade of a huge maple in the park by the baseball fields. Charlie had asked if they could all stay a little longer so he could play with some of his teammates in the playground. Austin had laid out a blanket and sat against the tree, his long, muscular legs extended in front of him. She remembered the day perfectly.

It'd been hot; the sun still high and bright at seven in the evening. She wore a white tank and blue shorts and sandals she'd slipped off her feet when she went to sit with Austin. Her head rested on his thighs, his hand brushing her hair back as they stared at each other. The love on their faces would be evident to anyone that saw the picture.

"Is this the only picture that was published?"

"No, there are others. None of Charlie, though," he said hurriedly.

"Good."

"Why are you smiling?"

"Because look at the picture, Austin. Even from that

angle, I can see the love in your eyes."

She looked up at him, knew she had a stupid smile on her face.

"People are gonna know now…about you…about us."

"Does that bother you?"

"No, of course not. I just didn't want this circus around us your first time I brought you home."

"It was bound to happen, though. Wasn't it?"

"Yes, but I just wanted it on my terms."

"Did you read the headline?" she asked him.

Austin shook his head. "No. I was staring at the picture."

"Listen to this…" she said and moved over to sit next to him. "'Could America's Most Eligible Bachelor Be on His Way off the Market?'"

"That's not true," he said. She looked at him, stunned. "I'm already off the market. Ain't nothing pulling me away from you, Claire."

"Good answer." She was surprised to find herself so calm over the matter. It was bound to come out. They couldn't hide in Springridge forever.

Austin seemed a little panicked. He knew firsthand what the circus he referred to entailed. She didn't know what the future would bring—his career was a thousand degrees different from hers.

Now, though, it wasn't just them. There was Charlie to

332

think about. She wondered how being outed would change them. Would he hide his feelings? Would he avoid holding her in public? Would they never lie in the grass together because photographers could be lurking behind trees or bushes? That's what scared her the most in that moment. She didn't want anything to change for them or between them.

"I don't care that they know about me."

"I don't care that they know about us either, Claire. I need you to understand that. I love you, and nothing will change that. But I want to keep Charlie out of it for now. I don't want him exposed to that craziness."

"You won't be able to protect him forever. At some point, photographers will get a shot of him. Whether he's with you or me, it will happen, and there's no hiding he's yours."

"I know," he said and smiled.

She leaned in and kissed him deeply. Their tongues mingled and their hands wandered. She wished they'd been alone on the plane and added the mile-high club to the list of places they'd made love.

"Hey, you took my seat," said Charlie.

"I was just comforting your dad. He gets a little nervous when he flies," she said and winked at her son.

He laughed and shook his head. "S'okay. Just stay there, I don't mind."

They all settled back in their seats. Claire double-checked Charlie's seat belt as the plane taxied for takeoff. Austin

333

grabbed her hand and she laid her head on his shoulder as she felt the plane speed up and ascend. Charlie's face was plastered to the window. Austin had closed his eyes, and she felt him take a deep, calming breath.

The descent into LaGuardia forty-five minutes later was incredible as the plane flew along the sandy shore of Long Island. In the far distance was the Statue of Liberty—a small, proud figure in the middle of New York Harbor. The East River was just ahead, and across from it, the economic and cultural center of the country—Manhattan Island. It was an impressive sight from the air. She imagined a lot was lost from the ground. In the middle of the concrete jungle, the sun shone off the Empire State Building—she was definitely going up there.

She looked over at Austin, who was wringing his hands on his lap. She'd never seen him look so nervous, and she knew it was the paparazzi that had him on edge. She reached over and slipped her fingers through his.

"I love you," he whispered.

"I know," she said, smiling up at him.

Charlie was nearly jumping off his seat in excitement. His expression changed when he felt the dip the plane took to position for landing. This was it. People would get confirmation that those pictures were the real deal. It still remained to be seen how much the press was able to dig up on her. There was nothing incriminating in her life file. She was an artist—an up and coming artist—and if the press would concentrate on that, she'd prefer it to her personal life. What she didn't want, and what she agreed with Austin on, was thrusting Charlie into the mayhem.

The terminal they arrived at was farther away from the main one. The pilot drove right to a hanger where the prerequisite black SUV with tinted windows waited. Claire unbuckled herself and helped Charlie gather his things. Books, DS, and iPod were all scattered on the seat next to him. His small backpack had been jam-packed with his precious belongings. The pilot walked into the cabin to advise Austin that the doors were open, and the driver was waiting and ready to take them wherever they wanted to go.

"Home is my only destination, Roger."

"Perfect, Austin. I'll let Henry know."

"Roger," he called out to him. "We got here a little late, and I didn't have a chance to introduce you. This is Claire, my...my..." he started, but couldn't find the right words to describe her role in his life.

"Girlfriend," she said quickly, saving him from any embarrassment. "I'm his girlfriend, and this is our son, Charlie."

"It's a pleasure to meet you, Claire."

"Can I see the cockpit?" asked Charlie from behind them.

"Of course. Why don't you follow me, and I'll give you the penny tour."

She started to walk after them, but Austin grabbed her

hand. He looked slightly ashamed and worried. They hadn't had to explain their status to anyone before. They'd been around family for the last month, and there'd been no point in justifying what they were doing. They were together. No one had asked any questions.

"I'm sorry…I don't know what came over me."

"It's no big deal, really."

"Yes it is. You're more than a girlfriend to me, Claire. So much more."

"The love of your life?" she asked, smirking at his embarrassment.

"For starters."

"For starters is good. Now come on. Let's get off this piece of tin and show me your house," she said and grabbed his hand. She couldn't wait to see where he lived.

CHAPTER TWENTY-SIX

Austin

He was nervous. Hell, he'd been nervous from the second he sat down on the plane. She wasn't going to just see his place, she was going to see the things in it. Part of that was the two walls in his living room that were covered with her art.

The drive into Manhattan was quiet, at least between him and Claire. Charlie, as usual, filled any awkward silence with his chatter. Their son was excited, flipping through a book his grandfather had bought him and pointing out all the things he wanted to see.

Austin had instructed the driver to head down I-278 so they could drive across the Brooklyn Bridge, instead of his usual route through the Queens Midtown Tunnel, which would have made the drive shorter. He wondered if they would have time or even be able to pull off taking a walk across the bridge. He'd done it a few times, very late at night or very early in the morning when there was no chance of being recognized. With the occasional jogger or cyclist and the East River below, he enjoyed every step he took.

Traffic was a nightmare, nothing unusual. But he wanted to get home and give his damned nerves a rest. He thought for an instant that he should have asked Celia to take the paintings down. Then thought better of the absurd track his thoughts had taken.

"What are you thinking about? You're very quiet over there," Claire asked.

"I was just thinking about something. I'll explain when we get home," he told her because he was sure he was going to have to do some explaining.

She looked at him quizzically; he smiled and leaned over to kiss her. Claire backed away, her inquisitive eyes asking for answers. He laughed at her and reached up, wrapped his hands around the nape of her neck, and pulled her in for the kiss she'd just refused him.

"Holy cow, can we do that, Daddy?" Charlie asked, pointing up to the pedestrian path on the bridge.

"If we have time. We're only here for a couple of days."

"Well, what can we do?"

"I want to visit The Metropolitan Museum of Art..." started Claire.

"I don't want to go there," Charlie expressed adamantly, cutting his mother off. She gave him what Austin called the look of death. "Sorry," he said, color rising in his cheeks.

Austin looked from mother to child. He'd suspected Claire would want to go to the museum, so he'd made arrangements for him and Charlie to visit The American Museum of Natural History, figuring dinosaurs would be a lot more interesting to a five-year-old. Claire looked like she was preparing for the argument when he cut in.

"No worries, buddy. Mommy can do her thing and we can head to the other side of the park and go see dinosaur fossils and skeletons and mummies."

"Yeah!" he cheered.

"What?" he asked when he saw Claire glaring at him. "You go do your thing. Us guys will go do our thing. It's a win-win."

"Is it now?"

"Yes, it is. We can meet at The Loeb Boathouse for a late lunch and voila, a little adventure for all in New York City to be had."

"What time is your meeting?" Claire asked.

Austin looked down at his phone and grimaced.

"At one."

"That's in an hour," Claire pointed out, looking down at her own phone.

He hated the thought that he'd have to drop them off at home and leave for his meeting shortly after. The ride from the airport had cut into precious time. He wanted to show them around the house, explain the paintings, and see what Celia had done with the room he'd designated for Charlie. He'd flipped her an email with instructions, hoping to surprise both

Charlie and Claire.

Aside from texts between him and Jackson, he hadn't talked to the band since they parted ways in Toronto. There was a time when they'd text, even call each other when they were on a break. Lately, they barely spoke when they were face to face. They put up a good front, pretended to be the best friends they were at the beginning of it all. He and Jackson were the only two that spoke to each other. The guy was a couple of years younger and always looked up to Austin. He tried very hard not to let him down.

Austin honestly believed that he'd never truly been happy in the band. He'd used the craziness to forget, to find a way to keep moving on. Feeling some responsibility to four guys he'd once considered friends was enough to take his mind off his life. Things had never been great for him. Claire was always on his mind, and his anger towards her and the situation she'd forced on him trumped any good thing that happened in that first year—the platinum albums, the cluster of number-one hits, the fans. The groupies, drugs, and alcohol were the only things that seemed to numb the pain. All their success had been at his expense, and he hated it.

He looked up at Claire; her face was in profile, staring up into to the sky. His hand was wrapped in hers. This time he wasn't just giving her back his heart and soul, but his whole life. He would do anything and everything to hold on to what they'd found again. It was all bigger, stronger, and more profound than anything they'd experienced in the past. He wanted to marry her, expand their family, and love her for the rest of their lives. To have that, he'd give up everything else.

"Oh no!" whispered Claire.

He looked up to see the crowd lined up across the street from his house. There were fans, passersby stopping to see what the commotion was about, and of course, the never-absent paparazzi. He'd been off the grid for months, and with the pictures of him and Claire being published, the bastards were thirsty. He dug in his pocket for his phone and called his assistant.

"Celia, are you at the house...Good, okay. We're three houses down. Be at the door in three minutes...Yes, but not Charlie, and I'm really not comfortable exposing him...No, she's okay with it. Our only concern is our son...Thanks. I don't know what I'd do without you... Yeah, probably...see you in a bit."

"There are so many of them," Claire said.

"I know. I'm sorry. I should have been prepared for this."

"It's fine. It's just a little daunting, that's all."

They stared at each other for a long while before either one of them moved. The car had come to a stop, and the only thing to break through the daze was Henry's voice.

"Should I open the door, sir?"

Austin held up a finger at his driver and turned to look into Claire's eyes. With a tug at her hand, he kissed her and said, "We've got this. You ready?"

"As I'll ever be."

He smiled at her and turned to their son.

"Charlie, listen to me. I want you to hold on to Mommy's hand and don't let go. Don't look up if you hear your name. Just jump out of the car and run up those stairs to that big black door as quick as you can," he told his son, pointing to his brownstone. "Can you do that?"

Charlie nodded, his gaze fixated on the photographers across the street. "Who are those people?"

"They just want our picture," Austin told him.

"Because you're famous?"

"Yes, but I don't want them to have your picture, buddy. I don't like how they go about getting it. That's why it's important you keep your head down, okay?"

"Okay."

Austin and Claire gave each other a nod. Claire reached for Charlie as Austin texted Celia. He saw the door to the house open just inside the entryway. He watched Claire adjust Charlie's backpack and then adjust a baseball cap on his head to further hide his face. He tapped Henry's shoulder. The man got out of the car, looked up to the house, and nodded. He and Celia had the move down pat. It was hard to find trustworthy people in this business; he'd gotten lucky and snatched up the two best people for their respective jobs.

Henry was a big man and had served as a bodyguard a time or two. If he was going to trust his family to anything, Henry and Tiny would be his pick.

"Celia is at the door. Go, I'll be right behind you."

Claire held on to Charlie, and like seasoned pros, heads down they made a dash towards the house, with Austin right at their heels. He ignored the calls from fans and photographers to approach the crowd or look up for a picture. He wanted to be in the sanctuary of his home where he would be able to, for the time being, keep his family safe and out of the hands of the photographic beasts waiting outside. No official word would be released until he gave his lawyer the go-ahead. Until then, it was the three of them.

Charlie was laughing when he entered the house. Claire was removing his backpack, and Celia was closing the doors to block out the yelling and pleading from outside.

"Well, that went well," she said and turned to Claire. "I'm Celia, Austin's savior most of the time. It's a pleasure to finally meet you."

"All the time…" he said, giving his assistant and friend a hug.

Celia's pixie cut fit her height, which was short; there was no other way to put it. Her brown eyes always shone with mischief, but she was reliable and unbelievably efficient.

"You seemed to be doing quite well, boss, until about last Thursday I'd say."

"It was a great last Thursday, Cel," he said, reaching for Claire.

"You looked very cozy and in love. I'm happy for you. Your moping was getting on my nerves."

"I did not mope!"

343

"He moped, Claire. A lot. Come on, Charlie, let's go check out your room." She laughed as she grabbed his hand and led him up the stairs.

"I have a room?" he heard his son say.

"Yep. A nice big-boy room," Celia told him. Their footsteps disappeared, then he heard the loud "wow" his son let out.

Austin watched Claire nervously as she walked into the dining room.

"Look at these stairs," she said as she looked up to where her son had gone. "This is beautiful. I love it. And these high ceilings…wow. Are they like that in the rest of the house?"

"No. On this floor, they're twelve feet. On the other floors, they're nine."

He followed her across the hall and into the living room. Her head was still tilted up to the ceiling. She was commenting on the door frames, which were original to the house, and raving about the wooden beams that ran across the ceiling. They'd been painted white when he moved in but had been restored to their original dark wood stain.

"This is magnificent. So much charm. And that fireplace…" Her words halted when she stopped in front of the large fireplace, every detail in the marble forgotten as she looked to the space above it. He couldn't take his eyes off her face. It was expressionless; nothing to tell him how or what she was feeling. Her hands went to cover her mouth, and her eyes moved over the painting.

"Say something," he said.

He'd moved to stand by the window, looking at her in profile, but he couldn't stand it any longer—he needed to be near her.

"I should have told you..."

"You bought it?"

"Yes."

"You paid a lot of money for it."

"It was worth every penny to have a piece of you in my home."

"Did you know my painting was going to be auctioned?"

"No. I had no idea what was being auctioned. In fact, I didn't even want to go. I almost didn't go."

She turned with tears in her eyes and just stared at him. The doubts and the fear all left him in that second. He knew the look she was giving him, had been at the receiving end of it many times in the last couple of weeks...love.

Her eyes shifted to look over his shoulder.

"Oh my God," she exclaimed in a loud whisper. "How many do you have?" she asked, looking on in shock at the other three paintings he owned.

"Whatever you see in this room is the extent of my Claire Monroe collection."

"What do they mean to you?" she asked, the question catching him off guard.

He didn't answer right away, wondering what exactly it was she wanted to hear. He stared at the painting closest to the door. A colorful piece of a man running through fields towards a child. He knew what fields they were, and he had no doubt who the man and child were now. Each painting was different. A woman by a window cradling her pregnant belly, tears running down her face. A couple walking through the same fields. And the last, the one that should have helped him piece it all together, a girl in a white dress with red flowers standing on what appeared to be a road leading nowhere. The paintings were blurry, the faces and details unclear. Each one was a message he hadn't put together until that moment. He'd sat in the large armchair and stared at those paintings countless times, always too angry to see the message she was sending. Tears were swimming in his eyes as he approached the picture of the pregnant woman and ran his fingers over her belly.

"Austin?"

He looked at her then, tears streaming down her face, realizing he'd made the connection. All this time, the truth had been right in front of him.

"Everything," he said. "These paintings mean everything to me."

"Where did you get them from?"

"A business partner of mine who lives in Toronto mentioned an artist to me. He said she had a stand at a farmers market in Springridge. He had no idea beforehand that I knew you. He bought a couple of paintings. I saw them at his house. When he told me the artist's name, I immediately offered to buy them from him. I offered him a ridiculous amount of money. He said no…" he told her, a smile on his face. "I asked him to stop at your booth next time he was in town and buy all the paintings you had. He thought I was insane of course. He brought those two home for me a couple of weeks later," he said, pointing to the pregnant woman and the man and child. "In the next couple of weeks, he bought the others. And that big one, I got myself."

She shook her head. "I don't know what to say."

"You don't have to say anything. I know this may sound crazy, but it was about supporting your art as much as it was about having a piece of you. I'd be on tour, and I couldn't wait to get home and sit in that chair," he said, pointing to a brown leather recliner by the window, "and just stare at the paintings. I had something to come home to. With your paintings hanging on my walls, I felt closer to you and not so alone."

She hadn't moved from the spot in front of the fireplace, hadn't reached out to him to either deny or confirm that he was indeed crazy. She simply watched and listened to his explanations. He wanted so badly to hold her. He had his meeting, and he didn't want to leave her with her thoughts. He truly needed to know what was going through her mind.

"Thank you," she finally said, making the decision for him. She didn't reach for his hands, rather his shirt, fisting it in her hands and pulled him to her. "Thank you," she repeated against his lips.

"For what?" he asked, his eyes locked on hers.

"For never giving up on me."

347

"I couldn't. If I gave up on you, I would have given up on myself, and I couldn't let that happen. You were all I had to hold on to."

He'd always held on to some hope where Claire was concerned. Knew that even the tiny bit of hope he had was enough to pull him through life and that some way, somehow, he would find his back to her. She was his beacon, the one true light he strived to never lose sight of. And he didn't; he sailed through every storm within him to finally get to her.

"I love you, Claire. I love so much I can't stand it."

"I love you, Austin. I never stopped. I couldn't," she said and leaned in to kiss him.

CHAPTER TWENTY-SEVEN

Claire

"I have to go," he whispered against her neck.

He'd buried his face in the crook of her neck to hide the tears in his eyes. She hated to see him cry, hated to know that he had needed her so much.

"Austin?"

"What?"

"You're going to be late," she said, laughing when he tightened his hold on her.

"I don't want to leave you."

"I'll be fine."

"I know, but I won't," he said, and they both laughed.

Claire put her hands on either side of his face, lifting his head. His eyes were red-rimmed, his lashes damp. Like she did with Charlie, she ran her fingers over his face, wiping away the trail his tears had left. She wanted to apologize, but she'd done that too many times already for it to have any significant

349

impact anymore. He knew how remorseful she was, knew that his pain was her pain—he knew everything. There were no secrets between them anymore. She smiled at him and pulled him towards her. His lips were soft and warm, and he moved with such gentleness over her mouth.

He grabbed her hips and walked back, his legs hitting the recliner. She fell on top of him, felt him reach for the lever, and all of a sudden she was lying on top of him. His hands wandered down her back to cup her ass, and she couldn't stop herself from wiggling over the very impressive bulge in his pants. Had it not been for the voices and footsteps she heard on the second floor, they might have completely forgotten they weren't alone. She went to move off him when she heard her son's voice and footsteps coming down the stairs. Austin gripped her hips, holding her in place.

"Don't move yet," he told her, his voice hoarse through his clenched teeth.

"What…why? I need to sit up."

"Claire, I don't want to embarrass myself. Please don't move," he told her. He arched his hips towards her to make his point.

What a point it was. He was incredibly aroused, and she wasn't sure if staying on him and applying further pressure to his groin was going to be of any help. She started laughing, which didn't help at all either. He growled in her ear, tightening his grip on her hips to keep her still.

"Daddy!" Charlie yelled from the doorway and ran to join them on the chair. "I love my room. It's the best bedroom I've ever had. Thank you."

"Well, thanks. I put a lot of thought into your room in Springridge," said Claire, feigning insult.

"I like that one too, but you have to see all the baseball stuff on the walls in this one, Mommy."

Austin made a brisk movement with his legs, and they were both suddenly sitting on his lap. Claire was sitting on one of his legs, her own legs between his. Somehow Charlie ended up on her lap with his legs hanging over Austin's. He squeezed them both.

"I love you both," he said. Then he yelled, "Group hug!"

Charlie laughed and squealed as the group hug quickly became a tickle fest. She screeched and tried desperately to move away from her son's kicking legs. She was elbowed, kneed in the stomach, and head butted.

"Ow! Stop. I want out of this game. You're both hurting me."

"Okay, okay. I have to go anyway."

"When will you be back?" asked Claire.

"Celia, what's the allotted time for this meeting?"

"They didn't say, boss. But we should really get going or my man will have me by the..." she started, but quickly caught sight of Charlie, "legs...if I'm late for dinner with his parents."

Austin kissed Claire long and sound, not caring who was around. He and Charlie did their dad-son handshake thing, and he flew out the door. Claire and Charlie stood in the middle of the living room, staring at each other, wondering what they were to do. They both jumped as the front door opened, banging against the wall as Austin walked back through it.

"Weren't you leaving?" Claire asked.

"Yes. I love you."

"Is that why you came back?"

"That, and to tell you to stay inside. I know it sucks, but paps are still hanging out across the street," he told her and kissed her once more before turning. "Oh, and don't forget this is your home too now. The fridge is full, the TV room is—"

"On the second floor," Charlie blurted. "Celia showed me. She also showed me how to use the remote."

"Great. I'll see you soon. I love you."

"I love you," they both yelled back, and once again, they were left alone.

The silence in the room was deafening. It wasn't often her son was left speechless, but she closed her eyes and relished in the quietness. She thought of the paintings Austin had purchased, and the bedroom he had decorated and furnished for their son, which she still hadn't seen. She thought of his face when he ran back in. He wasn't panicked, just happy to see her again, seconds after he'd walked out the door. To be in his home—their home—in New York, of all places, was mindboggling. She'd never let herself wonder if this moment would ever come. Sure, it sucked that they would be stuck indoors for the rest of the day, and what a beautiful day it was, but no matter how bored they got, she would not venture out.

352

The idea of being hounded by all those people scared the crap out of her. She wondered what would be printed about Charlie in tomorrow's tabloids—surely someone is out there wondering who he is and inventing some elaborate story with regards to his origin. She walked towards the window and peeked out through the side of the curtain, and sure enough, there were still some photographers and fans loitering on the sidewalk. Not as many as when they'd arrived, but too many for her liking.

How did Austin live with this attention—the fans she understood, but the press, invading every aspect of your life for the joy of it. Some of these people made millions off some of the pictures they took. The famous caught in the act of an unguarded moment. What would that be like, to live looking over your shoulder, wondering if something as simple as tying your shoes would make the cover of some gossip magazine. She shivered at the thought that that was exactly what would happen to them, no matter what they did to try and stop it. This was why keeping Charlie out of the public eye would be crucial. She didn't want his face or some crazy story about him splattered on the pages of trash. He was everything to her—to them—and she would bring out her mamma bear claws to keep him safe. If anything was going to be printed about their son, she wanted it to be the truth. Charlie wasn't up for public consumption or fictitious stories.

Charlie's voice broke through her thoughts. "MOM!"

"Yes, buddy? Sorry, I wasn't listening."

"I know," he said, rolling his eyes.

"What is it?"

"I'm hungry."

"All right then, let's go find the kitchen. Celia didn't happen to show you where that is, did she?"

"Yep. Right this way. So listen. The living room, eating room, and kitchen are on this floor. The master room and entertainment room," he paused, leaning into her as if to tell her a big fat secret, "that's where the TV and the Xbox are kept, are on the second floor."

"Yes, I gathered that. Thanks," she said drily, rolling her own eyes.

"Ha!" he yelled. "Daddy was right. I do get that from you."

"Get what?"

"That thing we do with our eyes, when we roll them in our heads," he said, smiling from ear to ear.

"Funny thing is, your father hates it," she told him, "and they are his eyes you roll…"

"I'm gonna tell him that." They both laughed and headed towards the back of the house.

The kitchen was a grand space. Homey, not at all what you would expect a world-renowned rock star to have in his house. White cupboards lined one wall of the L-shaped kitchen. The dark island framed by four bar stools had a beautiful light-specked marble countertop. The appliances were all stainless steel, and she nearly screamed with excitement when she took in the six-burner stove. It was a place you could walk into and feel instantly at home. Across the room, the sub-zero fridge, complete with an attached wine fridge, was inviting. She imagined more modern, straight-edged furniture, darker and manlier. This place was the opposite—airy, bright, and traditional—more Pottery Barn than Restoration Hardware. She loved it. It made her smile to realize they had the same taste.

A chair scraping on the floor made her regain her focus. Charlie had managed to drag a stool to the cupboard, where he now sat trying to open a box of Captain Crunch. She leaned her elbow on the island, her face resting on her hands and watched him. The way his face twisted as he struggled to open the plastic bag containing the cereal amused her. The triumphant look at finally getting it open and the blissful look in his eyes, when he popped a handful of the stuff into his mouth, made her laugh. God, he was so much like his father; the image always shocked her no matter how many times she studied his expressions. She reached for a bowl she insisted he use, and they sat down to eat.

She settled on an English muffin with butter and jam and a dark cup of coffee. Her nerves were a little shot—she peeked out the front window again, and she could swear there were more people out there now. It was the middle of the day—people obviously didn't work in New York.

After warning Charlie to stay away from any window facing the street, they headed up to the game room. She got out her laptop, answered some emails, and did something she'd sworn to herself she'd never do. She Googled Austin.

In images, the most recent result was pictures of them arriving at his house earlier, and him leaving. She let out her breath when she realized there were no pictures of Charlie. No articles speculating as to who he was. She saw one shot of her going up the stairs outside the entryway—Charlie was with her, but her body covered him, and they'd never gotten a clear picture. She could give small thanks for that, she supposed. For the moment, he was safe from the so-called media circus.

She scrolled down the page, glancing quickly at the links. There were links to a gossip site asking who she was, where he'd met her, how long they had been together. One site was already planning their wedding. She hit images again and scrolled through the results. There were millions of pictures dating back to the first year the band went on tour. She closed the search when the pictures of Kayla Aldridge appeared on her screen. She didn't want to see them together, had managed to avoid any media relating to him for her own sanity. She couldn't bear to imagine him with someone else. Out of sight, out of mind, the saying goes, and Claire took it to heart.

Austin had given her an idea of what his life had been like in the early years of the band. The insight he'd given her into his mood and behavior was upsetting, and she really didn't want to know any more. He'd been honest with her, told her everything he felt she needed to know, and she, in turn, had decided to trust him.

She closed the laptop and laid her head on the back of the couch. She looked around the impressive TV room. The thing hanging on the wall could hardly be called a television. It was a downsized movie theater screen. The ninety-inch screen seemed to fit the space nicely. Her son was currently playing some superhero game on it—a waste, if you asked her. She could picture Austin sitting on the large sectional she sat at, watching his sports. She wasn't a fan of any sport, but she imagined a football or hockey game looked fantastic on the large screen. There were no DVDs. The Apple TV on a shelf next to the television satisfied her movie watching needs.

The clutter in the space was minimal. Austin had always been neat, but the whole house looked like he barely spent any time there. The thought saddened her. To think he had all this, and that aside from wanting to come home to stare at her paintings, there was nothing else waiting for him. She let out a frustrated breath—they had both been so lonely in the past years. She walked to the window, stopping with her hand in midair a split second before she pulled the curtain aside, remembering the intrusive lenses of the paparazzi lying in wake outside the house.

Her ringing cell phone startled her. She reached into her back pocket for it. Relief came over her at seeing Alexa's number.

"Hey, how are you?"

"I should ask you that," Alexa said. "How's little old New York?"

"We got here not more than an hour ago, so we haven't seen much."

"How's his house?" Alexa asked, her voice conspiratorial.

She looked at Charlie, who was still absorbed in his game.

She warned him to stay away from the window once again and walked back down to the living room.

"He's got some of my paintings hanging on his walls," she told her friend as she stood in the middle of the room and stared at her paintings.

"Wow. How did he get them?"

"He bought them."

"When?"

She'd questioned Mr. Jameson's motives for buying all her paintings—of course, she never voiced her thoughts.

"Last fall, at the stand. Do you remember when I told you about a financier, Michael Jameson?"

"Yeah, the rich guy who bought your paintings for gifts…"

"Well, they weren't gifts. It was Austin who had sent him to buy them after seeing them at his place. Apparently they're business partners."

"Holy shit. How do you feel about that?"

"I'm okay with it, if that's what you're asking?" she took a deep breath and continued. "There's a story in those paintings, Alex. My truth was all there, right in front of him."

"I remember the paintings. Do you think he made the connection?"

"Yes. Today."

In the meantime, maybe the paintings had eased his pain

358

a little bit. She took comfort in that. Despite the fact that she hadn't been with him physically, he wasn't all that alone. She'd been with him all along. Austin carried her in his songs and his heart. They would make this work. They had to. There was no other way around it. She would support whatever decision he made, and they, without a doubt, would live happily ever after.

"This trip is good for all of you in order to continue bonding. I'm happy for you."

"Thanks. So, did you just call to hear my sappy arrival story?"

"Actually, I'm calling to say adios! I'm leaving for Cabo in the morning. Spoiled, rich, and hairy finally got his act together and made some decisions. Shit's finally moving forward."

"That's great. Are you excited?"

"Yes and no. Pemberton's not my easiest client. But I'll deal. Anyway, I have to let you go, I have tons of packing to do."

"Abby's still supervising?" asked Claire, the idea making her laugh for some reason.

"Yes. I'm certain that she'll take her job very seriously and do what most supervisors in Cabo would do. No supervising at all." Claire laughed. She had no doubt Alexa was right. Abby took the saying 'have your cake and eat it too' to a whole new level.

"Good-bye, sis."

"Later. I'll see you in a month. Have fun in N.Y.C."

"We will. Love you."

"I love you too. Now I'm saying bye before this sappy conversation gets any sappier."

Claire disconnected the call and took one last look around the room before going to join her son. She couldn't help but think that if Austin had connected the dots (or paintings) he would have been with her a lot sooner.

CHAPTER TWENTY-EIGHT

Austin

The scent of garlic reached him before he'd even turned the doorknob. He stood in the small entryway between the front door and foyer and realized that the smell of a meal being cooked had never traveled through his house. He'd never cooked in the kitchen, and to have Claire be the first delighted him. He dropped his bag on one of the sofas and walked into the kitchen to see her and Charlie dancing to some pop song on the iPod. They were both laughing, and he couldn't help the sense of joy and fulfillment that spread through him.

"Now this is a sight," he yelled over the music.

"Daddy!" Charlie cheered and ran to him.

"Hey, buddy. Did you have a good day?"

"I played on your Xbox, and Mommy was on her laptop."

"Oh yeah? I hope she was on it doing some shopping..." he said, looking at her questioningly.

She stopped midway through slicing some tomatoes. He could see her in profile, and he didn't miss it when she closed her eyes and let out her breath.

"I didn't Google further than a month."

"I'd prefer you didn't Google at all."

She looked up then, trapping her bottom lip between her teeth. She straightened her shoulders, preparing for a battle he didn't have the heart to endure.

"Something in the world wide web you don't want me to see?" she asked, her brows narrowing.

"Yes, lots," he said, his voice sharp. "I've told you everything, Claire. You want to know more, listen to my albums. Those songs will reveal things I can't speak about," his tone was frustrated.

"Can I go play video games until dinner's ready?" asked Charlie, briefly cutting through the sudden tension.

"Sure, go ahead," Austin told him. He watched his son run up the back stairs. He smiled, realizing his kid knew his way around the house.

"I'm sorry," she said.

"Don't be. You're curious, I get that. How could you not be? There's this huge gap in our relationship that we keep trying to breach. I'm tired of climbing, Claire. I need you to trust me."

"I do trust you. Please don't doubt that. I just got online to see if they'd printed anything about Charlie."

"There's nothing, I've already checked."

"I know."

She turned back to her task, her shoulders hunched. He couldn't bear to hurt her feelings. Even more, he hated to see doubt in her eyes still. He'd fucked up and made some questionable choices, but he'd be damned if his past mistakes would affect her or Charlie. He walked up behind her, wrapped his arms around her waist, and felt the relief drown his own doubts as she sank back into his chest. He needed to ease the sudden tension between them.

He'd had a shit few hours, had wanted nothing more than to come home to her and Charlie. He didn't want to fight or argue—he'd done enough of that for one day.

His band was in the process of unraveling. He'd refused to sign the new contract the record company had offered, and the guys jumped down his throat. It was a good offer, and he knew they'd come up with it to lock him in for God knew how long. If he signed on for a new album, he would be stuck in some recording studio for a few months, tours that could last years, and appearances he didn't want to be a part of anymore. He was exhausted, and he'd finally started to get his life back in order. He wasn't about to jeopardize any of it. No amount of money was going to tear him away from Claire and Charlie.

He had, he'd realized weeks ago, the two most important people in his life with him, and that was all that mattered. Jackson didn't say a word the entire time. His drummer wasn't surprised, and actually fucking smiled when Austin refused to sign. Lately, he'd gotten the impression that Jackson too wanted to slow down. Although he'd done his share of fucking around, he'd been getting quite serious with a certain actress and had successfully managed to keep the relationship under wraps.

Their bassist, Simon, was seething, and made reference to Austin's current situation in a much more vulgar way. The asshole had zero respect, and Austin wasn't able to contain his rage. He jumped across the table, grabbed Simon by the collar of his dingy T-shirt, and punched him in the mouth.

"Don't you ever talk about my family again. Get your head out of your ass and start paying attention to yours," he said through gritted teeth.

The jerk had a family, a great girl, an amazing kid, and he took it all for granted. He'd had enough at that point. Austin walked back around the table, grabbed his things, and left a stunned group of execs, producers, and lawyers behind. Yellow Scarlet was no longer his top priority. He wasn't sure if it ever had been. His job had been nothing but a distraction, something to pass the worst years of his life.

"I'm sorry, Claire. I didn't mean to snap at you."

"How was your meeting?" She avoided his attempt at an apology.

"Pointless. I'll tell you about it later. Right now I just want this," he said and turned her in his arms, kissing her like he hadn't kissed her in days. She gripped his biceps, her nails digging into his arms as if he was her lifeline. Did she have any idea that she was his?

"That was some kiss, McKinley."

364

"You're some kisser, Monroe."

He smiled down at her and wished for the thousandth time he could take away any doubt and questions she might still have. The old feelings had come back with a vengeance, but the truth was that they'd been strangers when he first arrived at her threshold. In that instant, he realized that despite whatever connection they'd made, they were still getting to know each other again.

"Can we eat now?" asked Charlie from the doorway. Neither one of them had realized he was there. He kissed her one last time, left her to finish the delicious-smelling concoction on the stove, and took on the task of setting the table.

Dinner was a quiet affair. Claire was lost in her never-ending thoughts, Austin was lost in his, and Charlie seemed too tired to say or do much of anything. His head wobbled, on the verge of falling asleep at the table. It wouldn't be the first time. It had happened a couple of weeks ago after a day at his parents' pool. Wearing the kid out was the only way to get him to bed early. He wondered briefly how much sleep his son had gotten, if any, with the excitement of going to New York. He was surprised to find that he too was quite tired. The early-morning wake-up, the travel, and the events at his meeting had made for a long day.

"He's going to fall into his food," he said, gesturing to his son.

"I should get him to bed. God only knows what time he woke this morning," said Claire, echoing his thoughts.

"I got him. Why don't you start clearing the table and I'll help you finish the cleanup when I come back down."

She didn't say a word, just started gathering the plates and silverware off the table. Her silence worried him; he hadn't meant to snap at her. The idea of her doing an Internet search horrified him. There was a lot out there he didn't want her seeing. Pictures of him at his worst had been printed frequently in the first couple of years. There were articles out there where he gave interviews while completely wasted, noted in graphic detail by the reporter. There were pictures where no amount of makeup or Photoshop would cover the dark circles or hide his bloodshot eyes.

It was disturbing stuff. His mother had seen some of those pictures. His family had worried terribly for him right up until he got his ass in gear and started taking better care of himself. In many ways, he had Kayla to thank for his recovery of sorts. She'd been patient, kind, and incredibly loving. Her kind of affection was just what he'd needed then, something good, genuine. He hadn't talked to her since just before he left for Springridge. She'd known of course why he was going home. They'd talked a lot about Claire, and had become good friends. Lately, she was involved with one of her directors, an affair he warned her about. He knew the guy. Matt Jacobs was notorious for fucking around with his leading ladies. Kayla, unfortunately, had fallen into his clutches. Austin hadn't been able to convince her to stay away; she was convinced the man loved her.

When he reached Charlie's room, he was out of breath. His child didn't weigh much, but three flights of stairs carrying

Charlie had his arms shaking. He changed him into his pajamas and tucked him safely into his bed. Back downstairs, there was more silence. The kitchen was empty, so he made his way to the living room. Claire stood in the dark room in front of the window. How many times, he wondered, had she done the same during the day. Her arms were crossed over her chest, her breathing calm.

"How do you do it?" she asked, unaware she heard him enter the room.

"Do what?" he whispered.

"Deal with all this attention? The fans are one thing, but the paparazzi. How do you let them dictate your life?"

"They don't dictate my life."

"Well, they dictated mine today. I hated being stuck indoors when we're in a city with so much to do."

"Is that why you're upset?"

She turned then, her face contorted in confusion. "I'm not upset. A little frustrated, maybe. What makes you think I would be upset?"

"You didn't say a word during dinner. I thought maybe it was because I snapped at you about searching the Internet."

"No, I get why that bothered you. For the record, there's nothing out there that I want to see unless it involves the last three weeks."

"I thought you were looking for…"

"No," she cut him off. "I know you had a rough time.

367

You've mentioned it enough times. I don't want to see the proof."

"Really?"

"Yes, really. Seeing Myra on her knees with your…well, that was enough."

He winced. That was one visual he wished he could make disappear from her memories.

"Come on," he said, holding out his hand. "I need to just be with you right now. Forget them," he suggested, tipping his head towards the window.

Although the crowd had dwindled, there were still enough people out there to put a dent in the already ridiculous traffic situation in the city. He had Tiny and Big Mike on duty outside. They'd parked two houses down in order to keep an eye on any wandering pap.

More than once he'd had some jerk try to sneak into his house. His small backyard, well, terrace was more like it, had a high wall and backed onto the neighbors'. Neighbors who were, thankfully, very protective of his privacy. He had sensors that triggered floodlights and a warning alarm on his phone announcing if an intruder had climbed the wall. He'd taken every possible precaution to ensure his safety, his guests', and now his family's. Claire looked down at her watch. The setting sun illuminated her face as an orange streak had snuck through a gap in the buildings across the street.

"I want to watch a movie," she said.

"Whatever you want, as long as I get to hold you."

She didn't say a word and led the way up to the game room, as Charlie had dubbed it. Her ass swayed in front of him, her longs legs calling for him to run his hands along their contours. Her hair was loose and fell in waves down her back. She rarely wore it loose, he realized as he took in the chestnut locks. Lately, her hair was always up in a ponytail or some sexy-as-hell bundle on top of her head. The sound of her flip-flops slapping against her heels brought his attention back to her legs. They were toned, defined, and beautifully tanned.

"Why don't you set up the movie. I'm going to change into something more comfortable," she told him, and he tore his gaze away from the ankles he wanted locked around his hips.

"What would you like to watch?"

"Surprise me..." she said with a wink.

He bent to pick up the game controllers and games that Charlie had left scattered on the floor. He smiled at finally seeing the house looking lived in. Things were out of place, in the kitchen dishes were drying by the sink, and a dirty pan still sat on the stove. The smell of the meal Claire had cooked lingered. He loved it.

Austin turned at the sound of Claire's feet padding along the floor just as she entered the room. He felt his mouth drop open and felt zero shame at the reaction she provoked in him. If by changing into something more comfortable she meant the damned yellow dress that barely covered her ass, he was fine with it—as long as she wore it indoors and in his presence.

"Did you pick a movie?"

"No, and it doesn't matter because I don't think I'll be able to concentrate on a movie with you in that dress."

"Why, what's wrong with the dress?" she said and twirled, allowing the skirt to rise, revealing nothing but silky, bare skin.

"Absolutely fucking nothing."

"Oh good. I thought you hated it."

"No, no I don't hate it," he said and rose to his feet to close the gap between them. "Come here," he told her as he reached for her hands and tugged her against him.

Her laugh was quiet, seductive. The visual of her smiling with her bottom lip trapped between her teeth would be something he'd never forget. He reached under her dress and grabbed onto her upper thigh with one hand while the other tangled in her hair. Austin leaned into her to take her lip between his lips, pulling it away from her teeth, sucking on it for a few seconds before he slipped his tongue into her mouth. He lifted his hand from her thigh to squeeze the luscious, soft flesh of her ass. Claire ran her fingers through his hair to the back of his neck and pulled him closer to her, so hard it was almost on the verge of pain.

"Couch, now!" she murmured against his lips.

He walked her back, his mouth never leaving hers, his hand on her head, guiding her back. The squeal she let out was the only indication that they were tipping over the back of the large sectional. Her dress flowed up, his groin landed where it was supposed to, and his left hand held her ass right where he wanted it. Reluctantly, he let go of her ass. He looked down at her expectantly and noticed for the first time since she walked into the room that the straps he'd ripped were sewn back on.

"Did you get this dress fixed?"

"Yes," she breathed and let out a soft laugh.

"Too bad it was for nothing," he whispered against her shoulder and ripped the flimsy strap with his teeth.

Claire let out a soft moan, and he took great pleasure in knowing that one: she didn't give a shit he ripped it again, and two: the strap fell away easily, exposing the gorgeous slope of her breasts. That right there was sexier than looking at her naked, hard-tipped breast.

"Jesus," was all he could think to say as he got to work on her exposed skin.

Her moans, her movements, and the way she gave him access to her drove him mad.

"Now, Austin. I need you now."

He didn't need to be asked twice. He slipped his shorts halfway down, the urgency too great to take the few seconds required to completely dispose of them. He wanted in her. He wanted fast and hard, just the way she liked. She reached down, wrapping her soft, warm hand around him, making him groan.

"I like that you've gotten into the habit of going commando," she moaned against his neck.

"Easier this way."

"For who, you or me?"

371

"I'd say it benefits both of us." He laughed. "God, you're so wet. Holy shit, this isn't going to be slow, baby. Shit, I don't think it's going to last long, I should make you come first, I..."

"Austin," she admonished, gripping his face in her hands. "You're wasting time talking, so shut up." She lifted herself to speak in his ear and whispered, "And fuck me."

"Jesus, Claire..." was all he could manage as he pushed her hand away and slipped inside her to the hilt.

They let out a unified sigh, and he began to move. Not the quick, hard movements she wanted, but rather the slow, tender possession he needed. He needed the connection that convinced him she was real. Her long fingers caressed down his spine, playing each joint of his backbone like a note she had finally figured out. The hair on his arms stood on end, and his breathing was ragged, each touch becoming harder to fill his lungs. She knew exactly what to do to him, exactly how to play him, how to love him. He nearly pulled right out of her when her fingers ventured lower, down the cleft of his ass to the top of his thighs where she pushed him down against her, in her.

"Fuck!" he growled against her neck.

"Yes, babe, you do that..." She giggled.

"Don't laugh. Please don't laugh, or this will be over sooner than we both want it to be."

She lifted her hips, pulling him deeper. He could take a hint, and he picked up the pace. His lips found hers, demanding, sucking, fighting for possession as he moved in and out of her. She let out a loud grunt.

"Shh. Babe, you need to keep it down," he smiled down at her.

"I can't...shit...oh God...babe..." Those were the last words that came out of her mouth before he clamped his mouth over hers to muffle her scream as her body shuddered beneath him.

He moved in and out of her once more before completely burying himself inside her and succumbing to his own release, along with a few muffled curses against her mouth. He leaned his forehead against hers, both their eyes closed, their breathing coming in shallow, ragged gasps as they came down from the best sex he'd ever had. There'd been lots of moments where he couldn't yet seem to fathom how mind-blowing it always was. Each time better, stronger. He opened his eyes to find her staring back at him. He was overwhelmed by the love he saw in her eyes. He kissed her briefly, attempted to move off her, but felt her legs wrap around his legs.

"Don't," she whispered, throwing her head back.

He looked down her body, right to where they were still joined, her hips moving subtly around him. He could feel himself getting hard again. He moved slowly in and out of her. His face was buried in her neck, hers buried in his. It didn't take long. They breathed out quietly, and holding on to each other like the damned world was ending, they came together. Not an explosive release, but intense nonetheless.

Austin lifted himself up on his elbow, ran the knuckle of his free hand down her face, her warmth all around him. With her legs wrapped around him and his cock still buried in her, he decided that was the moment.

"Marry me," he whispered to her, his eyes never leaving hers. He didn't want to miss her reaction, didn't want to miss her lips moving into the one word he longed to hear. He saw the tears slip out of the corners of her eyes. He wiped his thumb across her temple, waiting breathlessly for her answer. He felt her chest rise, saw the resolve in her eyes, and watched her lips curl into the smile he'd been waking to each morning for the past couple of weeks. A smile he wanted to wake to every morning for the rest of his life.

"Yes, I'll marry you, Austin." Although he expected her answer, it still managed to floor him. Finally. He leaned down to kiss her, their bodies moving again of their own volition. He couldn't control his desire for her any more than she could for him.

Home. He'd finally arrived.

CHAPTER

TWENTY-NINE

Claire

She didn't know why it always surprised her to realize her mornings were so disorganized. It hadn't always been that way. She'd had a routine, a system she stuck to, to keep her house, her son, and herself in order. It wasn't until Austin walked back into their lives that it had all gotten a little chaotic. They were always running out the door—late to one thing or other. Her fiancé put her off-kilter. She smiled at thinking of him as her fiancé—she was never going to get tired of saying that word. The only time she'd ever stop saying it was when she would call him her husband.

They'd fallen asleep on the couch the night before, a plush beige blanket draped over her legs with Austin's arm draped over her waist. The sofa was big, wide enough to fit both of them comfortably. They woke to their son's face peeking at them from over the sofa, declaring his hunger. Nothing new with that revelation—the kid was always hungry.

With breakfast eaten, the kitchen cleaned, and shoes on, they prepared to venture out into the streets of Manhattan.

Austin glanced out the window, checking for photographers. Most were gone. So were most of the fans. He'd mentioned last night, lying in the dark, that the paparazzi grew tired of him quickly. He hadn't given them anything worthy of their time. He also mentioned that being involved with her was considered significant news.

"Why?" she'd asked.

"I haven't been in a relationship in over two years. The press is well aware of this. You're interesting, our relationship is interesting. Although they aren't hanging around outside, it doesn't mean they aren't out there spying."

"That's a little creepy."

"Just try to ignore it. Don't look around for them. They'll know and feed on it. Just act normal."

"Right, cause that'll be easy."

"You'll have Tiny; he'll keep you safe," he told her

Tiny was a six-foot-four muscled gorilla of a man. He looked intimidating, his shaved head, tattoos, and prerequisite black shirt and jeans were sure to have anyone keeping off his path. She might have felt a little unsettled as well if she hadn't seen the guy playing Xbox with her son. The two laughed and joked, making friends quickly. His partner Mike was even less approachable—he stayed back, watched quietly. She wondered if the guy even talked. He was head of Austin's security, traveled everywhere with him. She figured if Austin trusted him, she might as well try to as well.

"Okay," Austin's voice interrupted her thoughts. "Tiny is

heading to the art gallery with you. Mike, Charlie, and I will head to the Museum of Natural History. We'll have lunch at The Loeb Boathouse. How's that sound?"

"Perfect. Where will I meet you guys?"

"At the Alice in Wonderland statue. It's right off of Fifth Avenue, down the street from the Metropolitan Museum of Art. Tiny knows where it is."

"Okay."

"Great. I have a cab waiting for each of us. I'll see you later," he said, smiling down at her.

"I love you, my fiancé."

"I love you too, my wife-to-be." He bent to kiss her, his lips lingering longer than they should in the company they were in. She didn't care much that Charlie was present. He'd been subjected to their affections often enough lately and didn't seem to care. She had caught him watching them a time or two, the goofiest smile on his face. He liked seeing them together. Their son was happy, and she would give anything to keep him happy, and most of all, safe. She looked up at Mike.

"Keep my baby safe, Mike."

"Count on it, Ms. Monroe."

"Please, call me Claire."

"Claire," he said, tipping his head.

She bent down to give Charlie a hug and wrestled a kiss out of him.

"Stay close to Daddy, okay? Be good, I love you."

"Love you too, Mom. Have fun looking at pictures," he told her.

She watched the large figure that was Mike. His dark hair was secured in a ponytail, and his big arms were barely contained by his T-shirt, which made him look just as intimidating as Tiny. The two men together were a force to be reckoned with. She doubted anyone got near Austin with them around. That gave her a small amount of comfort. Despite that, she couldn't help the unease that had settled in the pit of her stomach.

Wandering the halls of the Museum of Art for three hours, she'd stopped paying attention to the art. She couldn't shake the unsettled feeling in her gut. She looked at her phone several times, urging the time to move quicker. Tiny kept giving her strange looks. The guy was perceptive. He'd been the one to suggest they head to their meeting place early. They walked down Fifth Avenue. She heard horns blaring, watched people laughing and yelling, smelled the dense scent of seasoning and spices wafting from the falafel street vendors advertising the lamb over rice special. Combine that with the smell of horse manure, and there was no doubt she was near Central Park. The horse-drawn carriages were a small distraction in her determined steps. She was so focused on getting to Austin and Charlie, she nearly jumped when Tiny spoke.

"This way," he said, grabbing her arm and pulling her in the direction of the park. "We need to hurry."

"Why? What's wrong?" He ushered her around joggers and cyclists but didn't respond.

All morning she'd been fighting against the restlessness within. Tiny telling her to hurry didn't do much to calm her already uneasy stomach. He was walking fast; she had to run to keep up with his long strides. She kept her eyes on Tiny, trying to get a clue as to what the problem was because there was a problem. They crossed a street and got on a different path. She heard the crowd before she saw it. Mike looked flustered, trying to keep the hordes of fans back as they surrounded Austin. It was a large group, twenty maybe. She noticed Austin leaning down to speak to Charlie; the alarm on his face was unmistakable.

"Jesus. How did they find him?" she asked.

"They always manage," said Tiny, the frustration evident in his voice.

"But there are so many," said Claire, taking in the scene before her. "I have to get to Charlie."

All she could see was the top of Charlie's head, his face hidden by the crowd. Austin's arm was around him. Her only focus was getting to him and getting him out of the chaos in front of her.

"Stay here, Claire," said Tiny as he made his way towards the crowd.

She moved to walk with him, but his hand on her arm stopped her mid-step.

"Please, Claire. Don't go near that crowd. These girls are

crazy, and right now, you've got something that they consider theirs…"

With the realization of the situation dawning on her, Claire was more determined to get her son out of there. She waited, watched as pens, T-shirts, and cell phones were aimed in his direction, flashes going off like crazy. The clicking as picture after picture was taken echoed in the air. Women, girls, and a few men called out his name, eager to get his attention. Focusing on Austin, she saw him looking around frantically. He looked slightly relieved at seeing Tiny approach. Claire couldn't just stand there; she didn't stop to think of the consequences of what approaching the crowd would mean. She was in mama mode—Charlie was her only goal.

"Excuse me," she yelled, pushing her way through a group of girls.

"Hey, bitch, wait your turn. We were here first," said one girl, pushing Claire back.

"Get out of my way," shouted Claire. She pushed her way through, shoving the woman out of her way. "Austin!" she called as she got on her tip toes.

She looked down at the woman, saw her anger reflected on her face, and then there was recognition. She understood then. Right now you've got something that they consider theirs. A tremor ran through her. She had experienced fear before, but nothing like the threat she saw in this stranger's stare. Claire backed away, common sense telling her she needed to get away from these women. Claire didn't take her eyes off them. She backed away slowly and was met with another body. Claire moved away from that woman, only to be bumped by two others. She was being pushed around from one woman to the next.

"Bitch."

"Whore."

"He's mine."

"Stay away from him."

They yelled the insults at her at the same time, and hands and feet connected with her body. She lost sight of everything, could here Austin's voice calling her name, but couldn't spot him.

"Charlie," she whispered to herself, still aware that she needed to get to her son.

She began pushing, fighting back but was unable to take a step forward. She felt something hard hit her head. Claire heard Tiny's voice, pleading with people to move back, to move away. But he was so far away. Why was he so far away? She needed help. Why was no one helping her? Something hit her head again. No, not just her head, her whole body. Strange faces stared down at her. They were yelling, threatening, pointing. The trees beyond the faces were moving, falling...

"Claire!" Her name was the last thing she heard before everything went black.

●

When Claire's eyes fluttered open, the first thing she noticed was trees with very tall buildings growing out of them.

381

In her right mind, she understood that buildings didn't grow on trees. She tried to shake the absurdity away—her head protested. She reached for her face, feeling the oxygen mask that covered her nose and mouth. She pulled at it in panic, but a warm, familiar hand kept her from doing so.

"Don't try to take it off. Just a few more minutes, Claire."

She looked up, mildly aware that she was on the ground. How long had she been out? Austin stared down at her, worry and one other emotion she couldn't pinpoint evident on his face. She looked over to her right and saw the Alice in Wonderland statue, which didn't help her weary mind.

"Breathe, Claire." Austin's voice was calm, tender.

His fingers caressed her forehead, making their way into her hair. She felt something damp patting her face and smacked away the hand holding it reflexively. Someone she didn't recognize was reaching for her face. She cowered away from the hand. Claire noticed the patch on his right breast. EMS. The paramedic gently eased the oxygen mask off. She sat up suddenly, the world around her spinning as she reached up to grab her head, certain it was going to fall off. She looked around the area. It had been sectioned off. A large crowd and some press stood on the other side of the thick yellow tape. Police were asking questions; some officers gathered in a group, receiving what appeared to be instructions—there were dogs.

She looked around, searching for Charlie's fluorescent green shoes. She scanned the Alice in Wonderland statue. There was nothing—absolutely no sign of her son. She hadn't realized she'd gotten to her knees. Claire turned when she felt a hand on her shoulder. Austin stood right next to her. Her hand went to his chest, gripping his thin white button-down shirt. She gripped hard enough for a couple of buttons to pop.

"Charlie," she gasped, tears rimming her eyes. "Where's Charlie?"

Her heart was beating fast. She could feel the heaviness in her chest as she fought to fill her lungs with air.

"I don't know..." said Austin.

"What do you mean, you don't know?"

"I had him by the hand, Claire. I was holding on to him, I swear," he explained. He let out his breath. "I saw how those women were hurting you, and I tried to get to you. I was pushed, and we separated. I looked back to look for him, but there were so many people, Claire. I couldn't...I couldn't hold on to him..."

She looked at him, hoping that what he was saying was a joke. Maybe this was a dream—a really bad dream. Air wasn't making it to her lungs. Her chest felt tight, her head hurt, and her son was gone. She took small gulps of air and felt her head swirling. She was going to pass out. Shit, that hadn't happened in a long time. Not since they'd broken up. For months after, she had panic attacks. She knew the symptoms, felt it coming on.

"My son," she choked out, her voice hoarse. "Where is my son!" she shouted.

Her hands still gripped Austin's shirt as she looked up at

him. The look in his eyes was one she would never forget—fear, worry, and disappointment bundled into one numb stare. She vaguely heard the deep, demanding voices of Tiny and Mike talking on the phone, and the soft, crushed sound of Austin murmuring "I'm sorry…"

A sob tore from deep in her chest. All she could think about was her son. Charlie. Charlie. Charlie. "You lost him?"

"I…" he tried, but nothing came out.

She wanted Charlie back, to hold him and wrestle those kisses from him. She wanted to see him wipe his face when she finally did manage to steal a kiss or two. She scrambled to her feet, laying her hands flat on Austin's chest when he tried to help her, pushing him away.

"Don't touch me," she sneered.

"Claire…"

"No," she said, holding up a finger to stop him. "I need to find my son. I can't even look at you right now." She turned and walked away, her legs thankfully obeying.

She approached the first police officer she spotted. He looked like he was in charge, and she hoped to God he had answers.

"I'm Charlie's mother, Claire. What can you tell me?"

"Mrs. McKinley, we—"

"It's Monroe. You can call me Claire. Now tell me what you know?" she asked, sounding as strong as possible under the circumstance. She was going on pure adrenaline.

384

"At the moment, we don't know anything. He could have wandered away or maybe—"

"You think someone took him?"

"We are looking at any and all possibilities. Your hus—"

"He isn't my husband," she corrected before the word was out of his mouth.

"Mr. McKinley is a public figure, and people do all sorts of things for attention and money. We have to look at all the scenarios."

"He could have walked away, right?" A thought dawned on her. She looked in the direction of the restaurant. Water. There was a pond. "Oh God. Could he have...he can't swim very well." She felt the panic rising.

"Breathe, Claire," said Austin, his hand on her shoulder.

She shook it away. She didn't want him comforting her; she didn't want him touching her. All she wanted was her son, and he was nowhere to be seen.

"We have a team searching the lake, the reservoir, and the Harlem Meer. We have men throughout the park."

"He could be anywhere!"

"We're looking for him, Claire. We have a car waiting for you to take you to the precinct."

"I'm supposed to just leave and wait there?"

"There's nothing you can do here that we aren't already doing. You'll just get in the way. As soon as we have news, we'll let you know."

"I can't just leave!"

"Claire?"

"What?" she gritted out, turning to look at Austin.

"We should go. There's press here, and a crowd is gathering."

She looked around. It wasn't a crowd. It was a damned mob, and they were chanting Austin's name. The fans had no idea of the turmoil they were going through. These selfish people only cared about getting their fix—an autograph, a picture, and whatever else they felt they had a right to.

"The women that hurt me…where are they?" she asked the police officer.

"They're in custody. They're being charged with assault."

"You won't have to worry about that, Claire. Rick is taking care of it," said Austin.

"Thank God for small mercies," she snapped.

She looked at the crowd, a hatred for these people slowly seeping into her bones. There were photographers too. She didn't think they were there for any legitimate reporting. No, they weren't there for her, they were there for Austin. She and her son were just casualties.

Austin's grip tightened on her arm, pulling her in the direction of the waiting car.

"I said don't touch me," she hissed. "This is on you. You

lost my son because your lifestyle requires you to indulge a bunch of strangers, giving them the right to exact their misguided affections."

"Claire…" he gasped.

"I've spent every day since he was born protecting him, nurturing him, and making sure his wellbeing and safety were my number-one priority. You've spent three weeks in his life, and it all goes to shit. This is on you. If something happens to him…"

"Don't say it…"

"Mr. McKinley, Claire, you should head out," said the officer.

She hesitated for a moment, looked around one more time, and walked ahead of Austin, knowing that she couldn't get in the way if she wanted her son found. She looked out into the crowd and the park beyond them—he could be anywhere. Maybe, she thought, one of these people would bring him back. Maybe their devotion to Austin would encourage them to help. She didn't know these people, she didn't particularly care or like them, but she needed to have faith in them.

As soon as she had her son back, she would leave this madness behind.

CHAPTER THIRTY

Austin

They'd been waiting for six hours for any news. Six hours since Charlie disappeared from his side. A million scenarios ran through his head, and he couldn't escape them. Claire wasn't speaking to him. Her face was pale; she hadn't wanted anything to eat or drink. She'd barely said a word since they were dropped off at the precinct.

The ride had been torture. She hadn't looked at him since she yelled at him at the park. She sat in a corner, away from the windows and the prying eyes of the crowd gathering outside. They'd been escorted to an office that faced the street. The windows didn't have curtains or blinds, giving the photographers, press, and fans a clear view of their agony.

He blamed himself. The situation had gotten out of control fast, and his only thought when he saw those women hurting Claire was to get to her. To save her and take both her and Charlie somewhere safe. The memory of being shoved and feeling Charlie's little hand slipping from his grip was something that was going to haunt him for the rest of his life.

Fuck, he should have said no to that first fan and walked away. But then they descended on them like vultures fighting for their meal. He'd met aggressive fans before, but nothing like this. Today had been terrifying, further cementing the fact that he needed to get out of the band. This life wasn't for him anymore.

The fear and worry he saw on Claire's face was killing him. He'd tried to hold her hand at one point, only to have her pull away. She kept grabbing her stomach, rocking back and forth in her chair. He understood her agony; he felt it himself. Every few minutes he would watch a tear slip down her face, which she roughly wiped away. Austin sat in his own corner, praying for his son's safe return, promising the universe anything to never let this happen again. He wanted to turn back the fucking clock and live out their morning once again. Make different choices. Those what ifs were driving him mad. He was angry, and he had never felt so helpless. He was a complete Goddamn failure.

They'd let their guard down. He and Mike thought they were scot-free. There were a few tourists; none that would bat an eye in his direction. He'd even worn a different cap, opting to leave the Bubba Gump trademark at home to avoid recognition. The paparazzi, though, had been a dead giveaway. They'd been trailing them that whole morning.

They'd gotten a lot of footage, some video, and of course, hundreds of photos. The press had voluntarily handed over their cameras to the police, and they'd spent a couple of hours going through every single frame of video and photo. Claire had looked at everything at least four times, whispering to herself, willing for Charlie to turn back around as he walked away from the crowd surrounding Austin. He had his backpack, and they could clearly see what he was wearing, which helped for a clearer description.

Claire had mentioned to the officers that he had his iPod with him—he never went anywhere without it. They'd quickly gotten on the task of tracing it, only to discover its find feature wasn't enabled. She held her phone in her hands, typing a few words to him, hoping for an answer. He hadn't responded—a sign the damned thing could have run out of batteries.

"Is there anywhere he could have gone, Claire?" blurted Austin.

"What? No. Where would he go? He's never been here, he doesn't know the city. Where the fuck would he go?" she hissed.

"I know, I'm sorry."

"Oh, stop," she said, sounding so angry and scared. "Your I'm sorry's aren't going to bring him back, Austin. Why did you let him go? You should have held him tighter…damn you!"

"I…Claire, please let me hold you," he said at last, needing her.

"I don't want you near me," she cried into her hands. "I don't want you near me. I just want my baby…"

He backed away from her, shocked by her words. He understood her anger, but the rejection scared the shit out of him. All the steps forward they'd taken had suddenly come to a halt, the footprints fading with every tear that slid down her face.

There was commotion on the street, flashes going off like a red carpet had been laid out. There were shouts. They both stood just as the door to the office opened. Claire's parents walked in, hand in hand, approaching Austin first, giving him words of encouragement. Behind them were his parents and Analia, followed closely by Hunter. Austin let out a ragged breath and shook his head as his mother held her arms open for him.

"I fucked up, Mom."

"It'll be all right, Austin. Everything will be all right," she whispered as his father and sister surrounded him.

"He'll be found, Austin. He's your son, tough as nails," reassured his father.

He held on to his mother for dear life. She'd always understood him, knew exactly the pain he was in. The woman could read him like a book, and he could never hide anything from her. She understood the guilt he felt, the fear of losing the family he was fighting like hell to keep. As much as he loved his mother's arms around him, they brought little comfort. Claire, on the other hand, let out a muffled sob and ran into her father's outstretched arms.

"He's lost, Daddy. He's out there all alone, and we can't find him. We can't find him," she cried.

"Shhh, baby girl. He'll come back to us, you'll see."

"I want my baby...I want my baby."

Her sobs were painful to hear. He wanted to be the one holding her, giving her comfort. For the first time since he'd walked into her house, he wished he'd just stayed away. If it meant she'd have their son back, safe and sound, he'd go back four weeks and leave them to their lives.

Bruce pulled him aside briefly to ask what had happened. He told him everything, from the second they'd left the museum. He told him about the confrontation with the fans, the pap, and worst of all, being unable to get back to Charlie.

"I'm sorry, Bruce. I'm so fucking sorry," he said through a tortured cry. "If he doesn't... he has to be okay. I can't lose them...I can't lose them."

The worst part of it all was that he knew that no matter what happened, he'd lost the biggest part of his life. He raised his gaze to Claire at the exact moment she looked up at him. There it was, in her eyes, in her tears, all the confirmation he needed. The disgust with which she looked at him hit him in the center of a heart that was slowing its beats by the second.

He walked to the bathroom, lowered the toilet seat, and sat. With his elbows on his knees, he cried into his hands. His shoulders shook uncontrollably. He let go completely, coming to terms with the fear for his son, fear for the love he felt, for the anger he felt. After today, nothing would ever be the same.

Minutes later, he let the water run for a few seconds and bent over the sink. The cold water felt amazing on his swollen eyes. He was emotionally exhausted, drained. If he felt this way, he couldn't imagine how Claire felt. If she would only let him near her—all he wanted was to hold her. Tell her once again how sorry he was, that he loved her and Charlie more than anything. He was leaning against the sink, running his hands through his hair, when the door opened.

"They've got news," said his father.

Both men ran the short distance to the office they'd been holed up in. The captain was standing by the desk, putting down a pad of paper and pen. He looked at both him and Claire and it seemed like an eternity before he spoke.

"He's been found," he said simply.

Everyone let out their breath in audible relief.

"Thank God," Claire sobbed.

"Is he okay?" Austin asked.

"Yes. He was picked up at a Starbucks on Broadway and Forty-First Street."

"Jesus. That's almost forty blocks from the park. He walked straight down Fifth Avenue," said Austin, more to himself than for anyone's information.

"He'd been there for a while. He was waiting for his iPod to charge so he could text his mom," a fragment of a smile appeared on the captain's face.

"Who found him?" Claire asked.

"One of the baristas recognized him from the pictures that had been broadcasted. She called the precinct a few minutes ago. A cruiser is bringing him over as we speak. He's fine, not a scratch on him," the captain reassured her.

"Thank God."

"He should be here shortly. We're bringing him through the back. We haven't announced that he's been found. We won't do that until you leave. It's been a traumatizing day, and we want you to avoid the crowd out front, so you'll leave through the back as well."

A movement caught his attention, and he noticed two people in maintenance uniforms covering the windows with blankets. He sat heavily on a chair and let his shoulders drop. He didn't know if he should cry or scream or laugh. The relief the knowledge of Charlie's whereabouts brought was overwhelming. He felt the heavy hand of his father pat him firmly on the back. His mother's delicate fingers brushed through his hair, and he crumbled. Austin leaned against his mother's hip and cried, gripping her shirt for the support he so badly needed in that moment. What felt like eons later, they all looked to the door at the sound of the captain giving out instructions. Austin heard Charlie's footsteps before he made it to the door.

"Daddy!" yelled Charlie as he crossed the threshold.

Austin fell to his knees, opened his arms for his son, and held him tight to his chest. He felt Claire do the same, her arms coming around Charlie, careful not to touch Austin. Austin couldn't help it though. He let go of his son and reached out for her. She didn't fight him this time. He ran his hand up her back, to her hair, and pulled her to him.

"I'm sorry, Claire. Please forgive me. I'm so sorry, I love you both so much," he sobbed into her hair.

Her shoulders shook; she wasn't crying for Charlie anymore.

"Mr. McKinley. We need to get you folks out of here before it gets out that he's been found."

He nodded, helped Claire to her feet, who held on to Charlie's hand like he could disappear again at any moment.

"You need to make a statement," said Rick.

Austin looked up, surprised to see his manager standing there. "When did you get here?"

"Just now. I prepared two statements. One for when he was found and another in case he…" he trailed off, stopping mid-sentence at the irritation on Austin's face.

"I'm not making a statement, Rick. This isn't some sort of publicity stunt. You know better than anyone that my private life stays private. I have nothing to say."

"But you're Austin McKinley. People are going to expect something," he told his client.

"My girlfriend was assaulted, and my son got lost—all because the fans can't control themselves. I don't care what they expect—I owe them nothing. This is my family, and we've been through enough today. Our faces have been plastered on every TV screen. Enough is enough. I need to get them home."

He turned to the captain, took a deep breath, and asked, "How do we get out of here?"

"You'll be using the back door and hoping for the best."

He shrugged.

"Okay." He picked up Charlie and snuggled him into the crook of his neck, reached for Claire's hand before she could object, and motioned to one of the officers standing near the door to lead the way.

They could hear the unmistakable sound of a crowd gathered outside. He tightened his grip on Claire's hand when she tried to pull away. No fucking way he was letting her go now.

"What now?" he asked the officer, who put up his hand and called orders into his radio.

Several men in uniform marched down the hallway towards them. Beyond them was Rick, watching them with a malevolent glint in his eyes.

Bastard.

He'd tipped them off. Austin was sure of it. What the hell was he playing at? This was his life and family Rick was fucking with, and Austin was going to have none of it. He wouldn't be shocked at all if he was the one who tipped the pap off about Austin staying in Springridge. He shook his head. He'd have to deal with Rick later. Austin could hear screams when the door opened, and camera flashes went off like it was necessary to light the way.

"Charlie, I need you to keep your head tucked into my neck, okay? Whatever happens, don't look up. You too, Claire. And don't let go of my hand."

"They're ready, sir."

"Thank you." Austin looked back at their parents, who were coming behind them.

"You three go ahead," said Ben. "We'll find a way out and meet you at the house."

"Okay, Dad. And thanks for being here. All of you," Austin said, looking at his family members.

He looked at Hunter, who gave him a thumbs up. Austin simply nodded and braced himself for the storm brewing just outside the doors. He walked with Claire tucked under his arm, her arm across Charlie's back. Once the door opened, the screams multiplied to a deafening buzz. Flashes blinded him as they made their way to the police cruiser waiting for them just a few feet away. The officers that had gone out to tame the crowd were visibly struggling with keeping the people away. He let Claire in first, then handed her Charlie. He quickly followed, never acknowledging the crowd.

"Let's get out here," he ordered. "I don't want to give anyone the chance to follow us home."

The ride to the house was endless. Claire held a sleeping Charlie on her lap, her face buried in his dirty blond curls, her stare firmly aimed out the car window, deep in thought. The drive was taking forever. At three in the morning, it might take twenty to twenty-five minutes to get there. At eight o'clock in the evening, it could take as long as an hour. He was starting to feel his body give out on him; he was exhausted. It'd been a long day, and he longed for his bed. Looking at Claire, whose eyes were now closed, he wondered if she'd be joining him. Austin fought back against the urge to reach for her. She didn't want him near her, and that knowledge alone hurt like fucking hell.

After an eternal silent drive, the house came into view. He wanted to feel relief, but even after getting out of the car and then stepping into the house, it didn't come. He stood at the bottom of the stairs and watched Claire carry their son to his room. He would've offered to carry him, but she didn't give him the chance to ask. Their parents' steps sounded on the stairs outside. Austin opened the door before they could ring the doorbell.

"Where are Claire and Charlie?" asked Marcia as she walked into his house.

"Upstairs. Charlie fell asleep in the car. Claire carried him to bed," he said, resigned.

He ushered everyone towards the living room. With all the chaos of the last few hours, he had no chance to prepare himself for the reaction Claire's parents had to her paintings hanging on his wall. Bruce and Marcia stood staring in awe at the painting over the fireplace. Marcia looked back at him, questioning, and he shrugged, a barely there smile on his face. She smiled back, tears in her eyes.

"He wants you," said Claire from behind him.

He turned, stared for a long moment, capturing her gaze for a brief second before she turned away. She walked past him towards her parents. As he walked up the stairs, he heard her mother ask her if she knew he had the paintings. He didn't hear her answer, but obviously knew what it was.

Charlie was asleep when he entered his room. Austin kneeled next to his bed and ran his fingers through his soft curls. Charlie blinked once and looked at him between heavy eyelids.

"Hi, Daddy."

"Hey, buddy. You doing okay?"

"Yeah, I'm just really tired."

"I bet. It's been a long day."

"Daddy, I'm sorry I walked away. There were just so many people and—"

"Shh, it's okay. You're safe now, that's all the matters."

"Mommy says we're going home tomorrow."

His heart broke at those words.

"Go to sleep. We'll be downstairs if you need us." He leaned in and kissed him on the forehead. "I love you, Charlie…so much. Don't ever forget that."

"I love you, too, Daddy."

Austin walked out of the room, leaving a small gap in the door so they could hear him if called out. Their parents had made themselves at home in the TV room, coffees in hand.

"Charlie okay?" asked his father.

"Yeah, he's asleep," he said and stared at the four sets of eyes staring back at him. "Where's Claire?"

"She's in the backyard, said she needed some air," said Marcia. He nodded at them and went looking for her.

400

In the kitchen, he watched her for a few minutes from the doorway. She was shuffling her foot back and forth. Her arms were wrapped around her stomach, staring up at the sky. Her face was in profile, but he could see that her brows were furrowed. She'd put her hair up in a messy bun, tendrils curling at the nape of her neck. She was beautiful, and he knew in that instant that he would never, ever love another the way he loved her. He opened the door, and he knew she heard it because it made a loud suction noise that couldn't be quieted. He walked to stand beside her.

"Are you in any pain?"

"A bit, but I'll survive."

"Charlie said you're going home tomorrow."

"It's for the best."

"The best for who?"

"For everyone," she said, still not looking at him.

He didn't want to argue with her. He was tired of being angry, and he'd spent the whole day bouncing from one emotion to another. He was fucking exhausted. But he couldn't stay quiet.

"Bullshit," he spit out. "The only person this benefits is you because this is how you do things. This is how you've always done things with me."

"What are you talking about?"

"The way you push me away. It's so easy for you."

"Oh, please. Don't lay this shit on me. This isn't about

401

you; it's about Charlie and what's best for him."

"So taking him away from me is what's best for him?"

She let out her breath and turned to face him. The anger on her face made him take a step back.

"I'm not taking him away from you, Austin. Don't be so dramatic. I'm taking him home, to the place where we live. Away from the madness that is your life."

"I thought the madness didn't bother you?" he asked sarcastically.

"That was before it touched me. Before you lost my son in a crowd of your crazy fans."

"Our son," he hissed.

"What?"

"He's our son, and don't you forget it. You took him from me once, Claire. I won't let you take him away from me again. I have good lawyers."

"Don't threaten me!"

"I'm not. I'm promising you."

"I'm going into the house to pack our things. I've booked us a flight first thing in the morning. I am going home with my son. You can visit him anytime you want, but after what happened today, I'll be damned if he'll ever spend time alone with you."

"Claire," he called out when she walked around him and towards the house. "Please," he whispered.

She stopped, one foot in the door. "I can't do this right now, Austin. I need time to think. I'm not sure your life, your fans, and all the attention you garner fits into our lives. He was scared today. Hell, I was scared for my life. That's why he walked away. He's all I've had. He's my whole life, and I won't risk his safety. I'm sorry, Austin. But he does and will always come first."

He watched her walk into the house, and he wanted to scream, to beg for her to stay. There would be nothing he regretted more in his life than being the reason why their wellbeing was threatened.

He fell to his knees, desperately gripping his hair with both hands, and for the second time that day, he cried. Tears spilling nonstop down his face. For the second time in his life, he let the love of his life walk away from him. Things would be different this time. He knew what was at stake, and he needed to fix it. If she wanted time, he would give her time, but he wasn't losing her or Charlie again. Before he even made a move, he had to sort things out with the band. Determined, he got up and walked into the house that, despite his guests, felt empty already.

His father found him minutes later. Austin had a tumbler in hand, staring out the front window.

"You're not just going to let her go, are you, son?"

"Not a chance."

"Then why are you sitting in the dark moping?"

"I'm not moping, I'm thinking. She asked for time, Dad,

so I'm going to give her time." He looked up at his father and smiled.

"By the look on your face, I assume it's your time you're talking about?"

"Damn right."

CHAPTER THIRTY-ONE

Claire

"I'm going for a jog," Claire announced to her parents as they sat staring at each other. She had so much going on in her head. Her current separation from Austin was one thing. This news was just one more thing she would have to process. She needed an outlet, something to do, away from them and the kitchen that would forever remind her of the time her father told her and Hunter he had cancer. She pushed away from her stool, letting it scrape across the hardwood.

She couldn't listen to anything else he had to say. She was in shock. Her father had uttered the big C word, and there wasn't an ounce of fear in his revelation. Sure, his prognosis was good; stage one colorectal cancer had it perks—a ninety-two percent survival rate. But it was still cancer. The disease sat in his body, waiting to invade other parts while fighting against its most potent nemesis—chemotherapy.

She had to hand it to her dad, his optimism was commendable. "No worries," he'd uttered in reassurance. Sure, she looked calm, but inside she was dying. This was her

405

daddy. The daddy she'd finally gotten back after a long time away.

How was it possible that everything in her life was all of a sudden a giant leap backward? Move forward with her parents, step back. Move forward with Austin, massive leap back. What the hell was going on—when was she going to get her happily-ever-fucking-after?

She started to walk out of the kitchen when Hunter spoke. He'd remained quiet throughout the discussion of treatment and prognosis. The whole little gathering felt more like an information session.

"When did you find out?" Hunter asked.

Hunter had never been a talker, but she imagined he'd have some questions. He and their father were a work in progress. She turned to look at him—she could see the small glimpse of fear in her brother's eyes.

Her father cleared his throat, looked at her as if his answer would mean further revelation.

"Three weeks ago," he said and once again looked straight at her.

She thought back. They'd gone out for burgers. The realization she'd just come to terms with must have shown on her face. It was at the diner. You'll take care of them? her father had asked Austin. Of course, but everything will be fine. You need to have faith, was Austin's response.

"You told Austin," she said, remembering that he told her it was something big. "That day in the diner, that's what the two of you were talking about. He kept your secret, he wouldn't..." Tears rolled down her face. "You were making plans, making sure we'd be okay. Are you telling us everything, Dad?"

"Yes, Claire. I've told you everything. My chances are good. Your mom and I have finally found our way back to you and Hunter. I won't let this put a crack in the new foundation we've managed to build. I have lots to make up for. I'm not done yet."

"Does Alexa know?" asked Hunter.

"No. Your mom called her this morning and left a voicemail."

"I talked to her last night," said Claire. "She's been really busy, hardly gets reception where she is. It might be a while before she gets back to you."

"I'll keep trying her," said her mother.

Everyone grew quiet. Claire stared at Hunter, who was lost in thought, staring out the back door. His parents were leaning on each other, Bruce's hand making small circles on Marcia's back.

"I need air. I'll be at the high school. Can you stay here and watch Charlie?" she asked, directing the question to her parents. They never passed up a chance to spend time with their only grandchild.

She reached for her bottle of water, walked around the kitchen island, and headed out the door. She ran down the porch steps to temporary freedom from the insanity in her home and in her head.

She ran around the track eight times. The last time around she ran full speed, nearly passing out from the heat and exhaustion. She was never one to over-exert herself; she was mindful of how much her body could take. She'd been out of sorts in the last few days, barely able to stomach anything. The brief realization that she could be pregnant had crossed her mind, but a trip to the pharmacy and a negative pregnancy test later did nothing to put her at ease. If anything, she'd been disappointed. It was absurd to want a baby at this point in her life. Her relationship with Austin was nonexistent. They hadn't spoken at all in the last three weeks. He'd call the house, she would see the number and hand the phone to Charlie—it was him he wanted to speak to after all.

She ran to the middle of the football field and dropped to the ground, trying to catch her breath. The school brought back so many memories. It was in that very spot that Austin told her what they were naming the band.

"We're going to be called Yellow Scarlet," he announced.

"Most people associate scarlet with red. Are you sure that will fly?" she'd asked, laughing at the contradiction in the name.

"Why not? It's different." It had worked, of course, and the look on his face that day was unforgettable.

She was so tired of having just the memories to fall back on, and so tired of missing him. Not a day had gone by that she didn't think of him. Not a morning that she didn't reach out to his side of the bed for him. He had a side of the bed, she thought with a whimper. She stared at it every night before she closed her eyes. Tears filled her eyes. God, she needed him. She needed him to tell her it was going to be all right, that her father was going to be fine. She wondered if things had died down for him. She'd had some calls from major networks requesting interviews, all of which she declined. Her family's scariest moment wasn't up for public consumption. The calls had stopped a few days ago, and aside from Austin's nightly calls to Charlie, the phone was silent.

Her life was a mess. She felt lost, just as she had when she had let him go the first time. If it wasn't for Charlie, she would have completely fallen apart. The events in New York hadn't seemed to affect him in the least. Baseball was still a weekly obligation he took very seriously. Often, though, she'd find him staring into the dugout. He told her the week before that he missed Austin yelling instructions to him.

Her hands covered her face as her body shook with grief. She hadn't cried since the first night back, but she couldn't contain the despair. Not after her father's revelation. Despite his reassurances, she was fucking terrified. She screamed at the top of her lungs and felt her vocal cords strain at the action. She heard the hoarseness in her voice as she let out her sobs. She was alone in the field. The track was empty, too hot out for anyone to be jogging the shit out of themselves. How had her life gone from good, to great, to a downright disaster?

After their encounter on the terrace, she and Austin didn't speak again. She'd said what was on her mind, knew that most of her words were out of fear and anger for what could have happened to Charlie, because let's face it, she knew damn well that Austin would never let anything happen to Charlie. That realization had her regretting her actions and words towards him. She'd hurt him, again. Anger had taken over, and she didn't know how to take any of it back.

"You're so stupid!" she said and let out a growl as more tears fell.

She didn't hear the footsteps. His silhouette blocking the sun from her face was all she saw. She knew his build, recognized the slight slouch of his shoulders, the tilt of his head in the exact position Charlie tilted it. Most of all, she recognized the fresh, spicy scent of his cologne.

"Cry here often?" he said, giving her feet a soft kick.

"Nah, first time, you?" she said between sobs.

"I got no more tears left in me, baby. Just came over here to pick up your pieces."

"Such a gentleman." God, she'd missed the banter.

"Thank my mother. It was all her doing. Mind if I join you?"

"You want to join me?"

"More than anything," he whispered, his voice cracking.

She patted the ground beside her and had to laugh when Austin didn't hesitate. The second his body hit the ground, he reached for her hand. He was so close, she heard him let out his breath. She turned her head to look at him—his eyes were closed, his lips forming a small oh as he exhaled, trying to control emotions she knew he was fighting against.

She took in his features, his day-old stubble, those damn dark circles that were confirmation the past few weeks had been hell. Nonetheless, he was gorgeous. His dark blond hair, long lashes, and high cheekbones made him look strong and fearless—a contradiction to the fragile soul deep inside.

"Why do we do this to each other?" he asked, inhaling deeply before continuing. "What I really want to know, though—why is it so easy for you to walk away?"

"It's not. It wasn't easy to do five years ago. As for New York, I was angry and scared. I realized that maybe Charlie and I couldn't make it in your world."

"You're my…" His voice caught. "You're my world. I've always known that without you in it, I was nothing. But now, without Charlie, it's complete hell."

She turned to look at him—the agony marring his beautiful face tortured her.

"Austin…"

"You have to know, Claire, I would never intentionally jeopardize our son's life." The last word was a whisper. "I've gone over and over that day in my head, and what I should have done differently. It was my fault; I take full responsibility. We should have driven to pick you up. Walking through the park was a bad call. I'm so sorry. So sorry."

"I know, Austin. I know," she reassured. There was so much more they needed to work through. "I just need to know how we're going to move forward now."

"I need to know you trust me with your heart and our son. With everything."

"I do. I trust you implicitly. I was wrong to blame you, Austin."

"No, it was my fault. I should have taken better precautions, had more security with us. I let my guard down, and I will never forgive myself for that," he told her and turned onto his side to look at her. "What I need now more than anything is you, babe. I can't do it without you and Charlie. I've missed you so much."

She'd had the energetic distraction that was her son to keep her on her feet. In that instant, with him lying next to her, with his spicy cologne filling her senses, she was able to fully acknowledge how desperately she'd missed him. She'd struggled without him, emotionally, mentally. She had managed to depend on him in the short time they'd spent getting to know each other again. He was the baseball coach, the assistant carpooler, the cook, the partner she'd always known he could be. However, it was the physical connection they'd found that she had missed the most. The deep need and desire, the feel of his body next to hers, his hand brushing her hair away from her face, and the sex...how she missed the sex. Forget the next five years. She was hanging by the thinnest piece of thread imaginable. She couldn't make it another day without him.

"I missed you too. I need you, I want you, and Charlie needs you. I can't...Please tell me you came to stay," she sobbed. "I pushed you away, and I'm sorry, but I can't do this anymore without you."

Tears streamed down her face as she reached for him, grabbing his shirt and sobbing into his chest. The relief that swamped her when she felt his arms around her was rivaled only by seeing her son running into that police station in Manhattan.

"There's no way I would ever let you continue without me. You're my home, my sanity, my life. There's no question where I belong."

"Together we have the answer, Austin. Always together."

His smile unfolded across his striking face, making his eyes light up with joy.

They stood at the same time, giggling like children. He picked her up and carried her towards the parking lot, and she noticed the motorcycle.

"I didn't even hear you drive up," she said.

"You were too busy screaming."

She laughed. He put his arm around her shoulders, pulling her to him.

"I love you, Austin McKinley. I don't ever want to be apart from you again," she said, sliding her hand into his back pocket. "Charlie's going to be so excited to see you."

"I already saw him. I stopped by the house, and your mom told me where to find you."

He let her go, turned away, and fumbled through one of

the compartments on the motorcycle. His pants hung low on his hips, giving her a delightful view of his ass. He turned to her, a look in his eyes she'd seen often—mischievous yet determined. His hand was behind his back as he searched for words, his mouth opening and closing several times before he spoke. He was nervous.

"Okay," he said, more to himself than to her. "I just want to remind you that you've already agreed to this and I just need to make it official. Shit…I'm so nervous," he told her, smiling. "Before everything happened, Charlie and I didn't go to the museum. We went to Tiffany's. He helped me pick this out." He held out his hand.

In between his thumb and index finger, he held a diamond ring, encircled by a halo of smaller diamonds. It was stunning, reflecting the sun in a magnificent show of light.

"It's beautiful," she said simply.

"Your son has very expensive taste."

"He picked this?"

Austin nodded and they both laughed.

"Remind me to thank him when we get home," she said.

He got down on one knee, reached for her left hand, and stared at her as if it were the first time.

"Claire Alexandra Monroe, will you please accept this ring, here in the place I first laid eyes on you, and do me the extraordinary honor of becoming my wife?"

"Yes, yes, yes, a million times yes," she said without

hesitation.

He slipped the ring onto her finger, got to his feet, and kissed her like his life depended on it. And it very well did, she thought. "We're going to have a great life, sweetheart. I promise you that. Kids, dogs, the whole shebang."

"I look forward to it. Take me home, Austin."

EPILOGUE

"What's going to happen with the band?" she asked, hours later. Charlie was fast asleep, and Austin was helping her put away dishes from dinner with her parents.

"Come, leave that until tomorrow. I'm exhausted. Let's go to bed and I'll tell you everything."

He took the dish towel from her hand, threw it on the counter, and dragged her up the stairs. They checked on Charlie, closed his door, and headed to their bedroom. The light on the night table was on, giving the room a romantic glow. He closed the door behind them and immediately reached for the hem of the dress she'd changed into, working his way up as he walked her backward to the bed. He pulled the dress over her head and tossed it aside. He took a small step back, taking a minute to appreciate the fact that she wore nothing at all underneath.

"Commando?"

"Too hot for underwear," she said, echoing his words from a few weeks ago.

"Thank God…" he said between kisses.

She reached down for his jeans, groaned with frustration

when the button didn't budge. Laughing against her lips, he reached down and took care of the little dilemma. He grabbed her hips and gently urged her onto the bed. He felt his way down her body, his fingers checking her readiness, lingering a while. She writhed beneath him. He groaned against her neck. Not bothering with his shirt or wasting another second, he slid into her.

"Jesus…you're so wet… I'm not going to last, Claire." He moved in and out of her, his lips on her throat first, then moving to her face, her eyes, and finally her mouth. It didn't matter how long it would take him because she was on the verge of exploding. All it took was his body, moving and grinding against hers. She fell with him, an array of lights behind her eyelids, her body shuddering as the orgasm drifted through her.

"It's never the same," she whispered. "Every time we come together is different."

"I love you. You have no idea how much, Claire. I could spend the rest of my life trying to show you, and you wouldn't know. It's endless." He tightened his arms around her.

He had to know she felt the same.

Minutes later, they lay still on the bed, facing each other. She held her hand out in front of her, watching the diamond on her finger sparkle in the dim light of the room.

"Tell me what happened with the band."

"The long or short version?"

"The gist of it."

He took a deep breath and ran his hand down her arm, watching the path his fingers took.

"For the most part, I'm no longer part of the band. I will write four songs a year for them, though. If Yellow Scarlet breaks up, the songs belong to the record company. I get credit and royalties. They're going to hold some contest to find a lead singer."

"So you're out?"

"I'm out."

"Are you sure about that? I mean, is this really what you want, Austin? You've worked so hard."

"Right here is where I want to be, Claire. You and Charlie are my home."

"I don't want you to regret anything."

"The only thing I regret is not coming for you sooner."

"This is it, then?"

"It's you and me against the world, babe…"

They smiled at each other like fools. She gripped the hem of his shirt he hadn't bothered to take off and pulled it over his head, wanting desperately to feel him. They slipped under the covers.

"Thanks for being there for my dad all those weeks ago. He desperately needed your reassurance. He was really acting weird after we got back from New York. I didn't know why then, but I get it now. He trusts you, Austin, and my father doesn't trust many people."

"I promise to try harder with him."

"Thanks. I'd really like for the two of you to be friends."

They lay in silence for a bit, Austin's fingers still gliding up and down her arm. She smiled, feeling content. She had faith everything would turn out.

"Did your dad tell you he spoke to Alexa?"

"Yeah. I talked to her too. She wasn't too happy to be kept in the dark, but my dad had reassured her. I think her client added to her aggravation."

"Oh yeah. How so?"

"Turns out, Mr. Pemberton is a real pain in the ass. He's giving her a hard time. The way things look, she might be there for longer than a month."

"Cabo is not a bad place to be stuck for a month."

"But I need her here, and soon," she told him.

"For what?"

"To help me plan our September wedding…"

"You're not wasting any time are you?" he said and rolled onto her. "I like it. I can't wait to make you my wife."

She couldn't wait to be his wife either, and she hoped that someday her friend would find the love she had. Alexa had had her share of affairs but often closed herself off to relationships. Mexico would be good for her. Maybe she would let loose and not let Patrick Pemberton get to her. No billionaire was a match for her friend, however, there was no one tougher than Alexa. Pemberton had his work cut out for him.

"It's quiet and still early. Whatever are we going to do?" she asked mischievously.

"I can think of a few things," said Austin as he rolled on top of her. "Starting right here," he mumbled against her breasts.

Every night would be like this, if not better. Every morning she would wake up with him next to her, and she knew she would never get tired of it.

They both giggled as Claire brought the bedsheet over them and got down to starting again. The best day of her life was the day when he came back.

The End!

Acknowledgements

Writing is a solitary journey. You have to push yourself; often times sit in front of a computer and stare at a blank screen, searching for the words to build your story. It isn't easy. It helps, however, to have a cheering section, no matter how small. In this case it was a cheering section that consisted of my twin sister, Pamela, who was the first person I showed my words to. Thank you, Sis for always urging me to finish and for showing excitement over what I often thought was a pipe dream. To my little sister Denise, I thank you so you don't complain you're not in this section (and because I was on the phone with you while I was writing this) I love you. To my book pushers, cousins and best friends Cherie, Marcela, Paulina and Viani thanks for always introducing me to new and exciting reading material that was often inspiration to follow this crazy dream.

To my mother, for laughing the first time I told her I was writing a book and then finally convincing herself this was going to happen—I'll have to translate this into Spanish at some point for her—your strength motivates me. To my father, who still has no clue what I'm doing thank you, I love you both so much.

To Pam's friends, most of which I only connect with through social media (you know who you are) thank you. You girls rock! I'm holding you all to your promise to be the first to buy this book. To Pedro Miguel Arce thanks for taking the time out to read my work in progress and giving me the insight

I needed to make it better. You are my honorary beta reader. I owe you one.

To my editors Kerry Genova and Holly M. Kothe with Indie Solutions, thank you for your kind words and support. It was truly a pleasure to work with you. To Murphy Rae with Indie Solutions thanks for the beautiful cover and graphics. Your patience and support meant the world to this newbie.

Lastly I want to thank my boys. Mattias, Tomas and Elias, I do this for you, to show you that dreams are what you make them and that nothing is impossible. Thank you for your patience and understanding while Mommy spent so much time on her laptop. I admit it's my fault you got into the habit of wearing the same clothes every day. I promise you the laundry will get done. And to Luis, you are the single biggest source of support I have, thank you for believing in me when I sometimes doubted it. I love you all.

Happy Reading!!!

About the Author

Jessica lives in a small town outside of Toronto with her husband, three hilarious boys, one crazy, yappy dog and a fish she swears comes up to the glass when it's called. Her hobbies change all the time, currently she's obsessed with crocheting and chalk painting anything she can get her hands on. If you'd like to connect with her, she'd love to hear from you.

Website: www.JessicaBriones.com

Facebook: www.facebook.com/WriterJessicaABriones

Twitter: @JessicaBrio

www.ingramcontent.com/pod-product-compliance
Lightning Source LLC
Chambersburg PA
CBHW051514250626
47156CB00001B/86